FATAL PURSUIT

ALSO BY ELISABETH NAUGHTON

The Aegis Series
Extreme Measures
Lethal Consequences

Against All Odds Series
Wait For Me
Hold On To Me

Stolen Series
Stolen Fury
Stolen Heat
Stolen Seduction
Stolen Chances

Eternal Guardians Series
Marked
Entwined
Tempted
Enraptured
Enslaved
Bound
Twisted
Ravaged

Firebrand Series
Bound to Seduction
Slave to Passion
Possessed by Desire

Anthologies
Sinful Seconds
Wicked Firsts
Bodyguards in Bed

FATAL PURSUIT

THE AEGIS SERIES

ELISABETH NAUGHTON

Montlake
Romance

Published by Montlake Romance, Seattle

www.apub.com

Amazon, the Amazon logo, and Montlake Romance are trademarks of Amazon.com, Inc., or its affiliates.

ISBN-13: 9781503944800
ISBN-10: 1503944808

Cover design by Eileen Carey

Printed in the United States of America

For every reader who sent me a message asking about Marley and Jake.

Good things come to those who wait.

chapter 1

If she could shoot her boss and avoid the death penalty, Marley Addison would do it. Heck, she wouldn't even bat an eyelash at a few years in a federal prison, but Kentucky had that damn lethal injection sentence. A fact that was definitely making her think twice at the moment.

"There's nothing here." Jake Ryder's irritated voice sounded in Marley's headset, echoing in her brain, knocking her tension headache up another blistering notch.

"I said to take a right," she said again into her microphone.

"There is no right, Addison." On the screen in front of her where she monitored the op from the safety of Aegis headquarters, Jake shined his flashlight ahead and to each side so she could see the cement walls all around him. "There's no left either. No forward. Only back." He pulled off the headset and pointed the mini camera at his face. His rugged jawline, irritated expression, and dark eyes filled the screen. "Happy?"

No, she wasn't happy. Marley ground her teeth and typed quickly on the computer to her right because he'd clearly changed directions on her—again. "I said to hold still for ten seconds, not keep going." The schematics of the tunnels beneath the Pulaski Gallery and Jewelry Exchange in Washington, DC, zoomed in on the corridor he'd taken without waiting for her command. "I've almost got it. There. Go back ten feet, then take an immediate left."

Shuffling sounded in her headset, along with a string of muttered words Marley didn't have the patience to sort out. On the monitor at her side, Jake's light once again shone over his dark boots and the trickle of water on the cement floor as he headed in the direction she'd indicated. When he reached the corner, he lifted his light, illuminating a rusted gate, blocking his path. "No left, Einstein. What else ya got?"

She drew a deep breath and reminded herself patience was key with her boss. Arguing with Jake was as useless as banging her head against a wall. After three and a half years running operations at Aegis Security, the elite black ops firm Jake owned and operated, Marley knew that better than anyone.

Looking up at a multitude of screens in front of her in the high-tech communications room, she paged through the schematics until she found the route she'd told him to take in the first place. "Turn around, backtrack to the main tunnel, then *this time* take a left at the four-way intersection."

Jake's boot steps sounded in her ear. On the screen, he flashed the light over his wrist. "We're four minutes behind schedule."

Of course they were behind schedule, but not because of her. If *she* were in the field instead of stuck back at Aegis headquarters, they'd already be in the vault of the gallery because *she* actually did her research before a mission went into operation mode. But she refrained from saying so to keep the peace. She always bit her tongue with Jake to keep the peace. "There should be a ladder twenty feet ahead on your right. Access runs into a closet in the back office on the first floor of the gallery."

Jake didn't respond, but seconds later his light illuminated the metal ladder, exactly where Marley had said it would be. "Bentley, system check."

"Security system is down . . . now." The sound of keys clicking reverberated through the line, and Marley pictured Pierce Bentley, a former Secret Service agent, hacking into the gallery's security system in the back of the nondescript van parked a block away on the dark DC street.

That was where she needed to be in case something went wrong and she had to give the men inside split-second directions. On site in the van in the event the satellite feed went down, or the cops showed up, or any number of things erupted to ruin the op. But no, because she was a woman and not one of the guys, Jake made it clear her place was anywhere *besides* in the field.

That fact burned more than she liked. For the most part, working at Aegis was rewarding. She loved the guys, loved the work, and the pay was a serious perk. But Jake's gender bias was really grating on her last nerve. Especially lately, when his resistance to her having anything to do with fieldwork only seemed to be growing stronger.

He lets Eve participate in the ops.

Her brain skipped over the only other female who worked for the company. Yes, Jake let Evelyn Wolfe participate in the ops. Sent her all over the world, in fact. And his excuse when Marley called him on it was that Eve was ex-CIA and knew how to handle herself. He was right—Eve was as tough as they came—but that didn't mean Marley couldn't deal with the pressure. She'd grown up in the security game, for crying out loud. Her father was the CEO of Omega Intel and had dragged her all over the globe on his missions from the time she was old enough to carry her own backpack. When it came to fieldwork— raids, rescues, extractions—she'd seen it all. *And Jake knew that.*

"Addison."

Startled by the sound of Jake's voice in her ear, Marley flinched. "Yes?"

"I asked if you're monitoring the police bands. Where the hell did you go?"

Of course she was monitoring the police bands. "Still no chatter on the bands," she said clearly, then under her breath, "I'd tell you if there were. I'm not a freakin' rookie."

"Perimeter's clear as well." Mick Hedley's Australian accent echoed through the line.

Marley glanced at her map just to be sure. Mick and a couple of other guys were stationed outside the building, waiting for Jake's mark. Their op this time was simple: test the Pulaski Gallery's security system. No big deal. Aegis had done jobs like this dozens of times. But any number of things could backfire, and Marley still wanted to be there.

"What about Wolfe?" On the screen to her left, Jake's light shined over the interior of a small office made up of a desk, file cabinet, and a trio of chairs. If he'd heard Marley's muttered comment, he didn't acknowledge it. Then again, Jake rarely acknowledged her, let alone her feelings.

Marley pushed down the frustration and told herself to stick to the business at hand. What did she care if Jake noticed her? He was her employer, nothing more. Which was exactly the way she wanted it.

"She should be coming out anytime," Marley announced, flipping screens again so the layout of the gallery popped up. "Turn right when you open the door. A back hallway runs from the offices toward the kitchen."

"She better not be having too much fun in there," Zane Archer muttered over the line as Jake headed down the dark hallway. He, like Hedley, was also stationed outside, waiting on clean-up duty while his fiancée created a diversion and schmoozed with Washington's most wealthy at the black-tie affair happening inside the gallery's main rooms.

"Worried she's going to trade you in for a younger model, Archer?" Bentley asked.

"No," Zane huffed. "I just don't want her to spend all my freakin' money. There's a damn auction going on in there. You know how competitive the woman is. Knowing her, she'd start bidding just to prove she could."

"I heard that, Archer." Eve's clipped voice echoed in Marley's headset, followed by the click of her heels across the floor. "In a few minutes you're going to seriously wish you weren't talking smack about me behind my back."

"Ooh." Hedley chuckled. "You're in deep shit now, Archer."

"Babe," Archer said sweetly. "I wasn't talking smack. I was bragging about your sexy dance moves. I said, 'She'd start spinning just to prove she could.'"

Eve snorted.

"Jesus, Archer," Bentley mumbled. "You are so freakin' whipped. It's pathetic, man. I swear to God you've grown a vagina."

The team laughed. Over the line, Eve said, "I seriously hope not because I am so not into the girl-on-girl thing."

"Damn," Hedley mumbled. "There goes my fantasy. For a while there, Wolfe, I thought you were the perfect woman."

"Hey now, asshole," Zane interrupted. "I'm still on the line here, Hedley."

Laughter echoed through Marley's headset, but she didn't share in the lightheartedness. She never did, at least not until the op was over. "All clear?" she asked when the laughter died down.

"Yes," Eve answered, her voice growing serious as well. A beep echoed, and Marley knew Eve had just flashed the ID card she'd lifted from a security guard over the vault room's door sensor. The hiss of a heavy door opening sounded through her microphone. "Wilson just took the podium. You've got eight minutes, Ryder."

Marley started her stopwatch.

"Sam Wilson will talk for more than eight minutes," Jake said, moving out into the dark corridor and stepping through the door at the end of the hall that Eve held open for him. "He's as long-winded as they come. Holy hell it's hot in here."

"Vault air temperature is 98.6 degrees," Bentley informed him. "Infrared won't be able to sense you unless you're running a fever."

"Here's where you all hope I got my flu shot," Jake said.

The door clicked closed behind them. Eve turned and typed a code into the keypad near the door. "Seismic sensors are disabled."

Jake handed Eve a weapon. "Nice work, Wolfe."

"Feminine charm comes in handy now and then, especially with hunky male security guards."

"I heard that, too," Zane added.

"Relax, Archer." Even though Marley couldn't see Jake, she could tell from the sound of his voice he was smiling. "Her lipstick's only slightly smeared."

"Fucking relax," Archer mumbled. "I'd like to see you relax while your woman is in there rubbing up against some two-bit rent-a-cop."

"Not an issue." Jake handed Eve one of the two packs he carried. "Because I'm not stupid enough to get tied down to just one woman."

Eve grinned and shook her head. In the com room, Marley huffed.

"Problem, Addison?" Jake asked.

Marley cleared her throat and sat up straighter. "Not from me. That was a sneeze."

"Uh-huh." Jake chuckled. "Wolfe's on her way out to you, Archer."

Eve hefted the pack over her shoulder and looked toward Jake. "Try not to get shot."

"Try not to get mugged."

Eve smiled. "I'll do my best, boss."

While Eve disappeared back out the door, Jake moved forward.

And though there was a teasing tone in the air, once he was alone, Marley's stomach curled into a knot. Her mind instinctively tumbled through every awful thing that could happen to him alone in that vault. "Six minutes, fifty-eight seconds," she said into her mike.

The video feed swayed with Jake's steps, illuminating the hallway and, finally, the vault's door. "Won't even need half that." Jake dropped his backpack on the floor and reached for the dial on the vault. "Hey, Addison. What's your favorite color?"

Marley blinked twice as she watched the camera shift direction and knew Jake was pressing his ear against the vault's door, listening for the telltale click of the drive pin as he spun the wheel.

"You want to know my favorite color *now*?"

Jake turned the dial the other direction. "I'm guessing pink. You seem like a pink kind of girl."

Marley grunted. Of course he thought she was a pink girl. The same way he thought she couldn't take care of herself on an op.

"You're making an awful lot of funny noises," Jake said. "You coming down with something?"

"No, Jake." Why the heck was he having this conversation with her now of all times? "I'm as healthy as ever. And pink is not even close to my favorite color. I like blue."

"Blue, huh?" He turned the dial once more, then eased away from the door. The vault came into view along with his muscular forearm as he reached out and turned the hand wheel. "I never would have guessed that."

A hiss echoed through his mike, then he pulled the door back and open, and Marley's pulse jumped again, this time not from annoyance but excitement. "How the heck did you crack that so fast?"

"I—"

"Hands against the wall now!"

Several voices echoed across the line, followed by a rush of footsteps. Marley startled at the sound, then leaned forward for a better view of the screen as Jake whipped around. His camera scanned the room, now filled with seven, eight . . . at least nine security guards pointing weapons directly at him.

"Oh shit," Marley gasped.

"Well, hell," Jake muttered. "Looks like someone finally wised up."

"On the ground! Now!"

"Okay, okay. I heard you." He held up his hands and slowly lowered his body to the floor. "I don't suppose you boys are interested in a bribe, huh? Got an open vault here."

Marley typed quickly on her computer, backtracking through the system and pulling up cameras in the hall that led to the vault. "I don't know what we missed. Bentley?"

"System's still totally down," Bentley answered. "It's clean on our end."

No, it wasn't clean. This op was turning into a giant fuckup, which was exactly why Marley needed to be on-site instead of at Aegis headquarters. "Archer, Hedley, go three. Jake, hold tight. We've got a team coming your way."

"Take your time," Jake muttered. "I'll just take a nap down here."

One of the guards kicked Jake's backpack away from his feet. Perspiration dotted Marley's forehead as she zeroed in on the screen in front of her and focused on the gallery owner moving down the hall toward the vault room. "Jake, Wilson's heading right for you. Dammit, we missed a step somewhere."

"You didn't miss anything," Jake said quietly into his mike. "I tripped a sensor in the tunnels on purpose."

Marley's fingers froze on her keyboard just as the guard reached for Jake's headset. "You *what*?"

Jake didn't get a chance to answer. The guard tossed his headset on the ground, then hauled him to his feet. The camera clattered against the floor but continued to transmit a video feed. Not that it did a lot of good because it showed nothing more than boots and pant legs, but Marley leaned forward to see better anyway and flipped the volume up on her monitor. She could barely make out the voices. Some kind of commotion was happening. She recognized Jake's voice, and Wilson's, but she couldn't hear what they were saying. If they would just—

Gunfire exploded in her headset, and Marley jerked back in her seat. "Jake?" Her pulse shot up. "Jake, talk to me."

Shuffling sounded through the line, followed by more muffled voices she couldn't make out. Just when she was ready to send Bentley in after everyone, Zane Archer's voice sounded in her ear.

"All clear."

Marley's heart felt like it had taken up permanent residency in her throat. "What happened? Where's Jake?"

"He's fine. We—"

"Gimme that mike." Jake's voice was dim, then louder when he said, "Addison?" The camera shifted, and on the screen Marley saw Zane holding out a hand and helping one of the security guards up from the floor.

Marley breathed a sigh of relief. "Yeah, I'm here. What's the situation?"

"No situation."

"But I heard gunfire."

"The guard's gun discharged when Hedley and Archer arrived. No one was hit. Operation complete."

"*Complete?* Jake, you didn't even make it into the vault. What's going o—?"

"Bentley?" Jake asked.

"I'm here with Wolfe, boss," Bentley answered. "And wow. This

9

diamond is the shit. Puts the Hope Diamond to shame. Man, oh man. I would sure like to keep this one for myself."

Jake chuckled. "I've got an irritated gallery owner who might just take issue with that."

"You bet your ass I would," Wilson muttered.

Diamond . . . Bentley . . . Pierce was out in the van, not inside with the rest of the team. "Jake." It was all Marley could do not to climb through the airwaves and strangle the man. "Would someone please tell me what the hell is going on?"

"Jake cracked the vault earlier in the day when he went into the tunnels to do the system check," Eve answered. "Tonight's extracurricular activities were a decoy."

Decoy . . .

The word echoed in Marley's head, like the needle of a record player, skipping over the same note again and again as conversation continued through her headset.

"Gotta hand it to you, Ryder," Sam Wilson said in a dim voice. "I thought our system was foolproof. Your team proved me wrong."

"That's why you pay us the big bucks," Jake answered. "Just making sure you got your money's worth."

The men's relaxed voices continued to ripple through Marley's earpiece, but she barely heard the words. Jake had changed the op without telling her. She'd spent days planning this mission, and for what? So he could do whatever he wanted and leave her in the dark?

Shock rushed through her. Followed by a burst of stupidity. What was she doing? He clearly didn't need her. The team didn't need her. Everyone else had obviously been in on the change. But then, they were all in Washington and she was stuck in Kentucky. Right where Jake wanted her.

"Addison?"

Jake's voice pulled Marley out of her self-induced trance. She blinked several times and realized she'd been staring at a blank screen for she didn't know how long. He'd already turned off the camera in his hand. "What?"

Jake's footsteps echoed through his mike, but the voices had dimmed, telling her he was leaving the vault room. "Nice work."

Nice work? Yeah right. "For what? I didn't do anything."

"Not true. Your role was vital. Wilson knows us. His team was listening. I needed them distracted so they didn't notice the changes in the vault room."

"And tripping the sensor in the tunnels? What was that? Gloating?"

Jake chuckled. "I just wanted his team to see we could get to them twice."

Clearly. Because Jake loved rubbing shit like this in.

Marley sat up straighter and fought back her temper. "You could have filled me in on your plan."

"Wilson needed to believe we were really arguing."

She clenched her jaw. "News flash, Ryder. That wasn't an act."

Jake chuckled again. As if it were no big deal. As if she had no right to be frustrated. But to him everything that concerned her was simply status quo. He expected her to do what he wanted, when he wanted, no questions asked. And because she put up with it, she had no one to blame but herself.

A door opened and closed, then other voices sounded dimly in her earpiece—Archer's, Eve's, Bentley's—telling Marley that Jake was already outside in the van, celebrating.

She breathed deep while the team patted themselves on the back for a job well done. After tugging the reading glasses from her face, she flipped off the screens around her and pushed to her feet.

This was the life she'd carved out for herself. Hovering on the fringe of the action. Sitting back while everyone else made a difference and she watched from the sidelines. Being kept in the dark even though she *knew* the company would flop without her.

"Addison? You there?"

Jake's voice brought the fine hairs along the nape of her neck to attention. A low burn lit up her belly as she reached for her notebook and pen from the table. "Not for long."

"Wilson's secretary is going to contact you tomorrow with final payment. She's heading to India in the morning on a buying trip, so you'll need to be in the office early."

Of course Jake would think nothing of calling Marley in early. Forget the fact she'd worked late every night this week. Or the fact she was here before the sun most days. She ground her teeth to keep from telling Jake just what he could do with his final payment.

Laughter sounded in the background. "Addison? Did you hear me?"

She grabbed her bag from the floor and shoved the notebook and pen inside. "Yes, I heard you. But I'm not coming in early tomorrow."

"Why not?"

"Because I'm not. If it's so important for someone to be here, then you can get up early for once."

"Marley—"

That was it. All she could take. She slammed her bag shut. "No, you know what, Jake? You want to do things on your own? Go ahead and do them. Be my guest and do them all. I'm done with this."

"What does that—"

She pulled the headset off and tossed it on the table. Turning out of the com room, she marched down the hall and told herself it was way past time she set the man straight. She'd left her father's company four years ago because he'd been doing the same stuff to her then that Jake was doing now—holding her back, treating her like an expendable member of the team, not trusting her when it came right down to it. The difference was she expected it from her father. From Jake she'd stupidly assumed there'd be more.

She moved into her office, tossed her bag on the desk, then pulled open the bottom drawer and grabbed her purse. She wasn't taking any work home with her tonight. Wasn't giving Jake another moment of her precious time.

Her cell phone buzzed in her pocket. She pulled it out, saw Jake's name on her screen, and hit Decline. All she wanted right now was a bubble bath, a giant bottle of wine, a good book, and peace and quiet. Reaching into her purse, she found her keys and headed for the door.

Her phone buzzed again. She glanced at the device in her hand as she turned out of the office and moved down the stairs to the lobby. A number flashed on the screen, one she didn't recognize. Jake clearly knew she was upset, and he was smart enough to realize she wasn't going to answer. The man had grabbed someone else's phone.

She hit Decline again, crossed the lobby, and typed in the security code on the panel near the main door. Once the system was armed, she moved outside, locked the door, and headed across the dark and empty parking lot toward her Audi parked under a lamppost.

Her car door creaked as she opened it, reminding her she needed to oil the damn thing. She tossed her purse on the passenger seat. The phone in her hand buzzed again.

Dammit, she'd had enough of this. She was done being his beck-and-call girl.

She hit Answer and held the phone to her ear. "Look, as far as I'm concerned, you can—"

"Marlene? Oh, sweet baby Jesus. Marlene, is that you? I wasn't sure you had the same number. I took a chance."

The words died on Marley's lips. The voice was familiar but . . . No, there was no way it could be him. Jake had gotten her so riled up she was hearing things.

"Who is this? I'm not in the mood for games."

"No games. It's me, Marlene. It's Gray."

The air caught in her lungs. And for a moment, time seemed to stand completely still.

Grayson McKnight. No, it wasn't possible. Five years he'd been gone. Her heart beat hard against her ribs, and all those emotions she'd buried after he'd been lost in South America came screaming to the forefront. "This isn't funny. Grayson McKnight is dead. Whoever you are, I don't appreciate your sick joke. Go—"

"I'm not dead. And this isn't a joke. Marlene, it's me. It's Gray. I guarantee I'm very much alive. But I'm in trouble, and I need you."

She tightened her hand around the phone. "I don't know who you are, but—"

"Freckles, it's me. Please don't hang up on me right now."

Freckles . . . The nickname stopped her cold. Perspiration dotted her spine, and her hand shook against the phone pressed to her ear. Gray had only ever called her that in private. None of their friends had known he'd used that silly term of endearment. Not even her father. Her heart kick-started in the center of her chest with both disbelief and confusion.

"Gray? How . . . ? Where . . . ? What the . . . ? You're alive? Where the hell have you been for five years?"

"Yeah, Freckles. It's me. I'll explain everything, I promise. But right now I need your help."

Voices echoed in the background, and Marley shifted her weight as she stared out at the dark hills around her and tried to clear the lingering cobwebs from her brain. "Gray, what's going on?"

He didn't immediately answer. The voices grew louder. Shouts echoed, then dimmed. And as she waited, the hairs on Marley's nape tingled. "Gray? Tell me where you are."

"Look," he said quickly, his voice just above a whisper, "I don't have a lot of time. If they find me, they'll kill me. I gotta get out of this damn country."

"If who finds you? And what country? I don't understand what's going on. If you're in some kind of trouble, my father will—"

"*No!* You can't tell your father. I'm in this hell because of him. You can't call anyone. If you do, they'll find me. You're the only person left that I trust, Marlene. You have to do this for me. You have to come and get me."

Marley swallowed hard, and a quick shot of apprehension rolled through her belly. "I don't—"

"Go to the Hotel Chilimaco in Puerto Asis, Colombia. Check in under the name Sophia Alvarez. I'll call you there and tell you where to reach me. Bring documents, Marlene. I won't be able to get out of the country without them."

Colombia? Marley's mind spun. When she'd worked for her father she'd been a pro at faking documents to get his guys in and out of different countries under numerous aliases. And since working for Jake she did the same thing now and then. But still . . .

She pressed her hand against her forehead. "I can't just drop everything and fly down to South America. I have a job. Responsibilities. I have—"

"And I had a life before your father left me in this shithole to rot."

There was a bite to his voice, one Marley had never heard before, and it sent a chill straight down her spine.

"Look," he said softer. "I've got no money. No way to get out of this mess on my own. No one else to turn to. I stole this phone so I could call you. I just need you to come and get me. I'll explain everything when I see you. Please. *Please* say you'll help me. If you don't, I can't . . ." He swallowed. "I don't know what I'll do."

The desperation in his voice touched a piece of her she'd closed off years before. Memories bombarded her. The day she'd met Grayson McKnight when she'd been working for her father at Omega Intel. The weeks Gray had pestered her until she'd finally agreed to go out with him. The months they'd dated. And the moment her father had called to tell her that the op in Colombia had gone terribly wrong and that Gray had been killed.

A piece of her had died the day she'd gotten that news. Another part had been oddly relieved. She'd known before he'd left with her father's team that he wasn't the guy for her, and she'd planned to break it off with him when he got back. Then he'd died and she'd found herself off the hook. The guilt she'd felt over that relief and the frustration she'd experienced when her father hadn't given any explanation had formed a wedge between father and daughter. It had also been a major reason she'd left Mason Addison's company and never looked back.

Gray wasn't really dead, though. He was alive, alone, and in trouble. She didn't know what had happened, but if her father had lied to her and purposely left Gray behind, then she *owed* him her help. And at the very least, maybe she could make up for all those awful things she'd thought and felt after he'd disappeared.

Her throat grew thick. Her hand was sweaty against the phone. Her mind tumbled with options. What she'd need. How she could get there. She glanced at her watch. "I-it'll take me a few hours to arrange things."

"Thank you." He exhaled a long breath. "Thank you, Marlene. I'll call you at the Hotel Chilimaco in two days. I don't know what I'd do without you. I don't . . ." His voice hitched. "I knew I could count on you. I knew you wouldn't let me down. Thank you."

All that guilt she'd felt five years before came rushing back. But she swallowed it down and told herself she was doing the right thing now. "Where can I reach you?"

"You can't. I'll call you. Just hurry, Marlene. Get to Colombia as fast as you can. I need to get out of here. I need . . ." He hesitated, then his voice dropped to a whisper. "You're my last hope."

The line went dead in her ear. Marley pulled it away, looked down at the phone in her hand, and swallowed hard.

Yeah, she'd agreed to help him, but she wasn't stupid. Colombia wasn't exactly the safest place for a single American female to travel alone. She couldn't go by herself. She needed to take someone with her for safety. Jake's irritating face popped into her head, but she immediately dismissed him. He'd made it clear tonight that he didn't need her, so she definitely wasn't turning to him for help. She could ask one of the other guys at Aegis, but they all gossiped like schoolgirls. Even if one of them agreed to go with her, it would inevitably get back to Jake, and she didn't need any kind of lecture from him. Especially not when it came to her personal life. That left her father, but Gray had said something had happened between the two of them and that he didn't trust the man.

She bit into her bottom lip and glanced around the dark parking lot, the damp pavement illuminated by a shimmer of lamplight from above. She loved her father, but she knew how Mason Addison worked. He did what he wanted, when he wanted, and screw the consequences or what it meant for anyone else. In that respect, he was a lot like Jake Ryder.

She pushed thoughts of Jake aside and ran through her options. There was only one person she could trust with this. The only question was whether or not he'd agree to help.

Screw it. She was out of options.

She paged through her contacts and dialed. A male voice answered on the second ring. "Hamilton."

"Hey, Ronan. It's Marley." She hesitated, praying the whole time that he'd say yes. "I know it's been a while, but I need a favor."

chapter 2

"I'm done with this."

Jake Ryder slammed the door of his Escalade and crossed the parking lot toward the back entrance of Aegis headquarters. A light fog hovered over the damp ground and snaked through the barren limbs of the tall oak and hickory dotting the rolling Kentucky farmland in the morning light, but he barely noticed it. All he could think about were Marley's words from last night.

He tugged his jacket up to ease the cool March morning chill and stepped around a pile of dirty snow pushed up against a light pole from last week's storm. What did she mean by that—I'm done with this? Done how? And why wasn't she answering his calls? He'd left her a voicemail, but she'd yet to respond. Nor had she responded to his handful of texts.

Annoyance pushed at him from every side as he unlocked the rear door in the east wing of the twenty-thousand-square-foot monstrosity that used to be his father's house. He keyed in the security code, then moved up the back steps toward the Aegis offices on the second floor, his confusion growing thicker by the minute. She'd said no last night when he'd told her to come in early. She never said no to him. Yeah, he knew she was ticked he'd changed the op without telling her, but in the three and a half years she'd worked for him she hadn't once flat-out said no about anything he'd asked her to do.

He slid his hand into his jacket pocket and fingered the small white box holding the sapphire teardrop pendant he'd talked Wilson into selling him. The last thing he needed was for Marley to get the wrong idea, but he'd bought the pendant as a peace offering—a bonus really, for all her long hours and hard work. But as he reached the office level and heard her opening drawers and slamming them, rolling her chair along the hardwood floor and muttering under her breath, he wondered if instead of trying to keep the peace, the safer move might be to slink out of the building altogether.

"I'm done with this."

No. He didn't like what those words implied, and he definitely didn't like how she'd said them. Regardless of everything she did for the company, the decision for how the ops were run still fell on his shoulders, and she had no right to be upset with him. Tugging his hand from his pocket, he decided not to give her the pendant just yet. Instead they needed to have a chat about the whole employer-employee dynamic.

"Marley," he said loud enough so she could hear him, "my office. Now."

He turned for his office door, twisted the handle, and pushed the right side open with his hip.

"She's not here," a female voice called from the direction of Marley's office. "And where in the name of all things holy does she keep extra print cartridges? I can't find a damn thing in this place!"

Jake's brow lowered. He dropped his coat on a table near the door, then marched toward Marley's office. Evelyn Wolfe sat behind the massive desk, rummaging around in a drawer, her chestnut hair falling over her cheeks.

He looked around the empty room. "What are you doing here, Wolfe? And where is Marley?"

"That's what I'd like to know." Eve snapped the drawer shut, blew the bangs out of her face, and reached for the drawer to her right. "She called late last night and asked me to cover for her for a few days. God Almighty, all I want is freakin' ink for the printer." She shoved the drawer closed, rose, and moved to a cabinet along the wall.

Jake stepped farther into the room as he watched Eve rifle through Marley's supply closet. "She didn't tell me she was leaving. Where did she go?"

"Hell if I know." Eve's head disappeared inside the cabinet. "There. Finally. Of course it's way in the back." She reemerged with a box of cartridges. "I feel like I just struck oil." She swiped at her forehead. "And, Christ, I'm sweating." She waved the box at Jake and moved back for Marley's chair. "You both owe me big time."

A low hum kicked up in Jake's ears as Eve sat, swiveled toward the printer, replaced the cartridge, then whipped back to the computer and started typing. "What exactly did Marley say?"

Eve didn't bother to look his direction. "Just that she had a personal family situation she needed to deal with and that she was taking a few days off."

"I'm done with this."

That hum intensified, and Jake's hands grew damp. Marley never took time off. In all the years she'd worked for him, she'd only taken two weeks off total. And then only when he'd insisted that she needed a break. She was forever worried someone would screw up her filing system or mismanage an op for the guys or that the place was going to fall apart without her. So the fact she'd up and vanished, with no advance warning, didn't just strike him as odd, it told him something was seriously wrong.

He stepped closer to the desk. "Did she say when she'd be back?"

Eve's fingers stilled on the keyboard, and she shot him a frustrated look. "It's not like she left me a schedule. I'm not her personal secretary, you know." She held up a finger. "And I'm not your personal secretary either, so don't get any funny ideas." She resumed typing. "This is only temporary. I suck at office work, as you will soon find out. Archer should be doing this shit. Not me."

The buzz grew to a screaming roar in Jake's ears. He turned out of Marley's office and headed back for his. After flipping on his computer, he sat behind his desk and stared at the screen.

Where would she go? And why hadn't she told him she was leaving? Was she off pouting somewhere because of what had happened yesterday? What kind of personal situation would make her drop everything and disappear with no warning?

He tugged the cell out of his pocket and dialed. He knew there was a chance Olivia Miller wasn't at work yet, but he hoped maybe she could give him some insight. Luckily, she picked up on the third ring.

"Hey, Jake. You're up early this morning. Are you calling to talk to Landon? He should be on his way in to the office already."

Landon Miller, Olivia's new husband, was a former DIA officer and one of Jake's best operatives, but this had nothing to do with Landon. "Hey there, Olivia. No, I was actually calling to speak with you. Are you at work yet?"

"Yep, just got here. What's up?"

Olivia had recently started working as a trainer at Omega Intel, Marley's father's security company in Lexington. "Is Marley there by any chance?"

"No, not that I'm aware. Is she supposed to be?"

Jake sort of hoped so, because if she was in Lexington with her dad it would make his life a helluva lot easier. Something in his gut, though, told him his life was about to get way more complicated. "What about Mason? Is he around?"

"Yeah, I just spoke with him five minutes ago. He's in a meeting with a client. Do you need to talk to him?"

"No." Not yet, anyway. "So everything's normal over there? No family drama going on?"

"I don't think so. Everything's the same as it always is. What's up, Jake? Why are you asking these questions? Is everything okay?"

Jake hesitated. If there was nothing going on with Marley's dad, it meant her so-called personal situation didn't have anything to do with family. Marley didn't have any other family. And that meant she'd lied to Eve. His worry kicked up another notch.

"Everything's fine, don't worry. Thanks, Olivia."

"Jake—"

Jake hit End on his cell and pushed the intercom button on his desk phone. Eve answered with a huff. "I'm working, Ryder. Wilson's secretary needs a full invoice before she heads to India in like five flippin' minutes, and I only just found the damn file."

"I need you to hack into Marley's credit cards. Business and personal. I want to know where she's using them."

"Oh my God. Are you freakin' losing it? You can't just track an employee's credit cards because she took the day off. That's illegal."

"We do illegal shit ten times a day, Wolfe, and you know it. Marley never takes time off. Something's going on here."

"Well, gee. If you flip out like this on a normal basis, I can totally see why she cut and ran without telling you. In fact, I'm surprised she didn't do it sooner."

Jake's jaw ticked. "Just do it."

He hung up and stared at his computer screen again. Eve was right. He was bordering on losing it, but Jake didn't care. Marley's words from yesterday wouldn't leave his head. *"I'm done with this."* Done how? He had to know where she was. Why she'd left. When she was coming back.

He sat forward and opened a web browser. After typing in his cell phone carrier, he logged into Aegis's account and searched for Marley's number. He paid her cell phone bill. This wasn't an invasion of privacy. It was business. He pulled up her recent activity.

She'd called Eve late last night. A number he didn't recognize in Memphis. And his cell several times yesterday. None of her outgoing calls looked suspicious. He flipped screens to see her incoming calls. Another number he didn't recognize sat at the top of the list. He followed the line across the screen to see the location of origin: South America.

An odd tingle slid down his spine. He sat back in his chair and stared at the screen, confusion drawing his brows together. His intercom buzzed.

Leaning forward, he pushed the button while he continued to stare at the screen. "What did you find?"

"She went to REI yesterday," Eve answered. "Bought new hiking boots, a backpack, a canteen, energy chews, and matches among other things. Sorry to ruin your conspiracy theory there, Alex Jones. Looks like she took off camping. The world is not about to end."

"Call the airport. I want to know if my plane is still in the hangar."

"Jake, seriously? She didn't take your stupid plane. She went camping. Leave the poor girl alone. Employees are allowed to take vacation days, even from misers like you."

"Call the damn airport, Eve."

He released the intercom button, but he could still hear Eve bitching through the open office doors. Ignoring her, he paged back up to the top of the screen, then stilled when he saw Marley's cell phone plan.

International.

Her plan was domestic. She didn't travel overseas like the rest of the crew. On the rare instance she had to travel for Aegis, she changed her plan. But she always changed it back as soon as she was home to save the company a little money even though Jake told her not to worry about it.

International. South America. *I'm done with this . . .*

A hard, tight ball of worry rolled through his belly as he pushed out of his chair and headed for Marley's office. One that mixed with the sudden fear coursing through his veins. Fear he did not need to be feeling right now.

"Okay, thanks," Eve said into the phone. She replaced the receiver in the cradle and looked up as he entered the room.

"Well?" He stopped in front of her desk.

"You were right." Eve pushed to her feet. "Your plane's gone."

Sonofabitch. "The pilots had to file a flight plan. Where did she go?"

Eve pursed her lips. "You're not going to like this."

"Where, Eve?"

She blew out a long breath. "Colombia. South America."

Marley swiped the damp hair away from her face and tapped her palm against the desk bell. She was sweaty, tired, and in serious need of a drink, but she was also desperate to see Ronan. And she didn't want to give him any reason to leave by being late.

A chubby Colombian man who had to be in his sixties rushed out from a back room. Fans turned lazy circles above the lobby of the Hotel Chilimaco, but it did little to ease the oppressively humid heat. Late afternoon sunlight streamed across the white tile floor, warming the room even more.

"*¡Buenas tardes, señorita! ¿Le puedo ayudar?*"

"*Buenas tardes. Tengo una reservación.*"

"Muy bien," the man said. "You American?"

"Yes." Marley dropped her backpack on the ground at her feet. "Sophia Alvarez."

"Welcome to Puerto Asis." The man opened a book and scanned a series of handwritten names. "Ah, *sí*. Here it is."

He reached for a key from a series of hooks along the wall behind him while Marley fished out cash from her pocket. After she paid for the night, she hefted her backpack onto her shoulder, scanned the small empty lobby again that housed a couch, a couple of tables and chairs, and the oldest TV she'd ever seen. "I was supposed to meet someone here. Tall guy, American, dark blond hair, sharp blue eyes. Has he checked in yet?"

The man's eyes narrowed as if he were thinking. "I not sure. I check." He turned into the back room. Muffled voices echoed, but Marley couldn't make out the words. Moments later, the man returned and said, "US military, right?"

You could take a guy out of the army, but you couldn't change the way he carried himself. The clerk had obviously met his fair share of soldiers and recognized Ronan's type. "Yes."

"He register this morning. Asked about cantina." The man pointed toward the open doors that led out to the street. "Check outside."

Marley palmed the key on the desk. Of course Ronan had found a bar. She could always count on him to find the worst dive bar in the area.

"Gracias," she said as she turned for the stairs that led to the rooms. "I appreciate your help."

The room was nothing special. A double bed with a lime-green comforter, scuffed nightstand and side chair, and pink stucco walls. A freeway motel in the States, but down here, probably high-end luxury. After dropping her gear on the bed, she freshened up, grabbed her key and some cash, and headed out to find Ronan.

The first three cantinas were busts. Too nice, too clean, and filled with people who were way too normal. The minute she walked up to the fourth, though, she knew she'd hit the jackpot.

The tiny cantina sat on a side street off the beaten path. Litter was pushed up along the sidewalk outside, heavy smoke seeped from the open door, and raucous laughter echoed from inside. As she stepped through the doorway and paused to let her eyes adjust to the lack of light, she heard Jake's voice in the back of her head telling her she was being supremely stupid by not only traveling to Colombia alone, but walking into a place like this by herself. But she ignored it. Just as she'd ignored every other time her conscience had taken on Jake's voice as she'd been planning and executing this trip.

Conversation died down the minute she stepped into the room, and every patron turned to look her way. A trio of hardened, fifty-something Latino men sat at a small table. Two soldiers decked out in military green from head to toe with automatic weapons slung over their backs were bellied up to the bar. A kid who looked no more than twelve moved around behind the counter filling drinks.

There wasn't a single female in the room. And the way every man stared at her as if she were fresh meat made the hairs on her neck stand straight with both fear and doubt.

A voice cleared to her left. Marley glanced in that direction, then exhaled a long breath when she saw the figure sitting in the shadows, his hand wrapped around a glass on the table, his bright-blue eyes narrowed on her.

The fear slid to the wayside. She ignored the attention from the other men in the bar, headed toward the corner, then stopped in front of his table. "Couldn't just pick a normal restaurant, could you?"

Ronan Hamilton lifted the whiskey in his hand and took a sip. Ice clinked in the inch of amber liquid as he set the glass back down. "Nope."

Marley pulled out a chair and sat across from him. "When did you get here?"

He didn't move from his position—kicked back in his seat, head tipped to the side, eyes sharp and assessing as he glanced toward the door. "Late last night."

"That was fast."

The kid behind the bar moved up on Marley's right. He held a dishtowel in one hand, and an apron was tied around his waist. Startled, Marley looked up. This close she could see he was older than she'd originally thought, but not by much. And the fact he stood there without saying anything creeped her out.

She held up one finger. *"Uno cerveza."*

Ronan lifted his drink. *"Otra para. Y uno, mi amigo."*

The kid turned and left. In the silence, Ronan lifted his glass and threw back the rest of his drink. "I was in Cartagena when you called."

"The call said Memphis."

He shrugged. "I have my calls rerouted. Not smart to let too many people know where I am at any one time."

Marley nodded. She knew the way he worked. Here one day, gone the next. What the clerk at the hotel had missed was the fact he was *former* military and spent most of his life flying under the radar.

She studied him across the table. A dark-blond beard covered his jaw. He'd added a new scar along the right side of his temple since the last time she'd seen him, but other than that he looked the same. Dressed in jeans, boots, and a khaki button-down that was rolled at his forearms and damp around the collar, it was easy to see he was still as big and muscular as always. Still hard and edgy from his travels. And his striking blue eyes were tinged with an element of danger she remembered from the first time they'd met. But though a rational thinking woman would be scared, or, at the very least, intimidated by him, Marley wasn't. Because she knew he wasn't at all what people thought. And the fact he'd dropped everything to rush here and help her only confirmed that belief.

"Guess I got lucky, then."

The bartender set her beer and two glasses of whiskey on the table, then left.

Ronan huffed and reached for his new drink. "You're on the edge of the jungle, sweetheart. Nothing lucky about that."

Marley lifted her drink and took a long swallow. "I can hold my own, don't worry about me."

Ronan's brow ticked up as he brought the glass to his lips. "I don't doubt that. Does your father know you're down here?"

Marley didn't want to talk about Mason Addison, at least not with Ronan. She lowered her beer. "No, this doesn't concern him."

"What about that boss of yours? He know you're getting ready to tromp through the jungle?"

Marley thought of Jake. He'd throw a complete hissy fit if he knew she'd not only come to Columbia, but taken his plane to do it, but she only mildly cared. If Jake fired her, so be it. It was probably time for her to move on anyway.

"No, and this doesn't concern him either." She folded her elbows on the table. "This is personal."

Ronan took another sip of his drink and lowered the glass with a clink. "In my experience, personal can get you killed. Especially in a place like this."

Marley hoped the hell not. She didn't want to die for this. But she did owe Gray her help.

Ronan finally shifted in his seat and sat forward. "So tell me about this McKnight character. I never liked the look of the sonofabitch, but I want to know just what the hell your father did to the guy and why he's down here. And then I want you to tell me how you're involved."

Marley tightened her fingers around the beer bottle. "You're not going to like the answers."

"Tough shit, missy. Start talking."

Jake raked a hand through his hair and eyed the fifth and final hotel on his list across the dark street. If Marley wasn't here, he wasn't sure what his next move would be. She hadn't responded to his calls, hadn't checked in to any of the local hotels under her name, hadn't used her credit card since she'd landed in Colombia, and she hadn't made any calls from her cell. He knew she was still in Puerto Asis because he'd finally gotten a hold of Tony Hughes, the pilot who'd flown her to Columbia. Tony was currently hunkered down in a hotel near the airport awaiting Marley's instructions, but he didn't know where she'd gone, and at the moment, she wasn't answering Tony's calls either. Jake knew if Marley left the city before he found her, he'd wind up chasing her through the jungle, and right now, he did not have the patience to play her little game. Or to deal with the fallout.

He moved into the lobby, swiped his forearm over his sweaty brow, and stepped up to the reception desk. A portly Latino man emerged from the back room and lifted his hand. *"¡Buenas noches, señor! ¿Le puedo ayudar?"*

Shit. Today was one of those days he really wished he hadn't been flirting with Misty Swanson all through his high school Spanish class and had actually paid attention. *"Buenas noches. Habla Inglés?"*

"Sí, sí."

"Thank God," Jake muttered. He pulled a photo from his pocket and held it up. "I'm looking for this woman. Have you seen her?"

"You are American?"

"Yes. She is as well. I just need to know if she's been here."

The man chewed on his lip while he studied the picture. *"Sí,* but she not here now."

If Marley had been here, that was a start. Hopefully she'd be back. He slid the picture into his back pocket. "Is she staying here?"

The man's eyes narrowed. "We no want trouble."

Jake held up a hand. "No trouble. I promise. She's a friend. I was supposed to meet her but, silly her, she forgot to tell me the name of the hotel. I've been to every one in town. You're my last stop."

The man eyed him for several long seconds, then finally said, "I no idea where she went."

So she was staying here. Relief filled his chest. He nodded toward the keys hanging at the man's back. "Got any rooms left?"

"*Sí.*" The man's whole demeanor changed. He went from stand-offish and suspicious to helpful in the span of a few seconds. "You have money?"

"Yes." Jake pulled out pesos and set them on the counter. The hotel clerk quickly reached for a key from the wall behind him, handed Jake a registry book, and picked up his cash. "Second floor. Room twenty-two."

"*Gracias.*" Jake threw his pack over his shoulder, reached for the key, and moved to sit in the waiting area.

"You no go upstairs?" the man asked.

"No, I'm just gonna wait."

The man threw up his hand and turned for the back room. "I no care if you wait, so long as you pay."

Alone, Jake dropped his backpack on the floor and sat on the rattan couch. Five minutes passed before he checked his watch. It was close to ten p.m. No one had come in or out of the hotel since he'd arrived. He blew out a long breath, crossed his arms over his chest, and tapped his foot on the tile floor while he looked out the window toward the dark street.

Nothing was open except a few seedy bars. Marley was in a dangerous city, alone, at night. What on God's green earth was she thinking? And where the hell was she at this hour?

Unable to sit still, Jake stuffed his hands into the pockets of his cargo pants, pushed to his feet, and paced the length of the small lobby. People passed by on the sidewalk outside the windows, but still no one turned into the hotel. His jaw clenched. He flicked the key in his pocket, raked a hand through his hair again, thought about texting Eve once more to find out if Marley had checked in at Aegis yet, then thought better of it. Eve had said she'd call the moment she heard from Marley, and, knowing how moody Eve could get, Jake knew if he kept bugging her she might not respond at all.

Another fifteen minutes passed. Jake stopped near a potted ficus tree in the corner of the room and decided enough was enough. Nothing good happened to a single woman alone in a city like this at night. Determined to find her, he turned toward the door but only made it one step before familiar feminine laughter sounded outside.

He stopped, looked up, then stilled when Marley stepped into the room wearing a fitted black tank that showed off her breasts and the curves at her waist, dark-green cargo pants, and a pair of hiking boots that looked as if they were brand-new.

Relief immediately swept through him—that she was alive, that she wasn't hurt. Her blonde hair hung in waves past her shoulder, and a wide smile split her face, warming his insides. Then she turned to glance up at a tall, buff blond guy dressed all in black stepping into the lobby at her back, and Jake's relief morphed to confusion, then to flat-out disbelief.

"That is not even possible," Marley said over her shoulder as she crossed the lobby and headed for the front desk. "Now I know you're lying."

"No lie," the guy said as he followed her. "The kid was fifteen, sixteen tops."

Jake gave his head a swift shake, sure he was seeing things. But no, she was still there, laughing and flirting with some random guy as if running off to a dangerous country in South America was no big deal.

She'd come all the way down here to have an affair? To hook up with this loser? And she'd used his plane to do it?

Marley laughed again. Shuffling sounded from the back room, then the manager emerged and grinned. "Welcome back, *señorita*."

"Thank you. Room twenty-five, please."

The manager reached for a key at his back and handed it to her. *"Buenas noches."*

"Buenas noches," Marley repeated with a smile. She turned once more to the blond man behind her. "Fifteen, huh? If he'd been older, you'd have been in serious trou—"

Her gaze landed on Jake, still standing near the potted ficus, and the words died on her lips.

"Oh my God," she muttered, shock filling her light-blue eyes. *"You followed me?"*

chapter 3

"You're right, I followed you." Jerked out of his trance by Marley's words, Jake stepped out from behind the potted plant and leveled her with a hard look. "You stole my damn jet."

"I—" Marley's mouth snapped closed. "I didn't steal anything. I *borrowed*. But I have to say, I'm honestly surprised you even noticed."

She'd been drinking. Those pretty blue eyes of hers were slightly glossy, and her cheeks were flushed a soft shade of pink. He didn't like the idea of her getting drunk down here with some guy she'd just picked up in a sleazy bar. Didn't like the idea of her here, period.

She turned for the stairs, but Jake stepped in her path, preventing her from escaping to her room. "What exactly does that mean?"

She drew to an abrupt stop and swayed just a touch, confirming—oh yeah—she was tipsy if not already drunk. "It means nothing. Take your plane and leave. I don't need it anymore."

She tried to step around him, but he moved into her path once more. "I'm not going anywhere until you tell me what's going on."

Her eyes widened. "News flash, Ryder. This isn't the office. I don't have to tell you anything. If you want to fire me for borrowing your dumb plane, then do it. I don't care. I'm on vacation."

One thing registered. That she was still mad. But he couldn't tell if it was because he'd changed that op or if there was more going on.

She shoved her shoulder hard against his to get by. Twisting after her, Jake caught her by the wrist and tugged her back. "Marley, wait a min—"

"Whoa. Dude." The big blond guy who'd followed her into the lobby stepped between them and placed a large hand against Jake's chest. "Time for you to take a breather and back off, buddy."

Jake shifted his gaze from Marley to the oaf she'd picked up. His face was vaguely familiar, but Jake couldn't figure out how he knew the guy. And right now he was too frustrated to try to remember. "And you need to take your hand off me right this second before you lose it."

The blond guy's piercing blue eyes narrowed, but he didn't drop his hand. Several tense seconds passed, and without even looking, Jake knew the hotel manager was standing in the doorway to the back room, all but quaking in his boots.

"Oh for God's sake, Jake." Marley yanked her hand from his grip. "Stop being a bully." She looked toward the blond. "Ronan, I'm tired. Take me up to the room?"

She stepped back, swaying again with the movement. Jake tensed to catch her if she fell, but the blond—Ronan—reached his free hand out and captured Marley by the arm before she went down, never once looking her way. And as Jake watched the guy's big hand slide along her bare arm and the way she leaned into his touch, another wave of utter disbelief rushed through him.

She was drunk and upset, and she was going upstairs with this guy. Right in front of him, as if that too were no big deal.

Marley moved away from Ronan and weaved her way toward the stairs. Ronan dropped his hand from Jake's chest, but he didn't immediately step back. Instead his eyes hardened, and a muscle in his jaw ticked. That familiarity flashed in Jake's mind again. He knew this guy. Not personally, but he knew that face. And the name—Ronan—there was something about it . . .

The guy finally stepped back. "Way to piss her off. Thanks, man."

He turned and followed Marley. And completely dumbfounded, all Jake could do was look after them and say, "Marley, what the hell?"

With one hand on the banister, she hesitated on the third step and glanced over her shoulder. "I'm not in the mood to deal with you right now, Ryder. If you're here in the morning, fine. If not, have a nice life."

The two disappeared up the stairs. Alone, Jake stood where he was, staring after them.

Have a nice life? After all their years working together, that was all she had to say to him?

The hotel manager cleared his throat. Jake glanced in that direction. The man frowned, shook his head as if Jake were a complete idiot, then disappeared into the back room.

Jake looked back at the empty stairs. Have a nice life? She'd seriously said that, as if he were nothing but an acquaintance? *Have a nice life?* As if they hadn't spent every day of the last three and a half years together? Oh, fuck that.

His vision turned red. Every muscle in his body urged him to go up to her room and set her straight. He took one step toward the stairs, then heard Eve's voice in the back of his head, yelling, *"Are you freakin' losing it?"*

He stopped, held up his hands, realized his palms were sweaty and his fingers were shaking. He closed his hands into fists. Eve was right. He was crossing the line. If Marley wanted to hook up with some random loser, what did he care?

He didn't. That was the point. He'd only come down here for his plane.

He moved back for his pack, tossed it over his shoulder, then stepped out of the hotel and onto the street. It was still hot and muggy as hell, but at least out here he could breathe. He drew air deep into his lungs, blew it out. Did it again until the red faded from his vision and he could see straight.

Salsa music spilled out of a bar across the street. Determined to get Marley Addison out of his head for good, he crossed the street, moved through the open archways that led into the cantina, found a spot at the bar, and dropped his bag at his feet.

The bartender, a twenty-something Colombian man with dread-locks down to his shoulders, looked Jake's way from the end of the bar and lifted his chin. "You want something, *amigo*?"

English. Good. Jake wasn't in the mood to struggle through his limited Spanish. "Yeah, tequila."

The bartender chuckled, tossed a rag on the bar, reached for a bottle from the counter behind him, then moved Jake's way. "Here." He poured clear liquid into a shot glass and handed it to Jake. "You like this better. Trust me."

Jake eyed the bottle. "That's not tequila."

"It's guaro. Better than tequila. Colombian specialty." He nod-ded toward the drink in Jake's hand. "You like."

Screw it. As long as it was strong, Jake didn't care what the hell he was drinking.

He tossed the shot back. The taste of licorice splashed across his tongue. Then a burn like acid shot down his esophagus and ripped through his chest before settling like a rock in his stomach.

He coughed. Lowered the glass. Coughed again and gasped for a breath.

The bartender and the patrons sidled up to the bar around him burst out laughing. "That's firewater," the bartender said. "Good stuff, hey, *amigo*?"

He refilled Jake's glass, poured himself a shot, and tossed it back as if it were nothing. "Sure to cure anything that fucks with you."

Jake breathed deep and eyed the bottle in the bartender's hand. *Aguardiente* was written in cursive across the front. Several other people at the bar held up their empty shot glasses. The bartender made his way down the wooden surface, refilling shots with the nasty anise-tasting liquor as if it were liquid candy.

Laughter echoed around him. Salsa music floated in the air. The burn faded from his chest, and a growing warmth radiated outward from his belly. He glanced down at the full shot glass in his hand, already feeling the effects of the alcohol. The bartender set a beer bottle in front of him.

"To chase," the bartender said. "Drink up, *amigo*. You look like you need it."

Jake's mind flashed to Marley. Holed up across the street in the hotel with that loser. He tossed back the second shot, reached for his beer, and downed half of it to ease the burn.

What did he care if she fucked the guy? She was his employee, not his girlfriend. He didn't have time for a girlfriend. Didn't need the trouble of a girlfriend. And he'd sure as hell never pick Marley—headstrong and snarky as hell—to fill that role even if he *was* in the market for one.

He finished his beer, pulled cash from his pocket, then signaled the bartender and paid his bill.

The bartender held up the bottle of guaro. "Sure you don't want another, *amigo*? You missin' out on a good time."

Jake eyed the clear liquid, considered for a second the oblivion he knew the bottle held, then shook his head. "No. Thanks. I've got a flight to catch."

He grabbed his pack and moved around tables toward the bar's exit. Across the street, the dumb oaf who'd taken Marley upstairs stepped out on the sidewalk, rolled his shoulders as he looked up and down the dark road, then turned to his right.

Jake glanced at his watch, then to the blond dude heading away from the hotel. Twenty minutes. The loser had spent all of twenty minutes up there in her room. Oh yeah, he was a real catch. He'd gotten her wasted, taken advantage of her, then split.

Jake didn't think twice. He hefted the pack over his shoulder and followed. Ronan . . . Ronan . . . He knew that name. As he tailed the asshole, his brain skipped over the name, then finally made the connection.

Motherfucker. She'd hooked up with Ronan Hamilton?

Jake didn't know the former DELTA soldier personally, but he knew enough. A few of the guys Jake had served with had worked with Hamilton in the past. And Hamilton's reputation as a lone wolf was legendary. As was the reason he'd been dishonorably discharged from the military.

Hamilton stopped two blocks down the dark street and turned in the middle of the sidewalk. "Dude, whatever your problem is, I don't want it."

Jake dropped his bag on the ground, stepped over it, and advanced on Hamilton. "You're my problem. Stay away from her."

"Whoa." Hamilton held up both hands. "You've got the wrong idea, man."

"No, I'm pretty sure I've got the right one." Jake moved even closer, every muscle in his body bunched and ready for a fight. "She's not a toy for you to use and lose."

Hamilton dropped his hands to his hips, shook his head, and chuckled. "You've seriously got this all messed up. She and I are—"

"I know exactly what you are, Hamilton." Jake shoved his finger into the guy's chest. "And I know what you like to do to unsuspecting women."

Hamilton's eyes turned hard and icy, and all humor fled his features. His muscles tensed, and his jaw turned to steel beneath his scruffy beard. "You don't know shit, Ryder. And you need to back the fuck off, right this second."

So he knew who Jake was. Marley had probably told him, not that Jake cared. Jake searched the other man's features. Fury simmered beneath the cool blue eyes. A fury he sensed Hamilton only just held back.

Jake dropped his hand, but he didn't step away. "Leave."

"She asked for my help. I didn't volunteer."

"Well, she doesn't need you anymore now that I'm here, does she?"

"You're gonna stay? After that little show you put on in the hotel?" He shook his head. "Something tells me you're the last person she wants around."

"I'll stay." *Would he?* Shit, yeah, he would. There was no way he was leaving Marley alone in this country now. "Marley will just have to deal with me."

Hamilton's gaze searched Jake's face. Long, tense seconds passed before he finally shrugged. "Fine. No skin off my nose. Saves me a headache anyway. She's supposed to meet me tomorrow morning for breakfast at nine in the hotel restaurant. I'll split, but know this, Ryder. If you leave her here . . . If I find out you bailed on her, I will find you. And I will hurt you. That's a promise. If you know who I am, then you know I always keep my promises."

Hamilton turned and headed back down the street, disappearing into the darkness without another word. And alone, Jake looked back toward Marley's hotel and wondered just what the hell he'd gotten himself into. He still had no idea what she was doing down here, but now more than ever he was determined to find out.

Marley braced her hands on the edge of the sink in her hotel bathroom and hung her head, praying the throbbing against her skull would slow its relentless pounding. She couldn't drink with Ronan. She'd been stupid to try to keep up. The man had a gut of steel. Which went right along with his heart of stone.

Grinding her teeth against the pain, she finished getting ready, then headed downstairs. She just needed coffee and a little food. Then she'd be back to normal and ready to face Gray's call.

She drew a deep breath that did little to ease her queasy belly. Rubbing her temple as she turned the corner into the restaurant, she scanned the room for Ronan, then felt her stomach drop when her gaze landed on Jake.

He was really here. She'd sorta hoped she'd dreamed that entire scene in the lobby last night. Unease rippled through her. Why hadn't he just taken his plane and left as she'd told him to do?

He sat at a table near the windows, one arm slung over the back of the chair beside him, his white button-down rolled up at the forearms, his face freshly shaved, not a hair out of place. Knowing she had no choice but to deal with the man this morning, she headed toward his table. And as she did, she had a memory flash from last night. One she hadn't thought much about until right now. Of his shirt damp and sticking to his skin, one side untucked, his jaw covered in dark scruff, and his hair rumpled as if he'd run his hands through it again and again.

She'd seen Jake frustrated before, but this had been different. As if he'd been stressed. As if he'd been flustered. As if whatever had been bothering him was personal.

Not sure how to read his mood, Marley eyed him cautiously as she approached the table.

"Morning," he said with his ten-thousand-watt smile, the one he turned on a prospective client when he was about to seal a deal. He lifted his coffee cup to his lips. "Sleep well?"

Something was different about him this morning. Something she couldn't quite put her finger on. Gone was the combative man who'd gotten right in her face last night. In fact, the nice, agreeable Jake— the one sitting in front of her now—was one she rarely saw at work.

Hesitantly, she pulled a chair out opposite him and sat. She wasn't sure what was going on, but she knew a gloating Jake Ryder was never a good thing.

"I'd feel better if you'd stop shouting."

He grinned wider. "I'm not shouting. Too much Colombian beer last night?"

Marley pressed her fingers against her temple. "It could have been that. Or the tequila. Or the guaro. Ronan knows how to drink a person under the table."

Jake's irritating grin faded, and disapproval clouded his eyes. "Hm," he muttered. "Guy should know a person's limits." He looked away and signaled the waiter before Marley could respond. *"Uno café, por favor."*

What was that look in his eyes? Was he jealous? No, she had to be misreading things. Jake Ryder was never jealous of anyone. The man had everything a person could possibly want. Property all over the world, a thriving security company, people at his beck and call, not to mention women falling for him wherever he went. He was powerful, wealthy, attractive, and built. And there was no way in any scenario he would ever be jealous of anything that had to do with her.

The waiter rushed over with a cup and poured the bitter brew into Marley's mug. Shaking off the hangover-induced thoughts, she reached for the cream and sugar. "What are you still doing here, Jake? I thought you were leaving."

"I decided to stay. As you said last night, we're on vacation."

"*We* aren't on anything together," Marley clarified, circling the spoon in her cup. She braced her elbows on the table, lifted the cup with both hands, and took a deep drink. Warmth flooded her tongue and immediately eased the pressure behind her skull. "You were taking your plane and leaving."

"That's where you're wrong."

"No, that's where I'm right." The waiter rushed over again and handed each of them a menu. Marley set her coffee down and looked up. "*Gracias*. We have one more coming."

"Actually, we don't."

Marley's gaze snapped Jake's way. "Excuse me?"

Jake smiled at the waiter. The guy glanced curiously between the two of them and scurried off. Jake took another sip of his coffee, looking smug and victorious all over again. "Hamilton left."

"*Left?*" Marley's eyes flew wide. "What the hell did you do to my brother?"

"Nothing. I just explained to him that—" Jake's self-righteous smile faded. "Whoa. Wait. Your *brother*?"

"Yes, my brother, you idiot. Who did you think he was?"

Jake's mouth dropped open, and his gaze scanned her face. She could almost see the little wheels trying to catch in his brain. "But you don't have a brother."

"Half brother. And you don't know everything there is to know about me. Where is he?"

Jake stared at her another long beat, then seemed to relax even more. "He's fine. I told him he didn't need to stick around now that I'm here."

"And he *believed* you?"

One side of Jake's mouth curled. "I can be very convincing when I want to be."

Marley sat back and stared at him. No, he wasn't convincing. He was obnoxious as hell, and he bullied people until he got what he wanted. Though why he wanted to weasel his way into her business now, she didn't know.

"I don't need or want your help, Jake."

He eased back in his chair once more and laid his arm across the chair beside him, cocky as always. "Well, you're not getting rid of me. People are tortured and murdered every day down here. You were smart enough to know not to come down on your own. I think we both know you're smart enough to see I'm your only option at this point."

She clenched her jaw. She was going to strangle Ronan the next time she saw him. And right now Jake wasn't safe either.

The waiter came back to take their order. Marley's frustration shot up while she listened to Jake mutilate the Spanish language. When the waiter looked her way, she pointed to the first thing she saw on her menu, not caring what she even ordered.

As soon as the waiter was gone, Jake rested both muscular forearms on the table and pinned her with a hard look. One that was sexy and aggravating and made her want to slam her fist right between his eyes. "Now. Why don't you tell me what's going on. Who called that made you drop everything, steal my plane, and jet all the way to Colombia."

She leaned forward. *"You checked my cell phone records?"*

"Relax. I pay your cell bill. It's no big deal."

No, it was a huge deal. A giant deal. And just the fact he thought it was no biggie sent her temper right back to red-hot. "That's called invasion of privacy, Jake. Did you hack into my credit card records too?"

He winced and glanced around as if to see who had heard her. "I'd never do that."

"No, I'm sure you had Eve do it."

He exhaled a long breath and frowned at her.

Marley crossed her arms over her chest and sat back. "I really hate you sometimes."

"I know." A slow grin worked its way across his face. The big jerk actually *grinned*. "Start talking."

Exasperated, Marley debated her options. She could refuse to tell him anything, but that would only tick him off, and the hard truth was if Ronan had truly left, then she really was alone and needed Jake's help. She still wasn't sure why—aside from the obvious—Jake had flown all the way down here, but there was one thing for sure she knew about the man. He had a strong personal code that wouldn't let him walk away from someone in need. Ironically, that code was something she'd always admired and respected about him, but right now it was about to make her life hell.

She blew out a long breath and dropped her arms. "My friend is in trouble. He asked me to come down and get him. He's supposed to call anytime to let me know where to meet him."

"He who?"

Marley pursed her lips. This was so going to get sticky. There was a reason she kept her personal life private from Jake. Because she didn't need his disapproving looks or snarky comments about the men she chose to see. "Grayson McKnight."

The waiter set their plates in front of them. Marley's stomach rolled when she saw the fish, complete with fins and eyeball, staring up at her.

Jake reached for a biscuit, cut it open, and slathered jam inside. "That looks appetizing. Keep going."

Appetite gone, Marley pushed the plate away and draped her napkin over the fish so it couldn't stare her down. "He worked for my father."

"Worked? As in past tense?"

"Yes." She picked up her coffee and took a large sip.

"So, why did he call you?"

"Because we're friends. Were you listening, Ryder?"

"I meant, why not call your father?"

She shrugged while he ate his breakfast and she tried not to get sick. "I don't know."

"Here." He shoved the biscuit at her. "Eat."

"I'm not hungry."

"You're hung over. Eat it, Addison."

Reluctantly, she reached for the biscuit and took a tentative bite.

"Better yet," he went on, cutting into his eggs, "why didn't *you* call your father? If the guy worked for Mason, and something happened to him down here, which, let's get real, must have if he needs help getting out of the country, then Omega's responsible for him as his employer."

Jake was right. And that feeling that there was so much more to the story settled hard in Marley's stomach again. She swallowed the bite. "I'm not sure. I just know he called me."

Jake's fork hovered over his plate, and he looked up with pin-point focus. The same focus Marley saw whenever he was in black ops mode. A shiver rushed down her spine. "Just who is this guy to you besides a friend? Because random citizens don't take off without notice and go searching for people in dangerous countries. They call people like me to do it."

"No," Marley clarified. "They call you and you order your team to take care of it."

He tipped his head. "That's not exactly accurate and you know it."

Marley did know it. But she wasn't in the mood to be agreeable with him. He'd shown up unannounced, intimidated her brother, and wormed his way into something that didn't involve him.

Pushing the biscuit away that really didn't do anything but make her feel more queasy, she lifted her coffee, took another large sip, and told herself to play nice.

"So who is this guy, really?" Jake asked again.

Every instinct she had screamed not to divulge her relationship with Gray to Jake. The last thing she needed was any more of his judgment and disapproving looks.

Her phone buzzed in her pocket before she could think of an answer. Reaching for it, she glanced at the number but didn't recognize it. Heart beating hard against her ribs, she hit Answer. "This is Marley."

"Are you in Puerto Asis, Freckles?"

A relieved breath escaped Marley's lungs. "Yeah, I'm here. Tell me how to get to you, Gray."

"Do you have something to write on?"

"Yeah, hold on." Marley reached for a napkin and signaled the waiter, holding her thumb and forefinger together as if writing in the air. The waiter nodded and rushed over with a pen. "Okay, go ahead."

"I'm in Bruhia on the border of Colombia and Peru. It's only about a hundred and fifty miles from you."

Marley scribbled the name on the napkin. Jake twisted his neck so he could read her writing and mumbled, "Goddammit. That's in the middle of the rainforest."

Marley glared at him and refocused on her conversation. "How will I find you when I get there?"

"It's a small town, Marlene. I'm the only American in the area. Trust me, you'll find me."

"Okay, right. That makes sense."

"I need you to hurry, Freckles. I don't know how much longer I can stand this."

There was a note of urgency to his voice she hadn't heard in his previous call. And it pushed her to her feet. Whatever had happened to him was bad if he wasn't willing to call her father. "I'll be there as soon as I can. Hold tight, Gray."

He said goodbye, and she clicked End. Turning for the lobby, she muttered, "I have to get my things."

She made it all the way to the stairs in the lobby before Jake grasped her forearm. "Hold on a minute."

She'd reached the end of her patience where Jake was concerned, and she'd played nice long enough. Now it was time to act. "I don't have time to hold on. I need to call Tony."

"You're not taking my plane into the jungle."

Marley tugged back on his arm. "Then I'll find a car."

"No, *we'll* find a car."

The determined look in his dark eyes told her loud and clear that he wasn't going to give up. And that meant she was stuck with him whether she liked it or not.

Frustrated beyond belief, she tugged her arm from his grip and muttered, "Fine. Whatever. I still need to get my stuff."

She twisted to move up the steps, but her foot slipped on the carpet. She gasped and reached out for the handrail. But before she could close her fingers around the solid wood, her center of gravity went out from under her.

"Dammit." Jake wrapped his thick arm around her waist. His chest brushed her spine, his thighs skimmed the backs of her legs, then his hips cradled her butt as he pulled her back and into him to keep her from hitting the ground.

Heat encircled her. A heat she didn't expect. Her head grew light, and for a fleeting moment, she thought she was still drunk, but she couldn't be sure because, suddenly, she couldn't seem to think. All she could focus on was the warm, hard body at her back and the soft, sweet breath near her ear whispering, "Easy."

Oh man, that felt good. To be held close. To be protected. But as soon as the thought hit, she remembered who was holding her. She found her footing, let go of his arm, and tried to push herself upright. Then realized something else was hard against her ass. Something that hadn't been hard ten seconds ago.

She pulled quickly away. As if he'd just realized the same thing, Jake let go of her and stumbled back.

Marley turned quickly to make sure he hadn't just landed on his ass. Luckily, he hadn't, but he looked flustered.

Jake cleared his throat and nodded up the stairs, not meeting her eyes. "You should go get your stuff."

"Yeah," she said, eyeing him cautiously. "That's just what I was about to do."

He glanced past her toward the door, clearly not wanting to make eye contact. "I'll find us a ride."

He was rattled. She never saw the man rattled. A tingle lit off in her belly. The same one she'd felt over the last three months whenever he looked right at her at work.

She wasn't interested in Jake Ryder. He was domineering, aggravating, and he had more baggage than she wanted to deal with. And yet, no matter what she did, she couldn't stop that stupid tingle from spreading up her chest toward her heart.

He moved for the door, then turned back. "Don't think about disappearing."

Her heart made a weird little skip. *It's alcohol. It's stress. It is* not *attraction*, she told herself.

Bracing one hand on the handrail, Marley reminded herself this was Jake—her bullheaded, obnoxious boss—and flicked him a sassy look. "Why on earth would I possibly do that? We both know you'd just do something illegal to find me."

"So long as we're clear."

Marley rolled her eyes and stomped up the stairs.

No, they weren't clear on anything. And that stupid little bump in her heart said that was going to be a major problem for her. Probably soon.

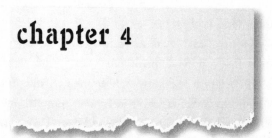

chapter 4

"Gracias." Jake climbed out of the beat-up Ford pickup and motioned to the driver he'd wrangled to take them to Bruhia. *"Un momento, por favor."*

The guy nodded behind the wheel, then looked down to tinker with his phone. As Jake headed into the hotel, he pulled out his cell and dialed Eve back at Aegis headquarters.

"Well?" Eve asked as soon as she picked up the line. "Did you find her?"

"Yeah." Jake moved up the stairs, pulled out his key, and unlocked the door to his room. "I found her."

"And?"

"And she's being evasive." He tucked the phone between his shoulder and ear and grabbed his bag. "I need you to run a search on a guy named Grayson McKnight. He used to work for Mason Addison over at Omega."

"Oookay. And why am I running background on some random guy who works for a rival company?"

"Because whoever he is, he's got Marley twisted up in knots."

"Ah," Eve said slowly. "Now it's making sense. Marley took off on a romantic vacation with this guy and you don't approve. Got it."

"Don't be a smartass." Jake slung his bag over his shoulder and pulled the door closed behind him. "I couldn't care less who she hooks up with. That's not what this is about. The guy isn't what she thinks."

"Says your super jealous black ops senses."

Jealous? He wasn't jealous. "Says my gut. I don't need your opinion here, Wolfe. Just run the damn search."

She sighed. "You've got a real way with women, Ryder. You know you're not going to be down there long with that attitude, right? Marley will kick your ass clear back to the States if you pull that on her."

He wasn't jealous, dammit. But even as Jake thought the words, his moment with Marley on the stairs rippled through his brain, drawing his feet to a stop in the middle of the hall.

Just what was that anyway? Marley was his employee, not a woman. At least not a woman *like that*. Not one he was interested in. She was a friend.

He swiped at the sweat beading on his brow. Yeah, that made more sense. She was a just a friend. The same way Miller and Bentley were his friends. He'd do what he could to help those guys too. This was no different.

Telling himself there was nothing to worry about, he stopped in front of Marley's room and banged his fist on the door. "Car's downstairs, Addison."

"Be right there," she hollered back.

He headed down the stairs, but a little voice in the back of his head whispered, *You don't get turned on by Bentley and Miller.*

"Ryder?" Eve asked in his ear. In the background, voices echoed as if from a TV. "Did I lose you?"

"No, I'm here." Irritated with himself, Jake clenched his jaw. "And I know you're in my office, Wolfe. I don't remember giving you permission for that."

"*Moi?* Why would you assume that? I'm only running the show while you're off gallivanting around South America playing lovesick tourist."

The woman could be such a smartass. Just like Marley. Why did he surround himself with sassy women?

"Don't mess with any of my shit."

"I wouldn't dare."

The smile in her voice lifted his spirits, if only for a moment. He moved from the lobby to the street. Midmorning sunlight beat down to mix with the humid air, making him sweat beneath the white button-down and cargo pants. "And if you call me a lovesick anything again, you'll be looking for a new job."

"Got it, boss." Her voice turned businesslike. "I'll call as soon as I have info on Marley's mystery boyfriend."

The line clicked dead in his ear. Pocketing his phone, Jake's almost-good mood plummeted. He hoped like hell the guy wasn't a boyfriend. That was just going to muddy things up for Marley, especially after five years. But his gut was already screaming that was the only logical answer. He couldn't think of another scenario that would make Marley drop everything—including him—and rush to a dangerous country alone.

This was cozy. Too close and cozy after her moment with Jake on the stairs.

Marley wanted nothing more than to shift to her left, closer to the driver, so she wasn't plastered against Jake on the bench seat of the rusted pickup. But if she did that, Jake would know she was awake. And that would mess up her plan to ignore him on the drive toward Bruhia.

The middle-aged Colombian man Jake had paid to drive them—Manuel—hummed along to salsa music on the radio. Normally, that wouldn't bother her, but she was hot, sweaty, and still a little hung over from the night before. And every time they went over a rock or pothole in the dirt road, it jostled her in her seat and knocked her into Jake at her side. Jake, who was radiating waves of heat that only sent jolts of awareness through every inch of her body. Jake, who wasn't taking the hint that she was too hung over to talk just yet and had spent the last two hours shifting in his seat, sighing repeatedly, and muttering under his breath.

The rig bounced over something big in the road, and Marley bumped into him, her arms flying up in the air. Before she could lay her head back down and feign sleep, Jake said, "Nice of you to finally wake up."

She closed her eyes and tipped her head away from him. "Wake me when we get there."

"I don't think so. You've had your sleep. It's time you continued talking."

Sighing, Marley shifted upright in her seat and moved as far from him as she could get, which really was only a centimeter. "You're like a dog with a bone, you know that?"

"Which is why I'm so good at what I do. Tell me about McKnight."

Marley exhaled a long breath. She'd been overly optimistic when she thought he'd let this line of questioning go. She brushed the hair out of her eyes. "I already told you he was a friend."

"What kind of friend? That's the question here, isn't it?"

Marley couldn't quite read him. The words were spoken in a calm and even tone, but she could tell from the tense line of his shoulders that something was bothering him. Something other than the fact she'd taken his plane. "Why do you care what kind of friend he was? Does it matter?"

"No." He glanced out the window. "Why would it matter? I'm just trying to figure out what you dragged me into."

Okay, he was definitely being moody about something, but Marley had no clue what. Before their little moment on the stairs, he'd been cocky as always. "For the record, I didn't *drag* you into anything. If you remember correctly, you forced your way in by bullying my brother."

"You're right, I did. And why didn't I know you have a brother?"

She could barely keep up with him. Now he was frustrated she hadn't told him about Ronan? He'd never seemed interested in her family life other than to play nice with her father, who was his closest rival for clients. "I wasn't aware we were trading family secrets, Jake. Tell you what. You go first. Let's talk about all your father's indiscretions."

He shot her a look. "Don't go there, Marley."

Manuel stopped humming and glanced their way.

She'd hit a serious nerve with that one. She knew it and immediately regretted the low blow. Jake's relationship with his father was a sore spot for him, even years after his father's death. Though she wasn't entirely sure why.

Marley reminded herself to stay calm. That was how she got through everything with Jake. She forgot how frustrated and hot he made her and focused on keeping the peace. "What do you really want to know?"

"I want to know who the hell this guy is we're risking our lives to rescue."

She nearly laughed. "We're hardly risking our lives. We're driving along a quiet jungle road. Sometimes you are so dramatic, Ryder."

"And sometimes you are just so"—Jake curled both hands into fists and clenched his jaw—"damn maddening."

"Hey, *señorita*," Manuel asked at Marley's side. "You want me kick him out of the truck?"

"Hm, I might." Marley grinned. She was kind of having fun with this. As much as she hadn't wanted Jake to tag along, watching him get worked up for no apparent reason gave her a little thrill. "Hold that thought." She glanced Jake's way and lifted her brows.

"God Almighty." Jake rubbed his thumb and forefinger across his forehead. "I give up. I don't know why I even try anymore."

Okay, enough was enough. She'd put him in his place. It was time to stop messing with him. "Gray and I used to date. He left on an op five years ago. Something went wrong on the mission. When my father came back, he told me Gray had been killed. Fast-forward to a couple of days ago when Gray called out of the blue asking for help, and you're caught up to speed."

Jake dropped his hands, but he didn't look her way. "So he's your boyfriend."

"Was. Kind of hard to have a relationship with someone who's been dead for five years, you know?"

"Now you're a comedian. Ha-ha."

There was no humor in his voice, but there was something different in his eyes. He was still irritated, but now there was a hint of . . . was that disappointment?

No, she had to be seeing things again. Why would he be disappointed? Because she'd dated Gray? He'd never cared who she dated before. He'd never cared about her personal life, period.

She gave herself a mental slap and looked back out the windshield. The more likely explanation was that he simply disapproved of her choice. Jake was one of the most opinionated men she knew. Another trait he shared with her father.

"That's all I know," she said.

"Why didn't you call your father for help?"

"Because he asked me not to tell my father. Whatever happened to him, he thinks my father was responsible."

When Jake's brow lowered, Marley sighed. "Let's get real, Jake. We both know how my dad works. He alienates people. It's his way or the highway. My father made it clear that he wasn't wild about my dating Gray right from the start. I don't doubt that Gray and my father clashed five years ago. Just as I don't doubt that my father had nothing to do with Gray's disappearance. But Gray was already agitated on the phone when he called me. If my father was the one to show up to help him, I'm not sure Gray would go with him. That's why I made the decision to come down here without Mason Addison."

She could see those wheels turning again in Jake's mind as he stared at her, but before he could respond, Manuel slammed on the brakes, bringing the pickup to a jarring stop, hurling both Jake and Marley forward.

Marley slammed into the dash with a grunt. Jake gripped her arm and pulled her back up on the seat beside him. "You okay?"

"Yeah, I'm fine." She winced at a stab of pain in her side. "Seat-belts would have been nice. What the heck was that?"

Manuel had already opened his door and stood in front of the truck, waving his arms. Marley's gaze shot past him to the giant tree lying across the dirt road.

"That," Jake said, popping his door open, "looks like a roadblock."

"Shit." Pressing a hand against her side where Jake must have elbowed her, Marley climbed out after him and stood in front of the truck with the men.

The jungle rose up on both sides of the road. Vines wrapped around tree trunks and hung from the branches above. Several different species of palms littered the jungle floor, and everywhere birds chirping and animals moving could be heard. Even along the road, there was so little light from the dense canopy above, it was hard to see in the distance.

Jake perched his hands on his hips and glanced around. "I don't suppose there's another way."

"No other way," Manuel said. "Not unless we go back. Must have come down during last week's storm." He threw up his hands. "We have to chop it."

Marley's brow lifted. The trunk alone had to be eighteen inches wide. They'd be here all night.

Manuel moved around the back of the truck and reached for an ax from the bed. The rat-tat-tat of something loud echoed through the trees off to their right.

Marley turned toward the sound. Manuel dropped the ax back into the bed. Jake grasped Marley's hand and pulled her around the driver's side of the truck.

"What was that?" Marley asked.

Jake's eyes scanned the trees. "Sounded like gunfire. Two hundred yards away."

Manuel pulled the driver door open and scrambled inside. "Paramilitary. Very bad men. Very, very bad." He grabbed Marley's backpack and threw it onto the ground.

Jake let go of Marley and stepped toward the door. "Hold on. Just what the hell do you think you're—"

Manuel chucked Jake's backpack onto the ground next to Marley's and slammed the door shut. "This as far as I go. Bruhia that way." He pointed to the left, into the trees, in the opposite direction of the gunfire. "Good luck, *amigos*."

He shoved the truck into reverse. Dirt and gravel spit up in the air. The vehicle whipped around, then tore away.

"Motherfucker!" Jake ran after the truck and smacked his hand along the tailgate, but Manuel floored it. Seconds later, all that was left was the crunch of gravel far off in the distance and the plume of dust he left in his wake.

The ricochet of gunfire sounded behind them. Closer this time. Marley looked in that direction, a sense of foreboding rushing down her spine.

"Son of a bitch." Jake marched back to her. "Grab your pack."

Marley scooped up her backpack and tossed it on. "What the heck are we supposed to do now?"

"Now we're getting as far from that"—he nodded in the direction of the gunfire—"as we can."

He knelt in front of his pack and pulled out a Glock. After checking the magazine, he drew out a holster, which he strapped to his thigh, slid the weapon inside, then threw his pack on. "Colombian guerrillas and paramilitary. Two groups we do not want to run into out here in the jungle."

Marley strapped the buckle of her pack around her waist. "What do they want?"

"The same thing all paramilitary groups want. Whatever the fuck they can get." Jake shoved a palm frond out of his way and stepped over a huge root. "Keep up, Addison. We need to put as much distance between us and them as we can."

He'd just taken over, but suddenly Marley didn't care. Her adrenaline surged as she shoved the damp palm out of her face and followed him deeper into the jungle. More gunfire echoed behind her, and she quickened her pace, working hard to keep up with Jake's big steps. Fear rippled down her spine, cooling her skin in the humid air, but two things became bitterly clear.

One, she wasn't just risking her life anymore, now she was risking Jake's. And two, there wasn't anyone she trusted more than him.

Jake unbuckled his pack and dropped it on the ground near some giant tree he couldn't name with huge roots sticking out from the base five feet high and extending downward to the forest floor. "We can stop here. I haven't heard any sign of our friends for the last hour. I think we lost them."

Marley stepped up next to him and gripped both shoulder straps of her pack. "We should keep going. If we keep up this pace, we could reach Bruhia in a couple of hours."

He glanced up at her as he knelt by his pack and flipped the top open. She looked over the jungle in the direction they'd been heading since he'd last checked his compass. She was right. If they kept going, they might reach the small town in three, four hours tops. But he didn't want to push her too hard. She was a city girl. And more importantly, he wasn't sure what was out there in the dark of the jungle.

He took in the supple line of her jaw, the bead of sweat that slid down her temple. Her hair was pulled back into a messy tail. Damp blonde tendrils hung around her face and down the back of her neck. The black tank she wore stuck to her curves, leaving nothing to the imagination, and her gray cargo pants were muddy up to her calves. But she didn't look tired or scared or overwhelmed. And she hadn't once complained as he'd led through foliage so thick she could barely move, across creeks that had soaked her boots to the point where they probably wouldn't dry in this climate, and up and down hills that had fatigued even his muscles. A fact that not only surprised him, it impressed the hell out of him.

Not that he was about to tell her that. The last thing he needed was her saying, *See? Told ya I could hold my own on an op.*

Frowning, he found his knife. After clipping it to his belt, he unhooked the machete he'd picked up in town before they'd left, just in case, and muttered, "Too bad this isn't an op."

"What?" She turned to look down at him. "Did you say something?"

He shoved his pack closer to the base of the tree between two wide roots. "I said we're not going anywhere. It'll be dark soon."

"I have a headlamp. Something tells me you do too in that magic pack of yours."

She was right. He did have one. But he wasn't about to use it. "There are all kinds of things in the jungle you do not want to meet in the dark. Trust me." He pushed to his feet. "Stay here while I cut some palms so we can build a roof over these roots for shelter."

He moved past her into the foliage. At his back, she mumbled, "I'm not an invalid, you know."

"Then do something productive while I'm gone." He glanced back at her. "Like find some berries for dinner. Just watch out for poisonous dart frogs, vampire bats, and anacondas."

"Yeah, thanks." She shot him a look that was cuter than it was frustrated. "I'll do just that."

He chuckled as he walked off, thankful the animosity was gone from her voice. He knew she was still miffed that he'd shown up and pushed his way into this little excursion, but he wasn't about to leave her safety in the hands of someone else. Especially not where she was headed.

It took longer than he thought to find the right kind of palm fronds. He had to make do with a variety that fanned out from a central branch. There were gaps between the spindly fronds that might let water in if it rained in the night, so he cut extra. By the time he had enough for the shelter, he was drenched in sweat, hot and sticky, cut and bleeding from the razor-sharp fronds and prickly vines around him, and irritated because it was growing dark quicker than he'd calculated.

He trudged his way back through the jungle. Stopped when he

was sure he should have already reached their camp, then pulled out his compass and checked his coordinates.

Damn jungle. Everything looked the same in the dwindling light. Backtracking, he made his way to the area where he'd cut the vines, checked his compass again, and headed in the other direction. Twenty minutes later, he slowed when he spotted a warm orange glow.

His adrenaline spiked, and his heart beat hard against his ribs. He squinted to see through the trees.

A fire. Someone had built a fire near their makeshift camp. A quick shot of fear raced through his veins. He reached for the Glock at his thigh. If those guerrillas had caught up with them . . . If they'd done something to Marley . . . A thousand scenarios raced through his mind, every one ending in something horrid.

A figure moved in front of the fire, circled around the other side, and knelt down. A curvy figure. One with blond hair pulled back in a tail. One he recognized.

Confused, Jake inched forward, careful not to make any sound, just in case. Ten yards away he realized Marley was the only one in the area. And their camp now looked nothing like it had when he'd left.

She'd laid the tarp on the ground between two giant roots. A fire sizzled ten feet away in a circle of rocks. Two Y-shaped sticks were stuck into the ground on each side of the fire, supporting another stick skewered through some kind of meat. On a piece of bark off to the right of the fire, a pile of purple berries sat untouched along with a cluster of bananas.

Reaching around the fire, Marley gripped the ends of the roughly made rotisserie and turned the meat. She winced when the flame got too close to her fingers, pulled her hand back, and sucked on her knuckle.

"What the heck is this?"

She turned at the sound of his voice and looked up as he stepped through the trees. "You're back. I was starting to wonder if I'd have to go look for you."

Jake dragged the fronds into camp, dropping them near the fire. "Who did all this?"

"I did."

He glanced from the fire to the berries and back again. "No, seriously. Is someone else here?"

She pushed to her feet. "No one but me." Stepping toward the tarp she'd laid out, she said, "The iguana needs a little longer to cook. In the meantime, we can get started on the shelter. It's getting more humid. I have a feeling rain's going to hit tonight."

"Iguana." Jake eyed the meat sizzling over the fire. "You're trying to tell me you caught an iguana."

"A green iguana. Fast little bugger." She picked up a wide-leafed frond, one that was easily three times bigger than the fronds he'd cut, with no gaps or holes. "I thought these might be good for the roof. What do you think?"

Jake glanced down at the spindly fronds at his feet.

"Oh," she said, following his gaze. "Yours are nice too. If you'd rather use yours, we can."

He looked up at her, widening his eyes in utter disbelief. Who was this chick? All this time, MacGyver had been sitting out in the other office?

A slow, gloating smile spread across her lips. One that warmed his belly in a way he didn't expect. "I told you I wasn't an invalid, Jake. My father dragged me all over the globe as a kid. I know a thing or two about survival in the wild. I also know how to take care of myself."

That was becomingly painfully obvious. Hidden survival skills, hijacking abilities, a mystery brother, and a not-so-dead boyfriend. The woman in front of him was turning out to be nothing like the one who'd quietly worked for him all these years. As Jake glanced around the camp she'd set up without a bit of his help, he couldn't help but wonder what other secrets were hiding behind those pretty blue eyes.

And just what the hell kind of trouble that meant was waiting for him down the line.

chapter 5

Marley turned her head in the darkness to look toward Jake, but all she could see was the outline of his shadow. "You really should let me look at those cuts on your hands."

"My hands are fine," he muttered next to her.

She smiled up at the roof of the shelter they'd built with her banana leaves. Mr. Moody was back. And this time she knew he was pouting because she'd surprised the heck out of him by setting up camp, catching and cooking dinner, and not being the needy and whiny female he expected her to be.

She really wanted to say, *I told you I could be an asset on an op, not a liability,* but held her tongue. She'd made her point. Rubbing it in now would just be overly satisfying.

She folded her hands over her belly, sighing as she listened to the bats and howler monkeys in the canopy above. After they'd finished eating, they'd laid Jake's palm fronds as bedding under the tarp. They were currently lying next to each other in the shelter, both of them quiet and lost in thought.

"Why the heck didn't I know Mason Addison has a son who was a soldier?"

Okay, maybe he wasn't quite as lost in thought as she'd assumed. "Ronan told you he was in the military?"

Jake crossed his arms over his chest beside her, his thick biceps straining the thin black T-shirt he'd changed into just before they'd left Puerto Asís. "He didn't have to. Once a soldier, always a soldier."

He recognized the stance too. That made sense. "The reason you didn't know is because he's not my father's son. We're half siblings. Through our mother."

"I thought your mom was dead."

"She is."

"Sorry. That was blunt. I meant—"

"I know what you meant." Marley's good mood took a nose-dive. This was not a story she enjoyed rehashing, but since Jake was here, helping her when he didn't need to be, she decided there was no reason not to tell him.

"Ronan's a year younger than me. Omega Intel was just a fledgling company back when we were both born. My dad's whole focus was building it up, gaining contracts, making a name for himself. He was gone all the time. Off running secret covert ops through different contracts with the government and private clients. My mother was lonely. I don't blame her. I mean, I know what it's like to live in this world. It's stressful and secretive and isolating at times. And he didn't make it easy on her. She was stuck on the outside looking in because my father didn't tell her anything. Maybe he thought he was keeping her safe that way, I don't know.

"Anyway, I was just a baby at the time, so I don't remember any of this, but according to my aunt Ginger who passed away from cancer a few years ago, my mother was in Nashville at the time visiting a friend and met some guy. My dad was somewhere in Africa at the time on this long mission—four months, I think. She hit it off with the guy and, well, got pregnant with Ronan."

"Ouch."

"Yeah. Ouch. Kinda hard to pass off a surprise pregnancy when your husband has been gone that long. She stopped seeing the guy in Nashville, but my dad didn't want to have anything to do with her. He kicked her out. The divorce got ugly, but he had a much better attorney and got custody of me. She moved in with her parents and had Ronan, but the guilt of it all got to be too much for her. She killed herself when Ronan was only a year old."

"Oh man."

"My dad never talked about her. For a long time I thought she'd died of cancer when I was a baby. It was only when I was in college that my aunt filled me in on the whole story. I didn't even know I had a brother until then."

"That must have been a shock."

"A good shock. I always wanted a sibling. I went and found him. He, as you can imagine, wasn't thrilled to see me. Unlike me, he knew all about my family. He was a pretty screwed-up kid then—raised by his grandparents, his dad was never in the picture, and he had a lot of anger—but I was persistent. Didn't let him push me away."

Jake chuckled. "Yeah, I can totally see you doing that."

Marley smiled in the darkness, remembering how resistant Ronan had been to her friendship at first. He still acted like he never wanted her around, but she knew it was all a façade. He wouldn't have hopped on a plane to help her if he didn't care.

"Just what did you say to him to get him to leave anyway? Ronan never would have left me in Colombia alone if you had threatened him."

"Yeah, well." Jake shifted on the tarp beside her.

"Yeah, well what?" She turned to look at his shadowy outline again.

He exhaled. "I just told him he didn't need to stick around."

No, there was more. She sensed it. "You recognized him, didn't you?"

"I don't know what you're talking about."

Marley looked back up at the makeshift ceiling. "I'm not stupid. I know SEALs run missions with DELTA guys now and then. You don't have to pretend as if you don't know who he is."

Jake was silent a minute, then said, "It just surprises me you'd turn to someone like him for help instead of asking me."

There it was. The frustration she knew had been at the root of his moodiness since the moment he'd stepped foot in Colombia.

She tried to figure out how to answer and came up empty. Because deep down she wasn't exactly sure why she'd been so adamant he not help her. It was more than the fact she didn't want to listen to his opinion. It had to do with the complexity of their relationship—more than colleagues, not quite friends, and the weird sexual tension she'd been feeling around him the last few months.

She cleared her throat. Crossed her ankles. Really wanted to put distance between them because her skin was suddenly tingling, but knew there was nowhere to go. Not knowing how else to answer, she finally said, "Ronan is not what you think. There's more to the story about how and why he was discharged than you and your SEAL buddies know."

Jake turned his head in her direction. She didn't have to see his *get real* expression to know it was there. "You know all guys say that, right? It's not what you think?"

"In this case it's true." Marley didn't want to talk any more about Ronan. What he'd been kicked out of the military for was pretty nasty. He'd been lucky he hadn't been court-martialed, but his judge advocate had gotten him off due to mishandling of evidence. He'd still lost his commission, and it had pretty well fucked up his life, but these days he seemed to be doing okay even if he was floating around South America doing mercenary work she didn't want to think too much about.

It wasn't worth her time or energy to try to convince Jake of that fact, though. No matter what she said, his rigid by-the-book ethics would make it impossible for him to agree with or understand the things Ronan had done.

"Where did he go?" Marley asked, changing the subject.

"I don't know." Jake looked back up at the ceiling. "Just threatened me if something happened to you."

Marley smiled again in the darkness. There was the protective little brother she knew and loved, even if he rarely showed it. "He knows who you are. He must have felt comfortable leaving with you here. Otherwise he'd have stayed."

Jake huffed, lifted his hand, and slapped a bug on his bare forearm. "Maybe he just didn't want to trek into this beautiful jungle to be eaten alive by mosquitoes."

Marley chuckled.

"Or maybe he knew you were being evasive about this so-called boyfriend and didn't want the headache."

Marley's smile faded. So they were back to Gray. She knew their respite from this topic had been too good to be true.

"Why didn't your father want you dating the guy?"

She was not in the mood to talk about this tonight. Especially when she was already so conflicted about Gray in the first place. And considering the odd tingle in her belly just from being close to Jake, she knew he was the last person she could talk to about her ex.

Rolling away from him, she rested her cheek on her hand and blew out a long breath. "I'm tired. We'll talk tomorrow. Night, Jake."

He sighed. Muttered, "You bet your ass we'll talk tomorrow." Then louder said, "Night, Marley."

And though she knew she was off the hook for the moment, she didn't have a clue what she'd tell him in the morning.

Jake blinked several times as he stared at a tree root inches from his face. Rolling to his back, he looked up at green banana leaves above. He was in the shelter they'd built in the jungle. The events of the last few days rippled through his mind, forming waves of consciousness that slowly sank in.

Man, he had to admit, Marley had shocked the hell out of him with her hunting and gathering skills. And she'd not only caught an iguana—which wasn't an easy task for anyone, him included—she'd skinned and cooked the bugger.

A slow smile spread across his lips as he thought back to the way she'd built a fire, cut and dragged banana leaves back, and set up camp without anyone's help. Did he know another woman who could do all that? Especially without a single complaint?

He couldn't think of any. Most of the women he knew didn't even like to kill a spider. And forget cooking. The last woman he'd dated—Karen, Kallie, no, Krista—hadn't turned on her stove in at least five years.

That awe came floating back. He shifted his head to the left, expecting to see Marley sleeping beside him in the shelter, but the tarp was empty.

He pushed up to his hands and looked out through the opening of the shelter. Rising to his feet, he stepped outside and glanced around the dimly lit jungle.

A bird cawed high above. The fire had died out, and the forest floor was damp from the drizzle they'd gotten last night, but it was still muggy and hot as hell. He moved past the fire pit and stepped into the trees, searching for her. "Marley?"

A howler monkey screamed somewhere off to his right, the sound echoing through the forest like an eerie premonition. Jake's pulse picked up speed. He scanned the forest but saw no sign of her.

"Addison!" he called, listening as his voice echoed through the rainforest. But there was still no response. His adrenaline spiked, and the same fears he'd had last night when he'd seen that fire through the trees came rushing back.

He darted back into the shelter and grabbed his Glock. Yeah, she might be able to set up camp on her own, but there were all kinds of dangers in the rainforest just waiting to strike. Not only were guerrillas and paramilitary troops wandering around out here, but snakes, jaguars, cougars, and poisonous plants and insects lurked everywhere.

He holstered his gun at his thigh and picked his way through the brush, cursing every time a thorny vine caught on his clothing and scratched his arms and hands. And he told himself if he found her alive—*Please God, let her be alive*—he was going to shake some ever-loving sense into her.

The splash of water echoed off to his right. He stilled, listened, squinted to see through the thick brush. When it happened again, he turned in that direction and shoved palm fronds and vines out of his way until he stepped into a patch of sunlight and stared dumfounded at the sight in front of him.

Marley stood under a waterfall across a small pond, her eyes closed, her hands brushing her wet hair back from her face while water sluiced down her naked body. The waterline hit at her waist, but Jake was too shocked to notice much more than skin and splashing water.

"Just what in hell do you think you're doing?" he asked.

Marley's blue eyes shot open. A tiny yelp slipped from her lips just before she dropped down into the water.

"Hey," she managed after several seconds. "I, uh, didn't know you were awake."

He stepped closer to the edge of the water. "Get out of that damn pond."

An amused expression crossed her dewy face. "Why? You got something against being clean, Ryder?"

"What? No." His brow wrinkled. Why the hell was she smiling like that? Didn't she know what could be lurking in that water? "You need to get out because there could be snakes or alligators or eels or God knows what else in there."

Marley laughed. "They're called caimans in South America, not alligators. And there aren't any here. I checked. Look down, Jake. If something were to swim up to me, I'd see it."

He glanced at the clear blue water, then to the waterfall that dropped from a rock face fifteen feet above. The edge of the pool was nothing but sandy loam. No reeds, no water lilies, nothing for snakes or alligators—correction: caimans—to hide under.

A little of his anxiety eased. But his irritation kicked up once more when Marley slapped her hand against the surface of the water, sending spray all over him.

"Hey." He jerked back and held out his arms. "What's wrong with you?"

"Not a thing. Take your clothes off and get in. The water's great. It'll ease your grumpy mood."

"I'm not grumpy."

"Oh. My mistake. It must be caffeine withdrawal."

His eyes narrowed. He couldn't quite read her. Her smile was one of ease. And there was a playful glint in her eyes he hadn't seen in a really long time. "Are you trying to get me naked, Addison?"

She rolled her pretty sky-blue eyes. "As if. No, I'm not one of your groupies. You stink, Ryder. I should know. I had to sleep next to you last night. If I have to spend the next few hours with you in this sweaty jungle, I don't want to smell you."

He shot her a look, which only made her laugh again. She turned her back. "I won't watch. How's that?"

That was good. Though a tiny part of him was disappointed that she'd turned around. Which totally made him frown because this was Marley. Not a woman he was the least bit attracted to romantically.

He glanced over the jungle, then looked at the pond and waterfall. She was right, it did look refreshing. And he was hot and sweaty and, yeah, grumpy as hell. And they *did* have a good long hike in front of them. A quick dunk would do wonders for his mood.

His frustration slid to the wayside. He bent over and unlaced his boots. "I don't know how I let you talk me into this shit. If I get eaten by piranhas or a Komodo dragon, you're in big trouble, Addison."

"Komodo dragons live in Indonesia, not South America. But if one happens to miraculously bite you here, I've got a first aid kit."

God, she was a smartass sometimes. But as he kicked off his boots and socks, tugged off his T-shirt, and reached for the snap on his pants, part of him was amused instead of annoyed. His gaze slid to her bare shoulder. Her toned, tanned, really sexy bare shoulder. "No peeking."

"Don't worry. I have to work with you every day. I don't need to be scarred for life."

He dropped his pants on the ground and waded out into the water, the silty bottom squishing between his toes. She was definitely right. The water was cool and felt damn good. He turned around and sank into the water backward, letting the clear liquid rush over his skin and bubble above his head.

When he came back up and shook the droplets from his hair, Marley was treading water feet from him, a wide smile on her pretty face. "See? Told ya."

Had he ever thought she was pretty before? Probably. When she wore a new blouse to work, or did her hair differently, or when she really smiled, like she was doing now. But for the most part he tried not to notice. Though her filing system aggravated the hell out of him, and she rarely did what he wanted at the moment he wanted it done, she managed the ops with precision, she could hold her own with each of the guys in the company, and she rarely complained—at least not about the job. He'd never wanted to mess up their working relationship by noticing something as silly as her looks, so he'd never really tried.

Except, he couldn't deny those looks now. As she dunked under the water and came back up, swiping her wet hair away from her face, he couldn't stop looking. She wasn't exotic like the last woman he'd dated, wasn't flashy like most of the women he went for. She was pretty in that girl-next-door way he'd told himself he was never interested in. And as he watched the water slide down her temple and inch its way toward the corner of her plump pink lips, something in his belly heated.

She opened those sky-blue eyes and smiled his way. "Nice, huh?"

Jake drew in a sharp breath and inched back from her. "It's okay."

What the hell was wrong with him? Noticing Marley's looks? Being turned on by her? Not good. Especially not with his history.

He turned around, glanced across the pond again, checking the edge of the pool and the water for any creatures. That, at least, kept his mind focused on something important and off the fact she was naked only inches away.

"So how is it you spent eight years as a SEAL and you're afraid of the water?"

He glanced over his shoulder and huffed. "I'm not afraid of the water. Sea, air, and land. Kinda had to get used to all three during SQT."

"What's that?"

"SEAL qualification training."

"Ah. Got it. But you clearly don't like the jungle."

He eyed the edge of the water. "I don't have a problem with the jungle. It's everything *in* the jungle I have issues with."

She laughed. "You worry too much, Ryder."

He turned to look at her. She was floating on her back in the water, her hair flaring around her head, the tips of her breasts skimming the surface.

Her very naked breasts.

He glanced quickly away and moved another foot in the opposite direction. The water was way too damn clear for his taste. Especially now, when that warmth he'd felt earlier was suddenly spreading lower.

She came back up and shook the droplets from her eyes before he had time to get to the edge of the lagoon and get the hell out. "Why did you leave the navy? I just realized I never asked before."

Oh gee. There was a topic he did not want to dive into. Especially not now when they were both naked and she was way too close to touch. Because talking about the past was like a giant knife slicing open a wound that would just leave him wrecked and vulnerable.

"My body couldn't take it anymore," he lied. "Sucks to get old."

She laughed and splashed water over her shoulders. "You're hardly old. You're what, thirty-six? And now that I've seen you without your shirt on, I know you're just as built as the rest of the guys at Aegis. I'm sure you've got a few more years left before you get all senile and decrepit."

Had she just implied she was checking him out? He turned in the water, watching as she ran her fingers through her damp hair, rinsing away the dirt and grime. A sliver of sunlight filtered through the canopy to highlight the different colors in her hair and make her skin glow, and though he knew he shouldn't look, he couldn't seem to tear his gaze away. If he didn't know who she was and had just stumbled across her in this pool, he'd think she was a water sprite, or a mermaid, or a forest nymph out for a quick dip. Yes, she was that fresh, alluring girl-next-door, but she was also confident and sexy, and that didn't just make her pretty, it made her drop-dead gorgeous.

That warmth in his belly spread down into his groin, making him hard and hot and achy.

She opened her pale-blue eyes and glanced his way. "Oh, I forgot to tell you. Before I—as you so eloquently call it—stole your plane, I sent that paperwork to the realtors."

"Realtors?" Why hadn't he ever noticed that spray of freckles along the bridge of her nose? The tiny little light-brown dots that seemed to dance across her olive skin, making it that much more alluring.

Because she usually wore reading glasses at the office, he realized. And because he'd never let himself take a close look like he was doing now.

"For the properties we talked about. The ones you haven't shown any interest in since your father passed. They should all be listed within the next week or so."

Just the mention of his father dampened his arousal and slingshotted his mood back to dreary. He blinked, looked away from her and out over the water, then blinked again. Before his death, Linus Ryder had cultivated quite the portfolio of land all over the world, most of which Jake had never seen. Real estate had been his father's one true love, and now, even four and a half years after his death, Jake was still trying to unload a good chunk of disgustingly ornate homes he had no interest in visiting—most out west where his father had spent the last years of his life schmoozing with celebrities and girls half his age in an attempt to stay young.

"That's good."

"I didn't mean to bring up your dad," she said quietly. "It just popped into my head when I was thinking about you not liking the jungle and how good it is that you don't have a house here you're trying to sell."

Marley knew Jake held no love for his late father, but she didn't know exactly why, and right now it wasn't a topic Jake felt like diving into. Especially not when just looking at her was short-circuiting his brain and making him think about things other than what they were really doing in this jungle.

He flashed her a smile, one that didn't come close to reaching his eyes, and moved for the edge of the pool. "It's fine. And you're right. This would be a shitty place to own a house. We should get going before it gets too hot."

"We're near the equator, Jake. It's *always* hot here."

She was right. But unfortunately, he was too hot near her. And being naked here in the water with her wasn't helping.

A fat raindrop hit his nose. He looked up toward the canopy but couldn't see more than layers of green. "All right, let's go before a giant alligator thinks we've taken over his home. Turn around again, Addison. I don't need you ogling my naked ass."

She laughed once more, the sound like a soft breeze. "They're called caimans."

"They can be called chompers for all I care. Same damn thing to me."

He climbed out and dressed. After pulling on his pants and shirt, he sat on a log and laced his boots. Another droplet hit his forearm. He glanced up again but still couldn't see any clouds through the dense canopy.

"Are you just gonna sit there, or are you going to leave so I can get out?" Marley asked.

"Shy all of a sudden?" He looked over at her. "You weren't shy ten minutes ago when your nipples were sticking out of the water."

Her eyes widened. "What?" She swam toward the edge of the pool and slapped her hand against the surface, sending water spraying all over him. "*You could see my nipples?* Why didn't you tell me?"

Laughing, he jerked off the log and moved out of her splash zone.

"Watch it. It's so humid in this jungle my clothes won't dry out if they get wet. Besides, you're the one who said the water was clear. All I was doing was checking for predators."

"I'll show you a predator," she mumbled. But there was no heat in her adorably annoyed look. "You're still here, idiot."

"Okay, okay. I'm going." He held up his hands and turned. "You win."

Just before he passed a palm that would block his view of her and the pond, he glanced over his shoulder. "They were nice nipples, though."

"Oh my God." Her eyes flew wide. "That's sexual harassment, Ryder!"

Feeling ten times better than he had in days, Jake laughed and headed back toward their makeshift camp. "Only if you can prove it, Addison."

He might be a moody pain in the ass sometimes, but Marley didn't mind Jake tagging along as much as she'd originally thought.

After breaking camp, they'd spent the next two hours picking their way through the jungle on their way to Bruhia. Jake had let her take the lead, and as Marley used the machete to chop palms and brush out of their way, she thought back over his teasing at the waterfall.

A silly smile toyed with the edges of her lips. She kinda liked him when he was in a good mood. When he wasn't grousing and nagging, he was actually funny and easy to be around. She'd even consider the nipple comment flirting if it had come from anyone but Jake, but she knew he wasn't interested in her. Interested in annoying her, sure. Interested in frustrating her, absolutely. But not interested in her romantically. Not even close.

Her smile faded. A little of her good mood ebbed. She hacked at a palm frond and shoved it out of her way. It wasn't like she wanted him to flirt with her. God no. That would just muck things up since they worked so closely together at Aegis. But, really. She'd seen some of the women he went out with, and she knew she was just as attractive and way smarter than all of them put together. So why on earth would he flirt with them and not her?

"Careful, Addison," Jake said at her back. Too close at her back. What was he, breathing down her neck? "You're hacking at those branches erratically. Sure you don't want me to take over?"

"I said I've got it."

"Oookay," he drew out. "Just trying to help."

Marley blew out a breath, hating that he had this innate ability to get her worked up even when he wasn't trying to annoy her. This was Jake. Her boss. Not a guy she even *wanted* to flirt with her. So what was her problem? She shoved another palm aside and kept moving,

"So this boyfriend," Jake said casually behind her. "Is he the only one?"

Marley stopped and turned, blinking in surprise. "What is that supposed to mean?"

"It means, I just think I should know if there's one, or more than one, or if you've got a string of guys in various countries I should be worried about."

Was he jealous? No, that couldn't be. She was clearly misreading things because of her messed-up thoughts. Facing forward again, she hacked at another vine. "You're worried? Seriously. Let's not tell lies, Jake."

He reached for her arm and gently tugged her back. "I think I've been pretty patient waiting for you to start talking. We'll reach Bruhia soon. I'd just like to know what I'm walking into before we get there."

He was talking about safety. Not her or them or any kind of emotions. She needed to pull her head together and start thinking rather than reacting to things that weren't even there.

She shifted her weight. Palm fronds closed in around them like a cave. Too close. Too cozy. Way too hot. A bead of sweat slid between her breasts, only frustrating her more. "What do you want to know?"

He let go of her arm and rested his hands on his hips. "For starters, why didn't your father want you dating him?"

It was the same question he'd asked last night, and she knew she couldn't put him off much longer. Besides which, he'd risked his life to come out here with her. She owed him an explanation.

"He didn't want me to marry a mercenary."

"Is that what he was? A merc?"

"Before he joined Omega, yes. Several of the Omega guys were. But it didn't matter what Gray did before he went to work for my father. My dad didn't want me involved with any of his black ops guys."

"Why not?"

Marley focused on a palm frond near his head. "He once said that he regretted dragging me all over on his jobs. As a kid, I thought it was pretty cool. I mean, the world was my classroom. But he didn't like the fact I never went to a regular school, that I didn't go to my senior prom, that I didn't get the full experience of being a teenager. I never felt like I missed out on anything, but he did. When it came down to it, I don't think my father wanted me dating Gray because he wanted more for me."

"And you disagreed."

Marley shrugged.

Jake's eyes narrowed. "Were you going to marry him?"

"No." She looked back at him. "We weren't engaged if that's what you're asking."

"But you thought about it."

Marley rolled her eyes, hating this whole conversation. "Every girl thinks about getting married, Jake. Doesn't mean she's stupid enough to go through with it."

Jake was silent for a few seconds, then said, "Were you in love with him?"

Marley looked up at the canopy and sighed. "I don't know."

"You either were or you weren't. It's not a hard question, Addison."

The bite to his voice told her loud and clear that he was back to being irritated.

She pinned him with a hard look. "I don't know, okay? For a while I thought maybe I was. Then I sorta freaked out and realized he wasn't the guy for me. Then he died—or supposedly died—on that op, and I didn't know what to feel. I was both heartbroken and relieved. And then racked with guilt because I felt that way. And now he's alive and I don't know what the heck to feel. It's been five years. I was pretty well resigned to the fact he was dead."

"Okay. I get it." Jake held up both hands. "I shouldn't have pushed."

Confused, Marley looked down and realized she was holding the machete out like a sword.

She dropped the blade to her side. "I'm not gonna cut you, Ryder. Sheesh."

"I'm just making sure. You do tend to dislike me more often than not."

No, she *liked* him. Liked him more than she should. That was the problem.

"All I'm trying to do is clarify what's going on here," he added. "Not piss you off."

Right. Because he cared about facts, not emotions.

Annoyed all over again, this time at herself, she turned and hacked at the palm fronds once more, pushing her way through the jungle, away from him. "Well, now you're caught up to speed. I don't know what to expect when we get to Bruhia, either."

The underbrush thinned—thank God—and Marley stepped out of the palm trees and into a small clearing, only to be smacked in the face by a giant raindrop. Jake reached for her arm again before she could take two more steps.

"Hold on."

Another raindrop hit her, and another, running in rivulets down her cheek. "What now?"

"Look, I know your dad. He's a good read on people. If he didn't want you dating McKnight, my gut says there had to be another reason."

And Jake listened to his gut over everything else.

"I said he didn't encourage my relationship with Gray. Not that he forbade me from seeing him."

"Because we both know what you would have done if he'd flat-out said no."

Marley frowned up at his already damp hair and the droplets pelting his nose and cheeks. "Are you implying I don't know how to listen to reason?"

Jake grinned. That irritating, obnoxious—dammit—sexy Jake grin. "I know that for a fact."

Marley tugged her arm from his grip. The hillside dropped to their right. She moved along a path some kind of animal had formed, ducking under branches and angling around prickly vines. The raindrops grew fatter, faster. Around them the echo of water splashing onto foliage increased. "Being independent is not a bad thing. And if my father *had* told me no—which he didn't, I'd like to point out—I would have listened to his reasoning."

Jake barked out a laugh at her back. "I say no to you all the time and you rarely listen."

Marley moved around a large puddle that had already formed in the dirt. "That's because the things you say no to make absolutely no sense. Like my working in the field. Look around you, Ryder." She held her hands out in the now heavy rain as she walked. "I know how to handle myself. I would have been just fine in the jungle alone last night. I don't really need your help, and we both know it."

"Are we back to this again? Give it a rest, Addison. I said—"

The wet ground slipped out beneath Marley's boot. Her eyes flew wide, and she tried to jerk back, but mud and water splashed in her face, making her gasp for air. She grappled for something to hold on to, but the thin rainforest sediments were already dragging her down the hillside in a roaring landslide that drowned out every other sound. Even Jake's voice calling her name.

chapter 6

Don't be dead. Please don't be dead.

The words echoed in Jake's head as he rushed down what was left of the hillside. Thick, fat raindrops pelted his body. Razor-sharp vines cut into his palms as he grappled for anything to hold on to. He ignored the blood and the pain, focusing only on getting to the bottom as fast as he could.

He'd been lucky the landslide hadn't taken him down with it. Lucky and horrified that he'd let Marley take the lead. It should have been him. He should be the one at the bottom of the ravine, not her. He was tougher, stronger. She shouldn't even be in this damn jungle to begin with.

After what felt like forever, he finally reached the bottom. Mud covered every inch of his clothes, his arms and face, even his hair. Water ran in rivulets down his cheeks, mixing with the dirt and mud to form streaks along his skin. "Marley!"

The mudslide created a fan-shaped area of sediments at the bottom of the hill. He tore off his pack and threw it on the ground, then forced his way through the hip-deep mud, searching for her, running his hands through the debris, afraid she was trapped underneath. Afraid she couldn't breathe. His heart took up residence in his throat. His pulse turned to a roar in his ears.

"Marley!"

Panic spread through his chest, beneath his ribs, making it hard to get air. Water rushed down his face. Mud splashed over every inch of him as he kept searching. "Goddammit, Marley. Answer me!"

His muscles ached. His breaths grew short and labored. Time passed. He wasn't sure how long, but every second caused his adrenaline to shoot higher, made his heart rate inch up. She had to be here. He wasn't giving up. "Marley!"

With renewed determination, he waded through the mud, searching a new section, hoping, praying—

Voices echoed through the trees. Jake slowed his frantic searching, jerked his head in that direction, and listened.

Male voices. Several. More than several—many. Coming toward him. Speaking a language he didn't understand.

The memory of those gunshots and the paramilitary group they'd just missed the day before ricocheted through his brain. Off to his right, another voice called, *"Aki! Aki!"*

He turned. Squinted to see through the foliage. A kid—no, not a kid, a native—was perched on his hands and knees, bent over, looking at something on the ground. More voices echoed through the rainforest. Jake took a step their way to get a better view. Several other natives rushed up, their bare legs and loincloth-draped bodies blocking his view. One native lifted branches and palm fronds and threw them at his back. The tallest of the bunch bent over, then hefted something into his arms.

No, not some*thing*, Jake realized, his eyes growing wide. Some*one*. "Marley," he whispered, his heart jackknifing all over again.

Her arm dropped to hang from her side. Her body was limp, her legs dangling in the air. Matted blond hair fell from her head as the native turned and headed in the other direction, but for a split second Jake saw her face. Dirty and covered in mud. Her eyes closed. Not a single muscle moving.

Jake's pulse went stratospheric. Frantic to get to her, he waded through the mud, pulled himself out of the gunk, then drew to a sharp stop when he got a better look at the group and the multitude of weapons in their hands.

Hunters. At least thirty. All armed with spears. Deadly-sharp spears.

He grappled for the gun at his thigh only to find it covered in mud. Cursing under his breath, he ducked behind a banana tree and swiped as much gunk from the weapon as he could, unsure if it would even fire. A handful he could take on his own, but not thirty. Not when they had Marley. He wiped the rainwater out of his eyes and listened as the group continued to chatter in that indecipherable language and moved through the trees away from him.

Scenarios, options, plans raced through his mind. He scrambled for his backpack, jerked it open and reached for his phone, then cursed again. His satellite phone couldn't pick up a signal thanks to the thick canopy. He dropped the phone back into his bag. Knew he had only one choice.

"I don't really need your help, and we both know it."

The last words Marley had said to him swirled in his brain. She was wrong. She did need him. And he wasn't about to let her down.

Groaning, Marley lifted her fingers toward her head and winced.

"Alasahe! Tu bet. Tu bet."

A hand gripped her by the wrist and gently pushed her arm down. Something soft pillowed her body. Struggling to pull her eyelids apart, Marley squinted up toward the face—no, correction: *faces*—staring down at her, then blinked in confusion.

Long black hair, brown skin, streaks of red and white across their cheeks. Women, Marley realized as she took in the full sight. Naked breasts, short fabric skirts, more of the red and white paint along their skin.

Gritting her teeth, she tried to move. The women chirped the same words they'd spoken before but which made zero sense and pushed on her arms again, but Marley struggled against them. The room spun. She managed to sit up. Tearing her gaze away from the women, she looked around.

A thatched roof, dirt floor, walls made of wood and grass. And a handful of naked children, staring at her with the biggest, brownest eyes she'd ever seen.

She glanced out the open doorway and could just make out other huts, a large central fire pit, and several natives milling around dressed and decorated in the same way as the women beside her.

Definitely not Bruhia. When Gray had called, she'd heard cars and the hustle of a modern town in the background. She was in some kind of remote village. Though how she'd gotten here, she didn't know.

She pushed to her feet. The room swayed, and she reached for her aching head then immediately sat back down on the pile of palm fronds and blankets she'd obviously been lying on. "Oh shit. That hurts."

"Tu bet. Makala hasa mati." One woman rushed over and reached for Marley's hand again, pulling it away from the wound on her forehead. To another woman, she said, *"Rusef. Nahala Rusef."*

The second woman motioned to another at her side, and the two rushed out of the hut. While the woman who was clearly in charge reached for a bowl on the ground at her side, the children continued to stand and stare as if Marley were from another planet.

Which, Marley realized, she might as well be. They were deep in the Amazon rainforest. She knew there were still several tribes that had limited contact with the outside world. The woman slathered some kind of ointment on the scrape on Marley's forehead, and Marley winced and tried to pull away from the sting. Slowly, the pain receded and warmth spread through the wound, relaxing her muscles.

"What is that?" Marley asked.

The woman blinked at her. Marley pointed toward the bowl in her hand, then up at her head. "What is this? Medicine?"

"Kohala asafi." The woman slathered more ointment on the edge of Marley's forehead, then twisted and did the same to Marley's leg.

Her pants were ripped open from thigh to ankle, the fabric hanging on each side of her leg. Marley watched as the woman smoothed the ointment over a large gash in her shin, not even remembering how she'd gotten it.

She'd been in the jungle. It had been raining. She'd stepped in mud and the ground had gone out from under her. Everything else was a blur. She couldn't even remember what she and Jake had been talking about as they'd walked through the—

"Oh God." *Jake.*

Her gaze snapped to the woman, rubbing more of the ointment into a smaller scratch on her bare foot. "I have a friend. A man. He was with me. He's tall. Dark hair. Is he here?"

The woman stopped what she was doing and blinked at Marley. She didn't understand a word Marley was saying. Marley glanced around the hut and spotted her backpack leaning against the wall.

"My bag." Marley tried to get up, but the woman pushed her down. Marley pointed toward her pack. "I need my bag."

The woman looked from Marley to the bag, then set her bowl down and pushed to her feet. Marley's heart pounded while the woman grabbed her backpack and pulled it over within reach.

Her pack was caked with mud. She flipped the top open and dug around inside until she found her phone. Thanking her good sense to put her phone in a plastic bag, just in case, she pulled it out and waited while it powered on.

"Come on, come on," she muttered. When the screen came to life, she opened her photo album and paged through until she found the shot she was looking for.

She'd taken it a few weeks ago. When the team had come back to the office after a training run in the mountains. She zoomed in on Jake in the middle of the group, sweaty and smiling from a day in the field, turned the phone, and held it up. "Have you seen him? Is he here?"

The woman's eyes narrowed. Cautiously, she took the phone from Marley and stared at it like it might just jump out and bite her. Heart beating hard, Marley pointed toward Jake's face on the screen and said, "Is he here? I need to find him. We got separated."

The woman shook her head. *"Notuli."*

The two women who'd left earlier ducked back under the doorway and entered the hut. The first woman looked toward them and held up Marley's phone, pointing to Jake. *"Makari ala falusi."*

Both women shook their heads. The one on the right reached for Marley's phone and turned it in her hands, studying every angle as if she'd never seen such a thing before—which, Marley realized, she hadn't.

The first woman glanced back to Marley. *"Notuli halem sahiko."*

Marley's shoulders dropped. She didn't understand what they were saying, but she could tell by their expressions they didn't recognize Jake's face. Which meant he wasn't in the village. And considering she didn't know where she was or how long she'd been here, that meant he could be anywhere.

A lump formed in her throat, and tears pricked her eyes. If she could go back to that conversation with him in the jungle, when she'd been so frustrated by her stupid emotions, she would. She'd go back and change her attitude, not get so defensive. Not take everything so damn personally.

"Shit."

She pressed her fingers against her burning eyes and tried to push to her feet. She needed to go find him. Needed to make sure he was okay. Before she could stand, the first woman grasped her arm and eased her back down. *"Notuli. Tu bet."*

Annoyed, Marley opened her eyes only to realize what the women were doing. The one who'd taken her phone dipped a rag into a bowl of water and began cleaning the mud from her face and arms. The other one reached for the edge of her tank and started to lift it up.

"Whoa. Wait. I don't think—"

"Don't worry," a voice said from the doorway. "They'll not hurt you. Only help."

Marley's gaze jerked toward the voice. An older woman with salt-and-pepper hair and a wrinkled face stood in the doorway holding fresh clothes.

"Who—?" Marley was suddenly afraid she was hearing and seeing things from the knock she'd taken to the head. "You speak English?"

"Yes. Though it may be a little rusty." The woman stepped into the room and set the clothing on the ground at Marley's side while the others went about cleaning her with the rags and water. She was small, no more than five feet tall, Caucasian, not native, and she wore shorts and a loose, weathered pale-green T-shirt instead of the skirt and paint.

"Who are you?" Marley asked.

"Darla. Was Darla," she corrected with a smile. "Now I'm known as Pakatito."

Maybe she'd gotten hit harder than she thought. Marley pressed a hand to her aching forehead, having trouble keeping up. "I'm not following."

"I'm an anthropologist," Darla said. "I came here a long time ago and liked it so much, I decided to stay. The Puketi people are friendly once you get to know them. You're lucky, though." She nodded toward the women fawning over Marley. "They don't usually take well to outsiders. They think you're a princess."

"A *what*?" Marley twisted away from the woman on her left who was still trying to pull her shirt up and off.

"There is an old myth in their culture about a woman born of the earth who rose from the mud to rule the rainforest. They think that's you."

"Do I look like Princess Leia or something?" Marley frowned at the woman reaching for her sleeve and pushed her hand away. "Stop that."

The woman didn't let go of Marley's arm, but focused on her mouth. "Lay-ah."

"What?" Oh, good God. Marley shook her head. "No, that's not my name." She tried to wriggle out of the woman's grip. "And stop trying to take my clothes off."

Darla laughed. "I forgot all about Princess Leia. Ah, I do miss movies. That Harrison Ford was such a stud." To the women she said, *"Pahali motalu. Asa kobeeli tan fu pa."*

The women let go of Marley and pushed to their feet.

Relief rushed through Marley, but before she could even sigh, both women grabbed her arms and hauled her up. "What the heck did you say to them?"

"I told them you didn't need a sponge bath. They're taking you to the river. They need to make you presentable for the celebration tonight."

The women dragged her toward the door.

"Celebration?" Worry rippled down Marley's spine. "What kind of celebration?"

Darla stepped aside. "The one welcoming you, of course. Do not fret. There will only be a few dozen suitors in attendance anxious to be chosen as your mate. The Puketi people value love and family over anything else."

"My *what*?" Marley pulled back, but the women had grips of steel and dragged her along as if she were nothing but a child. "Oh, I don't think so."

Darla's laughter echoed at her back. "This is going to be more fun than I've had in years."

Marley disagreed as she hobbled through the village toward the water with the women. Native men dressed in loincloths with their faces painted turned as she walked by. And every single one held a spear as tall as her.

Suddenly Grayson McKnight, snakes, caimans, and paramilitary troops were the least of her worries. All she could think about was Jake.

"Dammit, Jake," she mumbled. "If you're still alive, you better come and rescue me."

Because she'd lied when she said she didn't need him. Right now she needed him more than she'd ever needed anyone else.

Ever.

Jake swiped the sweat out of his eyes and peered through the foliage with his binoculars. He'd found the natives' village, a hundred yards in the distance down the embankment, but he hadn't seen any sign of Marley yet.

Worst-case scenarios filled his head, but he pushed them aside. She wasn't dead. She couldn't be dead. That wasn't even an option. She had to be in one of those huts. He just had to figure out which.

He glanced up at the sky. The village sat in a small clearing near a river, just down the hill from where he'd stopped. The canopy was sparse here, enough so he could see the filter of sunlight from above. It had stopped raining about two hours ago, but it was still hot as hell. He guessed it had to be close to late afternoon now. Rubbing his hand over his face, he lifted the binoculars again and took another look.

Natives hauled wood into the middle of the camp for what looked like a bonfire. Several warriors, complete with war paint and spears, milled around the central space. Naked children ran through the village. Women wearing only mid-thigh cotton skirts carried baskets and jugs.

His best bet would be to wait until dark. When they were all occupied with whatever ritual they had planned. Sneak into the huts one by one until he found her, then get them both the hell out. From the looks of those spears, he didn't want to go marching into their village unannounced. And he wasn't about to do anything to put Marley in more danger.

Plan made, he stuffed the binoculars back into his pack, threw it on his back, and inched away from the ridgeline. He'd wait until dark on the other side, where he had a better view of the huts, then he'd make his move.

His foot hit something solid as he was moving backward. He turned to look, then froze.

"Oh, shit."

At least ten native males covered in war paint stood around him, pointing deadly sharp spears right at his heart.

chapter 7

"No, I really don't need flowers in my hair." Marley reached up to remove the wreath the elderly native woman had set on the top her head. "Sorry, but I'm just not a flowery kind of girl."

The woman swatted at her hand. "*Notuli. A fusak,* Lay-ah.*"

Marley jerked her hand back and frowned. "Jeez. Fine. I won't touch it again." She might not speak the Puketi language, but she was quickly learning that *notuli* meant no. She glared up at the women standing above her. "But for the record, my name is not Leia. It's Marley."

"*Atuki mahatek,* Lay-ah," the woman painting red stripes on Marley's right arm muttered.

"*Ah, sutef,* Lay-ah," the elderly woman said in agreement.

Good lord. She was giving up. Marley sighed and focused on the far wall of the hut while the women continued to decorate her.

The second one, kneeling at Marley's side, laughed and tapped Marley's bare ankle, then went back to painting the geometric shapes on Marley's arm. Marley's gaze strayed to the decorated leather band strapped to the woman's ankle. Several of the women in the village wore them. As did a number of men. But Marley had no idea what they were for or why some wore them and others didn't.

Telling herself it really didn't matter, she glanced down at the bracelets on her wrists, then to the leather skirt and wrap top which crossed over her breasts and tied behind her neck that the women had dressed her in. It might not be her style, but at least she wasn't on full display. After she'd bathed in the river, she'd tried to get some-one to bring her pack so she could grab her change of clothes, but they'd refused. Instead they'd covered her in a blanket, then brought her back to the hut where they'd been "working" on her ever since. For a while, she'd been a little worried they were going to make her parade around in nothing but the short skirt most of the women seemed to be wearing, but thankfully Darla had intervened and sug-gested something a little more appropriate for their new "princess."

Princess. Yeah, there was a laugh. Marley had tried to correct them on that point several times, but no one had seemed to want to listen to her, so she'd finally shut up.

The old woman shifted her feet, and her saggy breasts flashed in Marley's peripheral vision. Wincing, Marley closed her eyes so she didn't have to look and sat still while they stuck more flowers in the wreath on her head. An image of Jake, smiling that obnoxious, sexy grin of his, flickered behind her eyelids.

He'd get quite a kick out of this if he could see her now. Where was he? She'd expected him to follow her. He'd come all the way to Colombia and refused to leave her even though she'd repeatedly tried to get him to go home. He wouldn't just walk away if they got separated. So the fact he hadn't already shown up meant either he hadn't tracked her yet or he couldn't because he was injured.

Another knot of fear wedged its way inside her chest. She'd heard him calling her name when the landslide had taken her out, but she didn't know if he'd been pulled down with it or if something worse had happened to him. She'd been lucky her injuries had been minor—bruises, scrapes, a knock on the head—but what if he'd broken his leg? What if a branch had speared him? What if he'd been buried in all that mud?

Voices echoed from outside, dragging Marley's eyes open. The women around her turned toward the open door of the hut. One rose and rushed over to look. In an excited voice, she exclaimed, *"Motani. Apukala tet."*

The women all let go of Marley and hurried for the door. Curious about what was going on, Marley pushed to her feet and followed, looking over their dark heads toward the group of warriors entering the village.

There were at least ten of them, all decked out in war paint and carrying nasty looking spears she did not want to be on the receiving end of. They moved in a pack. Several in the middle looked to be carrying something tied to a pole, which was perched on their shoulders. It had to be a hunting party. She'd noticed the bonfire they were building in the middle of the camp. They'd probably killed a boar or—her stomach rolled—she really hoped it wasn't a giant snake.

The men at the front of the pack stopped near the branch of a giant tree on the far side of camp and yelled something to the men at the back. One hastily moved over and threw a rope over the thick branch, then tied it off. Bodies shifted. Marley squinted to see better. They unhooked something from the pole and tied it to the rope. Something she couldn't quite see. Something that—

"Son of a bitch. Do not put me up there!"

Her pulse shot up. Eyes wide, she watched as one of the natives planted his feet in the dirt and pulled on the end of the rope. The warriors in the front moved back. Boots appeared over their heads, then familiar cargo pants, and finally Jake's arms and shoulders and face as he dangled upside down from the rope.

"Oh my God." Marley pushed past the native women in the doorway and ran across the camp toward the warriors. "Jake!"

"Marley!" He swiveled in the air and looked her way, but his momentum kept spinning him around. "Are you hurt?"

"No, I'm fine. I'm not hurt. I'm okay. Oh my God, Jake."

Footsteps pounded in the dirt behind her. She lurched for him but two warriors stepped in her way, blocking her path. "Wait. What are you doing? Get out of my way."

She reached past them for Jake, but they pushed her back and let off a string of words she couldn't follow.

Voices echoed all around her. Several other warriors moved in her way.

At their backs, Jake's frantic voice rose up. "Marley!"

She tried to see past the mass of bodies. Jake was still spinning in the air, his arms flying out to the side, trying to stop his movements. She struggled against the hands and arms trying to pull her back. "He's with me, you idiots. Let me go."

"Pahali acutef," Darla's voice rang out.

The warriors stilled and looked toward the voice, but Marley's gaze didn't follow. She rushed past the men toward Jake. "Oh my God, are you okay?"

"Fine, except for being strung up like a piece of meat."

She grasped his shoulders, hanging six feet off the ground, and pulled him around to hold him still. "What the hell happened?"

"What does it look like happened? I nearly got speared trying to rescue you."

Warmth filled her chest, and a silly smile she couldn't stop tugged at the corner of her mouth. "It looks to me like you're the one who needs rescuing."

"No thanks to—"

"Notuli aku tamen!" One of the warriors stepped close and drew his spear, pointing it right at Jake's side.

Jake tensed and reached out to grasp Marley's hand. "Stop gloating and do something, would you? I'm not in the mood to be dinner."

Marley let go of Jake's hand and moved between him and the warrior. "Whoa. Wait."

The warrior lifted his sword and yelled, *"Notuli aku tamen!"*

Two other warriors moved up on Jake's other side.

"Um. Addison."

From the corner of Marley's vision she could see Jake spinning at her back. Her adrenaline spiked. She held up her hands in a non-threatening way. "He's with me. He's totally harmless, I promise."

The warriors looked at each other, then refocused on Jake, their eyes narrowing, spears lowering.

"That's not working." Jake reached out for her arm, catching himself to slow his spinning. "If you've got any other bright ideas, use them. Like, *now*."

Marley's frantic mind caught on something Darla had told her about the Puketi people valuing family. Her heart rate shot up. Her hands grew sweaty. It was a long shot, but they were obviously out of options. "I've got one."

She whipped around and captured Jake's upside down face in her hands. "Hold still."

"Why? What—?"

She pressed her lips against his.

"Mar—"

"Just go with it," she whispered before kissing him again. Quick. Easy. Just a brush of lips against lips. But enough to make her belly warm and her fingers tingle against the scruff on his jaw.

Ignoring her body's stupid reaction, she drew back and glanced over the crowd, searching for Darla. "He's not a threat. Darla, he's with me. We're together. Tell them he's with me."

The crowd looking on parted. Darla stood at the back of the group with a perplexed expression and nodded toward Jake. "This is your mate?"

Mate? Whoa. That was a little more than she'd expected.

"I'll be your damn anything," Jake mumbled. "Just get me down from here."

"Um, boyfriend," Marley lied. "Yes. We're together."

Darla didn't respond. The warriors looked from Darla to Marley and back again. Tense seconds passed.

Finally, Darla said. *"Akutami peli aten fu maku."*

Two warriors stepped up on each side of Jake. Wide-eyed, Marley shifted back toward Jake to see what they were doing. Her heart beat hard as the males stared at her and then looked at Jake.

"Marley." Jake reached his hand out to her.

"I'm right here." She closed her fingers around his and squeezed. The warrior on her right pulled a knife from the strap on his bare thigh.

"They don't believe you." Jake tensed. His hand grew damp against hers.

Marley's heart shot into her throat. Jake was right. They didn't believe her. Fear jerked her forward. "Wait—"

The warrior reached up and sliced through the rope holding Jake's left leg. The one on the other side did the same to the second rope. Jake's "Fuck me!" echoed in the air as both warriors stepped back. He landed with a thud against the dirt.

Hands shaking, Marley dropped to her knees next to him. "Shit. Are you okay?"

"Yeah, I'm fine." Groaning, he rolled to his side and pushed up, then pressed a hand to his forehead. "Dizzy, but fine."

Relief swept through Marley like a tidal wave. She grasped his hands and helped pull him to his feet. "You scared me."

"I scared you? What the hell were you thinking stepping close to that edge? When I saw you go down that hillside, I thought—"

His mouth closed. His jaw clenched, and he shook his head.

Was that fear she heard in his voice? The usually calm, take-charge man she knew so well sounded rattled in a way she hadn't expected.

He turned those dark, intense eyes her way. "Are you hurt?"

Her pulse picked up speed all over again. And as the worry in his eyes registered, a new set of nerves lit off in her belly. Except these weren't rooted in fear. These rolled and churned and vibrated with an awareness she knew she shouldn't be feeling. "Um. No. Not hurt. Not really. Just a little bruised."

His dirt-streaked features relaxed, and he reached for her hand. "Thank God."

Before she realized what he was doing, he tugged her into the warmth of his body, then closed his arms around her and lowered his face into her hair.

Surprise made her draw in a quick breath. Her muscles tensed. Her hands opened against his pecs. The scents of dirt and sweat and *him* filled her senses until she felt lightheaded.

In all the years she'd worked for him, he'd never once hugged her. Her mind tumbled with an explanation, and then she realized it had to be the stress of the situation. They'd also never been lost in the jungle together, she'd never been swept away in a landslide, and he probably hadn't been dragged into a native village and strung up in the trees like lunch before either.

Relief came raging back. Along with a warmth that rippled through every part of her and eased the knot of worry inside. One she liked. More than she should. Sinking into him for just a minute, she closed her eyes and let him hold her. She wasn't one to need coddling, but this she didn't mind. Because it reaffirmed that he wasn't hurt. That they were both alive. And though she'd never admit it to him, this felt better than anything had in a really long time.

"So you told them we were a couple," he said into her hair.

His words popped the cozy bubble of relief. Marley blinked and looked up at the tree Jake had just been hanging from. "Um, yeah. Sorry. The Puketi people are sorta hopeless romantics as a culture. It was either that or watch them flay you. I figured this was the lesser of two evils."

"I definitely don't want to get flayed," he mumbled. "And since they're all still staring at me as if I might club you over the head and drag you off into the jungle, we better make this convincing."

"Make what convincing?"

Jake drew back. Confused, she looked up, then sucked in a quick breath when she caught the look in his dark eyes. A look that was soft, mischievous, and downright *hot* all at the same time.

He lowered his head and pressed his lips against hers. Gentler than she'd kissed him but more intense. More real. More *there*. Her whole body stiffened. Her head grew light, and her knees wobbled. Unsure if she should react, if she should kiss him back, she moved her hands from his pecs to his biceps and squeezed to hold herself upright so her legs didn't go out from under her.

His arms tightened around her lower back, drawing her tighter into the heat of his body as he skimmed his lips over hers again, teasing her bottom lip with the tip of his tongue. His thighs brushed hers. Those tingles in her belly blossomed and spread. Awareness morphed to arousal and then to a heat that flooded her veins. One she knew she shouldn't be feeling. One she couldn't seem to stop.

Sliding her fingers up his shoulders and around his nape, she played with the ends of his short hair, tried to hold back, but suddenly didn't want to anymore.

She opened, drew him deep into her mouth, groaned at the silky wet taste. It was wrong. It was just for show. But she didn't care. He tasted amazing. Felt even better. Especially after all the stress and worry of not knowing what had happened to him. And every time he moved his tongue against hers, she saw stars.

Her muscles grew lax, her body weak. His hand slinked up her back, slid into her hair, and cradled the back of her head. And then he kissed her deeper, his lips and tongue and seductive mouth drawing the thoughts right out of her head. Making her forget where they were. What they were doing. Why they were in this jungle in the first place. Made her think of nothing but him.

He drew back long before she was ready to let him go. Dizzy, she gripped his shoulders and pressed her forehead against his throat until the village stopped spinning. His warm breath fanned the sensitive skin of her temple, and then he whispered, "I think that time we fooled them."

It took moments for his words to register, but when they did, she slowly lifted her head and glanced over his shoulder.

The village women had already wandered back to whatever they'd been doing before the excitement. The males were heading toward the wood piled up in the middle of camp, spears in hands, their strides relaxed, as if nothing had happened. Even the children who'd stopped to watch wide-eyed were gone, probably off playing in the mud or river by now. Only one warrior stood by watching them, as if waiting to see if they'd flee.

She eyed the warrior's stoic face, swallowed once, then realized she was still pressed up against Jake's muscular body from thigh to chest. And, oh man, he wasn't as unaffected by their kiss as she'd thought. The rigid line of his erection pressed against her belly.

Letting go, she pushed back quickly, only to discover her knees were weaker than she'd thought.

"Whoa. Careful." He reached out to grab her, but she caught herself before she landed flat on her ass in the dirt, and wriggled out of his grip.

"I'm fine." *Holy hell. What the heck was that?* "You just surprised me, that's all."

He grinned. "It was your idea first."

A warmth she did not need flooded her belly. She looked up at his sexy grin, only to have a whole new set of tingles erupt in her belly.

Oh . . . crap. This is Ryder. Your boss. Mr. Emotionally Crippled and Aggravating as Hell. Do not *start thinking of him as anything else.*

She wouldn't. She was smarter than that. Way smarter. One kiss did not change reality. She squared her shoulders. "I said I'm fine, and I'm fine."

"You sure about that?" His heated gaze traveled down her body and back up again. Her half-naked body. And she realized then that even though she was wearing a tiny top and the shortest skirt on the planet, she was sweating. Profusely. "You look a little flustered."

Yeah, no shit, she was flustered. She was also flipping the hell out. Arousal and frustration and disbelief churned in her belly, leaving her confused, making her hot, pushing her right to the edge of control.

And he was enjoying it.

Drawing in a calming breath, she planted her hands on her hips and glared up at him. "If I'm flustered it's because I just had to save your life."

She eyed the warrior once more past Jake, thought about making a break for it, then realized her backpack, complete with her passport, phone, and money, was still back in the hut. Even if they got away, she needed her stuff. And more than anything right now she wanted clothes. Her clothes.

A child rushed up at Marley's side before Jake could answer and held up a flower. "*Atuen ma*, Lay-ah."

Marley took the flower and smiled down at the child. "Thank you."

The small naked girl ran off.

Jake tipped his head. "Leia?"

Marley pushed the hair back from her face. "Yeah. Um. They, ah, sorta think I'm a princess."

"Princess Leia?" He lifted one brow in total amusement. "You told them your name was Princess Leia?"

Heat rushed to Marley's cheeks. "No, I didn't tell them that. It was a misunderstanding." One she didn't want to get into with him now.

The soft, sexy chuckle that rumbled from his chest only made her cheeks hotter. She turned for the village, needing space, needing to get Jake and these crazy thoughts about that meaningless kiss out of her head. Needing to pull it together before she made a complete fool of herself. "And I wouldn't get too cocky if I were you. They're planning some kind of celebration tonight. Something tells me we're not getting out of here anytime soon."

His footsteps sounded at her back. "A party for Princess Leia, huh? As long as I'm not the main course, we're good."

No, they weren't good. They were as far from good as they could get. Because suddenly all those silly emotions Marley had been experiencing the last few months whenever Jake looked at her were rushing back. And that had bad news written all over it, because Jake Ryder was the last man on the planet she had any intention of getting involved with.

"Just try not to do anything to get us into more trouble."

He caught up with her and gripped her hand. Surprised, she looked up, then tried to pull away, but he only held her tighter and grinned.

"For effect," he said. "You may be the savior of the universe, but we are a couple, remember?"

Marley clenched her jaw and looked straight ahead. But a little thrill rushed through her. Forget about getting *into* trouble. That warmth flooding her belly all over again told her she was in trouble up to her eyeballs. And, dammit, she liked it.

chapter 8

Jake leaned forward and rested his elbows on his updrawn knees as he looked toward the enormous bonfire in the middle of the village.

Drums echoed in the darkness, and males decked out in grass skirts and feather headdresses with red paint in stripes down their arms and legs and across their faces chanted and shook to the beat. Children ran around the edge of the celebration, laughing and singing. Women moved through the villagers with large wooden platters in their hands, serving meats and fruits to those watching the festivities. Several elderly men were seated on the periphery near Jake, animatedly talking and smoking something in long pipes, but he barely noticed. The only thing he could see was Marley, standing on the far side of the fire, listening closely to a middle-aged woman trying to teach her how to dance like a native.

The woman, wearing nothing but a tiny skirt, grasped Marley's hand and twirled her around. Jake smiled as Marley's wavy blonde hair caught the light and swayed behind her. Firelight flickered over every inch of her bare skin—her long, shapely legs, her flat belly and the soft indent of her belly button, and her ample cleavage in the revealing top that was nothing more than strips of fabric tied together.

Why had he never noticed her breasts before? That was usually the first thing he spotted on a woman. And when had her hair gotten so wavy? Usually she wore it straight, either down to her shoulders or pulled back out of her face.

A woman passed in front of him, interrupting his view. She leaned forward with a platter of meat. Feeling stuffed from all the food they'd shoved at him already, Jake held up a hand and shook his head. "*Notuli*. Thanks."

The woman moved on. Jake leaned to his left to see past her. A wide smile split Marley's face, and she laughed at something the native woman beside her said. Mesmerized, Jake watched as torchlight flickered over her features, making her skin glow and her eyes dance as if fueled by flames.

"She's very pretty."

Startled by the voice, Jake pulled his gaze from Marley and looked up at the only other non-native person in the village. "Who?"

Darla nodded toward Marley and the fire. "Your girlfriend. I'm not so old that I can't see the obvious. May I sit?"

His girlfriend. Right. Everyone thought they were an item. Not employer-employee. Something in his stomach flipped over, but he figured it had to be the weird food. He seriously hoped that wasn't boa constrictor he'd eaten earlier. "Sure."

Darla lowered herself to the ground at his side and crossed her legs in front of her. "I'm not the only one who thinks so, either." She nodded toward the fire. "Look."

Jake glanced back at Marley. A tall, skinny male covered in red paint who looked to be no more than fifteen grasped both of her hands and spun her around. Marley's eyes widened, but she didn't pull away, and the smile rushing over her features told Jake loud and clear that she was enjoying herself.

He smiled again, just watching her, and wondered why he'd never seen her grin like that before. Yeah, she'd smiled earlier in the day when they'd taken that swim, but it hadn't been like this. This encompassed every feature, made the skin around her soft blue eyes crinkle, made the tiniest dimple appear in her cheek. And it lit up her entire face, bringing out a side of her he hadn't known existed.

The elderly male on Jake's left handed him a pipe. Pulling his gaze from Marley once more, Jake waved his hand. "Oh, no thanks."

"It's rude in their culture to say no," Darla whispered on his other side. "Take a few puffs and hand it back."

He'd said yes to food and drink way too much already tonight. Reluctantly, Jake forced a smile and took the pipe. On the third puff, he pulled the wood from his mouth and coughed until his eyes watered.

The males on his left laughed and took the pipe back. Blinking rapidly at the sting in his throat, Jake glanced toward Darla. "Thanks a lot."

Darla grinned. "They'll make you a native Puketi yet, just wait."

Clearing the smoke from his throat, Jake went back to watching Marley. "I think I'll pass. If I stay much longer, I'm pretty sure I'll wind up as dinner at some point." He nodded toward the warrior on the far side of camp, standing stoic with his spear, watching Jake as a predator watches his prey. "That one over there doesn't like me."

"Manaus is just protective of his village. Once he gets to know you, you'll be fine. The Puketi people lean toward peace and harmony with nature, rather than war."

Jake huffed. "I'll remember that the next time they're trying to shove a spear into my side."

"You scared them," Darla said. "They don't like to be scared."

Another male took Marley's hand and pushed the first out of the way so he could dance with her. "They don't seem scared of her."

"No," Darla said with a sigh. "They are not. She is special."

Marley glanced Jake's way and grinned, and his belly did that weird flip thing again as he watched her shake and move to the thump of the drums.

The man on Jake's left tapped his elbow. Halfheartedly, he tore his gaze from Marley once more and looked down at the bowl of liquid in the man's hand. "No, I'm not thirsty."

Darla nudged him from the other side.

"Shit," Jake muttered. "Okay, yeah." He reached for the bowl and lifted it to his mouth with a begrudging half grin. "It better not be jaguar urine."

Darla smiled. "Be sure to take a large drink."

The scent of something heavily fermented wafted to Jake's nose. Wincing at the smell, he opened his mouth and took a mouthful. The liquid was both sweet and bitter at the same time, and he coughed after swallowing, then handed the bowl back to the man at his side. "Holy hell, that's awful."

The elderly men next to him laughed again and pointed, speaking rapidly in their native language.

Jake swiped the back of his arm over his mouth and wished like hell for a beer to wash the nasty taste away. On his other side, Darla said, "It's *ayahuasca*. A very special drink used during ceremonies. A little goes a long way."

"I can see why. No one could drink more than a few sips of that without getting violently ill."

"You are more right than you know," Darla muttered. "Though it has other effects that are much more pleasant." Then louder, she said, "You do not wear a ring. Why are you not married?"

Startled by the change in topic, Jake glanced her way and realized she was staring at the fire and dancers and Marley.

His gaze followed, and he watched Marley brace her hands on her knees and bend forward, shaking her breasts and ass at the same time, her hair falling down around her face as she dropped her head and then lifted it again.

His belly flipped once more and then heated.

"Mr. Ryder?"

Jake blinked several times at the sound of Darla's voice. His head felt light. His skin hot. And every time he looked at Marley, he couldn't stop his mind from drifting back to that kiss. To the way her lips had felt against his, to the brush of her breasts across his chest, to the soft groan that had rumbled from her throat, and the way her fingers had drifted into his hair and her nails had scratched his scalp as if she'd wanted more.

That warmth in his belly drifted lower, sending tingles across his flesh.

"Hello?"

"Um." *Married.* Darla was asking why he and Marley weren't married. She still thought they were a couple.

Unable to look away, he watched as Marley turned in a circle. Damn, but the woman had incredible moves. She'd certainly never shimmied like that in the office. He'd have definitely noticed if she had.

"Mr. Ryder?"

Darla's voice cut through the haze sliding over every inch of Jake's body. He looked in her direction. "Yeah?"

One side of Darla's lips curled. "Feeling relaxed, are you?"

"A little."

The truth was he felt *really* relaxed. And hot as hell all at the same time. He focused on Marley. She flicked her gaze his way, smiled a sheepish, sexy little grin, then turned once more. And the way she swayed, the way her hips shook, the way she kept looking at him as if to see if he were watching, it sent the heat and tingles in his belly rushing lower, straight into his groin.

"And her?" Darla nodded toward Marley.

"I don't know." His blood pounded hard as Marley watched him, licked her bottom lip, then sank her teeth into the fleshy mass. And his mind flipped back to that kiss again. To the way she'd tasted. To the other parts of her he suddenly wanted to lick and sample and devour. "Just haven't found the right time, I guess."

"Time always gets in the way in the modern world." Darla folded her hands in her lap. "You should go dance with her. Something tells me she's waiting for that."

Dance. Yeah. That was a good idea. Why hadn't he thought of that?

Jake pushed to his feet and swiped his hands against the thighs of his cargo pants. "I think I'll do that."

"Have fun," Darla said at his back as he headed toward the fire.

The drums beat heavy in the air. The canopy slowly swayed above as if the trees too were dancing to the rhythm. Marley's gaze locked on his as he drew close, and the same spark of awareness, of arousal that he'd seen when she'd looked at him from across the fire flared hot in her sky-blue eyes.

He stopped in front of her and fingered the fabric tied at her shoulder. "I'm not sure this is appropriate work attire, Ms. Addison."

She swayed closer to him, her familiar scents of musk, sandalwood, vanilla, and some fragrant flower he couldn't name drifting toward his nose. Resting one slim hand on his chest, she tipped her eyes up and smiled that same sexy, for-his-eyes-only grin she'd cast him only moments ago. "And I think you are way overdressed for this party, Mr. Ryder."

He had just enough time to open his mouth before she grasped his shirt at the waist and pulled it from his pants. His adrenaline spiked. Every inch of his skin burst to life. He thought about stopping her but suddenly didn't want to. Her fingers shifted to the button at his chest, and she flicked him a challenging look. "Trust me?"

Heat and lust and need churned inside him, three things he never expected to feel around her, making him even more light-headed, making him desperate to see what she would do next. "Not for a second."

A sexy, seductive smile toyed with her lips. Her eyes were glassy, her skin luminescent in the firelight. And when she looked at him like that, like she wanted him, all he could think about was kissing her all over again. Everywhere.

She grasped both sides of his shirt and yanked, sending buttons flying into the fire.

Surprised, Jake glanced down at his naked chest, then to her victorious grin. "I might have to note that on your next performance evaluation, Ms. Addison."

She stepped closer and pushed the two halves of his shirt apart, then slid her palms over his bare skin. Electricity vibrated every-where she touched. "Then I'd better do something to make that note memorable."

She lifted to her toes, her lips a breath from his, and stilled.

Blood rushed into his groin and made him hard in an instant. His skin trembled beneath her soft hands. Unable to hold back, he trailed his fingers down her arms and then to the bare skin of her waist, needing to touch her too. Somewhere in the back of his head he knew this wasn't right. She was flirting with him, something she never did, and he was letting her, something he wouldn't do if he were thinking straight. And they were in the middle of a strange vil-lage, with people dancing and chanting all around them, watching their every movement. But as her shallow breaths lifted her breasts so they skimmed his bare chest and her thighs brushed his, bringing their bodies into even closer contact, he suddenly didn't care. Fire flared inside him, making him ache, making him need, making him focus on only one thing.

He closed his arms around her slim waist and jerked her in even tighter. She gasped, just enough to open her mouth in a sexy little O. And before she could protest, he lowered his lips to hers and kissed her as he'd wanted to kiss her since the moment she'd started to dance.

She groaned, opened at the first touch, slid her tongue along his, and wrapped her arms around his shoulders. She tasted of sin, of salvation, of something a little voice in the back of his head warned he wasn't ready for. But he ignored it. The same way he ignored the voices around him and the jungle and the fire and drank in only her.

He tipped his head the other way, kissed her deeper, reveled in the way she rubbed against him. One hand slid down her lower spine, over the swell of her sexy ass, and closed over her cheek, tugging her in harder against him. His erection pressed into her belly as he kissed her again and again, as her hardened nipples skimmed his chest through the thin fabric of her top. As her tongue turned frantic and hungry against his.

Hands landed on his shoulders, gripped the fabric and tugged. His hands dropped from Marley's waist, and the garment slipped free of his arms, but he barely noticed. All he could think about was Marley. How soft she was against him. How warm and perfect. How sweet and sinful she tasted in his mouth. How it would feel to have her legs closing around him, drawing him in.

She eased back from his mouth, stepped away from his body. Muttered, "Wait."

Unwilling to let her go, he opened his eyes and reached for her, only to realize a native woman had a hold of her arm and was tugging her away from the fire. Away from him. "Hey. Let her go."

The native woman mumbled something Jake didn't understand and pulled Marley toward a hut on the far side of camp. Marley stumbled as she was tugged along and tried to wriggle away, but another woman—the one who'd been teaching her to dance—rushed up and took her other arm.

Jake stepped forward. "Hold on—"

Two males grasped each of his arms. Startled, he looked down and tried to jerk back, especially now, when the camp seemed to be spinning around him.

"Akuten. Amalu matenku."

He had no freaking idea what they were saying, but they were dragging him in the direction the women had taken Marley, so he let them. For now.

They let go of him near the threshold of the hut. He had to duck down to enter so he didn't hit his head. Looking up, he stopped dead in his tracks.

Torches were set all around the perimeter of the hut, illuminating the space in a warm glow. A few women milled around the room, grabbing items he couldn't see. But what held his riveted attention was Marley, in the center of the hut facing away from him, her blonde hair hanging in a wavy mass down her back while the two women untied the strips of fabric from her shoulders.

The fabric fell to her feet. Jake's gaze slid down the supple line of her naked spine. The women brushed her hair to the side and reached for a bowl on the floor. Then they began rubbing some kind of oil all over her skin.

Blood pounded through every vein in his body. The room spun around him. In the corner, a woman lit some kind of incense and began chanting. Drums beat a thumping rhythm from outside. The men pushed him forward. As if in a trance, Jake stepped farther into the hut and stopped behind Marley.

The women slowly turned her to face him. And when they did all the blood in Jake's body rushed right into his groin. Her skin glistened in the torchlight. Her breasts were plump. Perky. Perfect. The tips of her nipples like pink erasers, straining for his touch. And the look in her shimmering eyes as her gaze locked on his told him loud and clear that she was as gone as he was.

The people, the village, the voices and drums all slid to the wayside. He fingered the edge of her hair hanging above her breast, felt the way she sucked in a breath and held it, and knew there was no holding back.

His hand slid up into her hair. He cupped the back of her head and pulled her in to him. Her mouth opened to his kiss, and her tongue brushed his without hesitation. A groan rumbled from her chest. Her hands gripped his elbows, tiptoed around his back, and tugged him in closer to her heat.

He wanted her. Needed her. Couldn't remember wanting or needing anyone the way he did now. He changed the angle of the kiss, slid his hand down her shoulder across her chest and cupped her breast in his palm. She sighed and kissed him deeper. He found her nipple and rolled the tip between his thumb and forefinger. She gasped and pressed her hips against his. His cock grew harder, hotter, pulsed with an urgency to get inside her.

Hands landed on his back and pushed. He stepped forward, forcing Marley backward. She pulled away from his mouth and hands before he was ready to let her go. He opened his eyes only to realize she was looking down at a pile of blankets near her feet.

Her gaze lifted back to his. Fire flared hot and wicked in her eyes. Footsteps faded away, but he didn't turn to look to see who was leaving. Because he couldn't. The only thing he could see was Marley.

She stepped back into him, lifted her mouth to his, and kissed him hard. Tingles rushed over every inch of his skin. He cupped both sides of her face and kissed her back, tangling his tongue with hers while her hands slid to the snap at his waistband.

"Marley . . ."

"Don't stop kissing me. Don't ever stop kissing me. I've wanted this for so long."

God, that sounded good. Sounded right. He kissed her again and again as she flicked the snap free and pushed her hand inside his pants. Her silky fingers skimmed his lower belly then brushed his cock. He groaned into her mouth and trailed his hands down her back then pulled her in tight. She moaned. Wrapped her hand around his cock and pumped. Fire and electricity raced down his spine. He kissed her harder and tugged her to the ground.

Lights danced behind his eyes. The thump thump thump of drums outside the hut pounded in time with his pulse. She let go of him and dragged her hands up his chest then trailed her fingers into his hair as he kissed her and rolled her to her back.

Her legs opened. He pressed his weight into her, rubbed his erection against her core. Kissed her again and again. Needed to taste her everywhere. Needed to make her as hot as he was.

His lips found her jaw, moved down the sexy column of her throat and across her chest. Cupping her right breast, he brought the tip to his mouth, licked and laved. She arched, dropped her head back, and moaned. Groaning himself, he moved to her other breast and did the same, then kissed his way down her ribs and over the soft indent of her belly button until he reached the waistband of her skirt.

His hand skimmed the skirt until he found the bottom edge. Pulling away from her mouth, he looked down as he slid the skirt up, baring every inch of her sex to his view.

He groaned again at the sight. She was naked. Sexy. Already swollen from her arousal.

"Jake . . ." She pushed up on her elbows.

He trailed his hand over her sex, parted her, then leaned in and licked.

She groaned. Dropped back to the floor, and pressed up against his mouth.

She was dripping. On fire. And she tasted like honey. He laved his tongue over her again and again, loving the sounds she made, the way she moved her hips against him, loving everything she did.

"More."

The word was a command, an order, a demand, and it only made him hotter. She gripped the blanket at her hips and lifted to his mouth, her body undulating beneath him. Sliding his fingers lower, he pressed inside her and twisted up, stroking her wetness exactly where he knew it would feel best.

She cried out. He swallowed her release as it washed over her, drawing it out as long as he could, savoring every shudder, every shiver, every single soul-shattering tremble. His cock throbbed, but he pushed his own need to the side, wanting only this. Relishing her pleasure as long as it lasted.

When her muscles relaxed, he kissed his way back up her belly and chest and captured her mouth. Her hands grasped the sides of his face. She moaned and slid her tongue along his, and then her leg hooked over his hip, and she rolled him to his back.

She pulled back from his mouth. His hands landed on her arms. He blinked up at her. Firelight made her skin glow and her gleaming eyes dance with arousal. She pushed away from him, crawled backward, and stripped his pants from his legs in one quick movement.

A tiny voice in the back of his head screamed this had gone way further than it should, but he didn't listen. Couldn't. Because suddenly she was crawling back over him, completely naked. Glimmering with the oil the women had spread over her skin. Her eyes blazing with the same heat and need erupting inside him.

"Come here." He lifted his torso from the floor, captured her face, drew her lips back to his. Kissed her with everything he had in him. She climbed over him, grasped his cock in her hand, and lowered her hot, tight, slick sheath, taking him deep.

Stars exploded behind his eyes. He thrust up inside her, needing to get deeper, needing to feel her everywhere. She lifted her hips and lowered, sliding along his cock, creating the most incredible friction. Her hands grasped his shoulders, her breasts rubbed against his chest. She rocked her hips against him as she pulled her body closer to his, taking him with long, deep, slow strokes that made him absolutely wild.

But he needed more. Needed all of her. He flipped her to her back and pressed her against the blanket.

"Jake . . ." She pulled her mouth from his and groaned.

He pushed up on his hands and thrust inside her. Her eyes glazed over. Her hands landed against his biceps. He did it again and again, feeling her grow wetter, tighter, feeling her body rush toward a climax they both needed more than air to breathe.

"Don't stop." She lifted her legs around his hips, tightened her sex. Gripped his arms to hold on tight.

He couldn't speak. Wanted to tell her how good it felt but couldn't do anything other than thrust harder, deeper, giving her what she wanted. He stared down into her gleaming eyes as she looked up at him. Felt every part of her. Couldn't hold back. And as his climax slammed into him, for a moment he was sure he could see into her soul. As if they were one. As if she were the answer to everything.

Her fingernails dug into his skin. She dropped her head back, closed her eyes, and cried out. Her sex pulsed and clenched around him through her release, and the delicious friction caused another tiny orgasm to slam into him, kicking his own pleasure right back to blistering, robbing him of all thought, of sight, of everything but her and this and them.

He collapsed against her. Couldn't seem to catch his breath. Couldn't move. But the room was spinning again. The drums once again pounding. And even though he'd just come harder than he ever had before, arousal was already rushing through his veins again, his body telling him once wasn't even close to being enough.

"Oh my God, Jake." Her hand slid up into his hair, and she scraped her fingernails across his skull. "That was . . . wow. Do that again."

He pushed up on one hand, looked down at her smiling, sweaty, gorgeous face, and knew before this night was over, he was going to have her again. Several times. Any and every way he could get her. And screw the consequences.

He lowered his mouth to hers and rocked his already growing erection inside her hot, slick core. "Yes. Definitely yes."

chapter 9

Okay, she thought she'd had the mother of all hangovers before. She'd been wrong. Marley felt like she'd slammed her head into the front of a semi going ninety miles per hour.

Pressing a hand against her aching forehead, she dragged her eyes open. Watery vision filled her sight and then slowly cleared. Blinking several times, she stared up at a thatched roof.

Voices echoed outside the grass walls of some kind of hut. Sunlight filtered around the edges of a blanket hanging over the doorway. She tried to sit up but couldn't. Something heavy pressed against her legs and waist. Shifting against the hard ground, she turned to her left. And spotted Jake's sleeping face resting against her shoulder.

Confusion clouded her mind. Her gaze skipped down to his bare arm wrapped around her waist, his leg draped over hers, then skipped up and over to his ass—his very naked ass—only inches from her hand.

"Oh my God." She shoved hard against his shoulder, knocking him off her, and jerked the blanket from the floor beside them, tugging it over her—oh holy God—own nakedness as she twisted away.

Jake grunted and rolled over on his belly. "Someone turn the damn lights off. It's too freakin' bright."

One quick glance over her shoulder confirmed—yep, she'd been right—he was completely butt-ass naked. And wow, he had a great butt. Totally muscular, squeezable, and hot.

Panic and heat rushed to her cheeks with that thought. Gripping the blanket tighter to her breasts, she averted her eyes once more. "What the hell did we do last night?"

Grumbling, Jake shifted behind her, then went utterly silent. And without even looking, she knew he'd finally cued in to the situation and realized the same damn thing she just had.

They'd slept together. No, that wasn't right. Her fuzzy mind was slowly clearing, bringing her brain back online synapse-by-synapse, making connections she'd rather forget. They hadn't done a whole lot of sleeping last night. They'd . . . Oh shit. She couldn't even think about what they'd done. Over and over. In a variety of positions. And she'd enjoyed every one. Multiple times.

She groaned and dropped her head into her hands. "Oh my God."

"Um. Wow." His voice echoed behind her, followed by the rustle of fabric. Then he chuckled. A nervous sound that only made her pulse beat faster. "I . . . Wow."

Wow? That was all he was going to say? *Wow?*

She pressed her fingers to her throbbing eye sockets. "This is such a monumental mess."

"Which part?"

She cringed. Definitely not wanting to remember all the different . . . parts. "Just don't even say it."

He chuckled again, as if the entire situation amused him. "Look, shock factor aside, there is a plus to all this."

"A plus? I can't see a single plus in this situation."

"I mean, if you had to lose control, at least you did it with someone you know you can trust instead of one of those natives. You're not going to get pregnant. And we're both clean. So there's no reason to stress over that part, at least."

A sick feeling passed through her stomach. "How do you know that I won't get pregnant?"

When he didn't answer, she glanced over her shoulder. "Jake, how do you know that information?"

A sheepish expression crossed his face.

And in a split second, the fact they'd just screwed each other silly was suddenly the least of her worries.

Her eyes flew wide. "Oh my God. You looked in my medical file?"

When he still didn't answer, she scrambled to her feet, tugging the blanket with her. Thankfully, he'd pulled another blanket over his hips so he wasn't flashing her. "That's an invasion of privacy. It's also illegal, and you know it."

He rolled his eyes. "You've looked in my file. If you hadn't, you'd be freaking out way more than you are now."

Her eyes shot even wider. "I schedule all the yearly physicals for employees of your stupid company. Of course I've seen your damn file. But that doesn't mean—"

"Yes, it does." He braced his hands behind him on the ground and leaned back, all relaxed and cocky and sexy as hell. "Don't get all high and mighty on me right now."

"That's just . . ." She glanced around the room, frustrated and, yes, freaking flipping out. "That's sexual harassment! Again!"

He barked out a laugh and eyed the flimsy blanket clutched at her chest. "If memory serves, you're the one who ripped my shirt off last night. I have the missing buttons to prove it."

Her mouth dropped open. Exasperation and disbelief killed the words on her tongue. She could barely think straight, let alone argue with him. Because he was right.

Oh shit. Oh holy shit.

"Hey." His brow dropped low. "You didn't drink from that bowl they were passing around last night, did you?"

Marley could barely keep up with him, but his question made her brain spin with the events of the night before, and she froze, remembering back to the women passing her that bowl of fermented smelling liquid as the fire was lit. "Yes." Several times, in fact. "Did you?"

"I might have had a sip or two."

"What was in it?"

Jake looked up at the ceiling. "I'm guessing some plant or vine with psychedelic properties. Did the room spin for you last night?"

"Yes."

"Leave you lightheaded, seeing stars and different colors?"

Her stomach dropped, and she closed her eyes again. They'd obviously gone for quite a trip last night. "Yes."

"Make you horny as hell? Oh wait, pretty sure I know the answer to that one."

She shoved her foot against his leg.

Chuckling, he bent forward and rubbed his hand over the spot. "Stop. I'm sore."

So was she. Everywhere. In a good way. She pressed her hand to her forehead. "Oh my God, I can't believe we—"

"Fucked."

She groaned and turned away, gripping the blanket around her. "Don't say that."

"Why not? That's what we did. Several times, I'm pretty sure."

"Ugh. That word is just so vulgar and descriptive. I can't—" Her gaze dropped to the dirt floor, the area surrounding their makeshift bed littered with flower petals, then to the woven bracelet around her ankle, and finally to the same bracelet on his ankle. Sketchy memories flittered through her mind. Ones that made her stomach flip over in a new, anxiety-inducing way. "Oh. Shit."

He raked a hand through his hair, then dropped his arm to his side. "Damn but I could really use a strong cup of coffee right now."

"Jake, look at the floor."

His gaze darted to the flower petals. "Yeah, so?"

"So, I don't think"—she swallowed hard—"sex was all we did last night."

"If you're talking positions, I'm pretty sure we covered most—"

"Just shut up. Do you remember the women in this hut last night? Look what's on your ankle."

His gaze drifted to the ankle bracelet. "Yeah, so? Someone gave me a gift. What about it?"

"They gave me the same one." She tugged the sheet up so he could see the matching bracelet on her ankle. "Couples wear them. You saw the men and women with matching anklets pairing off last night. Then that little ceremony thing they did when they brought us in here with the flowers and the incense." She pressed a sweaty hand to her forehead, and her stomach rolled all over again. "I think we might have gotten . . . married."

He went completely still and didn't utter a single sound. Then after several long seconds muttered, "Well, that's something I haven't been accused of doing before."

Panic pressed against every inch of Marley's skin. Gripping the blanket at her chest, she bent over and reached for the woven rope around her ankle.

"No, don't." Jake lurched to his feet.

Marley's eyes went wide. She jerked around. "Good God, Jake. You're naked."

He chuckled and reached for his pants from the floor.

She cringed and bent over to pull the bracelet off again. But before she could untie it, his hand closed around hers. "Don't."

She shoved his hand aside and stepped away from him. "Do not tell me you, of all people, want to be married. Or pretend to be married."

A mischievous smile curled his lips. His sexy and—now she knew from personal experience—way too soft and seductive lips. "No. I don't. But I also don't want to get skewered. If they really did some marriage ritual thing on us last night, which now I'm remembering back to, they might have done since there were people in this hut when we started to—"

"Oh God." Marley pressed a hand to her face as a new wave of complete and abject mortification washed over her. "We did—that—in front of them?"

"Relax. I'm pretty sure they were out of the room when we really got going."

"Oh holy God." Memories of the night before rushed through her mind. The women taking her top off and rubbing her up with oils, then Jake's scorching, intensely focused gaze as he'd stared at her and finally moved in to kiss her. She pressed a hand to her mouth. "I think I'm going to be sick."

She dropped to the edge of the blanket, pulled her knees up, and breathed deep, fighting the humiliation.

Jake rested his hands on his hips, barefoot, shirtless, and sexy as hell. Too damn sexy, especially now, when she knew just what he could do with his—

She groaned and dropped her head into her hands.

"That's one I haven't heard before either."

The hurt in his voice made her realize he thought she was talking about the sex. But she wasn't. That had been good. No, not just good, but mind-blowingly amazing. Only she didn't have a clue how to tell him that without making the entire situation worse.

"You can take the bracelet off if you want," he said in an irritated tone. "But I guarantee if you do, I'm not getting out of this village."

Marley lifted her gaze and eyed his bare foot. His khaki cargo pants covered the ankle bracelet, blocking it from view, but she knew it was still there. Matching hers.

"So what do you expect me to do? Act like we did get married?"

He reached for his shirt from the ground. "I know it's a stretch to act like you like me."

From his jerky movements, she could tell she'd upset him. But the thought was so foreign she wasn't sure what to say or do. Jake had never cared what she'd said or done before.

Confused, she watched as he pulled on his shirt, tried to button it, then gave up. And as he did, she had a memory flash. Of tugging his shirt from his pants, tearing the buttons off, and sliding her hands along his hard, muscular chest.

Warmth gathered in her belly and slinked lower, and she coughed and looked quickly away, fighting back the arousal she did *not* want to feel.

This was Jake. Her boss. *Her boss.* Not some random guy she could hook up with and fantasize about a future with. Jake didn't do long-term. Or serious. Or relationships. He was a casual sex kind of guy. And that kind of relationship with him was something she was not—never—interested in.

So okay, they'd slept together. They'd both clearly been high from whatever hallucinogen they'd ingested. If they'd been in their right minds, it would never have happened. And now that she was in her right mind, it was *never* happening again.

But she had liked it. Liked it a lot. And she liked him even more.

She pushed to her feet, grasped the blanket at her chest, and worked for calm when she felt anything but. "Your pack's in the other hut with mine."

"Which one?" He sat on the blanket and pulled on his boots, but, she noticed, didn't look up at her.

She'd hurt him. She didn't know how or why, but she had. She needed to do something to fix it.

She moved to the door, pulled the blanket back, and peered out at the rest of the village, getting her bearings. "Um, three doors down on the right."

"I'll get them."

He rose to his feet and tried to step past her. Moving in his way, she pressed a hand to his chest. "Jake."

"What?"

"I . . ." *Crap.* She was actually going to say this. It might ruin their working relationship, but right now she was more worried about their friendship than anything else. And that's what they were—friends. If she hadn't known it before this excursion into the jungle, she knew it now. She drew in a deep breath for courage and dropped her hand. "If I had last night to do over again, I wouldn't let it happen."

"Yeah, no shit."

"But"—she forced herself to go on—"that doesn't mean I didn't enjoy it. It was . . . nice."

His shoulders relaxed, and he tipped his head in a get-real move. "Just nice?"

Amusement lingered in his dark gaze. An amusement that did crazy, hot things to her blood. Things she didn't want to be feeling. "Yes. What's wrong with nice?"

"Nice is a walk in the park. Or a bike ride. Or a movie."

"How would you like me to describe it?"

A sexy smile toyed with the corner of his mouth. "Hot. Amazing. Fan-fucking-tastic."

She couldn't stop herself. A laugh slipped from her lips. The way he described it made the entire situation seem exactly what it was—completely and entirely, without excuse, insane.

"All right. You fried my brain. How's that?"

He grinned and leaned down toward her mouth, stopping millimeters from kissing her. She sucked in a surprised and—oh, wow—very aroused breath. "That will do, wife. That will do."

He moved away without touching her, and, more confused than she believed possible, Marley watched him pull the blanket in the doorway to the side, then disappear out into the sunshine.

Drawing in a shaky breath, she turned and stared at the ground where they'd slept. And felt her heart skip a beat in her chest.

Damn. She closed her eyes. Forget being in trouble with Jake. Right now she was drowning a long and torturous death. And she had no idea if she'd survive.

Jake shifted the pack on his back while he waited for Marley to say goodbye to Darla on the edge of camp.

After hugging the anthropologist, Marley stepped up next to him, her own pack slung over her shoulders. He gripped her hand and waved to Darla and the rest of the villagers, then tugged her after him into the jungle.

She waited until they were out of sight of the village, then pulled back on his grip. "You don't have to hold my hand anymore."

The dampness of her palm told him she was nervous. Something he found incredibly interesting. He tightened his fingers around hers, not letting her get away. "You never know who could be following. Better to be safe than sorry."

"Safer for you," she mumbled.

He smiled wider. She was *really* nervous. Which not only amused him, it excited him. Memories of the night before rolled through his brain as they pushed their way past vines and wide palms. She was right. If he had it to do over again, he'd never allow *that* to happen, but it had. And part of him wasn't sorry at all.

Because it hadn't just been fan-fucking-tastic as he'd teased her, it had been freaking incredible.

When they were at least a mile from the village, he finally let go of her hand and took the lead through the jungle. At his back, she muttered, "*Ayahuasca.*"

"What?"

"That's what they gave us last night. *Ayahuasca.*"

"I've heard of that." He ducked under a low branch.

"Darla said it's a brew created with the bark of the *Banisteriopsis caapi* vine, and that it's used in ceremonies to promote psychedelic and ritual inebriation."

And potency, he guessed. He'd been harder last night than he was sure he'd ever been.

Blood rushed into his groin. He drew in a breath and fought back the arousal as he used the machete in his hand to hack at the foliage in their way. "It worked."

"They also use it in rituals to revive the mythical past of the tribe."

"You're sure a mini-encyclopedia this morning." He glanced over his shoulder at her. She'd pulled her blonde hair back in a tie and changed into long cargo pants and a fitted black tank. Not exactly the conservative work attire he was used to, but it wasn't the half-naked tribal wear she'd been sporting last night. And he was both relieved and annoyed by that fact.

She shrugged. "I just think it's interesting. The whole mud-woman thing."

Darla had told him that story last night. He looked ahead and hacked at a vine. "They thought you were their savior."

Marley snorted. A sound that was not the least bit sexy but utterly adorable to him. "I'm definitely no savior."

Maybe not in her eyes. But the guys who worked for him wouldn't agree. She saved their asses on a daily basis from the safety of Aegis headquarters, and they all loved her for it.

He focused on the vines in front of him instead of the heat brewing again in the depths of his belly. "Luckily they realized you weren't her."

"Lucky for you, you mean," she said with a hint of amusement.

She was right. If Darla hadn't explained to the tribal leaders that Marley was just a lost tourist, they'd have tried to keep her. And from the way some of the local men were eyeing her, Jake had a feeling they wouldn't have wanted to keep him as well.

They moved through the jungle at a slow pace. Sweat slid down Jake's spine and dotted his forehead. Several times he had to stop to check their direction on his compass and cursed the fact his GPS still wasn't working thanks to the thick canopy.

Several hours into their trek they stopped for water. Jake handed Marley the canteen he'd filled before they'd left the village. Marley tipped it up to her lips and took a long swallow. A bead of sweat slipped down her temple and along her cheekbone to draw his attention.

That heat he thought he'd squelched rebuilt in his belly. A heat he didn't need on a good day, let alone out here when it was ten thousand degrees and more humid than hell.

She lowered the canteen and handed it to him. "Here. You look like you need this more than me."

He tossed back a large sip, then glanced over the jungle. "I figure we have another hour. Maybe an hour and a half."

"Thank God. I'm ready to be done with the jungle for the rest of my life."

So was he. But as he capped the canteen and shoved it back in his pack, he couldn't help but wonder if what they were walking into was better or worse than where they'd already been.

How could it be better? Last night was fucking amazing.

It was. But he was smart enough to know it was a one-time thing. Shoving that thought to the back of his head, he threw his backpack over his shoulder. "Come on."

Marley pushed to her feet and followed, and, to her credit, didn't grumble once.

She had to want to, though. If she was half as sore as he was, just walking had to hurt.

Fuck. Do not go there. And for God's sake, do not *think about fucking.*

Marley grasped his arm at the sleeve and drew him to a stop. "Shh."

Annoyed by her touch, by the way it lit up his skin, by the way he wanted it in other, more sensitive places, he turned and frowned at her. "What?"

"Listen," she whispered.

He stilled, looked out over the jungle, and realized what she'd heard.

Voices. Several. Speaking Spanish. Close. Coming from somewhere to his right. He'd been so wrapped up in thoughts of her he hadn't noticed.

"Shit."

Marley held up a finger to her lips, then let go of him and pushed through the brush *toward* the voices.

"Marley," he whispered. But she didn't stop. In seconds he couldn't see her anymore. His adrenaline inched up. Goddammit, where the hell was she going?

As quietly as he could, he followed. The voices grew louder. He pushed a palm frond out of his way, then drew up sharply so he didn't knock Marley to the ground where she'd stopped.

She turned and held her finger to her lips again, then pointed through the brush. "Sh. They're right there."

Yeah, no shit. He could hear they were close. He just didn't know who *they* were. Spying wasn't at the top of his list right now. The last time he'd done that, he'd nearly wound up as lunch.

She grasped his forearm and pulled him to the ground beside her. With no choice, he knelt close and drew in a sharp breath of that flowery scent mixed with sweet feminine perspiration. A combination that knocked his arousal right back to the forefront and sent flashes of their night together rushing through his brain.

She moved the brush a tiny bit so they could see into a small clearing. And then all sexy thoughts fled, because what he saw was a hundred times worse than the natives he'd tangled with last night.

"Fuck me," he whispered.

Marley elbowed him in his side to get him to shut up. Jake peered through the vines toward the six paramilitary soldiers clearly taking a break from their hike to drink and eat and shoot the shit.

The one on the right spoke rapidly in Spanish. One seated on a log nodded and responded. Marley glanced around the jungle as she listened, and when Jake could no longer take it, he whispered, "What the hell are they saying?"

"They're talking about Gray."

His eyes widened. "Your boyfriend?"

"Ex. Quiet, I can't hear."

Her brow dropped as she listened to the conversation, and something dark passed over her eyes.

"What?"

"They're looking for him. It sounds like he's been on the run about six days. They're frustrated they haven't found him yet."

"We're close to Bruhia. They had to have checked there already."

"They have." She shifted against the ground, and a twig snapped. "Their orders are to kill him on sight, and anyone he's with. They—"

Four heads turned their direction. At Jake's side, Marley opened her mouth in what he knew was about to be a gasp. Slapping his hand over her mouth, he tugged her deeper into the brush as soundlessly as possible. Her hands rushed to grasp his arm, and her feet shuffled in the dirt. Shoving her behind him, Jake pulled his Glock from the holster at his thigh and went still as stone.

Two paramilitary soldiers headed straight for them, guns drawn, faces somber. Marley tensed at Jake's back. Everything in Jake's mind slowed to the moment. To the two men approaching, to the four left in camp, visualizing where they were, how many guns they had, planning how he was going to take them down and get Marley out of here safely.

The first soldier reached the brush where he and Marley had just been and swept it aside. He stepped through the vines and reached out to move the brush directly in front of them. Marley held her breath at Jake's back. Jake locked his gaze on what little of the soldier's face he could see through the foliage and lifted his weapon.

A shout echoed from somewhere off to their right. The soldier's head jerked in that direction, then he yelled something in return. Tense seconds passed before he turned from where Jake and Marley were hiding and moved back toward the others.

Marley exhaled a long breath. Jake didn't take time to do the same. He grasped her by the arm and shoved her into the brush. "Move. Fast."

They picked up their pace. Neither one spoke. He let Marley take the lead, pushing her from behind and looking back to see if they were being followed. Sweat slid down his temples and dampened his hair. The back of her tank top was completely drenched from her own perspiration. Jake turned to look back again, but Marley's scream drew him to a bone-chilling stop.

chapter 10

A Colombian man decked out in camouflage from head to toe stepped out of the brush, directly in Marley's path. She screamed and jerked back. Before she could react, Jake swept past her, captured the guy by the arm and swung him around, then wrapped his arm across the man's throat and squeezed.

The man's eyes grew wide. His face turned red. In a matter of seconds, he was limp in Jake's arms. Jake laid him on the ground, took the guy's gun from his holster, and reached for Marley's hand. "Come on."

Wide-eyed, she stepped over the body and pushed her legs forward to keep up. "Did you kill him?"

"No. Just knocked him out."

By using the sleeper hold. Mick Hedley had taught her that one in the gym.

She pulled back on Jake's hand, drawing him to a stop in the middle of the jungle. "Wait. We can't just leave him."

He eyed her like she'd lost her mind, then turned and tugged her after him again. "The hell we can't."

She tried to pull back, but he held her hand too tightly. "Jake, he's going to wake up and tell them we were here. They're hunting an American. Two more show up in the same area. You don't think that's at all fishy? They'll come looking for us. They had machine guns."

"I know full well what they have. And by the time he wakes, we'll be long gone."

"So aren't you going to do anything to stop him? You're supposed to be one of those guys."

He pushed vines and palm fronds out of their way and pulled her behind him. "What guys?"

"Those SEAL guys. The ones who can stop a world war with their bare hands."

"Sorry to ruin your doe-eyed impression of SEALs, but in this situation we run. We don't hang around, and we sure as hell don't do something stupid."

"We could tie him up."

"We don't have time before those other soldiers come looking for him."

He was right. But they still couldn't just leave the guy. Something in her gut said that was just trouble waiting to happen. "There has to be something else we can do."

He whirled on her so fast she stumbled back, but his hand captured her upper arm so she didn't fall. "Don't even think it."

"But—"

"No buts. Forget the fact he's bigger and stronger than you and the tiny reality that you don't have combat training. You're not getting near that guy. It stays with you, Marley." The shadows lurking in his dark eyes were new and startling, and they lit off a wave of unease all through her belly. "It keeps you up at night. It doesn't matter if it's done in self-defense or to save someone else, when you kill another person, it haunts you for the rest of your life. You're not doing it."

He thought she wanted to kill the guy. Her eyes widened, and her stomach rolled. She was just about to tell him that wasn't what she meant when she realized it didn't matter. He was trying to protect her. From something similar in his past. Something he'd lived through that had shaped him into the controlling, domineering man he'd become. She wanted to ask just what that was, what had happened to him, but he cut her off before she could get the words out.

"Screw these soldiers and screw your ex." Letting go of her arm, he squeezed her hand in a death grip, turned, and dragged her behind him again. "We're getting you back to the States where you're safe."

Marley's mouth closed, and her questions died on her tongue. She didn't have to read between the lines to know what he really meant was *where she belonged*. Shock reverberated all through her, followed by a wave of disappointment. Even after everything they'd already been through on this trip, he still thought she couldn't hold her own.

She bit into her lip to keep from arguing and instead let him pull her through the jungle. What would it take to prove to him she was tough? That she was more than just a secretary? Would he ever see her as anything more? Or would she forever be stuck in this role—standing on the fringes, waiting for someone to view her as capable, waiting for *him* to see the real her?

She didn't have an answer. All she knew for certain was that she couldn't keep going like this. Not after last night. And sooner or later she had to make sure he understood that.

"Dumb fucking idiot," Jake muttered as he stood behind a beat-up truck on a side street in Bruhia and swiped the sweat out of his eyes.

The town, situated in a clearing in the middle of the jungle, was nothing but a handful of dirt streets, rows of dilapidated shacks, three cantinas, and one small store. Lingering out in the open like they were now, they stood out like big red here-we-are beacons, and all he wanted to do was to get out of this hellhole as fast as they could.

"He didn't give you any indication where he'd be?"

"No." Marley crossed her arms over her chest at his side. "Just said he'd be easy to find."

She was still upset about their moment in the jungle. He could tell from the rigid line of her shoulders and the way she wouldn't look his way. Yes, her logic made sense, but he wasn't about to let her do something she'd eventually regret. He lived with that shit daily and knew how it changed a person.

"He's American. He should be obvious to spot. Unless he's hiding. And if he's hiding, then you *know* that means he's into some nasty shit down here."

She didn't answer, and drawing in a calming breath that did shit to cool him down, he glanced over the dirt road, not quite sure why he'd grown more agitated the closer they drew to this town.

No, that was a lie. He knew why. Because her ex was somewhere in this hellhole. The ex she'd dropped everything for and raced to South America to help. As much as she wanted to believe the guy was on the up-and-up, something in Jake's gut said not a chance. And after last night, just knowing she was still so adamant about helping her ex-lover set off an irritating vibration in the center of his chest that he just couldn't shake.

He couldn't tell her any of that, though. And, luckily, his gaze caught on the men walking into town before he could think of a sane answer. Adrenaline surging, he grasped Marley around the waist and pushed her against the side of the truck, out of view.

"What are you—?"

"Shh. We have company."

She twisted to look toward the men decked out in camouflage, holding semiautomatic weapons, parading into town, the same ones they'd run across in the jungle. Against his chest, her heart rate shot up. "I told you."

He dragged her back from the truck and into the doorway of a cement building. Reaching back, he found the knob, then silently rejoiced when the handle turned. After pulling Marley in after him, he shut the door.

Darkness surrounded them, only a sliver of light coming from around the door and one small window covered by a tarp. But the way Marley pulled back from his touch told Jake loud and clear that the arousal she'd felt last night was long gone.

Good. Great. He didn't care. She could be as mad as she liked so long as she stayed alive.

The room was small, dark, and dirty. He glanced around, realizing it must have been used as a storage area for some kind of business at one time. Boxes of wiring sat against the wall. Broken, empty shelves lined the other side of the room. Shovels and rakes sat upright in the corner. Dropping to the ground, Jake tugged off his pack, rummaged around inside until he found his sat phone, then pulled it out. The light blinked green.

Relief rushed through him. He punched in the number and hit Dial.

"What are you doing?" Marley whispered at his back.

Jake lifted the phone to his ear. "Calling Tony. You saw the airstrip on the end of town. It's rough, but he can make it. That guy could land in sand if he had to."

"Wait. You weren't willing to risk your plane before on that landing strip, but you're willing to risk it now?"

"Hell yeah, I'm risking it. In case you haven't noticed, this town's about to be overrun by guerrillas looking for your boyfriend. We're not getting out by foot or car or train. The air's our only option."

"We're not leaving, Jake. We haven't found Gray yet. You wouldn't leave a man behind, and neither will I."

Jake pushed to his feet. *Come on, Tony. Pick up already.* "He's not my man."

"No, he's mine."

Jake's gaze snapped to her in the darkness. Her man? Now McKnight was *her man*? After last night, she had the balls to say that to him?

Tony's voice echoed in his ears. "I was starting to worry, Ryder. Another hour and I was going to take to the air and go look for you."

Jake looked quickly away and tried to ignore the sudden pounding in his ears. "We're fine, but we've got heat. The airstrip in Bruhia is going to be rough. How long 'til you can get here?"

"Hold on." Tony spoke in muffled words to someone else, and from the conversation, Jake knew he was at the airport, getting the down low about the conditions in Bruhia from the tower. "It's not far, Jake," he said louder. "But I can't land the jet there. The runway's too short."

"Shit."

"The guys here can get me a chopper. It'll take me a little longer to get there. If you've got heat, though, I'll need you at the airstrip. The Black Eagles are the dominant paramilitary group running that region. I'm being told they're famous for shutting down all air traffic in and out of Bruhia on a moment's notice."

"Black Eagles, huh?" Jake looked back at Marley. He couldn't see much more than the outline of her silhouette, but he knew she was listening to every word. His day had just gone from shitty to totally fucked. "They're associated with the Calindo Cartel, aren't they?"

"And the Muñoz Cartel. And the Rojas Cartel. Drug trafficking, extortion, racketeering, murder, and kidnappings are only a few of their most notable endeavors. And they do not like Americans. Not a group you want to cross."

"Yeah, tell me something I don't already know." And if they were looking for McKnight, it meant the fucker was definitely into something he wasn't sharing.

"We'll meet you at the airstrip in forty-five minutes, Tony."

"Got it. Stay safe, Ryder."

"You too, Hughes."

"Forty-five minutes?" Marley asked when he ended the call. "That gives us plenty of time."

"To play hide-and-seek with your ex? Not happening." Jake knelt and shoved the sat phone back into his pack. "We're heading for the airstrip so there are no mistakes."

Marley drew in a sharp breath. She was fuming. He didn't have to look to know there was steam coming out of her ears, but dammit, he was just trying to keep her safe. Why couldn't she that? This wasn't a game anymore. It had gotten way too real way too fast, and he wanted her out of it.

"Okay, listen," Marley said. "I realize this is the last place you want to be—"

"Got that right." He flipped the top closed on his pack.

"I also know this is my business not yours and that you don't have to be here. But I can't leave without searching for Gray. I won't be able to live with myself if I don't at least try." When he didn't answer, she said, "Dammit, Jake. Would you stop what you're doing and look at me?"

He didn't want to stop, he wanted to leave. But he pushed to his feet and faced her like she wanted because he knew there was no way he was getting her out of here until she had her say. "Your intentions were good, Marley, but it doesn't change the fact there are people out there who want us dead and that the safest thing for us to do is to get to that airstrip before the Black Eagles shut down the entire area."

"I know," she said calmly. "I know, and you're right. But if there's one thing I've learned from you over the years, it's that duty—your word—matters. You've never left anyone behind that you've gone after. I've watched you risk your life for people you don't even know, all because you gave your word to a relative that you'd do your best. You were willing to do it for Eve before you even knew she wasn't a traitor, and you'd do it for anyone at Aegis without a second thought. I'm not asking for special treatment here, Jake. I'm not even asking you to change your plans. All I'm asking is to use those forty-five minutes to look before we have to rendezvous with Tony. Because I did exactly what you've done your whole life. I gave Gray my word, and I can't break it."

His jaw clenched and unclenched. He wanted to tell her no way in hell, wanted to toss her over his shoulder and carry her to that damn chopper himself, but he couldn't because she was right. Once he gave his word, he stuck to it, no matter the consequences. And he'd be the biggest hypocrite on the planet if he held her to a different standard.

He glanced at his watch, hit the light button on the side of the face, and calculated time. Dammit, he so did not want to do this. And if something happened to her . . . Yeah, if that happened he'd never forgive himself.

Reluctantly, he let go of the watch and reached for his pack from the floor. "Fine. You've got thirty minutes. Not a second more. If we don't find him in that time, we drop back, regroup, and make for the airstrip. And you're not going to argue about it."

She exhaled a long breath. "I won't." Then her arms closed around him, startling him in the dark as she hugged him hard. "Thank you, Jake."

Heat rushed all through his body, everywhere they touched. A heat that shot his mind right back to that native hut and the wicked smile on her face just before she'd kissed him crazy. A heat that was warm and encapsulating and pushed aside his bad mood until lightness filled his chest.

Letting go of him long before he was ready, she moved quickly for the door and pulled it open just a crack, just enough so sunlight streamed over her face as she peered out into the street. Excitement shone in her eyes. An excitement that had nothing to do with him and everything, a tiny voice whispered, to do with McKnight. "We'll find him. I know we'll find him. Just watch."

Jake frowned as he slid his backpack on. And that bad mood came screaming back. Finding the sonofabitch was exactly what he was afraid of.

Marley ducked behind a dented car and waited until the soldiers turned the corner. Waving for Jake to join her, she stayed low as he drew close to her side.

"The edge of town is our best bet," she said softly. "He'd find a place out of view."

Jake glanced at his watch again. "You've got twenty-five minutes, Rambo. I know I'm going to regret saying this, but lead on."

A thrill rushed through her as she glanced at his profile. Two days' worth of stubble covered his square jaw, darkening his features, making him look sexy as hell even with dirt and sweat coating his skin. But all she could focus on was the fact he was letting her take the reins. Sure, he was doing it begrudgingly, but still. Mr. Forever in Control had just given her something she'd always wanted and never expected, and she was so moved by the gesture, she wanted to kiss him to say thank you.

Her gaze drifted to his lips. To his soft, warm, seductive lips that had made her absolutely wild last night. So close. So perfect.

He tore his gaze from his wrist and looked at her. "What? Change your mind already?"

Realizing she was staring—and wasting time—she blinked, looked away from his wicked mouth, and told herself not to think about sex. It had been one time. One amazing time. But the sooner she forgot about it, the better.

Right. Like she could ever forget that.

She cleared her throat and pointed across the dirt road. "I'm moving for that building."

Jake peeked over the hood of the car, looked right and left, then said, "Go. I've got you covered."

Her pulse shot up, and she rushed across the street and then slinked against the side of a dilapidated building. Sweat slid down her temple and dampened her shirt as she waited for him to join her. Her gaze followed a woman carrying a basket as she disappeared into a house. Laughter echoed from inside the building at her side, but she couldn't make out the voices. When Jake reached her side, she pointed toward the next building. He nodded, and she pushed to her feet. But just before she darted off, a barefoot kid who looked to be no more than eight, wearing nothing but shorts and a ripped T-shirt, stepped out of a doorway, directly in her path.

"You," he said in an accented voice. "You American."

Marley drew up short and gripped the gun in her hand. The kid wasn't armed, but that didn't mean he wouldn't alert the soldiers who'd just passed. Warily, she glanced down the empty street behind the kid, then over her shoulder toward Jake.

"What's the holdup?" Jake whispered.

She stepped aside so he could see the child.

"Shit."

"You no need those," the kid said, nodding toward the guns in both their hands. "He told me to look for American girl." He glanced up at Marley. "That you. I his friend." The kid shuffled backward and waved his hand for her to follow. "You come. I show you."

Marley's adrenaline spiked. She opened her mouth to ask who and took a step forward, but Jake's large hand gripped her arm.

"Wait." He looked toward the kid. "He who? Who's looking for an American girl?"

"The white man. The one with the dragon tattoo on his arm. Come. We hurry before the soldiers return."

Marley looked up at Jake, excitement pulsing in her veins. "That's him. He has a tattoo of hydra on his forearm."

She pushed past him. At her back, Jake muttered, "Of course he does."

The kid disappeared into an alleyway. Garbage cans filled with food and paper were pushed up against a building. Empty cardboard boxes lay scattered across the small space. Marley followed the kid through the alley, glancing at the doors on each side. She could feel Jake's adrenaline at her back, knew he was checking his watch and stressing over their timeline, but all she could focus on was getting to Gray.

Holstering the gun at her back, she followed the kid down another side street toward a house at the very end of town. "How far?"

"Almost there." The kid waved his hand for her to follow and jogged backward. "You come. I show you."

Staying low, Marley and Jake ducked behind a rusted old truck. The kid waved his arm for them to keep up, then headed toward a lean-to shack, overgrown with palms and vines at the very back of the property.

"He stay here." The kid pushed his way through the vines and moved around the shack.

Marley followed, stepping over weathered two-by-fours, plastic jugs, and garbage littering the ground. Jake didn't say a word, but she knew he was taking it all in, cataloging everything, scanning the area around them for dangers, and just knowing he was watching out for her, that he was supporting her instead of taking over made something around her heart warm.

The kid reached for a large piece of metal, what looked like it could be a section of corrugated roofing material, and pulled it away, revealing a doorway. "I bring him food. He promise to pay me when the American lady showed up."

The kid looked up at her expectantly. Marley's pulse beat hard as she glanced at the kid, then into the dark shack.

"It okay," the kid said. "He expecting you."

Anything could be in there. This kid could be working for the Black Eagles and could have just led them into a trap. But if she didn't at least look, she'd always wonder.

Jake gripped her hand before she could take a step inside. She was about to pull away when she caught his expression—stone face, jaw like steel beneath his skin, eyes focused and intense—but what gave her pause was the hint of fear she saw lurking in those dark irises.

Fear for them? Fear for her? She wasn't sure which, but fear was something she'd never seen in this man's eyes before. Fear meant he cared. Fear meant she mattered.

Her mouth went dry and her hands grew damp against her sides, preventing her feet from moving forward. He didn't say anything. Didn't order her to move or call her back. He just locked eyes with her and held her gaze, as if asking—not telling—her to let him go first.

Minutes later—or maybe it was seconds, she was so lost she couldn't tell which—he let go of her, stepped around her, and disappeared into the hut. And alone, all Marley could do was press her shaking hands against her cheeks and draw in a deep breath that did nothing to ease the vibrations suddenly echoing through her entire body.

What the heck was that? They could be overrun by guerrillas at any moment, and she was having a panic attack because Jake looked at her in a protective, caring way? No, she wasn't letting that happen. No matter what was going on between the two of them, the focus now was on Gray. It had to be or she might lose her mind.

She ducked under the doorway and stepped into the hut. Jake stood over a crumpled blanket on the dirt floor, his big hands resting on his hips as he looked down at the ground. "If he was here, he's gone now."

Marley's gaze skipped over the empty beer bottles scattered in one corner and the crumpled paper in another.

"He supposed to be here," the kid said at her back. "He be back soon. Never go far. Too dangerous. You see."

Jake glanced down at his wrist, then looked over at Marley. "We don't have time to wait."

A rumble sounded overhead, and Marley quickly looked at her own watch.

Her spirits dropped like a stone into the pit of her stomach. Jake was right. They were out of time.

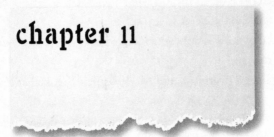

chapter 11

Dusk was just setting over the small town as Marley and Jake darted behind a parked car and hunched down out of sight next to Alejandro—the kid who'd helped Gray over the last few days.

The boy pointed between two buildings toward a clearing on the other side of town. "The airstrip is just past there."

"Thanks." Marley fished a wad of cash she'd converted at the hotel from the front pocket of her pack and handed it to him. "If you see Gray in the next ten minutes, tell him we're here but that we're leaving. He has to get to the airstrip as soon as possible if he wants to go."

"Thanks, pretty lady."

The kid pushed to his feet and turned to run off, but Jake caught him by the forearm before he could get a step away. "Don't tell anyone about this."

"No tell," the boy said quickly. "I promise." He winked toward Marley, tugged his arm from Jake's grip, and scurried off.

"I don't trust that kid as far as I can throw him," Jake said at her side.

Neither did Marley. The sooner they got out of here the better. Regret rolled in her stomach over the fact she was leaving Gray behind, but there was too much heat in this town. If they didn't leave now, they might never get out, and no matter what Jake thought about her intentions, the last thing she wanted was for him to get hurt because of her.

That weird vibration lit off in her chest again. The same one she'd felt when he'd looked at her outside Gray's hut. And it made her pulse turn to a whirl in her ears as their conversation from this morning echoed in her head.

"How would you like me to describe it?"

"Hot. Amazing. Fan-fucking-tastic."

Her cheeks heated once more. The memory of that wicked, sexy smile on his tempting lips when he'd said those words and leaned close but hadn't kissed her sent heat rushing to her belly.

Jake gripped her hand and pulled her to her feet, knocking her out of the memory. "Come on. We need to get a move on."

Dazed, she had no choice but to follow. But she only made it three steps before a hand darted out of a doorway, closed around her free arm, and jerked her from Jake's grip.

Marley yelped and swung out. Jake swiveled around, grasped the man by the shirt, and shoved the guy hard up against the side of the building. "Touch her again, and you're dead."

The man struggled. "Who the fuck do you think you are? I—"

Recognizing the voice, Marley darted around Jake so she could see better. And when she caught sight of the rangy man in front of her, her eyes flew wide. "Gray? Oh my God, is that you?"

"Yeah, it's me, Freckles." His focus stayed glued to Jake. "Do you know this guy?"

Marley scrambled to pull Jake back. "Yeah. He's a friend. Jake, it's him. Let him go. Oh my God, Gray. We've been looking all over for you."

Jake's jaw clenched, but he eventually released Gray. The man slumped against the wall and tugged on his frayed T-shirt. Marley took a good look at him, barely believing what she was seeing. He was still as tall as she remembered, Jake's height but leaner. His hair was long and ratty, dirty blond locks falling past his shoulders, and a thick, matted beard hung down to his chest. But the eyes . . . the deep-green eyes she remembered from five years ago were the same.

His gaze darted between her and Jake. Taking them in, assessing the threat. Confusion passed over his features. He seemed to be having trouble adjusting. But then he looked Marley's way, and it passed.

"You have no idea how good it is to see you." Gray captured her in a bone-crushing hug before Marley even saw him move. The scents of dirt and sweat and body odor assailed her nostrils, and her nose wrinkled at the hideous combination. "I thought you weren't coming. I waited and waited but I didn't see you. Then I heard the helicopter and I thought maybe."

Marley could barely make out what he was saying. Her eyes were watering too much from the smell. Carefully, she rested her hands on his shoulders and tried to push him away, but he was like a rock, immovable and unyielding. And the suffocating hug shot her anxiety over seeing him again straight through the roof.

"We need to go," Jake said in a gruff voice. "Tony's landing in five minutes, and we've got zero leeway to fuck around."

Gray let go of her and looked toward Jake, as if he didn't realize the man was still there. "Oh. I didn't realize you were coming with us."

"You got a problem with that?"

Marley shot a look at Jake. His irritated expression said he wasn't enjoying this little reunion at all. And though that aggravated her—he always kept his cool with every other hostage he'd ever rescued, good or bad—she cut him some slack this time because she knew he was simply stressing about their timeline.

"Yes," Marley said, trying to keep the peace. "Jake's pilot is the one picking us up. Grayson McKnight, this is Jake Ryder, CEO of Aegis Security, the firm where I now work."

Gray glanced between them. "You left Omega?"

"Yes," Marley answered.

"What kind of work does Aegis do?"

"The same."

"Better," Jake corrected. "None of my men have ever been incarcerated in a third world country."

Gray's spine stiffened and his eyes narrowed on Jake.

Okay, that was uncalled for. Unable to believe he'd just said that, Marley fought the urge to reach over and smack Jake upside the head. He was being rude again, his gaze locked on Gray as if the man were a bug Jake wanted to squash under his boot. But he turned before she could tell him to knock it off, and as she watched him walk toward the airstrip, that feeling hit her again. The one she'd experienced back at Gray's shack and again only moments ago. The one that told her the reason she was so irritated with Jake now, the reason she'd been growing more frustrated with him these last few months, wasn't because he was acting any differently than normal, but because she was falling for the man.

Falling for Jake Ryder? No. *No*, she couldn't be. Her hands grew damp. Her cheeks hot. The man wasn't relationship material. He didn't *do* relationships. He'd made that clear on numerous occasions. She'd have to be stupid to ever open herself up to someone like him.

"Marlene?" Gray said somewhere close. "Are you okay? You don't look so good."

Slowly, because the street seemed to be spinning, she looked to her right, toward Gray's unfamiliar face hidden by that long rangy beard and all that dirty hair, and for a moment had no clue where she was. The last few days spun in her mind like a carousel set on supersonic speed—making her lightheaded, making her stomach roll, making her skin burn—then came to a screaming halt in that torch-lit hut she'd shared with Jake.

Oh shit. Oh holy shit. She leaned forward and rested her hands on her thighs while she focused on sucking back air. She wasn't just falling for him, she was falling *in love* with him. With a man who was just like her father. With a man who made her so crazy sometimes she wanted to pull her hair out. And she had no one to blame but herself. "I-I think I might pass out."

"Right here?" Surprise lifted Gray's voice, and he rested a hand on her back.

"Yes, right here." She focused on the ground beneath her. Tried to push the panic down.

"Ryder!" Gray yelled.

Jake's footsteps echoed close. "What's wrong with her?"

"I don't know. Said she feels lightheaded."

"Marley?" Jake reached for her.

"I'm fine." She stood quickly and moved out of Jake's reach, not able to bear his touch just now. Not when her emotions were so raw and unguarded. She couldn't be in love with the man. She couldn't be. She was too smart for that. Wasn't she?

He dropped his hand when she moved out of his reach, frowning at her in clear annoyance. And though she knew she was confusing the heck out of him, she didn't care. Because she was fucking confused right now too. And more than anything she just wanted to get out of Colombia and back to the States where things made sense. Or used to, at least.

"I'm fine," she said again, drawing a deep breath that did nothing to settle her nerves. "Let's just go."

Jake's expression said he wasn't convinced, but she swallowed hard and stepped past him, careful to stay out of his reach. And told herself she could fix this. As soon as they got home, as soon as everything got back to normal, she could make herself *not* love the man.

She had to. Because there was no way she'd ever survive loving Jake Ryder.

Something was up with Marley. Jake didn't know exactly what, but ever since Grayson McKnight had shown up on the scene, Marley's demeanor had done a complete one-eighty.

She definitely wasn't being her normal sassy self. Wasn't challenging Jake as she always did or gloating that she'd found McKnight, wasn't even questioning Jake's decision that they wait for Tony's chopper in the dark on the edge of the airstrip. Since they'd found McKnight she'd barely said two words to Jake. And forget looking at him. The last time she'd glanced his way, when she'd felt sick on that street corner and he'd tried to help her, the look she'd shot him was one of complete disbelief. And at the moment her don't-touch-me vibe was completely clear as she sat on the other side of McKnight, as far from Jake as she could get.

He ground his teeth and glanced over the domed airstrip, telling himself whatever was going on with her wasn't his issue. But he couldn't stop thinking about it. And every time McKnight turned to talk to her and the two exchanged quiet words, the urge to slam his fist through McKnight's face just for the fun of it curled Jake's fingers into the palm of his hand.

You're jealous, a tiny voice whispered in his ear.

He clenched his jaw hard. He wasn't jealous, dammit. He was hot, sweaty, dirty, and ticked he was sitting out here, hiding from the Black Eagles, but he definitely wasn't jealous. Not even close.

Red lights blinked above, drawing Jake's attention, and he looked up, relieved the wait was finally over without any more drama. Grabbing his pack, he pushed to his feet. "That's our chopper. Right on time."

The single-engine helicopter lowered to the ground. Ducking low beneath the blades, Jake rushed forward. After pulling the cabin door open for Marley, he tossed his pack inside, then reached for the cockpit door.

"Haul ass, Ryder," Tony Hughes said over the roar of the blades. "We've got company."

Jake glanced over his shoulder, then muttered, "Fuck me."

No more drama? In his dreams. At least twelve paramilitary soldiers were bearing down on the runway with automatic weapons in their hands, pointed straight at their chopper.

Jake slammed the cabin door, climbed into the seat beside Tony, then snapped his harness and pulled on a headset. "Buckle in," he hollered at Marley over his shoulder.

She yelled something Jake couldn't hear over the whir of the blades. At her side, McKnight reached for his seatbelt. Outside, the soldiers moved closer to the runway.

"Hold on, folks." Tony pulled up on the collective, and the skids lifted off the ground. "Things are about to get dicey."

Bullets pinged off the side of the aircraft as they rose in the air. McKnight shoved Marley's head between her knees. Gripping the handhold above, Jake looked down toward the troops rushing the runway and spotted the rocket launcher being holstered onto one soldier's shoulder.

"Son of a bitch." He reached for the Glock at his thigh, braced his foot against the inside of the cockpit, then unstrapped his harness and gripped the handhold tighter. To Tony he said, "Don't drop me."

"Roger that, boss. Get the fucker."

Jake kicked the cockpit door open. A gust of air rushed over his face, blowing his hair around. At his back, Marley yelled, "Jake! What the hell do you think you're doing?"

He ignored her. And the way the wind jostled him in his seat. And the sound of her voice melding with the hum of the rotor blade. His focus zeroed in on the guy holding the rocket launcher. And everything else—her, McKnight, this damn situation, and, mostly, what would happen to her if he missed—drifted to the background. Closing one eye and clutching the handhold above, he lined up his shot.

Jake fired just as the warhead in the rocket launcher burst free of the weapon in a plume of smoke. Tony muttered, "Motherfucker," then cranked on the cyclic, angling the chopper Jake's way. "Hold on!"

Grunting at the shift in gravity, Jake tried to scoot back but his foot dislodged from its brace. His body weight pitched him toward the open door. He reached up for the handhold above, but his fingers only grazed the metal. Then he was falling.

chapter 12

Marley's heart lurched into her throat as Jake's body fell toward the open cockpit door.

She scrambled to free her seatbelt. Before she could get it unbuckled, Gray jerked from his seat and grabbed Jake's arm, hauling him back into the chopper. Relief swept through her. She opened her mouth to scream at Gray not to let go, but Tony pitched the helicopter the other direction. The cockpit door slammed shut. The rocket went screaming past them and slammed into the canopy of the jungle with an explosion that shot a fireball straight into the air. Jake crashed into the center console between the two cockpit seats with a grunt.

He glanced up at Gray, muttered "Thanks," then looked toward Tony. "A little warning would have been nice."

Tony chuckled and pushed forward on the cyclic, gaining speed and putting distance between them and the airstrip. "Just trying to keep you on your toes. You're getting soft in your old age, Ryder."

Jake laughed, twisted in his seat, and looked out the window. Heart pounding, hands shaking, Marley's gaze followed. Jake's shot had hit the man holding the rocket launcher. He lay motionless on the runway. Others were hoisting the weapon to line up another shot, but the helicopter was quickly moving out of range.

They sailed out over the jungle. Jake and Tony joked in the cockpit as if falling out of a helicopter was no big deal. Gray relaxed back into the seat at her side.

But Marley couldn't settle her whirring pulse.

Panic and a new sense of fear pummeled her chest. Followed by a blistering disbelief that colored her vision red. She squeezed her hand into a fist, clenched her jaw, didn't know why she was getting so worked up now that everyone was safe, but couldn't stop it from happening.

Did he have a death wish? Was he trying to prove how macho he could be? This was exactly like that mission in DC when he'd changed the op on her without notice and done his own damn thing. He hadn't known what those security guards would do. Hadn't known Wilson would be there to tell them to stand down. He could have been killed then like now. He was always doing shit like this while she sat back and worried. While she tried to act like it didn't faze her. While she pretended she didn't care.

She did care, dammit. She cared too much, and he didn't deserve it. Breathing deep through her nose, she blinked up at the ceiling, forcing back the burn in her eyes, forcing herself not to give in to the urge to climb over the seat and slap some sense into him once and for all.

Gray brushed a hand over her arm. "Hey, you okay?"

"Yeah. I'm fine. I just want to get the hell out of here."

He reached for her hand and wrapped his fingers around hers, then laid his head back against the headrest. "You and me both. You have no idea how much."

She didn't pull her hand away, instead she studied his face because it gave her something to focus on *besides* the man in the front seat still acting as if almost dying was *no big hairy deal.*

Dirt streaked Gray's cheeks. His hair was nothing but a rat's nest. He didn't look a thing like the man she'd once known, but she sensed that guy was under there somewhere. And all those questions she'd had about what had happened to him and where he'd been for so long came rushing back.

Now wasn't the time to ask them. Pulling her gaze from Gray's face, she looked up, and caught Jake twisted in his seat, staring at her with narrowed dark eyes. Her stomach tightened as his gaze dropped to Gray's hand still holding hers against her thigh. Without a word he looked back up at her, clenched his jaw, and turned to look out the windshield of the copter, his shoulders tight, his head shaking as if he couldn't believe what he was seeing.

Great. Just great. Now he thought there was something going on between her and Gray? She didn't have the strength for this. Didn't have the emotional fortitude to care what he thought because in the long run she knew it wouldn't even matter.

Right now all that mattered was getting home and forgetting this trip had ever happened.

Jake tossed his pack on the leather seat in the cabin of the jet. The Bombardier Global 8000, parked at the airstrip in Puerto Asis, sported three different zones—the galley, where they entered; the main cabin complete with swivel chairs, a dining area, and couch; and a back stateroom. Tony's copilot, Ben, already had the aircraft's engines fired up and ready to go, and Jake moved out of the way so McKnight could pass, then headed for the cockpit to check in with the pilots to make sure they hadn't been followed.

Marley mumbled something to McKnight at Jake's back, but Jake didn't hear what she said, nor did he care.

He pushed the cockpit door open. Tony was already sitting in the pilot's seat. He glanced back at Jake, then flipped a switch above his head. "We've been cleared for takeoff."

"No sign of our friends?"

"Not yet. That doesn't mean they don't have eyes and ears on the ground, though. Better to get out of here quickly."

"I couldn't agree more."

"Grab a seat so we can lift off."

Jake debated heading into the cabin with Marley and McKnight, then thought better of it. He wasn't in the mood to watch her being all touchy-feely with McKnight again. Pulling the jump seat down, he decided he'd stay right where he was.

Ben, in the copilot seat, hit the intercom button. "Folks, we're about to take off. Find your seats and buckle in."

Tony maneuvered the plane toward the runway and rattled off instructions to Ben. Crossing his arms over his chest, Jake stared at the instrument panel and tried to keep his mind from wandering over the last few hours, but he kept seeing Marley holding hands with McKnight. And every time he thought of her, he couldn't stop his brain from skipping back to last night. To the sounds she'd made when he'd been kissing her. To the way she'd felt above him, beneath him, closing around him. To the tiny droplet of sweat that had slid down her temple when she'd straddled his hips, lifted and lowered and taken him deeper. And finally to the adorable flush of her cheeks in the morning when she'd remembered what they'd done.

His skin grew hot. He frowned as the plane lifted off the runway, unable to stop the arousal and irritation from swirling in his belly. She was acting like last night hadn't happened. Which was fine, because they'd both agreed it was a mistake, but seriously. She was letting McKnight get all handsy with her only hours after she'd rocked Jake's world? Was that normal for her?

He didn't know a hell of a lot about her personal life. He'd purposely never asked. But now he couldn't stop himself from wondering. Was she this cavalier with all the guys she slept with or just him? And why the hell was she acting like McKnight was her long-lost love when she'd told Jake in the jungle that she'd known McKnight wasn't the guy for her before he'd even disappeared?

"So what's up with Marley and that McKnight character?" Tony asked.

Jake glanced toward the pilots only to realize they were in the air and that the plane was already leveling off. Shit, he'd zoned out all through takeoff. If that didn't prove his head was in a really fucked-up place, nothing did.

He released the buckle on his harness and pushed to his feet. "Nothing."

At least nothing he wanted to witness. She could do whatever the hell she wanted with McKnight when she got home, but not on his plane.

"I'll check in with you guys later."

The pilots exchanged curious looks, but Jake ignored them. He closed the cockpit door behind him, moved through the galley, and stepped into the main cabin.

Marley sat in a swivel chair by the window, a magazine in her lap, flipping pages with a perturbed expression. She'd pulled her hair back into a ponytail, swiped the dirt off her face, and tugged on a clean blue V-neck T-shirt that dipped down to her cleavage. But she was still wearing the slim-fitting cargo pants that made her ass look way too good, her cute little feet were still covered by the clunky boots he was sure had to be as damp as his, and she still looked adorably sexy in that rugged jungle girl outfit when he needed her to look anything but.

He clenched his jaw, told himself sexy was an opinion, not a fact—one he could change if he tried hard enough—and rested his hands on his hips. "Where's McKnight?"

"Taking a shower."

His gaze shot to the closed stateroom door ahead. "You let him use my shower?"

"And I gave him some of your clothes."

Jake bit down. "I don't want him wearing my damn clothes."

"Get over it, Jake." She slapped her magazine closed and pushed to her feet, pinning him with a hard glare. "I think you can afford to donate a few items of clothing to a good cause."

She pushed past him and stepped into the galley. Shocked by her blasé attitude, he turned to look after her. "What I can afford isn't the issue here. And whether or not he's a good cause remains to be seen. I'm still not convinced he was worth rescuing."

"Oh, for crying out loud." She opened the cupboard above, pulled a glass off the shelf, then shoved the lower cabinet door open and poured a generous shot of whiskey. "He saved your life in that helicopter. If it weren't for him your brains would be smashed all over that runway."

"I didn't ask for his help."

She tossed her drink back, then set the glass on the counter with a click. "No, you didn't, did you?"

She moved back into the cabin, but the animosity radiating off her in waves made Jake suddenly too fired up to let her pass. "Hold on." He reached for her arm and tugged her around. "I don't know what your problem is, but ever since McKnight showed up you've been acting like a completely different person."

"I don't have a problem. And this has nothing to do with Gray. It has to do with you."

"What's that supposed to mean?"

"It means you have two rules, one for everyone else and one for Jake Ryder, and I'm tired of it."

He frowned down at her. "I don't know what you're talking about."

"Yes, you do. You go all ape shit on the Aegis guys if they react without thinking, but you do it all the damn time. Unsnapping your harness and kicking that helicopter door open is a prime example."

"Wait." He let go of her arm, unable to keep up. "You're mad because I saved your life? If I hadn't done that, we'd probably all be dead."

"Or we might not be. But we'll never know because you didn't think about anyone else in that moment besides yourself."

She turned away again, but he grabbed her arm and whipped her back once more, his own temper shooting up to the point where he knew he needed to close his mouth and back away from this, but for some reason couldn't. "Hold on. Just who the hell do you think I risked my life to save back there? Who did I chase around the jungle these last three days? Who nearly gave me a heart attack every time she disappeared? Who did I spend two freaking days tracking to Colombia, when everyone else ignored the fact she'd up and left with no explanation? Who, Marley? Do you need a hint? Because I'll tell you right now, I sure as shit didn't do any of those things for your boyfriend in there."

She stared at him, her chest rising and falling with her heavy breaths beneath the thin T-shirt, her eyes hard and fiery. He knew he'd just crossed a line, that he'd let himself get worked up when he should have just bit his damn tongue. But the woman had a way of getting under his skin, digging in until he wanted to scream, and the words had spilled out before he'd even thought to stop them.

He drew in a deep breath, let it out slowly, tried to settle his frayed temper, and realized—belatedly—that maybe she had a point.

A small one. But he wasn't ready to yield to her on it yet. Not when McKnight was the bigger problem hanging over everything.

"Marley, look, I—"

"Shut up." She moved toward him. "Just don't say another word."

Her fingers captured his jaw. She rose up on her toes and pressed her mouth to his. Startled, he looked down at her, couldn't figure out why she was kissing him. Thought—

Holy hell. What did it matter what he thought? *She was kissing him.*

He opened to her. Didn't even hesitate. His hands found her hips and pulled her into him. Their mouths fused, their tongues tangling in an erotic dance. Everything else drifted to the background—their argument, the reason they were here, McKnight. Only one thought circled his head. Only one need.

Just *this*.

Her mouth turned greedy, hot, wild. She pushed him back into a captain's chair and devoured his lips. She tasted like whiskey, felt like fire, and when her hands streaked down his chest and found the hem of his shirt, he knew this kiss wasn't nearly enough.

He maneuvered her around and back into the galley, shoved her up against the cabinet. She pulled her mouth from his and gasped, then leveled him with a searing look. Pushing him against the opposite cabinet, she rose up on her toes and sank her teeth into his bottom lip.

He jerked back at the pain. Tasted blood in his mouth. Looked down to see her smoldering, wanton, challenging eyes. Lust reflected in her irises, flushed her cheeks, pushed him forward so he suddenly didn't care if she bit him a hundred times just so long as she never stopped.

He lowered his mouth to hers and took her lips in a bruising kiss. She opened at the first touch, tangled her tongue with his as if she couldn't get enough, and pushed him toward the back of the galley then around the corner so his back was plastered to the flat wall near the entrance of the plane.

"God, Marley." He wanted her. Needed her. Right now. Kicking her legs apart, he trailed his hands down to the hem of her T-shirt so he could feel her skin. Moved between her legs as he tasted her deeper and slid his fingers along the silky flesh of her flat belly.

She groaned, pressed her hips into his. Rocked against him, rubbing her steamy center along his hardening cock. Tingles erupted in his groin, sent a shockwave of heat through every cell in his body. Her fingers found his shoulders, his neck, then trailed up into his hair. Pulling hard on the locks, she yanked his head back then lowered her mouth to his throat.

Her teeth sank in. A shot of pain seared his skin. Then her tongue was there. Stroking the sensitive spot. Her lips sucking, driving him absolutely mad.

It was a battle of wills. Of strength. Of blistering passion. And he loved every minute of it. Only wanted more. Capturing her head in his hands, he pulled her back, then took her mouth again. She groaned and tasted him. He dropped his hands. Slid one under her shirt, then up to cup her breast in the silky bra. Found the snap on her pants with the other and flicked it free.

He was hard. Hot. Ready. He kissed her again and again. Let go of her breast and slid his hands to her waistband then pressed his hands inside the back of her pants so he could grab the fleshy globes of her ass.

She wrapped her arms around his shoulders. Groaned deep in her throat and pushed her hips against his. He needed her naked. Needed her spread. Was just about to shove her pants down and pin her to the wall when a voice echoed from the main cabin.

"Marlene? Where did you go?"

Marley pulled back from Jake's mouth so fast his head snapped back. But before he could tug her back, she pushed him away, then quickly snapped her pants and fixed her shirt. "Shit. *Shit.*"

Bracing a hand on the wall at his side to steady himself, Jake reached for her, desperate to pull her back. "Marley."

"No, don't." She moved out of his grasp. "I . . ." Her eyes met his for a brief second, then quickly darted away. "Dammit. I wasn't going to do that again."

She ducked under his arm before he could stop her. Before he could get his head on right. Before he could think of something to say.

"I was in the galley getting something to drink." Her voice drifted from the main cabin. "I—oh my God. Gray."

Confused, Jake turned so he could see her, then realized her surprise. McKnight hadn't just showered. He looked like he'd gone through a complete makeover. The beard was gone, his jaw freshly shaved, and he'd cut his hair. It wasn't a salon-quality cut by any means, but the above-the-ears trim was a hundred times better than the shoulder-length shaggy locks he'd sported before. And cleaned up, wearing a fresh set of Jake's cargo pants and a blue button-down rolled up to his forearms, he didn't look a thing like an escaped convict. He looked like Mr. *GQ* on vacation.

"Wow," Marley muttered, standing in the middle of the aisle, staring at him.

"Better?" McKnight held his hands out wide and looked down. "Feels better."

"Um. Way better."

All that animosity Jake had felt before when he'd seen the two of them holding hands in the helicopter came rushing back. But this time it was accompanied by a searing burn in the center of his chest. If McKnight was the one she wanted, then what the hell was she doing shoving her tongue down Jake's throat?

Yep. Totally fucking jealous.

Son of a bitch. Jake raked a hand through his hair when he realized where his thoughts were going. He was a mess. Three days in the jungle had turned him into a giant wuss.

Okay, enough is enough.

Jaw tight, he moved into the main cabin, careful to step around Marley as he leveled a look on McKnight. "I hope you didn't leave a mess in my bathroom."

McKnight looked up and grinned. "No mess. Thanks for the change of clothes, man."

Jake didn't answer. Wasn't in the mood to be civil just yet. He headed for his stateroom, needing space, needing his own damn shower to cool himself out.

"Jake," Marley called at his back. "Wait a second. We need to talk."

She wanted to talk? Now? Not a chance. He'd had enough talking. And kissing. *Way* too much kissing for this trip.

Alone, he closed the stateroom door at his back, leaned his head against the solid surface, and drew a deep breath that did shit to ease that burn still smoldering in his chest.

Problem was, he liked that kissing. Liked it way more than he should. And that didn't just fuck with his head, it scared the shit out of him.

chapter 13

A sick feeling brewed in Marley's stomach as she watched Jake go.

What the heck was going on between them? And why couldn't she get a handle on the crazy emotions pulsing inside her? She knew she'd overreacted by being angry with him. He was a grown man. He could do whatever he wanted. He didn't have to answer to her or anyone else. And if that meant he wanted to take stupid risks, that was his choice to make, not hers. So why was she upset with him? And why did she suddenly feel depressed for pulling away from that reckless kiss when they both knew it was a major mistake?

Warmth brewed in her belly and her lips tingled from the memory of his mouth moving against hers. But the look in his dark eyes after she'd moved back and finally glanced up kicked her in the stomach all over again. A look that was a mixture of yearning and anger and rejection.

"Marlene?"

Startled out of her ricocheting thoughts by the sound of Gray's voice, Marley looked away from the stateroom door and blinked several times. "Yes?"

She barely had time to focus before Gray pulled her in for a tight hug. "I'm glad we finally have a few minutes alone. You have no idea how much I've missed you."

He smelled like Jake's citrusy soap, his body strong and warm against her. And though there'd been a time—years ago—when she'd looked forward to embraces like this from him, right now it felt wrong. Because he wasn't the man she suddenly wanted holding her this way. He wasn't the man she wanted to kick and scream at and kiss like crazy all over again.

Her eyes slid closed. Her heart dropped like a stone into her stomach. She didn't have the energy to pull away from Gray. Wasn't sure her legs would hold her up if she tried. Because that little voice in the back of her head whispered she was on the verge of losing it. Losing it over a man whose high-handedness didn't just frustrate the hell out of her, but who was emotionally crippled in every way and who she'd vowed years ago to steer clear of when it came to her heart.

"You're trembling," Gray said into her hair. "I'll take that as a good sign."

He eased back and smiled, and in a daze, Marley realized he thought she was overcome with emotion for him.

Heat rushed to her cheeks. A heat she didn't want and definitely didn't need. Followed by a wave of guilt that slammed into her belly. She let go of him and pressed a hand to her suddenly aching forehead. "Gray, we need to talk."

"I know." He reached for her hand and pulled her toward the couch that ran along the wall opposite four chairs and a table. "I know you've got questions. I'll try to answer as much as I can. Things are a little fuzzy in my head though. Weeks without food . . . well, it messes with a person's memory."

Marley let him pull her toward the couch, but confusion colored her vision as she sat beside him.

"Gray," she said as she turned toward him, choosing her words carefully because she knew he'd been through a lot, but wanting—no, needing—answers. "You said you were imprisoned and that you escaped, but you don't look like someone who was held captive in a South American prison for five years."

"I know. But trust me, the way I look now is nothing compared to the way I looked six months ago."

He was still holding her hand and she wanted to pull away, but the stormy look in his green eyes made her wary about reacting in any way that might upset him. "I don't understand."

He sighed. "They were getting ready to ransom me. I couldn't go on video looking like a skeleton. So they were—"

Her sat phone buzzed in the cargo pocket of her pants. She'd forgotten it was even on because the whole time they'd been in the jungle it hadn't been able to connect. Letting go of Gray, she said, "Hold on."

One quick glance at the number pulled at the corner of her lips. "Who is it?" Gray asked.

The last person she wanted to talk to right now. "My father."

Shit. She couldn't ignore him. She pushed to her feet, but from the corner of her eye she saw the way every muscle in Gray's body went tense and rigid and his eyes locked on the phone in her hand.

Steeling her nerves, she hit Answer, then tried like hell to keep her voice calm and unrevealing. "Hi, Daddy."

"Marley Addison," her father said on the other end of the line in his ever-commanding voice, "if you're in any kind of jungle, you're in big trouble."

Marley closed her eyes and opened them again quickly. Part of the reason she'd left her father's company was because he was too overprotective. He'd never had a problem with her providing support for his ops from base camp—which, at least, was more than Jake ever let her do at Aegis—but whenever she'd asked about actually working in the field, her question had always been met with a resounding no.

From her father she understood the overprotectiveness—even accepted it. From Jake it was a whole other issue. One she needed to address soon rather than stressing about some stupid kiss that meant nothing.

One kiss? Yeah right.

She forced thoughts of her moody boss aside and focused on her current nightmare. "I'm fine, Daddy. And no, I'm not in a jungle." *At least not anymore.*

"Don't lie to me, pumpkin. I might be old, but I'm not stupid. I know you went to Colombia. I want to know why, and how in the hell Ryder let you go."

He was hardly old. At sixty he was in the same impeccable shape he'd been in all his life. The only part of him that showed his age was the silver at his temples.

She ground her teeth and forced back her temper. Unleashing it never worked with her father. Clearly worked even less on Jake.

Stop thinking about Jake!

"First of all, Ryder didn't *let* me go anywhere. He's not my keeper. And second of all, I went to Colombia on my own. But if it makes you feel any better, when he found out I'd left, he was as angry with me as you obviously are now. He flew down to tell me as much."

"Ryder's with you?"

With her? Marley glanced toward the closed stateroom door, and her stomach pitched like a fish flopping on dry land. No, Jake wasn't *with her*, at least not in any way that made sense. And she wasn't even sure if she *wanted* him with her. Especially after the way he'd just stormed off. Yes, she could admit there was something bubbling between them, and every time she thought about what they'd done to each other in that hut it only made this—*thing*—bubble that much hotter. But lust was not a good basis for a relationship. And lust—for him, with him—would just make her loonier than she already felt.

"Marley? Are you still there?"

She blinked several times. "Yeah, I'm here. Sorry. The signal must have cut out. What did you say?"

"I asked if Ryder is there with you."

She turned away from the stateroom door. "He's in the shower. We're on the jet heading back to the States."

"That's one small relief." Her father sighed. "You had me worried sick. When Olivia mentioned you were in South America, I didn't know what to think."

Olivia. Of course that's how he knew. Jake had obviously told someone at Aegis where she'd gone, and being Landon Miller's new wife, Olivia must have heard the news from her husband. The fact Olivia now worked with Marley's father at Omega Intel was just an unlucky coincidence on Marley's part.

"I'm fine, Daddy. Nothing to worry about."

"I'm glad to hear it. But I'm still waiting for you to explain what you were doing in Colombia."

There was no way she was getting out of this. Her father was more stubborn than Jake when he set his mind to something. Marley looked toward Gray.

Something hard flashed in his eyes. Something she couldn't read. She didn't know how her father was involved, didn't know what had happened or why Gray hadn't wanted her to ask for her father's help, but in her heart she believed her father would want to know he was still alive. Gray's death had haunted Mason Addison ever since the op to rescue him had failed.

"Dad, listen. I know this is going to sound crazy, but I went to Colombia to help Grayson McKnight."

Silence echoed across the line. And across from her, Gray didn't say anything, just stared at her with blank, unreadable eyes. Though she did notice a muscle in his jaw tick ever so slowly.

"What did you say?" her father asked quietly.

"I said I went to Colombia to help Gray. I'm standing in front of him right now on the plane."

"Grayson McKnight?" her father muttered. "He's alive? I don't believe it."

"Believe it, Dad."

Silence again, then, "Put him on the phone."

Gray shook his head, obviously having heard her father's words, and softly said, "Tell him I'll talk to him later."

Marley wasn't sure why he was being evasive, but she wasn't about to push him. Not after everything he'd been through. "He's sleeping right now. It's a long story. I'll explain everything when I see you."

"Oh." Disappointment echoed in his voice. "But he's okay?"

"Yeah. He's fine. Rattled, I think, but fine."

"I still can't believe it," her father muttered. Then, "When will you be back?"

"Um." She glanced at the clock on the wall. "About seven hours, give or take."

"Okay. Seven hours." She could almost hear the wheels turning in his head. "We'll talk then, I guess. Stay safe, pumpkin. Grayson McKnight. I can't believe it. Tell him . . ." His voice trailed off, but Marley heard the emotion in his words. "Tell him I can't wait to see him."

"I will. I love you, Dad."

"I love you too, pumpkin."

She hit End on her phone and slid it back into her pocket. Then she looked toward Gray. "I don't know what happened between the two of you, but I need you to know that whatever it was, it was an accident. My father had a hard time of it after he thought you'd died. He's been racked with guilt for years, mostly because of how your death affected me. I know if he had it to do over again, he'd have treated you differently."

Gray reached out and drew her to sit next to him on the couch once more. "I believe you. I'm just not ready to talk to him yet. The truth is, though, no one had a harder time of it than me."

The questions, the answers she desperately needed, took up center stage all over again. "Gray, I need to know—"

He let go of her hand and wrapped his arms around her in another tight hug. This one strong enough to cut off her words. "You're what kept me alive. So many times I just wanted to give up and die, but then I'd think of you and I knew I had to stay alive. I had to stay alive so I could find my way back to you."

The rest of her question died on her lips. And that guilt she'd felt five years ago came rushing back to stab her hard in the belly.

"I will make it up to you," he said softly, still holding her tight. "I promise, if it's the last thing I do, I'll make all of this right. Say you believe me."

Marley didn't know what to say, was having trouble getting air. Then he squeezed her harder, and the words squeaked out before she could even stop them. "I-I believe you."

"Of course you do." He eased his hold, at least enough so she could breathe, then drew his hand down her spine as if he were petting a dog. And though he was close, his body heat warming her skin, a shiver rushed down her spine. "Because you're my Freckles. And you always will be. Just the way I planned."

Jake flipped the water off and ran a towel over his dripping hair. He'd shaved, then spent the last ten minutes under the cold spray trying to cool himself down and chill the hell out.

So far it hadn't done a bit of good.

Stepping out of the shower stall, he wrapped the towel around his waist and tried not to think about what was going on in the main cabin of his plane, but failed. Marley was out there with McKnight, doing God-knew-what. Probably enjoying it more than she'd enjoyed it with him.

Fuck. He braced his hands on the edge of the sink, dropped his head, and drew in a deep breath. That—what had happened in the galley—was pure stupidity. Last night had been hallucinogens. But this . . . this had been too much adrenaline, too little self-control, and not nearly enough brain cells.

She was his employee, not his girlfriend. He didn't even *want* a girlfriend. His track record with women proved he wasn't relationship material—just like his father. Besides which, *this was Marley.* If he wasn't careful from here on out, he could lose her for good.

An image of her dancing around that bonfire pinged through his brain. Followed by the way she'd kissed him in that hut, then dragged him to the floor and completely rocked his world.

His skin grew hot. His hands sweaty. More frustrated than he'd been when he'd come in here, he turned out of the bathroom, found fresh clothes in his bag, and pulled them on. What he really wanted to do was stretch out on the couch in his stateroom and sleep for seven hours, but he was too fired up to get any kind of rest. The only thing that was going to cool him out now was a bottle of Jack and a few hours of mindless television.

He opened the stateroom door, intent on finding that bottle, then drew to a stop. Marley sat on the couch, her back angled Jake's way, holding McKnight close. His hand ran up and down her spine in an intimate way as he whispered words Jake couldn't make out. Neither seemed to notice him, but Jake's stomach twisted into a tight, hard knot at the sight, and before he could retreat back into the safety of his stateroom, McKnight's eyes lifted and zeroed in.

If he'd seen gratitude or relief or even happiness in the other man's eyes, Jake would have turned around and left them alone. But he didn't see any of that. What he saw was victory. A flash of gloating, then a whisper of something dark.

Every alarm bell he had went off all over again. This guy was not at all what he seemed. Jake didn't care what Marley believed. No way in hell he was leaving her alone with McKnight.

He stepped past the pair and headed toward the galley. At his back, Marley said, "Jake. I didn't hear you come out."

No, of course she hadn't. Because she was too wrapped up in McKnight to notice what he was doing. Another fact that burned more than he liked. He moved into the galley and reached for a glass from the shelf above. "Don't mind me. I'm just getting my laptop and something to drink."

He poured a generous glass, added ice, and took a big sip. From the corner of his eye he watched Marley push to her feet and look toward him with worried blue eyes.

"We need to talk." Yeah, they did, but he wasn't in the mood to deal with her right now.

Carrying his glass into the main cabin, he found his laptop in a storage compartment, then sat in the chair farthest away from the duo. After flipping up his screen, he powered on the machine and pretended to work.

"Freckles," McKnight said. "Why don't you come back and sit down so we can finish talking."

Freckles? McKnight had called her that in Bruhia. What kind of nickname was that? Clenching his jaw, Jake pretended to type, but he was so on edge he could barely see the screen.

Marley turned and looked down at McKnight, who was still sitting on the sofa. But McKnight's gaze skipped from her to Jake and back again, and Jake knew the fucker had already figured out there was something going on between them. Something, Jake guessed from the seething look McKnight shot his way, that put a crimp in the man's plans.

She's not all yours, after all, asshole.

Of course, Marley didn't back Jake up on that. She went and sat next to McKnight again. "Okay, explain to me why you didn't want my father to help rescue you."

McKnight reached for her hand and, contrary to what Jake wanted, she didn't pull away from his touch. "I know this is going to be hard to hear, but your father lied to you. He knew I was still alive in that South American prison. He left me there on purpose."

"Go back to the beginning, Gray. Originally, you went down to Colombia to rescue an American hostage."

"No. Your father lied about that too. He didn't want you to know the truth. It wasn't a rescue mission. It was a hit. Contracted by the US government to take out a ruthless drug lord who was taking Americans hostage. We were awarded the contract after the third American in two weeks was executed. Your father sent me and two other guys in to do the job. I don't know what went wrong, but they were waiting for us. Jones and Reynolds were killed. Me they took hostage."

"Then what happened?" Marley asked.

"I was there about a week. Let's just say they weren't wild about American black ops. I knew your father wouldn't leave me behind, so I toughed it out, figuring he'd come back for me."

"He did. I was there when he and the second team left to bring you back."

"You're right, they did. I was in a room high in the compound when they arrived. I watched the firefight from the tiny window. Your father saw me. But his team never made it inside the compound. I was still alive when he ordered the retreat. And he knew that."

Jake's fingers hovered over the keyboard. He remembered hearing about Omega's failed rescue attempt. He'd just been starting

Aegis back then, so he'd been paying close attention to what was happening with his competitors. The drug lord was Jose Moreno. One of the most ruthless drug lords in all South and Central America. And he'd been killed by US forces three weeks after Omega pulled out of that op.

"Hostages are big money in Colombia," McKnight went on. "The drug cartels pay paramilitary groups to run their security. And those paramilitary groups are often in bed with corrupt Colombian military officials. They decided to hold on to me for a bit, let me suffer before they tried to ransom me back to Omega. They handed me over to the Black Eagles, who threw me in a Colombian prison. The conditions were . . ." A dark look filled his eyes as he gazed at the windows across the cabin. "Well, let's just say they weren't pretty."

He blinked and looked back at Marley. "I was there for several years. I don't know exactly how long. I heard through the grapevine that the general who'd thrown me in that clink was killed with Moreno. Basically, they forgot about me. Then about six months ago, someone wised up to who I was. They pulled me out of that hellhole, put me in isolation in the drug cartel's compound, and started feeding me. I was sickly. Weak. They brought in doctors. I knew what they were doing. I knew if they were getting ready to try to ransom me back, then it meant my days were numbered. Your father left me in South America. He wasn't going to pay to get me back. My only play was to get strong enough and then find a way to escape. Which is what I did."

The story made sense on the surface. But one thing didn't sit right with Jake. Namely, why the Black Eagles had kept McKnight alive in the first place. They'd killed the other two members of his team. Why let him live?

There was a whole lot McKnight wasn't copping to. Every instinct Jake had screamed that this guy was not at all what he seemed.

He paged through his inbox and found a message from Eve. Hitting Open, he leaned forward and read her note.

Ryder,

Where the hell are you? I'm starting to worry, and you know how much I like to do that. I left a message on your phone but figured I'd e-mail this as well. Here's the info I was able to find on McKnight.

He's thirty-four years old. Went to high school in Arizona. Joined the army when he was eighteen. Did two tours—East Africa and the Middle East. Rose to the rank of staff sergeant in his infantry unit. Had a history of being difficult to work with but always got the job done. No stellar commendations. Left the army and went to work for Mission Elite, a defense contractor based out of North Carolina. Spent most of his time overseas, primarily in Central and South America. Basic merc stuff. Five and a half years ago, he joined Omega Intel. Spent six months with them before he was listed as missing in action.

No red flags in his background. The guys at Mission Elite didn't have anything positive or negative to say about him. Just said he was a hard worker and sort of a loner. I didn't contact Omega to get their take on him, but I can if you want me to.

Call me when you get this so I know you're alive. FYI—I like being in charge less than I like worrying, so get your ass back here soon.

~Eve

Jake leaned back and read through the e-mail again. Nothing stood out, but that didn't mean he wouldn't find more when he dug deeper.

"How did you get out?" Marley asked.

Jake glanced over his laptop toward the pair. McKnight was still holding her hand, but instead of sitting back all relaxed and confident as he'd been before, he was now leaning forward, his elbows on his thighs, his fingers slowly stroking the back of Marley's hand as he stared down at the floor with a dazed expression. Jake frowned. The guy's mood switched faster than a chameleon changes color. But the kicker was Marley. She didn't seem to notice. Or if she did, she just didn't care.

Clenching his jaw, Jake looked back at his screen. He hit Reply and sent Eve a quick response, gave her an update on their status, then opened a new e-mail and typed a note to his contact at the State Department.

"Security at the compound wasn't as tight as at the prison," McKnight said to Marley. "I paid attention to the guard's patterns, watched for weaknesses in their routines. When I felt comfortable with the timeline, I faked an illness. The guards took me out of my room and walked me to the doctor on site. I made my escape while we were in transit."

"And then what did you do?" Marley asked.

"Then I made my way to the first phone I could find and called you."

"We ran into paramilitary soldiers in the jungle. They were looking for you."

"I know. I stayed out of sight. Made friends with that kid who brought me food. The soldiers came and went in Bruhia. I knew they were looking for me, so I sat tight and waited."

"We went to your hideout. You weren't sitting tight."

"That's because I heard the helicopter. I was trying to get to the airstrip when your friend over there intercepted me."

Jake glanced over his laptop once more. McKnight wasn't looking Jake's way, but Jake could see Marley's skeptical expression.

And a tiny shot of relief bounced through him. She wasn't buying McKnight's story. At least not all of it.

That's my girl.

Marley's brow wrinkled, and she pulled her hand from McKnight's. "I'm sorry you went through all that. It sounds awful. But you need to know that my father did look for you. I'll be the first to admit he has his faults, but I believe if he'd known you were alive, he wouldn't have just walked away."

"Sometimes the people closest to us are the ones we're blinded by most."

Marley stared at him for several seconds, and the statement hit Jake as odd. Just as everything about McKnight seemed odd.

Sighing, Marley braced her palms against her thighs and pushed to her feet. "I'm sure you're hungry and tired. There's food in the galley, and these chairs all recline. Since you both had a chance to get cleaned up, I guess it's my turn."

She moved for the stateroom, but McKnight pushed to his feet and caught her by the arm. "Marlene."

She turned back to face him. "Yeah?"

"Just . . . thanks. For coming to rescue me. You know, things are foggy in my head. I might not be remembering right about your dad."

She stared up at McKnight, and Jake couldn't help wondering if she was thinking the same thing he was. That McKnight's sudden capitulation about her father was a complete one-eighty from what he'd believed about the man earlier.

Marley nodded. "Okay." Gently, she pulled her arm from his grip. "I'll be back in a little while."

She disappeared into the stateroom and closed the door behind her. And in the silence, Jake leaned back and crossed his arms over his chest.

Slowly, McKnight turned and caught Jake's gaze. Only Jake didn't see gratitude or relief or warmth in the man's green eyes. He saw darkness.

McKnight averted his gaze and headed for the galley. "I'm just gonna get something to eat and then take a nap."

"Yeah, you do that," Jake mumbled as McKnight stepped past him into the galley.

But sleeping was the last thing on Jake's mind. He rose from his seat and headed for the stateroom. Before this got any more out of control, he planned to make sure he and Marley were on the same page where this guy was concerned. And if they weren't, well, he'd just have to set her straight.

chapter 14

Marley ran a comb through her wet hair and then tucked the towel tighter around her breasts. The shower had helped—at least now she felt clean—but her head was still spinning with everything that had happened and all she'd learned in the last hour.

She wasn't sure what she thought about Gray. He was different. One minute he seemed angry, the next vulnerable. Five years in a South American prison would mess with anyone's head, but she couldn't seem to get a handle on his mood from one moment to the next. And that bit about her father . . . She'd seen deep distrust in his eyes when she'd first defended her dad, but by the end of their conversation, Gray had acted as if he'd been wrong about the entire situation.

She tipped her head the other way and combed the opposite side of her hair as she thought back through their conversation, then stilled when she realized she had no plans for what to do with him when they got back to Kentucky.

"Shit."

Her father had boxed up the belongings from his apartment and stuffed it all in storage. Gray didn't have a home to return to. And she wasn't about to let him stay with her. She might have flown down to Colombia to help the man out of guilt, but she didn't really know him anymore, and she wasn't about to be stupid.

That meant she'd have to get him set up in a hotel, then find him a more permanent place to stay. Her spirits dropped. All her plans for this to be a quick extraction were crashing and burning before her very eyes. And in the back of her head, she couldn't stop hearing Jake's irritating voice whispering, *"There's a reason I keep you out of the field."*

She looked up at her foggy reflection and straightened her spine. Planning was her strong suit. She did this kind of thing for the guys at Aegis all the time. And she'd already proved herself in the field. She didn't need Jake's approval one way or the other.

Shoving the bathroom door open, she stepped into the state-room, then drew to a stop when she saw the man she'd just been thinking about sitting on the long couch that folded down into a bed.

Marley's stomach tightened, and she tugged the towel tighter around her breasts. "What are you doing in here, Jake?"

"Waiting for you. We need to talk."

She'd said the same to him just before he'd taken his own shower. The memory of that kiss spiraled through her brain. The way she'd grabbed him. Pushed him. Bit him. Her skin prickled with aware-ness and anticipation and a host of nerves. In the center of her chest she knew he wanted to talk about that kiss. About what was happen-ing between them. About where it was going. And she didn't know what the hell to say.

She'd liked that kiss. Liked it way too much. Knew it was a bad idea but probably wouldn't have stopped if they hadn't been inter-rupted. And she had no clue about what that meant or where they went from here.

Her throat grew dry. She drew the towel tighter around her. Was he as confused as her? Did he feel the same way? What the heck were they going to do about this—*thing*—that seemed to be smoldering between them?

"O-okay."

He leaned forward, rested his elbows on his knees, and clasped his hands in front of him. His big, masculine, talented hands. Marley's gaze followed, and her pulse raced when she remembered the way he'd lifted her shirt and run his warm, rough fingers over her belly only minutes ago.

"You do realize McKnight's not telling you the whole truth, right?"

Her gaze slid up, over the faded SEAL tattoo on his forearm he usually kept covered, then to his strong biceps and the dark T-shirt pulled tight across his muscular chest. Her skin warmed. Nerves danced in her belly. Just being in the same room with him made her body feel alive in a way it hadn't felt in a very long time.

When had that started? In the jungle, obviously. No, she realized, thinking back. It had been happening for a while now. Over the last few months she'd been feeling this way whenever he walked through the damn door or called her on the phone or looked at her when they were together at the office.

"Marley."

She tore her gaze from his chest. "What?"

"You do realize he's keeping things from you, right?"

She stared at Jake's clean jaw and the dark hair still damp around the edges from his own shower and tried to remember what he'd been talking about before she'd been distracted by his hands and muscles and *him*. "Who?"

"McKnight. Aren't you listening?"

Gray. He was talking about Gray. She blinked several times, tried to get her brain back online, and suddenly realized he wasn't here to discuss what had happened between them in the galley. He was here to lecture her about Gray.

All that warmth cooled, and though she told herself not to be disappointed—after all, this was Jake, the most emotionally closed off person she'd ever met—she couldn't stop her heart from sinking just a little bit.

"I heard you." She moved for her backpack on the far side of the room, lifted it to a chair, and rummaged around until she found clean clothes. "But you're wasting your breath."

"And you're naïve if you buy everything he's selling out there without considering the source."

God, this man was so aggravating. And it wasn't because she was in love with him, dammit. It was because he was just completely bullheaded sometimes.

She tossed her pack on the floor, gripped the fresh clothes in her free hand, and tugged the towel up with the other. "And what source is that? He's been through hell, Jake. You saw the people who were after him. Cut the guy a break."

She moved back for the bathroom, but Jake stepped in her path. "Have you even once asked yourself why they were after him?"

"Because he escaped. Duh."

Irritation darkened his eyes. "Don't get smart with me. You know what I'm getting at. Why him? Why not the other guys?"

"Because they're dead."

"Right. And why did the cartel kill them and not him?"

She exhaled and stared at him. She'd asked herself that when Gray had been explaining what had happened to him. But no matter the answer, she couldn't see how the facts of his imprisonment changed his situation now. "Regardless of why, he was still imprisoned. I didn't go to Colombia to figure out what happened five years ago. I went to help a friend."

She stepped past him and moved for the bathroom.

"Is that all he is? Just a friend?"

Marley's feet slowed at the quiet question, and her pulse ticked up all over again. Resting one hand on the bathroom door, she turned to look Jake's way. "Does it matter if he's just a friend?"

He watched her carefully, but he didn't immediately answer. And in the silence she tried to read his blank expression and figure out what he was thinking—what he was feeling—but couldn't. His face was as guarded as always.

"No, it doesn't matter," he finally said. "But the truth does. And my gut's telling me there's something off about the guy. You need to be careful."

Disappointment rushed through her—way more than she wanted to admit, even to herself—and she looked away. What did she expect? That he was suddenly going to open up to her? That he'd tell her how he felt? He'd never done either of those things before, so why would she expect him to start?

She turned back for the bathroom and stepped through the doorway, more exhausted than she ever remembered being. "Thanks for the concern, but I know how to take care of myself. I think I proved that the last few days."

She pulled the door closed.

"Marley, wait."

She couldn't. Because right now she just needed to be alone. Flipping the lock on the door, she drew a deep breath that did nothing to ease the burn in the center of her chest, and told herself this was all for the best. Once they got home, she could forget about the last few days, forget about everything that had happened between them, and focus on what really mattered. Namely, getting everything back to normal.

The only problem was, her heart screamed there was no more normal. Nothing with Jake would ever be the same again.

Jake stuck his head through the cockpit door to thank Tony and Ben for the easy flight. They'd made good time on the way back to Kentucky, but he hadn't been able to sleep even though they'd flown through the night. All he'd been able to think about was Marley. About the disappointed look on her face when she'd closed that bathroom door. About the way he felt as if she'd expected him to say something more.

The hard truth was, he didn't know what to say. Didn't know what to do, either. Talking about what had happened between them would only remind him just how hot kissing her had been. And how much hotter making love with her was. And while a big part of him wanted only to do both of those things again and again, an even bigger part knew it could never happen. Not with how closely they had to work at Aegis.

To his relief—and disappointment—she hadn't seemed up for talking when she'd emerged from the bathroom. Dressed in fresh jeans that molded to her body and a fitted white sweater that accentuated her breasts, she'd feigned exhaustion. Then she'd found a chair near McKnight in the main cabin and closed her eyes. Jake had no idea if she'd actually slept, but just the fact she'd gone to sit by McKnight set off a weird vibration in his stomach. One that had kept him awake all the way home. One he didn't like.

The pilots killed the engines. It was close to four a.m. and darkness pressed in through the windshield, but Jake could see the remnants of another snowstorm littering the edges of the runway.

Frustrated—with the weather, with McKnight's presence, mostly with himself—Jake said goodbye to the pilots, walked back into the main cabin, and then stilled. Marley stood near the couch in a lightweight red jacket, tugging her backpack over one shoulder while she reached for her extra bag from the seat. Her shoulders were tense, her blonde hair hanging past her shoulders. He knew she'd heard him walk back into the room, but she refused to look up.

She was upset. About their argument? About what had happened in the galley? About their conversation in the stateroom? Probably all three, but he couldn't stand the distance between them any longer.

Say something, idiot, and fix the giant mess you made with your dick.

He cleared his throat. "Where's McKnight?"

"Washing his hands." She tossed the strap of her pack over her shoulder and took a step toward the exit, but as he was blocking her path, she had no choice but to stop. "You're in my way."

He drew a quick breath. "Look, Marley. I know you're upset with me. I get that. But I'm just keeping your best interest in mind here. This guy . . ."

She glanced up at him. Her gaze narrowed, and as their eyes held, he realized there was only one thing he could say that would hopefully get through to her.

"I'm worried about you," he said softly. "That's all. I don't want to see you make a mistake."

"Why not?"

Why not? The question took him back. "Because I care about you."

"How?"

His skin grew hot. His mouth opened, but the words wouldn't come.

She shifted the bag on her shoulder and tipped her head. "How do you care about me, Jake? As your assistant? As a friend? As something more? As what? After everything that's happened these last few days, I think I deserve to know what, exactly, you mean by that."

She wanted an answer. About the night they'd shared in the jungle. About that kiss in the galley. About what it all meant in the long run. Only, he didn't have a clue what it meant, and he had even less ability to explain it.

The palms of his hands grew damp, and his mouth couldn't seem to find any words that made sense. But he needed to give her something, and the only thing that kept circling in his brain was the fact he didn't want to lose her. "Marley, I—"

"I'm all set, Marlene." McKnight stepped through the stateroom door with a shit-eating grin on his clean-shaven face. But the grin faltered when he saw them standing together. "Oh, Ryder. I thought you'd already left." That same contempt Jake had noticed before flashed in McKnight's eyes before quickly clearing. "I'm not interrupting something, am I?"

"No." Disappointment flashed in Marley's eyes, and she turned away before Jake could say, *Hell yes.* "We were just saying goodbye. Are you all set?"

That aggravating grin returned to McKnight's face, only this time it was laced with victory as he glanced toward Jake and then focused on Marley. "Yeah. Ready to get on with my life, that's for sure."

Marley brushed by Jake and headed for the door. Jake turned, wanting to reach out for her and pull her back, wanting to finish what they'd started, wanting to hold on to her. But McKnight moved past him before he could do just that and said, "I can't wait to see what you've done to your place."

The air whooshed out of Jake's lungs, as if he'd been sucker punched in the gut. She was taking McKnight to her place? To her house? In the three plus years the two of them had worked together— closely together—she'd never once invited him to her place. Hell, she'd never once let him drive her home after work when the roads had been icy.

Pull it together, man. She's not yours. You don't even want her to be yours, remember?

Jake's head grew light and an odd tingle took up space in his belly. Reaching for his coat, he swallowed hard to distract himself from his shaking fingers..

Crisp, cool air slapped him in the face when he stepped off the plane, but his feet drew to a stop when he spotted the sleek black Escalade parked on the tarmac, and Mason Addison standing near the hood.

"Dad." Marley dropped her bag on the ground and closed her arms around her father's broad shoulders. "What are you doing here?"

Mason's salt-and-pepper hair caught the light from the plane as he drew back from his daughter, highlighting the silver strands. At five-eight, Marley wasn't a small woman, but next to her father's six-four frame, she looked tiny.

"Eve told me when you were due back. I wanted to meet you." He looked over Marley's shoulder toward McKnight, and a worried look passed over his weathered features. "Holy mother of God. I don't think I really believed it until this minute. He really is alive."

Marley let go of her father and turned toward McKnight. From his vantage, Jake couldn't see McKnight's face, but he could read body language. And McKnight's was so rigid, Jake could tell the man would rather be back in a Colombian jungle than with Marley's father.

The animosity in McKnight's voice when he'd been talking to Marley on the plane about her father ricocheted through Jake's mind. He moved quickly down the aircraft's steps, unsure what the guy was going to say, what the hell he'd do for that matter.

"Addison." McKnight spread his stance, clenched his hands into fists at his side. His voice dropped to a menacing whisper. "It's been a long time. Too long."

Shit. Jake glanced at Marley. She was standing way too close to her father if McKnight decided to launch himself at the man.

He pushed his feet forward to get to her, to pull her out of the way. Before he could reach her, Mason stepped past his daughter. Every muscle in McKnight's body went rigid.

"Marley!" Jake lurched for her. She twisted at the sound of her name. McKnight glanced his way. Jake was still two steps away when Mason wrapped his arms around McKnight's shoulders and hugged the man.

Jake's feet shuffled to a stop. Marley looked up at him like he'd just lost his mind. "What the heck is wrong with you?"

McKnight's body was still as stiff as a board, but his hands were no longer clenched into fists, and Mason was muttering something about being sorry, about being glad he was back, about making everything right.

McKnight nodded once, then Mason let go of him and, with a beaming smile, turned Jake's way. "Ryder." He captured Jake's hand in both of his. "Thank you. I can't tell you how grateful I am that you brought this man back. I wish someone would have told me. Omega would have been down there in a heartbeat."

"He didn't do it on his own," Marley said before Jake could answer. "In fact, it wasn't even his idea."

"She's right." Jake glanced down at Marley, relieved nothing had happened and that she was okay. But the minute his eyes locked on her, he had a flash of her in the jungle, building that camp and taking care of both of them, saving him from those natives, even planning and finding McKnight. Awe rippling through him. Awe for everything she'd accomplished, even when he'd thought she couldn't handle it. "It wasn't me. It was her. It was pretty much all her."

Marley turned wide, surprised blue eyes up to meet his. And like it had in the jungle, when he'd watched her dance around that fire, heat exploded in his belly, and every inch of his skin burst to life.

Mason grinned, let go of Jake's hand, and wrapped one arm

around his daughter's shoulders. "For some reason that doesn't surprise me. She's just like her old man." He looked over at McKnight. "The guesthouse is yours. My personal doctor is on his way to look over you. Anything you want, you just have to ask." He glanced down at his daughter. "You're coming back to the farm with us, right?"

"I . . ."

Marley's gaze was still locked on Jake's, and Jake's pulse was suddenly pounding, his hands inching to pull her away from her father and into his arms.

She blinked, breaking the connection, and looked toward McKnight, then up at her father. "Yeah. I-I guess so."

"Great." Her father let go of her and moved toward the SUV. "McKnight, take the front. We have a lot to talk about. Marley, hurry up. Amelia should have breakfast ready by the time we get back."

The two men moved for the vehicle, and Marley reached down to pick up her bags. Jake grabbed her pack and duffel before she could and lifted them, anxious to keep her with him, frantic to come up with any reason for her not to leave just yet. "Amelia?"

She looked toward the bags in his hands, then took a step toward the back of the SUV. "Thanks. Amelia's my father's new assistant. I'm pretty sure she's more than his assistant if she's at the farm at four a.m. Even you don't make me come in that early."

No, but he suddenly wanted her around that early. And not for work.

"She's also my age." She opened the back of the vehicle so he could toss her bags inside. "How's that for ironic?"

"More like awkward. Been there. My father never dated a woman his age—ever."

A half smile curled her lip. "Yeah, I guess you would understand."

She knew all about Linus Ryder's love of younger women. Luckily, Jake's father had never been stupid enough to marry any of them, so Jake wasn't continuously supporting them. But every now and then, one would call Aegis looking for the man, completely floored that he'd actually had the nerve to keel over from something as ordinary as a heart attack. And Marley, the saint that she was, usually handled the calls because she knew how much they upset Jake.

She tugged on the door and closed the back, then looked up at him. "So, thanks for, you know, going with me. I know you had other, more important things you could have been doing these last few days."

No, there wasn't anything more important than her. Going after her hadn't even taken a second thought. That tingle came back to his skin, and he tucked his hands into the front pockets of his jeans so he didn't do something stupid—like grab her and kiss her.

"You mean thanks for pissing off your brother, getting in the way, aggravating you beyond reason, and generally mucking things up all the way around? You're welcome."

She smiled. A wide, beautiful smile. One that lit up her eyes and made him remember the way she'd danced and smiled around the fire. One that sent the blood pounding in his veins all over again. "Yeah, that. But I guess I deserved it since I stole your plane."

He glanced toward the jet, then back at her. "Well, maybe just a little."

Her smile faded, and she bit into her lip. A sexy nip that made him think of the way she'd bit his lip in the galley. How it had surprised him. How it had made him absolutely *wild*. "I guess I'll see you on Monday?"

"Right. Monday." Damn, he'd lost track of days. Today was Saturday, which meant he had an entire weekend to sit and think about everything that had happened between them and try to decide what the hell to do about it all.

"Okay." But she didn't move. Didn't step toward the back passenger door. And neither did he.

Part of him wanted to grab her and never let go. Another part wanted to run. His track record with women was such shit, he was afraid of making a giant mistake and ruining what they already had. And as much as he complained about her sass and independence, he couldn't imagine his life without her in it.

"Well," she finally said. "They're waiting."

Right. Waiting for her.

She took a step past him, but he moved faster and reached for the door handle before she could. Without opening it, he said, "You sure this is a good idea?"

A frown tugged at her lips. "Jake, do you honestly think my father would put my safety in danger by bringing someone he didn't trust back to the farm? You're worrying for nothing. You saw the way my dad reacted to him. You yourself have told me numerous times that Mason Addison is a crazy-good read of people. Gray is exactly what he appears to be. Nothing more. Trust me, I'm perfectly safe with him."

Jake looked over his shoulder toward the silhouetted men inside. They were both facing forward, deep in conversation, neither paying an ounce of attention to them.

Maybe Marley was right. Maybe the guy was harmless. Maybe Jake was just reading into things because he was jealous her ex was still alive and getting in the way of whatever this was going on between them.

"You're losing it . . ."

Eve's words in the office just before he'd rushed off to Colombia to find Marley echoed in Jake's head. At the time he'd ignored her, but now he couldn't deny the fact there was a big chance his radar was off because his emotions were all over the stinkin' map where she was concerned. And they had been for longer than he'd realized.

Pulling the door open quickly, he moved out of her way. He needed to take a giant step back before he did something he'd regret. Before he ruined things for good.

"Monday," he said, holding the door open for her so she could climb in. "Bright and early."

She didn't move. Just stood still and stared at him. And he knew she was waiting for him to say something else, but he couldn't. Because as much as he still didn't trust McKnight, the one thing he could say to make her stay wasn't something he was ready to admit, even to himself.

She pulled her gaze from his and climbed into the car without another word. And as he shut the door and watched the vehicle pull away, he caught McKnight's gaze in the side mirror.

No, that wasn't just jealousy in the other man's eyes. There was something more there. He was something more.

And Jake was determined to find out what.

chapter 15

Marley pushed the potatoes around on her plate, then moved her fork to the steamed broccoli, unable to focus on anything Gray was saying. She wasn't quite sure how she'd gotten herself into this situation, but the last place she wanted to be was having a quiet, candlelit dinner with the man in her father's ritzy guesthouse.

"You're not eating."

"Huh?" She looked up. He was sitting across from her at the dining room table wearing a green sweater that matched his eyes and stretched across his broad shoulders. Firelight flickered over his handsome features and accentuated his blond hair. And not for the first time since they'd come home did she wonder why she wasn't attracted to him like she'd been before.

"Your food." He nodded toward her plate. "You've barely touched your dinner."

"Oh." She glanced down. "Sorry. I had a late lunch. I didn't realize you were cooking. If I'd known," she lied, "I would have waited."

Her phone buzzed on the table beside her plate, and she reached for it quickly, a shot of disappointment rushing through her when she realized it was just her father texting to see how dinner was going.

He was pushing her toward Gray. She wasn't naïve enough not to notice. Five years ago, he hadn't wanted her dating the man, but now it was like he was waiting for her to fall into Gray's arms. She knew it was because her father felt guilty over everything that had happened to Gray and because he was trying to mend his battered relationship with her, but his one-eighty in attitude was making her head spin.

"He's not going to text you, you know."

She let go of her phone and glanced up. "Who?"

"Ryder."

Marley's pulse picked up speed, and she quickly let go of her phone and reached for her fork. "I don't know what you're talking about."

"You know exactly what I'm talking about. I saw the way he looked at you. Judging from your reaction, you saw it too."

Marley's pulse turned to a whir in her ears, and a whisper of guilt—all that guilt she'd carried for five years—rolled over her like fog creeping along the valley floor. "Ryder and I are just colleagues."

"You sure about that?"

His posture was relaxed, one forearm resting on the table, his other hand gently swirling the red wine in his glass. But his eyes were as focused as she'd ever seen them, and she knew what he was asking even though he didn't come right out and say it. More of that guilt rushed in, making her feel even worse. "Gray—"

"It won't work between the two of you. You know that, too, right?"

"I—"

"He's not a team player," Gray went on. "He's an I-guy. He always has to be in control, always has to call the shots, is always the one telling everyone else what to do."

Marley's throat went dry, and the protest died on her lips. Gray was right, that was Jake to the letter, but she didn't want to agree with him. Not when she didn't know where he was going with this.

"Tell me if I'm wrong. I bet he's never had a long-lasting relationship. He views women as expendable. Good for a night or two but not much more. The people who work for him probably don't like him all that much, but they put up with him because he pays them well. And I'm guessing he doesn't hire too many women to work in his little black ops company. Why would he when women just get in the way?"

Marley's stomach rolled, and she reached for her wine. "You seem to know a lot about a man you've barely met."

"I know him because *I was him*, Marlene."

She swallowed the sip of wine and met his gaze. His unwavering, intense, burning gaze that seemed to look right through her.

He sighed and leaned back. "Five years in a Colombian prison makes you reevaluate your priorities. I was Ryder. I did all that shit. I told people what to do, had to be in control all the time, and I used women because I didn't have a reason not to. I started dating you to get in good with your father so he'd give me the best assignments. It was a stupid thing to do. I knew you deserved better, but I didn't care. I even knew you were planning to break things off with me before I left."

A lump formed in her throat. "Gray—"

"No, don't try to make me feel better. I was a shit, and we both know it. But I'm not that guy anymore."

He leaned forward, gently pulled her hand away from her wine glass, and closed his fingers around hers. "I wasn't lying when I said the thought of you kept me alive. It did. It also made me realize you were the best thing in my life. I have a lot to make up for, but because of you, I have the chance to do that. And I want to do that with you."

Marley's heart beat fast against her ribs. "I don't—"

"Look, I know your life is different now. I know you think you've got this thing going with Ryder, but we both know that's never going to work out. It's a fantasy. It can't be anything more because he doesn't appreciate you the way I do. I won't hold you back, Marlene. I'll never tell you what to do. If you give me a chance, I'll prove to you that I'm the guy you should be with."

"Gray, I . . ." Pressure condensed in her chest, made it hard to breathe. She let go of him and pushed back from the table, needing air, needing a moment to think. Grabbing her phone, she turned, frantically searching for her purse. "I-I have to go."

"Marlene, wait."

There it was. On the entry table. Hands shaking, she crossed to it and tossed the strap over her shoulder.

"Let's," he said at her back, "let's talk about this."

She stopped at the door and looked up at him. She didn't want to hurt him, but she needed to make him understand. This was too much. It was all just too much.

"I heard what you said. I did. And I get it. I'm just . . ." She looked around the entry, searching for the right words. "A week ago I thought you were dead, and now you're asking me to make a decision about a future I didn't even know was out there. I can't think. It's happening too fast. I can't—"

"Okay." His big hands landed on her shoulders and then slowly traveled up and down her biceps. "Okay, just breathe. I know that was a lot to throw at you. It's just . . ."

He hesitated. Blew out a breath. Stared at her. "When you see the end of your life, you realize what's important. It's not money or possessions or the past. It's people. And when you have a chance to live again, you don't want to wait to start that living. Time is precious. Life is precious, Marlene. It can be gone before you know it. We spend our lives worrying about things that don't matter. Spend way too much time wasting it on people who will never be able to give us what we need. I don't want to do that anymore. I know what I want, and that's you. I can make you happy. Your father knows it too or he wouldn't be pushing us together." One side of his lips curled in a sexy half smile. "All you have to do is give me a chance to prove that to you."

Her mind drifted to what a future with him would look like. She'd loved him once—or thought she had. But how could she be sure she'd ever feel that way again when that so-called love had faded so fast? And if she did what he asked, if she gave him a chance, what would happen with Jake?

The memory of Jake's mouth moving over hers, of his hands traveling down her spine to grab her hips filled her head. Jake's. Not Gray's. She'd sensed Jake wanted to say something to her when they'd been standing beside her father's car, but he hadn't. And suddenly, she needed to know what he'd been holding back. Needed it like she needed air to breathe.

"I have to go, Gray." She reached for the door handle at her back and pulled the door open. "I-I'll call you tomorrow."

"Marlene, just stay. Finish your dinner."

No, she couldn't stay. She needed to see Jake, needed to talk to him, needed to figure out what the heck was really happening between them once and for all. She stepped out on the front porch and then moved down the steps, snow crunching under her shoes as she headed for her car.

Her fingers shook as she shoved the keys in the ignition and started her Audi. One glance up as she backed around told her Gray was still standing on the porch, watching her go.

She gripped the steering wheel in both hands as she passed the monstrous main house on her father's property and turned down the long tree-lined drive that led to the highway. Lights burned in the windows, but she didn't stop. Couldn't handle listening to her father drone on again about Gray, at least not right now.

She flipped her headlights to low beam as she pulled onto the highway and headed toward Louisville. Cars passed going the opposite direction. Horse farms with their white pristine fences rolled across the snowy, dark hillsides, but she barely saw them. All she saw in her mind was Jake. All she thought about was their night together in that village. All she felt was a warm, aching thump in the center of her chest, followed by a flutter of nerves that rushed through her belly.

The drive into Louisville seemed to fly. It wasn't until she was already in the suburbs, moving slowly through neighborhoods, looking for Jake's street, that she realized she didn't have a clue what she was going to say to him.

She couldn't just barge in and demand to know how he felt about her. He'd never answer. Those nerves kicked up until her fingers trembled against the wheel. A little voice urged her to just go home, but she didn't want to. She *needed* answers once and for all. Which meant she had to come up with a legitimate reason for going to his house after dark on a Sunday night.

She found the street, took a right onto the icy road, and drove slowly as she glanced at house numbers. The street was wide, with big old oak trees lining the road on both sides and two-story middle-class homes on large lots. Snow was pushed up against the curbs, and the houses were nice—wide porches, shutters hanging on windows, neatly manicured trees and, she guessed, lawns under all that snow. But they were a far cry from the mansion where Jake had grown up, which now housed Aegis headquarters. And they were nothing like any of the luxury properties he owned around the globe.

The properties. She could use that as her excuse. She still had the paperwork he'd yet to sign for the properties he wanted to sell somewhere in her car.

She spotted his house at the end of the cul-de-sac. A two-story craftsman style home that looked only a few years old. His Tahoe was parked out front. She pulled around and parked in front of his house. Killed the engine. Tugged off her seatbelt. But couldn't get out. Looking up at the house, she sat where she was and stared at the warm glow inside.

Her heart pounded hard. Her skin grew damp. What the heck was she doing? This was a stupid idea. He was going to see through her excuse like tissue paper. She could get the paperwork signed tomorrow—Monday morning—at work. As soon as she walked up to that door, he was going to say just as much. But even if he let her in, even if they started talking, what would she do if he told her something she didn't want to hear? Was she ready for that?

She swallowed the lump in her throat. Stared down at the steering wheel. She didn't know what answer she wanted from him, but tonight was not the night to ask the question. Not when she was still so tired and stressed and . . . scared. Scared of making the wrong choice, scared of not having a choice, but, mostly, scared to death of getting her heart broken. And as much as she didn't want to admit it, he was the one person who had the power to do just that.

Decision made, she started the engine, pressed down on the gas, and turned out of the cul-de-sac. But in her desperate attempt to flee, she gave the engine too much gas, and the car lurched forward. The tires skidded toward the right. Her adrenaline shot up when she realized she was going sideways. She tried to turn into the skid to gain traction, but there was nowhere to go. Before she could even correct, the front of her car slammed into the base of the streetlight.

Her head cracked against the window to her left. Her body shot forward. Pain spiraled across her skull as she slumped over the wheel. Wincing, she tried to lean back, but the car felt as if it was suddenly spinning.

She pressed a hand against her forehead, drew her fingers away, and saw the blood. Her stomach rolled. Glancing out the windshield toward the front of her car, she spotted the dented front end of her vehicle.

The engine had died, but the lights were still on. She tried to start the car again. Panic pushed at her as she turned the key, but nothing happened. She pressed down on the gas and turned the ignition. "Come on. Please."

A banging sound against the glass made her jump and yelp. Marley jerked away from the driver's door, then felt her heart sink.

Jake stood outside her window wearing a loose sweatshirt, jeans, and snow boots. And he was looking at her like she'd just lost her freakin' mind.

Which, considering everything that had happened, she was pretty sure she already had.

Jake's heart shot into his throat when he looked through the glass. Reaching quickly for the car's door handle, he jerked the door open. "Marley? Holy hell. What are you doing?"

"I . . ." Marley pressed a hand to her head and hissed in a breath. "Ouch."

Blood trickled down her temple from beneath her fingers, making his heart race even faster. Leaning inside the vehicle, he quickly reached for her seatbelt only to realize she wasn't strapped in. "God Almighty, woman."

She slid one leg out of the car, but he captured her before she could stand and swept her up into his arms. "Don't move."

She scrunched up her face and pushed her other hand against his shoulder as he kicked the door closed and carried her away from the car. "I'm fine, Jake."

"Yeah, we'll see about that. You're bleeding. And why weren't you wearing your seatbelt? Seatbelts save lives, you know. And heads."

"Lapse in judgment, I guess."

"You seem to be having a lot of those lately."

"Is that a crack about my driving or my life?"

"On this one I'm keeping my mouth closed." He caught the doorknob with his hand, turned and pushed it open with his hip, then carried her into the entry and closed the door with his boot. Moving down the two steps into his sunken living room, he headed for the leather couch near the fireplace, then set her down. "Don't go anywhere. I'll be right back."

"Don't worry." With her hand still pressed against the cut on her forehead, she winced. "I won't."

Jake's pulse thumped as he rummaged around in the medicine cabinet of his bathroom. What the heck was she doing here late on a Sunday night? She'd never just dropped by before. And holy shit, what was she thinking driving around in the dark when it was icy?

He found bandages, antiseptic, and acetaminophen. Carrying it all back into the living room, he couldn't stop his mind from spinning. Had something happened with McKnight? Had the prick tried or done something to hurt her? He'd like nothing more than to drive out to her father's house and pound his fist into the guy's face just for the fun of it.

His feet stilled as he stepped out of the hall and caught sight of Marley on his couch. She'd taken off her jacket and the loose blue blouse beneath and tossed them both over the arm of the sofa. Wearing nothing but a fitted white tank that accentuated her breasts and made her skin look darker, slim jeans that molded to her hips and legs, and tiny black flats she never should be walking on snow with, she pulled her hand away from the cut on her forehead, grimaced at the sight, then reapplied pressure to the wound.

She shouldn't look sexy sitting there, but she did. Warmth gathered in his belly, slinked into his groin. Clearing his throat, he pushed his feet forward and moved down the steps toward her. Told himself she wasn't sexy, she was hurt. Then mentally ticked off all the reasons he needed to stop looking at her like a woman and go back to seeing her as just his assistant.

"Here." He sat next to her on the couch. "Turn toward me."

She shifted one leg underneath her and twisted to face him, then pulled her hand away from her forehead. "How bad is it?"

He focused on her forehead, not the cleavage staring him in the face. Carefully, he swiped at the blood with gauze. A nice-size lump had already formed and had to hurt like a bitch. "I don't think it needs stitches, but you're gonna have a nasty bruise."

She winced when he gently applied antiseptic and then blew over the wound to ease the sting. "Serves me right."

He set the antiseptic on the coffee table, then reached for a bandage. After pulling the tape off, he gently placed it over her wound. "How is it you can tromp through the jungle where ten thousand dangerous things are trying to kill you and not get a scratch, then get hurt doing something as simple as driving a car?"

"I don't know. I'm just lucky, I guess."

"You're something, that's for sure." He set the plastic tabs from the bandage on the coffee table, then turned to face her. "Just look at me."

"Um." She stilled and blinked several times. "Why?"

He captured her face in his hands and tipped her eyes up to his. "Because I'm checking to see if you have a concussion."

"I'm fine, Jake."

"Says the girl who just plowed her car into a light pole. And don't roll your eyes at me, either."

She sighed but held his gaze. And though he was supposed to be checking her pupil size, he couldn't keep from noticing the ring of navy around her sky-blue irises. Why hadn't he ever noticed that before? And why hadn't he ever noticed the different shades of blue in her eyes? They weren't one continuous color; they were a kaleidoscope of different hues.

"Well?" she asked, breaking the spell he seemed to be falling under. "Satisfied?"

"Not yet." He pulled one hand away. "How many fingers am I holding up?"

"Two."

"Now?"

"Four. Three." She narrowed her eyes when he pulled another finger down so only two remained. "Okay, stop changing the damn number. I feel like an idiot enough as it is."

She didn't look like an idiot. She looked beautiful.

He quickly released her and moved several inches away. Dammit, that was the kind of thinking that was going to get him into trouble. He cleared his throat again. "Headache, nausea, dizziness?"

"Only briefly when you were whipping your fingers around." When he glanced at her, she frowned. "No, no, and no." She reached for her sweater and coat. "I'm fine. And I need to be going."

A whisper of panic raced down his spine. He captured her arm so she couldn't stand, then reached around her and took her coat and sweater. "You're not going anywhere. You might not have a concussion, but you're obviously rattled. Besides which." He pushed to his feet, tossed her coat and sweater on a chair out of her reach, and rested his hands on his hips as he looked down at her. "You're not going anywhere in that car until a mechanic looks at it."

"It's barely dented." She twisted to look out the front window across the dark cul-de-sac. "Isn't it?"

"Barely or not, it's getting checked out." He headed for the kitchen. "I'll call a tow truck in the morning."

She sighed and leaned back into the couch.

Since he'd seen her drink tea at work in the afternoons, he fixed her a cup of English Breakfast and grabbed the bottle of acetaminophen. Before he could head back into the living room, his cell on the counter buzzed.

He thought about ignoring it, but flipped it over. Then wished he hadn't.

After typing a quick response, he tucked the phone into his back pocket and headed into the living room. Marley was hunched over her cell tapping on the screen when he entered.

"Here." He handed her the cup. "Drink. It'll make you feel better. And give me that." As soon as she took the mug, he plucked the phone out of her free hand.

"Hey. I need that to call a cab."

"Not right now you don't." He dropped her phone on the coffee table and eased back into the opposite corner of the couch.

She frowned and lifted the mug to her lips. "You're awfully aggravating when you're bossy."

"I know. Deal with it. After three years you should know how."

She rolled her eyes, took a sniff of the hot brew, then sipped. "Mm. I thought you were only a coffee drinker."

"Contrary to what you might believe, I'm a man of many varied tastes." Not that he wanted to get into those tastes with her right now. Especially when his favorite taste at the moment was her.

Shit. Don't go there.

The cell in his pocket buzzed again. Relieved by the distraction, he pulled it out, read the response, then frowned and typed a quick note.

"Problem?" Marley asked, sipping her tea.

"Nothing I can't handle." He set his phone next to hers on the table.

Her eyes narrowed. "I know that look, Jake. What's going on?"

He debated whether he should tell her, especially with everything she was already dealing with, then figured the easiest way to get their relationship back on solid ground was to go back to what they did best. Which was dealing with crises.

"That was Miller. Someone's looking into my properties."

"What does that mean?"

"I don't know." He shrugged, crossed his arms over his chest. "Could be nothing."

"Or it could be something. Which ones?"

"Here. Italy. The Caribbean."

Her face paled, and she lowered her mug. "Do you think it's the Red Brotherhood trying to figure out where you are?"

"No." He knew it was possible the terrorist organization that had targeted Landon and Olivia six months ago could be gunning for him, but his gut said this was something else. Something he probably shouldn't mention to Marley, all things considered. "And even if it were, they'd go after Miller, not me."

"You helped bring down the head of their organization. I'd say that gives them every reason to go after you."

Possibly. But he didn't want her stressing about this now. "Don't worry about it."

She huffed and lifted her mug again. "I do. The same way you worry about me getting a bump on the head."

Something in his chest turned over as he watched her sip her tea. Something he hadn't felt before. "I know how to take care of myself."

"That's what worries me."

His brain flipped back to the plane, and how angry she'd been that he'd taken that risk and almost gotten killed trying to save them from the Black Eagles. Then fast-forwarded to the way she'd kissed him crazy in the galley until he could think of nothing but her.

Those tingles intensified until it felt like his entire body was vibrating.

"What are you going to do about it?" she asked quietly.

The Red Brotherhood. Not their kiss. God, he needed to get his brain back online. "Nothing."

But the bigger question was, what was he going to do about her?

His heart raced, and he knew he needed to change the subject before he did or said something that would make things worse. Perching one bare foot on the edge of the coffee table, he said, "So. Wanna tell me why you're plowing your car into a light pole on my street at nine p.m. on a Sunday night?"

"Oh." Her cheeks turned a soft shade of pink, and she lowered her mug to her lap. "I, um, was on my way home when I remembered those papers I need you to sign."

He had absolutely no idea what she was talking about. "What papers?"

She frowned like he was a complete idiot, and the expression was so cute, he had to physically restrain himself from leaning over to kiss the scowl off her face. "The papers we've talked about several times. For the properties you asked me to list because you have no intention of using them."

"Oh." A familiar bitterness rolled through his stomach when he remembered the handful of houses he'd asked Marley to sell. One that dampened his awareness of her in a good way. "Those properties. Right."

All were homes he'd inherited from his father when the old man had passed. All had meant something special to his dear old dad. And all were nothing more than ugly reminders of a father who cared so little for his kids, he'd preferred spending time gallivanting around the globe with strangers rather than being present in their lives.

"I have the realtors' contracts. I just need you to sign off on each one."

"Yeah. Fine. I'll do it."

She leaned forward to set her mug on the coffee table, and knowing she was about to get up and go out into the snow to get the papers in her tiny, slippery shoes, he laid a hand on her thigh to keep her from standing. "Later. Finish your tea."

She shot him a look, but he just gave it right back to her. If there was one thing he knew about Marley Addison, it was that pushy was the only real action she responded to. And right now he'd be as pushy as he needed to be because she wasn't leaving this house until he knew for sure that she didn't have a concussion and wasn't in danger of doing some kind of other bodily harm to herself.

Their eyes held, and electricity sparked between them. A familiar electricity charged with conflict and exasperation. But tonight there was a whole lot more. A heat that was simmering beneath the surface. The same heat they'd both felt in the jungle. On that plane. A heat he knew from the color in her cheeks she felt as strongly as he did.

She sighed, eased back into the cushions with her mug once more, and took another sip. Silence slid over them, the only sound the flicker of the flames popping in the fireplace. But that heat was still there. Bubbling and rolling with energy, kicking up his pulse and making him twitch. And even from his end of the couch, he could smell her delicious scent rolling over him like a warm, luxurious wave, drawing him in, making him forget all those reasons her being here late on a Sunday night was a bad idea.

She lowered her mug and looked up at the far wall. "I like your house. It's not at all what I expected. You live in the suburbs."

Chitchat. He could do chitchat. It, at least, would keep his mind off the way her breasts pushed against her tank and the long, shapely line of her thigh. "What did you expect?"

"I don't know. A fancy downtown penthouse with a doorman and security up the wazoo."

"I've got security up the wazoo. You just can't see it." He glanced at her. "But a stuffy penthouse? Seriously?"

She shrugged. "You have the money for it. And you do dress all Mr. *GQ*." Her gaze dropped to his favorite faded jeans and the ratty Notre Dame sweatshirt he'd pulled on earlier. "Well, usually."

"Don't let the image fool you. Underneath I'm just an ordinary nobody." Leaning back farther into the cushions, he laced his fingers behind his head. "A giant disappointment, as my father always liked to point out."

"I hardly think you're a disappointment. You graduated top of your class at Notre Dame. You were a Navy SEAL. You run an incredibly successful security business. If your father was disappointed, then I'd say his standards were more than a little skewed."

Jake stared at the blank TV screen on the wall across the room. The one he'd flipped off when he'd heard Marley's car slam into that light pole. "He died before I started Aegis. But I doubt he'd be proud, especially with the way the guys run roughshod across his pristine properties."

"Which is why you let them do it."

He tipped his head her way and grinned, a feeling of supreme pleasure rushing through him. "Yeah. It is."

"So tell me why he wasn't proud you were a SEAL."

He sighed and looked back at the TV. "Because he wanted me to work for him. Take over the day-to-day operations of his mega-empire so he could run off with his latest girlfriend who was half his age. I only joined the navy because it was the very last thing he ever expected or approved of. Wasting my degree. That's what he told me the day I informed him I was enlisting."

"And when was that?"

"College graduation. Took me out to lunch after the ceremony. Actually carved out two whole hours for me. It was a monumental feat for him."

He heard the sarcasm in his own voice and clenched his jaw. All that victory slipped away as he stared at the blank screen and remembered how ticked his father had been that day. "Man, he was pissed. Almost as pissed as the day my mother walked out on him."

"How old were you when that happened?"

"Seven. Just turned seven." Too old to go with her, too young to take off on his own. *"Happy birthday, Jakey. Momma has to run to the store. I'll be right back."* Only she hadn't come back, and she'd never meant to. He'd spent the last thirty years resenting her for that. Not for the fact she'd wanted to escape her emotionally detached husband—hell, Jake had been trying to do that most of his own adult life, and he still couldn't manage the feat even with the old man dead and buried. No, he'd resented her for leaving her son—her own flesh and blood—with the man instead of taking him with her.

That day was still fresh in his mind. As fresh as if it had happened yesterday.

"I guess that explains why you let the board of directors manage his companies and aren't involved in any of them," Marley said quietly.

Her voice pulled him back from the depressing memories spinning in his head. "Yep."

"And I'm guessing that's why you don't live in any of the properties you inherited either."

"Right again." Jake looked around the living room. It was sparse— light gray walls, a few prints hanging here and there, worn furniture he could easily afford to replace but didn't feel the need to get rid of. "He'd hate this place. So below my potential." He shook his head and looked down at his foot against the coffee table. "Just like me."

"Well, I like it. It's cozy. A real home. Not institutional like Aegis."

He glanced over at her. Her gaze skipped over the room, taking it all in, and the twinkle in her eye said she was telling the truth. All that animosity he'd been feeling for his fucked-up parents trickled away. "You think Aegis is institutional?"

"Maybe institutional is the wrong word. Stuffy."

"Stuffy?"

"Formal?" She turned her smiling eyes his way. "Sometimes I'm afraid I'm going to knock a sculpture or a plant over and some ancient butler will poof out of the walls and jump on me."

Jake chuckled, feeling better with every passing second. "Don't tell anyone, but that's the way I feel there too."

It also explained why he was usually in a bad mood at the office. Even though he loved his work, there were days when he wondered if setting up his company in his father's eccentric mansion had been a good idea. He'd done it to prove to the old man—even in death—that he could make something of himself. But these days he was starting to think there were too many ghosts lingering there. Too many reminders of a childhood spent mostly alone.

"Why don't we remodel?"

"Huh?" He glanced over at her.

"Start with the offices and the reception area and go from there. Make it your space and not his. I think it would make a difference."

The idea revolved in his head. It had potential. He could easily afford it. And it might make all the difference in how he felt every day when he had to go to work.

But as he stared at her, his mind drifted away from Aegis and settled back on her. How the heck did she do that? How did she so easily see through his bullshit when no one before her ever had?

"I'll talk to some contractors this week." She sipped her tea. "Get some estimates."

And there she went. Taking charge like she took charge of everything else. Awing him with not only her independence, but her ability to know exactly what he needed long before he did.

She lowered her mug to the coffee table, then moved for her phone. "I should probably get going."

Jake glanced over his shoulder out the window. Snow had started to fall again, which meant the roads were going to be slick.

And that panic re-forming in his chest told him loud and clear that she shouldn't be out in it. Even in a cab.

He reached for her cell phone on the table before he thought better of it and pushed it out of her reach. "You're not going anywhere tonight."

"Jake, really. This is silly."

Not to him. "No, it's not. It's a safety thing. You're staying here tonight."

She shot him a look. One he knew was meant to be exasperating but was so damn sexy, it brought a flood of warmth to his belly all over again. "We both know that's not a good idea."

Heat sizzled between them. A heat he knew might just burn him if he wasn't careful. "When has that ever stopped me?"

He pushed to his feet before she could protest, grabbed both their phones, and tucked hers into his back pocket. Then he ignored the little voice in the back of his head saying he was playing with fire. "You're still not leaving. End of story. Now get up. Since you don't have a concussion, you're going to bed."

chapter 16

Marley followed Jake up the steps to the second level and eyed her phone in his back pocket.

This was silly. She didn't need to stay overnight. She didn't have a concussion, just a bump on the head. And she wasn't feeling the least bit tired. Only embarrassed and way too turned on to deal with his overly sexy bossiness at the moment.

Dammit. When had his being bossy ever been sexy? *When he's being bossy to keep you safe. When he's being bossy to look after you, like now.*

She swallowed the lump forming in her throat and eyed the curve of his ass in the worn, faded denim. His words on the jet, just before they'd parted ways Saturday morning flashed in her brain.

"I care about you . . ."

Yeah, she knew he did care deep down. But the question was how? If she hadn't known he had attachment issues before, she did now. Holy cow, his mother had abandoned him when he was seven, when he was just starting to figure out how the world worked. And she hadn't just left him with any father. No, she'd left him to fend for himself with a man who'd been as warm as a piece of steel.

Thinking about Jake's childhood made her own years growing up seem downright peachy. No wonder he didn't have a wife or a girlfriend or even a steady relationship. After that kind of upbringing, she was impressed he even had the emotional ability to form friendships.

"This is the guest room." Jake pushed the first door on the right open with his hip and held it so Marley could pass. "It's not much, but it should work."

The room was small, just big enough for a queen-size bed and two bedside tables. Double doors opened to a closet on her right. To her left, she peered past Jake toward what looked like a bathroom.

The space was cozy, with pale-yellow walls, a white bedspread, and four simple pillows. There was nothing sexy about the room. Nothing that should make her feel uncomfortable. But then she stepped inside and her arm brushed his chest, and a rush of heat spread across her skin where they had touched, telling her this was the very last place she should be.

Nerves kicked up in her belly. She'd been stupid to think she could come here and force some kind of emotion out of him. He wasn't ready for that, and she didn't want to push him. "Jake, I really need my phone back."

"This phone?" He pulled her cell from his back pocket and held it up. "Why?"

"Because as sweet as this is, it's not necessary. I'd rather sleep in my own bed. I only live across town."

Forty minutes across town, but still. He didn't know that. She was sure he didn't even know where she lived.

"We've already been through this. You're not leaving." He turned for the door. "Just try to relax and get some sleep."

Panic rushed through her. She couldn't stay here when every inch of her body wanted him. Not when he didn't want her back. She'd be miserable, and she could just as easily be miserable in her own home. Stepping forward before he could reach the threshold of the room, she closed her fingers around the phone in his hand. "Give me that."

He jerked the phone out of her reach and twisted toward her. "You're not getting this phone."

"Yes, I am."

She swiped at it. He moved it behind his back. Leaned toward her while he held it farther behind him so she couldn't reach it. Heat radiated from him into her. She tried to move around him, but he stepped in her way and kept the phone out of her grasp.

"Dammit, Jake." She shoved one hand against his shoulder, knocking him into the wall at his back. All she wanted was to get away from his overheated body and that scent of sandalwood, citrus, and leather that always made her a little lightheaded. "I'm not fooling around anymore."

"No." A smile twisted his lips—his plump, playful, way too tempting lips—as he switched hands and wiggled away from her so she still couldn't reach the phone. "I can tell you're not."

"Then stop being such a brat"—she maneuvered one hand around his back, tried to ignore the way that brought their hips and thighs into contact—"and give me my damn phone."

From the corner of her eye she could tell he was staring at her face as she struggled, that he was amused by this little game. And— dammit—she couldn't even feign being irritated because *she liked* that he was watching her. Liked that they were touching. Liked that she amused him in any way, because most days she wasn't sure he even noticed her.

And that made her the biggest fool on the planet because this was Jake.

"Okay, enough." She put on her most serious face, pulled her hand back, and glared up at his dark, mischievous eyes. "Drop my phone."

The phone clattered to the ground at their feet. And even though it had fallen between their legs and now was her chance to grab it and run, she suddenly couldn't move. Because she recognized that look in his eyes. The same look she'd seen from across that jungle village when she'd been dancing around the fire. One filled with heat, with yearning, with a lust that wasn't just spontaneous, it was downright combustible.

"I kinda like that tone," he murmured, his voice rough and low.

"Jake—" She'd meant to reprimand him, but his name came out more like an invitation than a warning.

With one step, he closed the space between them, his hands capturing her face in warm, strong palms, the same way he had downstairs. But this time, instead of letting her go, he held her gaze, his own dark eyes glittering with fire and need. "Order me, the way you told me to drop the phone. This is your chance to boss me around. However you want. Take it. You never know when it will come around again."

Was he talking about . . . ? No, he couldn't be. But when she saw the desire burning in his eyes, her resistance wavered. Suddenly, she was the one breathing hard. Her mind pinging between right and wrong, should and should-nots, actions and consequences.

The corners of his lips tipped up, and those hot eyes slid to her mouth. The muscle in his jaw pulsed, like a tiger holding itself back from pouncing on its prey, waiting for the perfect moment. "Do it."

The dark, gritty order threaded heat and need down her chest, and straight between her legs. Pushed aside every last rational thought. "Kiss me, dammit."

A flicker of a grin, edgy and victorious, flashed across his handsome face before his mouth covered hers. The familiar feel of his lips brushing hers instantly relieved the tension pulling her body tight, and she swayed into his heat, into his support, into that delicious body she'd been dreaming about for way too long.

As if he couldn't help himself, as if it were ingrained in his DNA, he took control again, demanding with his mouth, the same way he had that night in the jungle. Like he couldn't get enough. Like she was the only thing he wanted. Like he couldn't live without this. Without her.

And she let him. Gave herself over to the need that had been building between them ever since that night. She opened and slid her tongue along his, groaned at the warm wetness of his mouth. Knew it was wrong but didn't care. She needed this. Needed him. He was right. This was an opportunity she might never get again.

Her hands tightened in the denim at his hips, then stroked up, her fingers pushing the thick sweatshirt away, then the soft cotton of his T-shirt. Finally reaching skin. Heat. Muscle.

He kissed her deeper, his tongue wild against hers. Greedy. Demanding. Heat flooded her body. Every inch of her skin tingled where they touched. All she could think about was more. More of his kiss, more of his hands, more of his warmth sinking in, grabbing on, never letting go.

He pulled back long before she was ready. The room spun, and she gasped. Hung on to his sides. Tried not to fall over.

"Shit," he whispered. "I wasn't going to do that again."

The sexual fog cleared, just enough so she could focus on the Notre Dame emblem across his wide chest.

Right. They weren't supposed to be doing this at all. They'd both agreed what had happened in the jungle wasn't supposed to happen again. It didn't matter how much she wanted it. She didn't want it if he was already having regrets.

Pulling out of his arms, she pressed the back of her hand against her mouth. Glanced around the room, and tried to remember where she was.

His guest room. Her gaze shot to the dark window and the snow falling outside in an orange glow from the streetlight beyond. She needed to call a cab. Needed to get the hell out of here. Her gaze dropped to the phone on the floor between them.

He stepped past her, toward the door, looking sheepish and guilty and—dammit—still sexier than any man had the right to look. "I'm just gonna go."

Go. Right. At the moment she was thinking that would be a good move for her too. But she knew he'd never let her leave with the snow falling outside. He was too protective for that. The only thing she could do would be to wait until he went to bed, then call a cab and sneak out before he could stop her.

"Yeah," she managed. "Probably a good idea." But even to her the words sounded weak and disappointed.

"Right." He reached for the door handle and stepped out into the hallway. "Night, Marley."

She didn't get the chance to answer. The door snapped closed before she could find the words, and alone, Marley dropped her face into her hands.

God, she was pathetic. One crazy, impulsive kiss and she was right back where she'd vowed she'd never be. In love with a man who was more freaked out by what was happening between them than she was. Gray was right. This thing between her and Jake was never going to work. Not when they couldn't even be in the same room without—

The door creaked. Startled, Marley lowered her hands and looked up. Jake stepped back into the room and shut the door at his back.

"I want it on record that I left." His gaze was a little wild. Hot. Oh God . . . *smoldering.* "I actually walked out the door and left the room. I walked away."

Her pulse raced. All that heat and energy splashed in her belly again, followed by a quiver of excitement. "You did."

"It's just . . ." He stepped close, reached for her hips, and gently drew her toward him. "If there's a chance you have a concussion, even a mild one, I don't think you're supposed to go to sleep."

A half laugh scraped out of her throat. Jake Ryder, for all his domineering, overbearing traits, had a wicked-sharp sense of humor. One that made her entire body sizzle.

She bit her lip, lifted her hands, and laid them carefully on his chest. His warm, solid, chiseled chest that did crazy things to her libido. "Isn't that an old wives' tale?"

The corner of his lips curled. Just a touch. Just enough to form a sexy little smirk that made her insides absolutely melt. "Sounds logical though, right?" His gaze swept over her face, trickled down to the top of her breasts just visible near the edge of her tank, then slowly returned to her eyes as if trying to decide where he wanted to start his feast. "I'm pretty sure we need to do something to keep you awake. It's a medical emergency, after all."

Oh, holy God. Yes, yes, yes.

"Right," she whispered. A blistering desire rushed through her veins. One she knew she should squash but suddenly didn't want to. "A medical emergency." Her hands shifted to his shoulders. His strong, toned, muscular shoulders. "It's the only thing we can do."

She lifted to her toes, slid her hands around his nape, and pressed her lips against his before he could change his mind. If he needed an excuse, fine, she'd let him have one. She just wanted—no, she needed—this. Needed to feel wanted, needed to feel desired, needed to feel beautiful, with him.

He opened to her kiss, and his tongue stroked along hers, slowly, sensually, so very different from the way he'd kissed her only a moment before. Marley sank in, let him take the lead, forced herself not to overanalyze him or them or this. Forced herself to simply enjoy.

She pushed her hands into his hair, let her fingers sift through the soft dark strands. Jake moaned deep in his throat and changed the angle of the kiss. One arm left her waist, and the light flipped off, then he walked her backward until her legs hit the mattress.

He pulled away, grabbed the hem of her tank, and tugged it over her head. "God, Marley. You make me fucking crazy, you know that?"

Excitement pulsed through her, the words stimulating something deep in the center of her chest that she hadn't known was there. Before she could respond, his mouth covered hers again, his tongue sliding along hers, tasting, savoring, teasing. His hands stroked her ribs, creating an electric sizzle all across her skin that made her belly quiver.

Impatient for more, she pushed his sweatshirt and the T-shirt he was wearing beneath higher, and ran her hands over the smooth skin of his back. Pulling away from the kiss, she murmured, "More. I need skin. Give me skin."

He groaned, released her, and reached behind his head, tugging both shirts off before tossing them aside. "Like this?"

"Yes," she exhaled, the word dripping with an almost evil pleasure. "This."

She touched him everywhere, memorizing the delicious feel of him beneath her fingertips, the intoxicating and unique scent of spice and skin, one hundred percent Jake. Pressing a kiss to the center of his chest, she inhaled deeply, savored the heady rush, and smiled. "Mmmm. The smell of you makes me higher than that freaky jungle juice."

His deep chuckle vibrated beneath her mouth as she laid a trail of kisses toward his nipple, then pulled the tight flesh between her lips.

A low, animalistic sound rumbled through his throat. His fingers dug into her waist, and his head dropped back. "I know I shouldn't, but I love your mouth on me."

She knew she shouldn't too, but she loved the sound of her name on his lips. Wondered how she'd ever lived without it. She rolled her tongue around and around his nipple, thrilled with his pleasure. Wanted only to spend the night discovering every single thing that excited him. Hoped he'd give her the time.

Lowering one hand, she slid it between their bodies and popped the button on his jeans. His head righted, his lips pressing hard to her brow, her temple, her cheek, then, using his forehead to nudge her head aside, his mouth dropped to her neck.

Marley floated in lusty heaven, wishing it could last forever. Searching for the tag of his zipper, she nudged his erection, then pushed her hand lower, rubbing her palm along his length.

"Ah, God, Marley."

She smiled, her chest full and light as she stroked him again. "I like it when you say my name." Not her given name. Not her last name. Not that stupid nickname Gray used. This name. *Her* name. On his lips. "Do it again."

He growled first, then obeyed. "Marley."

She kissed his chest, stroked his cock through his pants. Brushed her lips across his neck, ran her hand up and down his steely length. "Again."

One hand fisted in her hair and pulled her head back until he was looking directly into her eyes, searching her face in the dim light. Tension hummed from his big body. Lust flamed in his gaze. But his expression was tight with something else. Something more. Affection. Unfulfilled desire. Longing. Something—

"Marley," he whispered. He kissed her forehead, slid the tip of his nose down hers. "Marley." He touched her lips with his. "Marley." Licked her lips. "Marley." Pressed his mouth over hers and swept a long, slow stroke of his tongue along hers, kissing her until she was breathless, then pulling away with a soft, hungry, "Marley."

Need hit her low and hard. Urgency made her fingers shake. She fumbled with his zipper. Before she could free him from his jeans, though, he lowered his mouth to hers again, then captured her lips in a deep, heart-stopping kiss filled with passion and need.

One that consumed her. Overwhelmed her. Made her absolutely dizzy with the thought of only him.

God, he tasted good. Like a hint of the beer he must have had earlier, like sin and sex and oblivion. And she wanted all of that. Wanted to let go, wanted to feel. Wanted to forget everything else and just focus on this. On him. On a moment she could never get enough of.

His strong, warm hands gripped her waist and lifted her off the floor. He laid her back on the bed, took her hands in his, and pushed them overhead. Wrapping her fingers around the wooden slats in the headboard, he covered hers with his own, then looked directly into her eyes.

"My turn." His voice was husky and breathless. So damn arousing it made her entire body tremble. "Say my name."

"Jake." The word came out on a soft breath, and she worked her hands free, needing to touch him anywhere. Everywhere.

"Uh-uh." He held her hands in place. "I said it was my turn. I'm in control now." His gaze rolled down over her body. "And you are still wearing way too much clothing to get that skin you wanted."

Yes. Oh, yes. "Definitely."

He eased the hold on her hands, then skimmed his fingers down her arms and over her breasts, sitting back, his thighs flanking hers.

Streetlight washed over his bare skin. Over muscles carved from hours in the gym. Across scars from his years in the military. Highlighting the fine dusting of hair along his chest and the ripple of his ab muscles. And she wanted to lick every spot. Every muscle and scar and dip and plane. She wanted it all.

Releasing the headboard, she swept her hands over his chest and down his abs.

Jake grabbed her wrists and met her gaze with a hot, sharp look that pierced her belly with excitement. "No touching. Not until I say so." He replaced her hands on the headboard. "Don't move again."

Oh man, she liked this side of him. Liked it way more than she should. "Figures you'd get bossy."

His lips curved in that hot little grin that made her wet. One finger traced a line down the center of her chest, slipped beneath the clasp of her bra, and flicked it open. Marley sucked in a breath of surprise.

"This bossy," he said, his gaze hot on her breasts as they spilled from the parting fabric, "is in your best interest. I promise."

When he did nothing more than stare, running the back of his fingers across her exposed skin, she growled, planted her feet on the mattress, and lifted her hips, pressing them into his. His cock pushed against that sweet spot between her legs already aching for him. "Take control, Ryder, or I will."

He chuckled. "That's an offer I'll take you up on later."

Later . . . Later, tonight? Later, tomorrow? Later, next week? Her mind flitted to the future before she caught it and reined her thoughts in to the now. Just now.

His head lowered, his lips kissing a path down the center of her chest and over the mound of one breast. She was already arching when he finally took her nipple into his mouth. Her head fell back, her eyes closed on a sound of pleasure that erupted from her throat.

He pulled his mouth from hers for a husky, "Say my name." Then covered the other breast.

She whimpered with pleasure. "Jake. More, Jake."

He moaned against her, the sound vibrating her nipple, sending shockwaves straight to her core.

Oh . . . She released the headboard and threaded her hands into his hair. "I can't—"

"Addison." He pulled her hands from his hair and slammed her arms above her head. "What did I tell you?"

Really? He was playing games *now*? Frustration and need coiled hot in her belly, making her tremble, making her sweat. "I'm feeling sleepy, Ryder. Step it up already and focus on the importance of this medical emergency."

His gaze snapped to hers, and something dangerous, something scorching brewed in their dark depths. "Sleepy, huh?" He reached between them and pulled her jeans open—button and zipper—in one hard tug. "I guess I'm gonna have to do something about that."

Oh yes, he would. She grinned. Held on to the headboard as he moved back and stripped her jeans and panties roughly over her hips and down her legs. Shook with excitement. But she didn't care if he ripped them. Didn't care about anything right now except taking him deep inside.

"It's about time," she said on a breath of both anticipation and relief. "I think I'm waking up."

"Well then, we'd better make sure you stay that way." His gaze seared her legs, her hips, and her sex as he scanned every inch of her flesh with fierce hunger. Then he gripped one thigh and pushed it wide, slid the other hand beneath her ass and lifted at the same time he dropped his head, covering her with his mouth.

Sensation rocketed through Marley's body, taking control. "Jake. Ah, God, Jake."

He hummed against her, lips suckling, tongue stroking, exploring, tasting. "Mm," he murmured between kisses and licks. "You taste incredible."

As if to prove it, he took her clit between his lips and suckled.

"*Oh.*" Marley arched, unable to stand the intense pleasure, unable to stop herself from lifting into his mouth.

Her orgasm came out of nowhere, rising too fast for her to do anything but hold on. She gripped the headboard in her hands. "Jake . . ." He hummed in response, licking faster, stroking harder. "Jake . . ." She pulled one hand from the headboard and fisted his hair. "Holy Go—"

Pleasure peaked, closing her throat and twisting through her body in hot shards of ecstasy. The pressure eased, his tongue gentled its frantic stroke, but the friction continued to create little spasms of excitement that coursed all through her.

He kissed her inner thigh, her hip, her belly as her limp muscles finally relaxed and she melted into the bed beneath her. Then he shifted to the side, and she realized he was sliding off the mattress.

She grasped his arm, pushed him back before he could get away, rolled him over, and straddled his hips. "Don't you dare leave."

"Like I could."

He was breathless as he looked up at her, his voice gruff with lust. And as her gaze raked his bare chest, down to the open button of his jeans, every inch of her desire roared back to life. Inching back, she grasped the denim and pulled it from his legs, then dropped the garment on the floor. But before she could explore with her hands and lips and tongue the way she wanted, he pushed her back, climbed between her legs, knelt down, then sat on his heels, gripping her hips so he could roughly pull her into his lap.

Gasping, she wrapped her arms around his shoulders and looked down into his face. The dim light cast shadows across his intense expression, made her heart beat faster. But his erection pressing against her wetness sent a shiver through her entire body, one she couldn't ignore. Groaning, she lifted her hips and slid over his length until they both trembled.

"God, I want you." He pressed a gentle kiss across her collarbone. "Want you so much I can't stand it. But I need to get a condom."

She tightened her arms around his shoulders, preventing him from leaving. "If you walk out of this room I might fall asleep. We can't chance it with this possible concussion I've got going."

He chuckled. Kissed the base of her throat. Smiled against her skin in a way that made her entire body shiver. "Are you sure?"

She'd never been more sure about anything. Cupping her hands on each side of his face, she lifted so he could see her. "Absolutely."

He growled, closed his eyes a brief second, then lifted his lids to look directly into her eyes. Rocking his hips, he positioned his cock at her entrance, then slowly pushed into her. The head pressed past the tightness, and he paused. "Mm, I like that. Tell me you like it too. Tell me."

"So good." Her eyes drifted shut at the delicious stretch he created. Her hands slid to his shoulders, holding on as she tightened around him. She tried to lift to cause friction, but he held her too tightly, preventing her from moving.

"Open your eyes, Marley. Look at me. Say my name again. Tell me where you belong."

The possessiveness in his words should have annoyed her. But instead it excited her. Electrified her. Made her hotter than she'd ever been. And it also confused her because she didn't know what the words truly meant, and right now she didn't want to wonder. She just wanted *him*.

"Jake." She rocked her hips to take him deeper. Needed more. Needed all of him. "I belong right here with you."

He pulled her mouth down, swept his tongue in and circled hers. His hips lifted, driving his length deep. Then he stilled, broke the kiss, and pressed his face to her neck. "Ah, God. Just want to stay here. Just want . . ." He lifted into her again, spread his knees, pushing her legs farther open, forcing himself deeper. "Just want all of you."

Warmth spread through her chest, circled her heart. Using his thighs, he lowered and lifted in full, deep, slow strokes, murmuring confusing, almost desperate words and phrases against her skin that didn't make sense—*"want it all, can't, need more, yes, don't let go, Marley, fuck, Marley . . ."*

Every stroke grew stronger, harder, deeper, rocking her beyond mind and body, straight to her soul. He sounded desperate, sounded frantic, sounded lost. And all those things he'd told her about his parents, about growing up alone, about being nothing but a disappointment, they echoed through her mind, shot straight to her heart, and made her love him even more. Because underneath all his aggravating alpha male-ness, he was just like her. Struggling to find his way, fighting to make something of himself, searching for a moment that would make everything else worth the battle.

"Right here." She gripped his face, tipped it up to hers. "I'm here." Holding on tight to his shoulder, she lifted and lowered, driving him toward his climax, wanting to go over with him. She pressed her lips against his. "I'm right here, Jake."

He pulled back, clasped his hand against the back of her head, placed the other at the base of her spine, guiding her hips to his thrusts. His hair clung to his handsome, damp face, and his eyes looked both dark with passion and open with vulnerability. He pressed his forehead to hers. "Crazy. This is so fucking crazy. Crazy hot. Crazy good. *Ah, God.* Come with me, Marley."

Finally. "Yes."

With a groan, he picked up the speed of his thrusts, dug his fingers into the base of her spine, holding her steady. And as soon as Marley relaxed into him, her orgasm blossomed in stages—first mild, then intense, and finally, a blinding spasm of ecstasy spilling through her body as Jake released his own climax in shudders and guttural growls of pleasure.

She fell against him. Sweaty, limp, unable to move. Heavy breaths lifted and lowered his chest. His damp skin pressed against hers—everywhere. He drew in a deep breath, then muttered, "Holy hell. That was . . ."

Her eyes squeezed shut tight. *Don't say a mistake. Please don't say it was a mistake.* She wasn't sure her heart could take that right now. Not after the things he'd said and the emotions he'd made her feel. Tomorrow she could handle rejection but not now. Not when—

He fell back on the mattress and pulled her on top of him. "That was fucking amazing."

The tension leaked out of her. Relief rippled through her belly. She relaxed into him and pressed her face against his neck as his arms wound around her back, holding her close.

"I think my muscles are broken," he mumbled into her hair, "but it was amazing."

She smiled, pressed her lips against his throat, loved that he was *him*.

And oh, the truth she'd tried so hard to ignore was plainly obvious. So obvious her heart squeezed tight. She wasn't just *in* love with him. She was *head over heels* in love with him. She loved what he'd made of himself. Loved his determination and drive. Loved the way he cared about the people in his life even when he acted like he didn't. She even loved his moodiness because it meant he wasn't the hard, cold shell of a person his father had been. He might see himself as a disappointment, but she didn't. She saw a man who'd risen above neglect and abandonment and become more than a child of abuse, he'd become a warrior.

"You're not falling asleep, are you?" he asked, his voice rumbling in his throat, tickling her lips.

"No." She blinked back the warm wetness threatening her eyes. Told herself she was being silly and that she needed to get in control of these stupid emotions before he saw them. "I don't know. Maybe."

He rolled her to her back, drew away, and gazed down at her. And though she tried not to look, the minute she met his heated, sultry gaze, she knew she wasn't tired. And neither was he. Not even close. Fire flickered in his dark eyes. A fire she knew just how to stroke to a full-blown flame even if the result might burn her in the end.

The edge of his lips curled. "Then we better do something about that. Don't you think?"

Her pulse raced. Her stomach tightened in anticipation. She braced her hands on his muscular forearms and then bit her lip. "What do you have in mind?"

"This." He lowered his mouth to her throat. Kissed her neck. Slid his lips to her collarbone, then lower to the edge of her breast. "And this." He moved down and laved his tongue across the tip of her nipple, sending shards of arousal straight back to her center. "And a hell of a lot more of this."

Oh yes . . .

He lifted his head before she got lost in the sensation and captured her gaze. "But mostly, tonight, I just want you to be mine."

Those were the words she'd been waiting to hear. Warmth bloomed all through her chest, and a hope she'd been afraid to let herself believe in spread through every cell. It was foolish and reckless and made zero sense, but she wanted that too. Wanted everything.

She drew in a breath for courage. Licked her lips. And decided now—right now—she'd finally take the chance. "Then do it, Jake. Make me yours."

chapter 17

Jake rolled to his side, spooning in against Marley's back. His skin tingled everywhere they touched, from the top of his head to the tips of his toes. Draping his arm over her side, he pulled her back into him, loving the soft little moan that drifted from her lips, loving the way every inch of his skin heated, loving mostly the way her hand slid over his against her belly and her fingers closed to hold on tight.

She was asleep. Or maybe she was drifting in that semiconscious state between rest and alertness. He'd been there for a while, enjoying the feel of her against him, not wanting to think too much about how what they'd done in this room was going to change things between them. Savoring the moment for what it was: pure delight.

It was different from what had happened in the jungle. He knew that even without opening his eyes. Then, they'd both been a little high and way tipsy. Adrenaline had been pulsing. Drums had been beating. Neither of them could have stopped that night from happening if they'd tried. But this . . . this was a definite choice. He'd come back to her even though he'd known the smart move was to leave. She'd welcomed him without a single protest.

His eyes slid open. He glanced toward the window beyond her. It was still dark outside, but he knew it was getting close to dawn. In a few hours he'd have to figure out what he was going to say to her about all this. What it all meant. God knew she'd want some kind of answer—this was Marley after all. The woman planned everything.

He glanced down at the soft skin of her neck, her jaw, the edge of her lips. Remembered the things he'd whispered, the things he'd felt. Gently tugging his hand out from under hers, he brushed a lock of hair away from her cheek, awed by the silkiness of her skin and the way her lashes fluttered against her flesh.

What was he going to say? He wasn't quite sure. But he liked this. Liked the feel of her against him, liked the way she reacted to his touch, liked being with her way more than he ever should.

His chest grew tight. A familiar sense of panic pushed in, one he'd learned long ago meant he was getting too close. One that made him vulnerable. Pushing away from her, he rolled to his back, rested his hand on his bare chest, and stared up at the dark ceiling while he tried to get hold of the crazy emotions pinging around beneath his ribs.

This was why he'd kept his distance. Not because he didn't care, but because he cared too much. She thought the reason he'd chased her down to Colombia was because he thought she couldn't handle herself in the field, but that wasn't the truth. The truth was simply that he couldn't handle the thought of anything bad happening to her. Not when he knew he could be the one to make sure she stayed safe.

The pressure intensified in his chest. He rubbed his hand over the spot. He needed to tell her about Gabby. Marley knew about his parents, but she didn't know about Yemen. Maybe if she did she'd understand why he was the controlling ass he'd become. But even as he thought the words, he knew there was no way he could come right out and tell her. It wouldn't change the past. It wouldn't make any kind of difference. It wouldn't change him or this relationship growing between them.

Relationship . . .

He blew out a long breath. Wished like hell that spot against his sternum, the one that seemed to be cinching down tighter with every passing second, would just go away. That was the crux of the issue here, wasn't it? She wasn't just his assistant anymore. She wasn't his friend. She was more. And the hard reality was that he wanted more. Wanted more of this, wanted more of her, wanted more of the lighthearted warmth he felt whenever she was close.

What-if scenarios filled his head. Ones that didn't scare the shit out of him, surprisingly. He rolled toward her once more, needing to touch her, needing to feel her, needing to pull her close, and draped his arm over her waist again as he pulled her in tight. Something rigid brushed along his foot.

He pushed up on his elbow and glanced down her leg. The sheets were tangled between them, but her bare foot was tucked on top of the white cotton, and even in the darkness he could see the woven leather band tied around her ankle. The one that matched the band still tied around his ankle, which they'd both gotten in that jungle village.

The pressure eased. Warmth filled his chest when he realized she hadn't taken it off. She'd had multiple opportunities to do just that—in the helicopter when she'd been pissed at him, in the shower on his plane after they'd argued, at her father's house the last two days—and still hadn't. Which meant, to her, this was more than just physical too. It meant—

A buzzing sound echoed from the floor. Startled out of his thoughts, Jake glanced over his shoulder toward his jeans lying in a heap. The buzz sounded again. He looked toward the clock on the bedside table, thought about ignoring the call—after all, nothing good happened at 4:47 a.m.—then cursed under his breath and slid out from beneath the sheet.

He had a couple guys stationed overseas. If something had gone wrong on one of their ops, he needed to be available. Plus, if Miller had more info about who was checking into his background and properties, he wanted to know.

He grabbed his pants from the floor, tugged his phone out of the front pocket, and stared down at the screen. The message wasn't from Miller, though. It was from Dominic Brooks, his contact at the State Department, and it simply said, Check your e-mail.

Thoughts of McKnight pinged through his head. Marley would be pissed if she knew he'd been digging around in McKnight's background, so he purposely hadn't told her. But curiosity got the best of him, and he tugged on his pants. He'd just take a quick peek, then come back. Glancing once more at Marley to make sure she was still asleep, he tiptoed out of the room and closed the door softly at his back.

A smile tugged at the corner of his mouth as he moved down the steps and thought about sliding back into bed with her. About waking her with his hands and lips and tongue. It was crazy—this whole thing was crazy—but for the first time in he didn't know how long he was starting to think maybe he'd been wrong to keep his distance from people all these years. Maybe what he really needed to break his father's cycle of neglect was someone who could see through his bullshit, who knew how to deal with it, and who didn't take no for an answer.

Maybe what he'd needed all this time was Marley.

He moved into his office and sank into the chair behind his desk. After powering on the monitor, he pulled up his e-mail, then opened the message from Dom.

Ryder—

Interesting bit of info I was able to dig up. Omega's raid on Jose Moreno was indeed a State Department contract. Addison sent four men in on the job—McKnight, Sanders, Jones, and Reynolds. Jones and Reynolds were both killed in action. Sanders and McKnight were officially listed as MIA. McKnight eventually turned up. No clue where Sanders is.

Also found these photos, which I thought you might want to see. Doesn't look like your assistant has the same worries you do.

—Brooks

Jake sat back and read the first paragraph again. Before looking at the photos, he grabbed his cell and texted Pierce Bentley.

RYDER: I need you to find Darren Sanders. He worked for Omega until he was listed as MIA on a raid in Colombia five years ago. Find him or find me his death certificate. I need to know if he's still alive.

He set his phone down, confident Bentley would get right on it in the morning. The man was fresh from a week's vacation and didn't have another op scheduled for a while.

Setting his finger back on the touchpad, Jake scrolled down to look at the pictures Brooks had sent, then drew in a breath as if someone had sucker punched him straight in the gut.

The photo was of Marley and McKnight. It was clearly several years old—her hair was shorter and a little darker, and her face appeared younger, not as mature as it was now—but it didn't change Jake's gut reaction. They were standing on the patio of what looked to be a golf course. He was dressed in a charcoal suit, and she wore a formfitting red dress that hit just above the knee. Both were holding drinks and smiling. But what caught Jake's attention was the way she was looking up at McKnight as he stared at the camera. As if he were the center of the world. As if she'd found the key to happiness.

Jake scrolled down to the next picture. In this one, the two of them were seated at a candlelit dinner, neither looking at the camera, both focused only on each other. He paged down again and found one where they were both dressed in camo gear, green paint smudged over her cheek, his arms wrapped around her from behind, both holding paintball guns and laughing toward whoever had snapped the photo.

In every picture she was happy. In every picture she looked relaxed, content, not a thing like the snarky, worry-about-everyone woman he knew so well.

His stomach churned, and he forced his fingers to page down once more.

The last three photos were lined up side by side. As if taken in succession. And they didn't include Marley. They were only of McKnight. Opening a shop door, about to step inside. Coming outside holding a small, pale-blue box. And the last, standing on the street with that open box, looking down at a ring.

The first photos were clearly taken by friends. These last three—time-stamped after the others—looked to be from security footage from a store. Jake focused on the building and immediately recognized the name. Cartwright's. One of the most prestigious and well-known jewelers in all of Kentucky.

A hard, cold knot formed in the pit of his belly, chilling all the warmth he'd been feeling before. Sitting back, he scrolled up to the first picture and stared at Marley's smiling face as she looked up at McKnight.

She rarely smiled like that with Jake. He could only remember one time with him when she'd been that happy, and it was when she'd danced around the fire in that jungle village. The rest of the time she was irritated or frustrated or ready to pull her hair out because of him. Incredible sexual chemistry didn't equal happiness, and it sure didn't change any of the other issues still simmering between them or in his past. And holy hell, the guy had bought her a ring.

Out of nowhere, Marley's words in Colombia echoed in his head. *"Every woman thinks about getting married."*

His hands grew sweaty. That knot tightened in his belly. Is that what she wanted? Marriage? McKnight had obviously been ready for that. It didn't matter if the guy had given her that ring or not. Just the fact he'd bought it meant he was ten thousand steps ahead of where Jake was now or ever would be in the future.

He pushed to his feet. Covered his mouth with his hands. Tried like hell to settle the sudden pounding in his veins as he paced the length of his home office.

He didn't want to get married. Knew he'd make a shitty husband. Didn't even want to think about kids. And holy hell, Marley probably wanted that. Wanted *them*. Probably several. All women did at some point. The last thing he could fathom was screwing up some poor kid's life the way his had been screwed by his selfish parents. All that panic came raging back, only this time it rushed over him like a tidal wave, filling him like water fills the lungs of a drowning man.

Shit. *Shit!* He hadn't just messed things up, he'd fucked them royally. He'd let lust get in the way of the only thing that really mattered. And now, thanks to his inability to keep his hands to himself, he might just lose the second-best thing in his life.

She's the first. Stop fooling yourself.

She was. Which was why he couldn't let either of them be tricked into thinking this—thing—between them would ever work. Because it wouldn't. His father was right. He was a major disappointment. He'd fuck up her life sooner or later, whether he wanted to or not.

The only way to save her from himself was to let her go. And hope that maybe her loyalty to the guys, to Aegis, would be enough to make her stay.

You are so totally fooling yourself. She's gonna ditch Aegis so fast your head will spin.

She would. His eyes slid closed. But even as he accepted that, one solution came to mind. One he hoped would get through to her.

It was a long shot. She might balk. Acting like he didn't care just might kill him, but he had to give it a try.

Decision made, he flipped off the monitor and stared at the dark screen. Thought about her lying naked in his guest bed upstairs, and fought the urge to slide back between the sheets with her one more time.

His chest stretched so tight he thought it might just tear open right down the middle. But it didn't. It just kept on aching like a motherfucker.

Screw it. He headed up the stairs for the shower in his master bath. Drew up that wall that had protected him most of his adult life. Bypassed the guest room and didn't even slow his steps. And told himself that no matter what happened in the morning, he was doing the right thing.

He just hoped someday he believed it.

Marley blinked into the morning light and focused on the window only feet from the bed where she lay. The snow had stopped falling sometime in the night, and crisp winter sunlight streamed over her and the mattress, warming her underneath the thin sheet.

Her muscles were sore, but her body felt relaxed, her limbs loose, her skin alive. Memories of the night before echoed through her mind, making her skin tingle, making a sultry heat roll through her belly and slink between her legs.

She couldn't stop the smile from pulling at the corners of her mouth. Rolling to her back, she looked up at the ceiling and tried not to grin but couldn't seem stop it. She hadn't expected *that*. Hadn't expected anything really. Wasn't even sure why she'd come to Jake's house. But she'd liked it. Liked it a lot. And wanted more right this minute.

She rolled to her other side to entice Jake into another round of mind-blowing lovemaking, then frowned when she realized she was alone. Pushing up to sitting, she tugged the sheet up to her breasts and glanced around the empty room.

His jeans were gone but his sweatshirt was still on the floor in a pile. She listened, hoping to hear him somewhere in the house, but the only sound came from her—slow, uneven breaths. A whisper of worry rippled through her, and then she caught the scent of freshly brewed coffee hovering in the air. She glanced at the clock. 6:09 a.m.

It was Monday. A work day. Before she could stop it, another smile pulled at her mouth when she pictured him downstairs making coffee, trying to get her up so he could get her to the office— slave driver that he was.

She slid out of bed, reached for his sweatshirt from the floor, and slipped it on. Coffee sounded heavenly right now, but not as heavenly as dragging him back to bed for another hour or two. No one would miss them—at least not for a few hours. And what was the point of being the boss if you couldn't play hooky without consequences every now and again?

The sweatshirt hit her mid thigh, and the sleeves bunched around her wrists because they were so long. But she liked the way the cotton felt against her skin, and more than anything she liked the scent of him all over her body. Cups clinked in the kitchen, and she smiled wider when she imagined him pouring her coffee wearing nothing but that grin she'd put on his face when she'd taken him into her mouth late last night and made him forget his own name.

She was just about to reach for the door handle when she noticed her cell on the bedside table. Picking it up, she glanced at the screen, then winced. Nine missed calls. All from Gray.

She didn't want to talk to him. Didn't want to think about him right now. Replacing the phone on the nightstand, she headed out the door and down the steps. The scent of freshly brewed coffee pulled at her, but it was the man making the coffee she really wanted to see. The one who'd done and said things last night she was never going to forget.

Her feet stilled when she turned the corner and caught sight of him standing at the counter, pouring steaming liquid into two cups. The smile faded from her lips. He wasn't naked like she'd hoped. He wasn't even wearing the worn jeans he'd snagged from the floor before leaving her. He was dressed as he always was for work—Hugo Boss dress shirt, crisp Brooks Brothers slacks, Prada dress shoes that probably cost more than his couch.

He glanced over his shoulder. "Oh, you're up. I was about to wake you."

He'd clearly been up for a while now. He'd showered, shaved, and dressed. This from the man who never made it into the office before nine. Her gaze skipped to the kitchen table, where work folders were stacked as if he'd just gone through each one. And open on the table was the blue file filled with the property contracts she'd left in her car. Contracts, she could tell from where she stood, he'd already signed.

That whisper of worry morphed to a knot of apprehension in the pit of her stomach. When had he left her bed? She'd thought he'd stayed the whole night, but now she was starting to wonder if he'd stayed at all. Without making eye contact, he crossed to her, handed her the mug, careful, she noticed, not to touch her, then moved for the table.

"These are all signed, so you can fax them to the realtors." He flipped the folder closed and dropped it on top of the others. "Your car's already at the mechanic's. Should be ready this afternoon. In the meantime, you can drive the Explorer in the garage to work when you're ready. It's smaller than the Tahoe. Figured it'd be easier for you."

Two things hit her at once. They weren't going to work together, and he was leaving soon without her. The apprehension inched up to unease. An unease that made her skin prickle, and not in a good way.

She took a step toward the table, hoping she was reading too much into things and that he wasn't trying to avoid her the way it seemed. "You're up early."

"Yeah." He flipped another folder closed and tossed it on the stack. "Eve's going bat-shit crazy at the office. Said if I didn't get my ass back there today she was going to light the place on fire. I really don't want to have to file an insurance claim thanks to an unstable employee."

Marley's apprehension eased and slowly drifted away. Okay, that made sense. They'd both been away from the office for a week. Eve was probably going nuts with the paperwork and managing the guys on the ops.

Marley pulled out a chair at the table, tucked her leg under her, and sat down. She really wanted to slide over there and tug that tie off his neck, but she restrained herself—just in case. "You asked Eve to cover for me?"

"It was either her or Archer. She volunteered both of them. I said no way. Last thing I need is the two of them having sex on my desk."

Marley smiled and wrapped her hands around her warm mug. "What makes you so sure they haven't already done that?"

"Because I sent Archer to meet with a client in Dallas."

"Ah." Marley lifted the cup to her lips and sipped. "And therein lies Eve's bad mood."

"Yep." He tucked the files into his computer bag on the chair beside him. "Look, I gotta go before she sends one of the guys into a combat situation just for the fun of it, but feel free to help your-self to any food you can find. Coffee's hot, keys to the Explorer are on the hook near the garage door, and there are fresh towels in the upstairs bath if you want to take a shower."

He was running. The thought hit her hard in the stomach, made that unease come rushing back. She knew he was running because she'd done the same thing to Gray last night.

He pulled the strap of his bag over his shoulder and moved through the kitchen and then out into the living room. And feeling like an idiot, she rose and followed, unsure what to say.

This was awkward. This was morning-after-sex awkward. And way more awkward than their morning after in the jungle.

"Jake, I—"

He turned in the entryway, but he didn't meet her eyes. And though she couldn't be sure, it looked as if he were focusing on the Notre Dame emblem on her chest. "Look, about last night . . ."

When he hesitated, her unease shifted to full-on panic. Those words never preceded anything good.

His gaze finally lifted to hers. But she couldn't read his emo-tions. His dark eyes were as guarded as she'd ever seen them. "It was great. No, it was better than great, it was amazing. But—"

Oh shit, here came the *but*.

"—we can't let it happen again. It would be irresponsible con-sidering we work together and that people are relying on us to keep them alive. This last week has been way out of character for both of us, and I just think . . . I think it would be better all around if we went back to the way things were before. When everything was simple and we were just friends."

A sick feeling brewed in her stomach, one that threatened to inch its way up her throat. She swallowed it back, unable to come up with a response, unable to think about anything besides the word "friends."

A bitter reality settled hard in her gut. She was a fool. A giant, pathetic fool. She'd stupidly thought his coming to her had been the start of something incredible, when the hard, cruel truth was, to him, it had been nothing more than another one-night stand in his string of easy hookups. And now that it was over, he wanted to go back to being "friends."

"You're not saying anything, Marley."

What the hell could she say? "There really isn't anything to say, is there? It's already been said."

His shoulders relaxed. "I knew you'd see it the same way. Honestly, I'm surprised you didn't say it first." He turned and reached for the door handle behind him. "Take your time coming in this morning. I'll make sure Eve puts all your stuff back where it belongs. I know how much it irritates you when people mess with your system."

He winked at her, stepped outside, then closed the door behind him as if nothing had happened.

Marley stared at the door, listening to the sound of his engine starting. When it faded in the distance, she sank to the ground.

Her body ached, no longer in a good way, but from exhaustion. From fatigue. From knowing she'd spent three years wasting her time. Jake was never going to change. Nothing between them was ever going to change. And no matter how long she stayed, he would never see her as anything more than his secretary.

Emptiness rolled through her. No anger, no sadness, just . . . nothing. And she knew right then that she had a choice. She could keep living this life that would never be what she wanted, or she could make a change.

She pushed to her feet before her foolish heart could change her mind, moved into Jake's office, and flipped on his monitor. An e-mail popped up, but she closed it, then pulled up a Word document. Typing quickly, she hit Print, then hurried up the stairs to find her clothes and her cell phone.

Five minutes later she was dressed in the same jeans and sweater she'd worn last night. She grabbed the letter from his printer, took it into the kitchen, and used the pen he'd left on the table to sign her name. Leaving both next to the file folder he'd grabbed from her car, she stepped toward the garage door, then remembered the band around her ankle.

She perched her foot on a chair, tugged her pants up, and eyed the woven leather anklet. A sense of loss rolled through her, but she pushed it aside. The stupid bracelet didn't mean anything. It was nothing but a reminder of something that never should have happened. And now more than ever, she was ready to put it and the last three years behind her for good.

She untied the band, dropped it on the paper she'd signed, then grabbed the keys from the hook near the garage door, and headed for his Explorer.

She closed the car door at her side, then hit the garage door opener. Sunlight streamed into the garage as the door went up. Her gaze caught on her purse sitting on the passenger seat.

And for the first time since Jake had made his little morning-after announcement, anger rolled through her. A hot, bubbling anger that gave her purpose. He'd thought of everything. Everything but her.

She shoved the car into reverse, backed out of his garage, hit the button to close the door. And she didn't once look back at everything she was leaving behind.

Jake checked his cell phone for the tenth time, glanced at the clock on the wall in his office, and tried to fight back the wave of panic. It was three thirty in the afternoon, and Marley still hadn't shown up.

She wasn't coming in. He'd known she'd probably balk. He'd just hoped her loyalty to the guys would outweigh her hatred for him. Obviously he'd been wrong.

A hard, sharp ache settled beneath his breastbone. One he couldn't get rid of no matter how he tried. And it hadn't helped his mood. He was being short with anyone who came into the office, but he just couldn't stop himself. More than anything, he wanted to drive to her house and tell her he was sorry, that he was a dick, that he didn't mean it, but he couldn't. Couldn't because this time he was determined not to make things worse. He had to hold on to the hope she'd eventually see the logic in his pathetic argument, take pity on him, and come back to Aegis.

Knowing he was doing no good here, he grabbed his coat and decided—for once—he'd cut out early. He stepped out of his office and caught sight of a framed painting his father had bought at some stuffy auction. A familiar bitterness trickled through him. One that reminded him of his conversation with Marley last night.

She was right. He needed to remodel the damn place. Get every memory of his father out once and for all so he could breathe. He just prayed he wouldn't be doing it without her.

"Don't tell me you can't find the file. I know it's in there!"

The male voice coming from Marley's office drew Jake toward her door. Mick Hedley sat behind her desk, his surfer blond hair falling in his eyes as his big hands hacked at her keyboard. "What are you doing here, Hedley?"

Mick glanced up, frowned, then refocused on the screen and hit another key. "Trying to get my flight information. I'm heading to Canada to meet with a client. Marley was supposed to send it to me, but didn't."

Jake's heart pinched, but he ignored it. Moving around behind Marley's desk, he eyed the folders on the screen. "Try that one. AU."

Mick moved the cursor and clicked. Sure enough, all his information came up—personnel files, itineraries, health information. "What the hell?"

"You're Australian. Sometimes she files shit by where you guys come from."

"What if she's got two guys from the same place? How does she keep that straight?"

"Hell if I know." Jake shrugged into his coat, fighting back a small smile. Yes, her filing system aggravated the hell out of him most days, but he liked depending on her. Liked that she'd made this company part hers. Liked that every morning he could look forward to seeing her, and that he knew she'd always be there.

His smile faded. And that ache re-formed. What if she wasn't?

He needed to get out of here. Needed to clear his head. Couldn't sit around waiting. If he did, he'd just go mad. "Listen, I need to run out. Since you're here, if Marley calls, give me a ring."

Mick glanced up at him. "Where is she anyway? She's always here."

"She's taking the day off." *Please let it just be today.*

Turning out of the offices, Jake jogged down the curved staircase and moved through the reception area. Johanna, the twenty-something girl Marley had hired to man the front desk, waved at him from behind the tall counter. Voices and laughter echoed from the back room, and Jake knew Eve and Archer were in there with Raleigh Stone, but he didn't stop in to say hi. Didn't feel like shooting the shit. He just needed air. Needed space. Needed to chill the hell down before he did something that would make things worse.

Crisp air slapped him in the face as he pushed one side of the wide double doors open. Snow littered the ground but the temperature was already warming up, which meant in a few days it would be gone, and he was glad. He was ready for spring, ready for new beginnings, ready to put the last week, especially, behind him for good.

He tugged his keys out of his pocket and hit the lock button on his Tahoe twice so he could start the ignition remotely. His thoughts automatically drifted to Marley once more, and he hoped like hell she hadn't run to McKnight. He could handle a lot of things, but he wasn't sure he could handle that.

His thumb slid to the remote ignition on his fob. He pressed down on the button as he crossed the slippery parking lot toward his rig parked fifty feet away. A roar sounded, and then the vehicle erupted into a giant fireball that lifted the car off the ground and hurled Jake back through the air.

chapter 18

Marley's phone buzzed for the third time in a row. Glancing over her shoulder at it on the floor outside the closet in her bedroom, she eyed the thing like it was a two-headed dragon.

She didn't want to talk to Gray. She was already dealing with enough emotional turmoil over her night and morning with Jake. She didn't need to add in Gray's baggage as well.

Tossing a pair of shoes she hadn't worn in over a year into the pile she'd started for charity, she clenched her jaw and told herself at some point physical exhaustion would set in and she'd pass out. But she was starting to think maybe she was fooling herself. She'd already organized her panty, and the counter under the bathroom sink, and the storage closet in her guest room. The master closet was her last hope.

Her phone buzzed again before she could even reach for the next set of hideous shoes she didn't remember buying, rattling the gray matter against her skull.

"Goddammit." She snatched the phone, sat back on her heels, and hit Answer before she looked at the number. "Look, Gray. I—"

"Marley, it's Eve. Jake's on his way to the hospital."

"What?" The blood rushed from Marley's cheeks, and fear burst inside her chest. Pushing to her feet, she let go of the ugly clog and stood. "What happened?"

"His Tahoe exploded. We think it was a bomb. Paramedics just left for the ER."

Her heart lurched into her throat, and the conversation she and Jake had last night in his living room rushed through her mind. "Which hospital?" She ran for the entry closet, where she yanked out her snow boots and tugged her jacket from the hanger. "Is he okay?"

"Norton Suburban. I don't know. He's pretty banged up."

Oh God, oh God, oh God. Please be okay. "I'm on my way."

She bolted out the front door and slid behind the wheel of her Audi, which she'd picked up earlier in the day from the mechanic, and backed out of her drive. Her heart pounded hard as she maneuvered through traffic and found a parking space outside the ER.

Jogging into the building, she rushed up to the counter. "Jake Ryder. The ambulance just brought him in."

"Hold on while I check." The nurse fiddled on her computer, and Marley only barely held back from climbing over the counter and shaking the info out of the woman. "Ah, here he is. Are you family?"

"Yes."

"Bay fourteen. Go through the double—"

Marley didn't wait to hear the rest of the woman's words. She hurried toward the double doors and pressed the button on the wall to open them. The doors slid back way too slowly. Her adrenaline spiked. As soon as the doors parted, she sprinted through the opening and scanned numbers along the curtained rooms on each side of the hall.

"I don't need stitches. I just want to get the hell out of here."

Jake's voice echoed in her ears, and she stopped, turned, realized she'd passed his bay, and rushed back. Grasping the curtain, she jerked it open. He was sitting on the bed, his chest bare, his eyes red, his hair and face covered in a thin layer of soot from the explosion. A nurse stood next to him, rubbing an alcohol pad over a gash in his arm with gloved hands.

The nurse looked over. "Miss, you can't be in he—"

"Marley," Jake said, swiveling his head her way.

She stepped into the room, swallowed hard to keep the contents of her stomach from shooting up, and eyed the blood rushing down his arm and smeared across his chest. "Eve called. Oh my God. Are you okay?"

"Fine." He glared at the dark-haired thirty-something nurse wearing blue hospital scrubs. "Nurse Ratchet over here was just going to slap some butterfly bandages on my arm and call it good."

The nurse shot him an irritated look and then glanced toward Marley. "He needs stitches, and he's being difficult." She grabbed a gauze pad from the bed at his side and slapped it against the wound on his arm. Jake winced in pain, but it didn't even faze the nurse. "Hold this here." She tugged her gloves off and dropped them in a bin, then stepped past Marley. "I'm getting the doctor. Don't let him leave."

The nurse disappeared around the corner, and, holding the pad against his arm, Jake turned his scowling expression Marley's way. "Did Eve tell you what happened?"

"Yes. Oh my God." She took a step toward him. "Jake—"

"I told you he was up to no good. But you didn't listen."

Her feet stilled before she reached him, and her brow wrinkled. "He who?"

"McKnight."

It took a second to realize what he was saying, and then her eyes flew wide. "You think Gray did this?"

"I know he did. He's got you on the radar, and he's been shooting daggers at me ever since we rescued his ass. I saw how many times he called your damn cell phone last night. Doesn't take a rocket scientist to put two and two together and figure out where you were. And he's been checking out my background and properties."

"You said that was the Red Brotherhood."

"No, *you* said it was the Red Brotherhood. I had a hunch it was McKnight. I just didn't say so to keep from pissing you off."

Frustration and disbelief rolled through her stomach, pushing aside whatever compassion she'd been feeling about his injury. "You've crossed paths with plenty of bad guys in your life, Jake. There are a thousand people who probably want to see you dead. You are seriously losing it if you think Gray had anything to do with this. I know him. For all his faults, he's not a murderer."

Jake's jaw clenched down hard, and he looked toward the white board on the wall. "Then fine. Get back to the office and help me figure out who did this to me."

Her mouth opened, and the word "yes" dangled on her tongue. But then she remembered his blank eyes this morning and the way he'd brushed her off like their night together hadn't meant anything.

She couldn't go back to that. Not when she knew for sure that she did love him, and that he didn't love her back.

"I'm not going back with you. I can't. You'll have to figure this one out on your own."

His gaze snapped to hers. "Mar—"

"I'm done with Aegis. I left my resignation letter on your kitchen table this morning." Oh God, this hurt more than she'd thought it would, but she pulled up her strength and didn't let that stop her. "And considering everything that's happened between us, I think it's smarter all around if we both bypass the two-week notice and call things quits right here."

She turned for the door. At her back, she heard him scramble off the bed. "Marley, hold on."

Every muscle in her wanted turn back, to go to him, but her battered heart wouldn't let her give in. She stepped through the doorway, desperate now to escape. To her luck, the nurse moved into the room just after her and held up both hands. "Whoa. Where do you think you're going? Get back on that bed."

"I'm leaving."

"Not like that you aren't," the nurse said.

Marley slipped around the nurse. A young doctor in blue scrubs with a stethoscope around his neck stepped into the room as well.

"Goddammit, Marley," Jake said behind them. "Please. Just wait."

She couldn't. Without looking back, she headed down the hall for reception, her hands shaking, her body vibrating with a heartache that came out of nowhere and stabbed at every inch of her skin. But as much as it hurt, she knew she was doing the right thing. The only thing she could do. She just hated every moment of it.

Jake lowered the Glock in his hand, grabbed the second magazine from the counter in front of him, lifted his arms, and fired toward the target in rapid succession. A burn lit up his biceps where he'd been injured by flying debris in the explosion four days ago, but he ignored it.

On the range around him, gunshots echoed through the shooting earmuffs protecting his eardrums. He lowered his weapon and set it on the counter. Gunfire in the next booth halted. Jake pulled the muffs off his ears, then hit the button on the wall to draw his target toward him.

Mick Hedley chuckled as he hit his own target return. "That time I know I beat you."

Jake wasn't feeling particularly competitive at the moment. Or friendly. But he'd let Hedley drag him to the range when the man had walked into the office after returning from his assignment in Canada because he knew he was being a bear to anyone who walked by. He also knew if he didn't do something to release the pent-up frustrations inside him, someone else might try to take him out, and he didn't want it to be one of his own employees.

He eyed the target as it drew close. One shot dead between the eyes, a series of holes right through the heart, exactly where he'd aimed. But he barely saw the outline of a body on the paper. All he could see was Marley's face in the hallway of the ER days ago, when she'd stood behind that doctor and told him she was done with Aegis for good.

That sinking feeling grabbed on to his stomach and pulled hard. The same one he'd felt when he'd gone home and found her ankle bracelet on his kitchen table and read her letter of resignation.

"Shit," Hedley said in the booth at his side. "That's not fair. You're fucking ticked and you still shoot like that. It's not right, man. It's just not right."

Jake reloaded his magazine, desperate for something—any-thing—to take his mind off Marley. "When I'm drunk I don't shoot so well."

"I'll remember that." Hedley rolled up his target. "So the party starts at seven. A few of us are going over around eight. Don't want to get there too early, don't want to be too late, you know?"

Jake slid his weapon into the holster at his side, then tugged his target from the clips. He didn't normally carry a weapon unless he was in the field, but his car exploding hadn't just rattled him, it had pissed him the hell off. "What party?"

"Addison's big shindig. You are going, aren't you?"

Confusion clouding his mind, Jake stepped out from behind the wall separating the two booths and looked toward Hedley. The Aussie was wearing jeans, a black button-down, and boots, and, standing on the range with a gun in his hand, the former Special Air Service Regiment of Australia soldier looked every bit the badass Jake knew him to be. He was also looking at Jake as if Jake had grown a second head.

"Dude," Hedley said. "Tell me you know about this. Eve left the invite on your desk two days ago. Marley's dad's throwing a big welcome home celebration for McKnight."

A roiling anger brewed in the pit of Jake's stomach. He grabbed his stuff and turned for the door. "I didn't know about it, and I'm definitely not going."

"You have to go," Hedley said at his back. "You helped rescue the guy."

Jake pushed the door to the parking lot open and stepped out into the crisp March air and fading light of late afternoon. "He blew up my fucking rig."

Hedley sighed. "You don't have any proof of that. Cops haven't found anything that points to him, and your own team hasn't been able to prove it. You could be wrong about the guy, you know."

He could be. But in his gut, Jake knew he wasn't. "It was him."

"So that's why you won't go? Because you think he did something he probably didn't do?"

"Yes." Jake opened the door of his Explorer.

"Bullshit."

He glared over his shoulder toward Hedley. "Excuse me?"

"Excuse nothing. You're being a pussy and we both know it. This isn't about McKnight, it's about Marley. Whatever shit's going on between you two, you need to suck it up and get over it. I don't care if you think he's a douchebag or a fucking idiot or even if he did blow up your truck. You need to be there for her. You owe her that much after the years she's invested in you. And if you can't do that for her, then she's not the only one you're gonna have to replace."

Jake's eyes narrowed. "Are you threatening me?"

Hedley slid his hands into the front pockets of his jeans in a very nonthreatening way and rocked back on his heels. "No. I'm just saying plainly that you're no peach on a good day, but ever since Marley left you've been a complete pain in the ass. I'm not the only one who's noticed. If you don't trust McKnight and you don't want Marley anywhere near him, then don't stand here pouting like a little bitch. And don't take it out on the rest of us. Go get her back."

Jake's stomach tightened. He did want her back. Wanted her back at Aegis and wanted her back with him. Like they'd been that night at his house. That was all he'd thought about for the last four days. But he was scared. Scared he'd mess things up again. Scared he'd never be what she really needed. Scared of taking a chance and failing with her like he'd failed with everyone else he'd ever cared about.

Hedley turned for his truck. "Eight o'clock. If you're not there by eight, I'm coming after you. And trust me, you do not want me dragging your ass there by the scruff of the neck."

Jake climbed into his vehicle, closed the door, and just sat behind the wheel in silence as he stared out at the melting patches of snow and thought of Marley.

The cell in his pocket buzzed before he could decide what to do, and he pulled it out and hit Answer without looking at the caller ID. "What?"

"Hey, it's Bentley. I checked into that text you sent me. I can't find a death certificate on Sanders. I've got a buddy in Colombia, though, who thinks he might have come across the guy in the last year or two."

Jake sat up straighter. That meant Sanders could still be alive and might know what had really happened on that raid. "Fucking find him."

"Are you authorizing travel to Colombia?"

"You bet your ass I am. Take my plane."

"All right. Ridin' in style. You got it, boss. I'll call when I know more."

Jake clicked off his phone. Thought of Marley again and frowned. Sonofabitch. He did not want to go to any stupid party, least of all one for McKnight.

chapter 19

Marley swallowed the last sip of champagne in her glass and noticed the waiter walking by with a fresh tray. "Oh. Wait." The waiter turned her way. "I'll have another one."

She placed her empty glass on the tray, grabbed a fresh one, and took a large sip of the bubbly liquid.

At her side, Gray muttered, "You might want to go easy on that. You haven't eaten much today."

Irritation pulsed through her. She hadn't eaten much in several days, but she wasn't about to confess that. And she didn't like his telling her what to do.

"I'm fine." Sipping again, she glanced around the ballroom of her father's stuffy country club and tried to settle her frazzled nerves.

Tables and chairs were set up around a dance floor. A three-piece orchestra played a depressing tune in the corner, and food was laid out on a giant table along one wall. Several double doors opened to an enormous deck that ran around the clubhouse, and twinkle lights in the potted plants and trees and space heaters out-side shone through the glass.

Several couples danced in the middle of the room, and clusters of her father's friends chatted and sipped their drinks. Before Marley could take another sip, Gray plucked the flute from her hand and set it on a passing waiter's tray. "Come on. I've been dying to dance with you all night, and your father's buddies have finally left us alone."

He grasped her hand and dragged her out onto the dance floor. Not wanting to make a scene, she let him pull her into his arms and rested her hand on his shoulder while his slid around her lower back.

He tugged her in tighter than she liked, turned their clasped hands in close to his chest, and hummed along to the tune.

It was too close. Too romantic. And she hated that her mind drifted to Jake.

She hadn't seen him in four days. Not since the emergency room. He hadn't texted, hadn't called, hadn't once tried to reach out to her, and though part of her wanted him to, another part didn't even know what she could say in response. She'd let her emotions get the best of her in the ER, and now that her temper had cooled, she felt wretched about that scene and especially about how they'd ended things. Worse even than the morning after their crazy night at his place. Because then she'd just been heartbroken. Now she felt as if she'd lost her best friend.

"It's nice of your father to host this party," Gray said softly in her ear. "He didn't have to."

She tried not to think about the reason for this party. Tried not to remember those steamy days and nights in the jungle with Jake and how much she'd enjoyed them even though she'd acted like she hadn't. "He's glad you're back."

"I know. But the big question is, are you?" Gray leaned away and looked down, his green eyes brimming with emotion—an emo-tion that hit Marley hard in the belly. "Are you glad I'm back?"

He wanted an answer, wanted to know how she felt about him, and the truth was that she didn't have a clue. Yes, she was glad he was back, and yes she wanted him to be happy, but she just wasn't convinced that happiness would ever happen with her. And she didn't want to hurt him when he'd already been through so much. He hadn't said a word about their conversation over dinner Sunday night, but the way he kept doting on her, the way he wouldn't leave her side, the fact he was looking at her now as if she was his everything, it made her hands grow sweaty and that panic re-form beneath her ribs.

"Gray, I—"

"You know, before I left on that mission, I bought you a ring. I didn't buy it for the right reasons, but I put it in a safety deposit box, and I still have it. I can't make up for the past, but I can promise you that the future will be very different. And I want to give that ring to you now because this is all that matters." His hand tightened around hers against his chest. "You are all that matters. I want you to be my wife, Marley."

The blood rushed out of her cheeks. Her feet stilled, and she stared up at him, unable to believe he'd just said those words. One phrase echoed in her head—*Oh my God, oh my God, oh my God*—but she couldn't make her lips and vocal cords work to get it out.

"I know it's sudden," he said, pulling her against him once more so her chin rested against his shoulder, "but we're going to be happy together. I promise. You'll see. We'll be so very happy together."

She was completely speechless. Didn't know what the hell to do or say. Her wide eyes scanned the ballroom over his shoulder. She caught her father's eye across the room where he was standing next to his new assistant or girlfriend or whatever the hell she was. He smiled and winked at her in approval. And right then Marley knew she was in deep shit.

She had to put a stop to this. She had to set Gray straight, set her father straight, stop letting them manipulate her into something she wasn't ready for. They'd both done that to her once before—in very different ways—but she wasn't that person anymore, and she wasn't going to fall back into old patterns.

She let go of his hand and pushed against his shoulder. "Gray, I—"

"Hm," Gray said into her hair. "Looks like your friends from Aegis finally showed up."

Hope bloomed in Marley's chest, pushing aside every other thought and worry. She swiveled her head and watched as Eve and Zane stepped into the room, Eve decked out in a sparkly black cocktail dress that showed off her curves, and Zane wearing smart back slacks, a white dress shirt, and a black tie that made his hair look even darker. Behind them, Mick Hedley and Raleigh Stone were dressed in much the same way, while Landon and Olivia Miller followed hand in hand. But there was no sign of Jake. And though Marley had tried not to expect too much, her spirits dropped lower than they'd been before.

She swallowed back the disappointment, told herself she was being foolish—again. She didn't even know what she'd say to Jake if he did show up. But she knew she had to get away from Gray right this minute before she had a mental breakdown.

She pushed out of his arms. "I-I need to go say hello."

"Sure." He released his hold on her, but before she could get a step away, he caught her by the hand and drew her back. Then he leaned close and slowly brushed his lips over hers in a move that was every bit possessive and made the hairs on her nape stand straight, especially as it was the first time he'd kissed her since being home. "Don't be gone long. I can't live without you, you know."

Her stomach rolled. She wanted to jerk back and say hell no, she didn't know that, but restrained herself. After the party, when everyone was gone, then she'd set him straight. Right now she didn't want to ruin her father's night and draw unwanted attention, especially when what she really wanted to do was scream.

Carefully, she eased away from him and headed across the ballroom toward Eve and the others. But her legs felt like gelatin, and by the time she reached the group, she was shocked she hadn't melted into a puddle right in the middle of the room.

"Hey. You all made it." She shored up her strength, hugged Eve and Zane, Raleigh, Mick, Landon, and finally Olivia. "I wasn't sure if any of you were going to come."

"Are you kidding?" Mick slipped an arm around Marley's waist and drew her to his side. "Free grog and tucker? Don't have to twist my arm."

The group laughed. Eve rolled her eyes. "Jesus, Hedley. Speak English. We're in America, not the land down under."

"Leave the poor guy alone," Olivia said, brushing her blonde hair to the side. "I think he's cute."

Mick placed a hand over his heart and smiled. "Someone loves me." He winked at Marley, then angled his thumb toward Landon. "That's because I taught her a few moves for when this guy gets out of line."

"Don't get any ideas, idiot." Landon glared at Mick. Then to his wife at his side, he said, "Hedley is not cute. Annoying as hell. But definitely not cute."

Olivia slid her fingers over Landon's cheek. "Don't be jealous, sweetie. I know a little secret. I'm going home with you, and I'm a sure thing."

He leaned down and kissed her. Mick made gagging noises, and the rest of the group laughed.

Unable to stand too much happiness, Marley focused on Eve. "Is anyone else coming?"

"Walker's in Nashville with Grace," Zane said, sliding an arm around his fiancée's waist. "Tierney's still in Europe on assignment,

Bentley's—hell, I can't remember where he went—and Blackwell's at a premiere for his wife. Lucky sonofabitch gets to walk the red carpet with Angeline Jolie."

"Hey." Eve elbowed Zane in the ribs. "Stop fantasizing about Hollywood celebrities. I'm standing right here."

Zane grinned and rubbed the spot, but didn't loosen his hold on Eve. "Trust me, I know. I have the bruises to prove it."

The group laughed again, and Hedley—already eyeing the buffet table—released Marley. "I see some ribs with my name on them." He smacked Raleigh in the stomach with the back of his hand. "Come on, mate."

Raleigh shook his head and glanced toward Marley before stepping away from the group. "He ate before he got here. The guy's like a bottomless pit."

Marley smiled. She knew full well how much Mick could eat. "Luckily, my father can afford it."

As soon as the two men moved away, Eve's smile faded. "I haven't heard from Jake. I don't know if he's coming."

"Hedley said he talked to him," Landon added at Marley's side. "Reminded him about tonight."

"Yeah, well." Marley tried not to be disappointed again as she crossed her arms over her chest. She shouldn't have let her father talk her into wearing the tight green satin dress. She'd have been much more comfortable in black, like Eve. But she'd wanted to please him—something else she was going to stop doing. "Jake does what he wants, when he wants. That's no surprise."

"Holy crap, you don't even know the half of it," Eve said. "He's been a complete nightmare the last week. Seriously, Marley. You *have* to come back. If he makes me work in the office one more day, *I* might try to blow him up."

Landon chuckled. Zane grinned. But Marley didn't share in their humor. Not a bit. Because just the thought of the way Jake had looked in the ER made her pulse skip up and nausea roll through her belly.

"What's happening with that, by the way? Did you figure out who did it?"

"No," Landon said. "Investigators said the bomb was attached to the ignition. They don't have any leads yet, but whoever placed it obviously didn't expect Ryder to use a remote starter. Which is pretty freakin' stupid if you ask me because most cars these days have those. Ryder got lucky."

Very lucky. Marley had a memory flash of the panic she'd experienced when she'd heard he'd been injured, felt it echo in her chest. But her mind drifted toward what Landon had just said. "Maybe they weren't trying to kill him, just warn him."

"About what?" Zane asked. "Whoever it was hasn't made any kind of demand. If it was a warning, none of us know what it was for, even Ryder."

Marley chewed on the inside of her lip. She knew full well there were plenty of people who disliked Jake Ryder. He'd been a hard-ass in the navy. And an even harder-ass since opening Aegis. And recently, she could think of a number of individuals who wouldn't bat an eyelash at killing him in retaliation for messing up their plans, including one well-known terrorist group based in Europe and another CIA mole Jake had helped expose.

"Speak of the devil," Olivia murmured. "I guess he decided to show after all."

Marley's heart jerked, and she glanced toward the ballroom doors. Jake stepped into the room wearing a crisp black suit and a pale-blue tie against a white shirt. His shoes were shiny, his hair was perfectly combed, and though Marley saw him in slacks and a dress shirt every day at work, something about this outfit—not just the clothes but the way he wore them—ignited a burn low in her stomach.

He scanned the room, then his eyes locked on hers, and her pulse shot up even higher. He didn't smile, but he didn't glance away. And as he headed for their group, her pulse turned to a roar in her ears.

He stopped between the two couples, shook hands with the men and nodded at Eve and Olivia, then slipped his hands into his pockets. "Where are the other yahoos?"

The question was directed at the group, but his dark gaze was locked solidly on Marley, and she felt the heat of his stare across the distance. Felt the electricity sizzling between them. Felt the same fire sparking that had consumed her not once, but twice before.

"Already raiding the buffet," Zane answered. He glanced down at Eve. "Which is where I think we ought to be."

Eve looked at Marley, then at Jake. "Um, yeah. Definitely. Olivia? Landon? Want to join us?"

"Absolutely," Olivia said, already stepping away and dragging Landon with her. "Catch you both later."

Marley watched them go and knew they were all cutting and running from what they thought might be an explosive confrontation. She couldn't blame them, but she didn't particularly like the guys at Aegis knowing her business. And she liked even less that this was happening in the center of the ballroom.

Okay, say something. Anything. She swallowed once. "I, uh, wasn't sure you'd come."

"I wasn't sure I would either."

His face was stoic, his expression guarded. And she couldn't read his eyes, which only frustrated her more. "How's the arm?"

"Sore but still working."

She exhaled a slow breath. He wasn't making this easy on her. But then, she couldn't really blame him. She knew she'd left him in the lurch at work, but she was still hurt over the fact the only thing he cared about was Aegis.

"Marley, Marley, Marley, Marley . . ."

The way he'd said her name over and over that night at his house when they'd made love echoed in her head. And the emotion in his voice, the urgency, the need . . . it all hit her hard, right beneath the breastbone.

She was lying to herself. She knew he did care about something more than Aegis. He cared about her. He was just afraid to admit it, even to himself.

"I need to tell you something," he said before she could find her voice. "Something important."

Surprise rippled through her. "Um. Okay."

"Outside, if you don't mind." He glanced over her shoulder, and his features hardened. "Away from prying eyes."

Without turning, Marley knew Gray was staring at her from across the room, watching her as he'd been watching her all night. A shiver rushed down her spine.

"Yeah," she said. "I think that's a good idea."

A whisper of relief rushed over her as he took her elbow and turned her toward the glass doors that opened to the veranda. Tingles raced over her flesh where his fingers grazed her skin, and nerves brewed in her belly. What did he want to say? What was so important that he had to say it now? As they headed for the door, every cell in her body vibrated with uncertainty and anticipation.

"Ladies and gentlemen." Just as they reached the doors, her father's voice boomed over the sound system, interrupting the music. "Thank you all for being here tonight to welcome home not just a former employee of Omega Intel, but a man who has become a true friend to us all."

Dammit. Marley turned near the doors and looked back to the center of the dance floor where her father stood with a microphone in one hand and the other perched on Gray's shoulder. She couldn't leave now. Not when her father was making his big speech. At her side, Jake looked back toward the two men as well, but the scowl on his face said he wanted to stay even less than Marley.

"He won't be long," Marley whispered, leaning toward Jake, trying like hell not to get lost in his familiar scent of leather and citrus and spice. "I read his note cards earlier. Should be short and sweet."

Jake angled toward her as well, and his hand slid around her lower back, igniting a rush of tingles straight down her spine. "Let's hope he hasn't been drinking and decides to wing it."

Oh God. His touch . . . It was all she could do not to turn in to it and pull him close. But then she realized what he was remembering. Her father's Christmas party only a few months before. When Mason Addison had one too many whiskey sours late into the night, grabbed the microphone, and started singing "I Will Survive."

That easy, relaxed sensation she'd always felt around Jake until recently came raging back, making her think . . . maybe. Maybe this wasn't the end. Maybe there was hope for something. She was just too afraid to think what that something could be just yet.

"As many of you know," her father went on, dropping his arm from Gray's shoulder and looking out over the crowd, "we come into this business from varied backgrounds, many of which are not all that pleasant. The first time this man walked into my office five and a half years ago, I saw a cocky, arrogant soldier who didn't know the first thing about being a team player. I'll admit, there was a time when I wasn't sure about his intentions or his loyalties. But I was wrong. The man standing beside me now hasn't just lived through more than any man should have to endure, he's come through the ordeal stronger, more confident, and with a will to live like I've never seen. His survival is a testament to the strength of his character, and I for one am happy to welcome him back not just to our community, but to Omega as well." Her father turned toward Gray. "You'll always have a job at Omega, McKnight. As long as you want one."

Gray shook his hand. Over the noise of guests clapping, Gray said, "Thank you."

Jake let go of Marley and begrudgingly clapped at her side. Another whisper of disappointment swept through her over the loss of his touch. Then he leaned close again, distracting her from anything but him. "Looks like Omega's going to be stuck with him."

Marley watched the two men embrace, and a sinking feeling filled her chest. If she took her father up on his offer to work for him, like he wanted her to do, she'd be working alongside Gray as well. And that meant what she had to say to Gray after the party was going to make things complicated.

Her father clapped his hand on Gray's shoulder and faced the crowd once more, a beaming smile across his weathered face. "And on a personal note, I'm thrilled to welcome McKnight to the family." Her father's eyes locked on hers across the room. "A little bird just informed me that my daughter said yes. Consider yourselves all invited to the wedding."

Cheers erupted in the ballroom, and all eyes turned on Marley. A ringing sounded in her ears as she glanced around at the sea of smiling faces focused on her. A ringing that rose in decibels until it was all she could hear.

Did her father just say . . . ? No, she had to have heard him wrong.

"Oh, they're getting married!" someone exclaimed. "After all this time. That's the sweetest thing I've ever heard!"

Married.

Wedding.

Shaking, Marley turned to Jake, desperate for him to help, for him to do something to get her the hell out of there. But when her eyes met his, everything inside her chilled. His dark gaze was as hard and icy as she'd ever seen it.

"I . . . But . . . He . . ." She couldn't get the words out. They stumbled on her tongue, came out as a brainless stutter.

The muscles in his jaw clenched down hard, and his voice dropped to a hoarse whisper. "Congratulations."

He turned and left, moving behind the crowd that was pushing toward her from all sides. Marley's legs wobbled. She took a step to follow him, but Gray rushed over and pulled her with him, back toward her father in the middle of the room.

"Don't be mad," he whispered near her ear. "He misunderstood. I asked if I could propose, not that I already had. But this is a good mistake. Now that everyone knows, we can focus on the ceremony and what comes after."

His words floated in Marley's head like a fog. The room spun around her. Her vision blurred. A line of people she couldn't identify hugged her and wished her well. The orchestra played a festive song as muddled faces passed. Champagne corks popped and glasses clinked through the room, but her head grew lighter and lighter, and the only thing she could hear was Jake's hurt voice echoing in her head.

Congratulations . . .

Panic trickled through her chest. He'd wanted to tell her something. He'd said it was important. But her father had interrupted him before he'd had the chance. Oh God. He thought . . .

Congratulations.

Panic turned to a fear that shook every part of her body. She gripped Gray's arm on her left, then her father's on her right, but she didn't look at either man. "I'll be right back."

"Marlene," Gray said as she turned away from them both. "Wait."

"Marley?" Her father's voice rang out at her back. "Are you okay?"

Was she okay? Hell no. She was about to lose it. And she needed to find Jake before that happened.

Voices echoed. She didn't stop, couldn't turn and look, didn't answer. She headed for the exit, didn't even bother to search for Jake in the crowd. Knew instinctively that he'd already left.

Cool air slapped across her face as she stepped outside the clubhouse and scanned the main parking lot, every space full. She couldn't see him. Couldn't see his Explorer anywhere under the lights, either. Turning for the path that veered off down the hill to the lower parking lot, she picked her way around patches of melting snow, prayed she didn't slip on the ice in her heels, and hoped like hell she caught up with him before he drove off.

She rounded the corner. A utility building sat ahead and to her left. Trees lined the dark areas of the golf course to her right. Two hundred yards below, the flicker of parking lot lights shone down the hill in the distance, and Jake's silhouette strode away from her on the path.

Urgency coiled insider her, pushed her feet forward, colored every thought and feeling and emotion she had. "Jake."

He turned at the sound of her voice, and she saw then what she'd missed in the ballroom when he'd kissed her cheek. He was livid. His eyes on fire. His body humming with a fury he only just held back.

"Go back inside to your fiancé," he ground out.

"That's all you have to say to me?" She closed the distance between them. "Nothing else?"

His eyes narrowed to hard, sharp, dangerous points as she drew close. "What do you want me to say? Your father said it all inside."

He turned away again, but she caught him by the arm and yanked him back to face her, her own temper ticking up that he would so easily believe what her father had announced in there. "Bullshit. There's a hell of a lot more only you're too afraid to say it. Tell me how you really feel. Get mad at me. Yell. Do something, dammit. Because I know it's in there. I deserve to know what that is after everything you've put me through the last few days."

"Everything I've put *you* through?" His eyes flew wide. "You're the one getting *married*."

Shock rippled through her. He really did believe it. "I told you in the jungle that I wasn't in love with him. You know how manipulative my father can be. I can't believe you'd accept this as truth without talking to me about it. I can't believe you'd just walk away like it—I—mean nothing."

"Are you saying you're not engaged to that asshole?" He held up his arm and pointed back toward the clubhouse. "Is that what you're telling me? Because everyone in that damn ballroom thinks you are, including me. God Almighty, your father invited everyone to your fucking wedding."

Just the fact she had to explain herself to him told her loud and clear that he didn't get it. That he didn't get her. And he never would. And the longer she stood here beating her head against a wall with him, the worse off she'd be in the long run. "It's a misunderstanding, Jake. My father wants it. Gray wants it—"

"And what the hell do you want?"

Her jaw clenched down hard because he should already know, dammit. And the sting of his words told her didn't have a freakin' clue.

She held her hands out to the side. "I don't know what I want anymore. I thought I wanted you, but now I know that was just a giant waste of time." She dropped her arms. "I'll tell you what I definitely don't want, though. I don't want a man who's so blind he can't see what's right in front of him."

She turned back up the path, heartache and stupidity vibrating in her limbs as she moved. But his hand closed around her bare arm and jerked her back to face him before she could get two steps away.

She gasped in surprise. His other hand closed over her opposite arm, and he shoved her off the path and up against the wall of the utility building. "You think that's what I am?" he growled. "Blind? You don't have a clue. I see everything. I see you. I see—"

ELISABETH NAUGHTON

He squeezed her arms, but she barely felt it. All she could focus on was his hard body pressed against hers and the fire simmering in his dark eyes as he stared down at her. A fire she knew burned hotter than the one that had consumed them before.

His gaze darted to his hands where he held her and widened, as if he hadn't realized he'd grabbed her. Releasing her quickly, he stepped back. But she wasn't ready to let him go. She tangled her fingers in the fabric of his shirt, pulled hard, and drew him close to her once more.

"You see what?" She rose up on her toes and jerked harder. "Tell me. Stop pretending like you don't care. I know you do. I know—"

"Dammit, Marley."

He moved so fast she barely saw him. Gripping her face in his hands, he shoved her up against the side of the building, and closed his mouth over hers. And the instant he did, that fire raging between them completely imploded.

chapter 20

Heat was all he felt. Heat and a driving need to prove to her—and himself—that he wasn't afraid.

Jake's hand closed around Marley's breast in the tight, strapless green gown and squeezed hard as he bit down on her bottom lip. He licked the spot and pushed his tongue back into her mouth. She groaned, shoved at his jacket, tangled her tongue with his in a ferocious battle for control. The jacket got stuck at his shoulders. He didn't bother to take it off.

His hands streaked down to the hem of her dress just above her knee. He yanked it up to her hips as he devoured her mouth. She groaned and kissed him harder. Reaching between her legs, he wrapped his fingers around her panties and yanked hard.

Lace tore. She pulled her mouth back from his and gasped. Leaning forward, he breathed hot over the soft column of her neck, pushed her legs apart with his knees, stepped in close, then slid his fingers down her hot, steamy center, already wet and ready for his touch.

"Oh," she groaned.

Her hands streaked up into his hair, grabbed on, and pulled tight. He bit down on her slick flesh, and she cried out. The sound excited him, aroused him, made him frantic for more. Sweeping his tongue over the spot again and again, he pushed two fingers up inside her, found her clit with his thumb and circled.

She dropped her head back against the wall, moaned low in her throat. He twisted his fingers inside her, swirled his thumb faster. Needed to hear her cry of release. Needed everything.

"Jake . . ." She wiggled against the wall, tried to inch herself higher in his arms. He thrust his fingers in and out, harder, deeper, frantic to make her feel all the things he couldn't say.

Grabbing his head, she tugged his mouth back to hers. Her tongue pushed between his lips, her taste seared his soul. The need to get inside her, to consume her, overwhelmed every inch of him.

He pulled his fingers from her tight sheath, unsnapped the button on his slacks, and pushed down the zipper. Licking into her mouth again and again, he freed his erection, dropped his hands to her ass, and lifted. Then he pressed her back into the wall and plunged inside her in one hard thrust.

"Oh fuck." She pulled her mouth from his and groaned. "Jake . . ."

He couldn't see anything but her. Couldn't feel anything but the tight, slick pressure all around his cock, making every inch of his skin absolutely burn. He drew out, thrust back in deep. Did it again. And again. And again. She moaned, tightened around him, dropped her head against his shoulder, and hung on while he drove into her.

More. Deeper. Harder . . .

The words echoed in his head. The friction grew hotter. And her moans . . . her moans of absolute pleasure grew higher and faster and longer and sweeter.

He needed to own her, to make sure there was no room left inside her for anyone else. Slapping one hand against the wall, he tightened the other around her ass and thrust again and again, desperate to prove to her and to him that she was his.

Her fingers gripped his hair. Her body tightened all around him. And before she lifted her head and cried out, he knew she was coming. Knew the orgasm he was desperate to feel was already washing over her, dragging her down and devouring every part of her.

He drove harder, couldn't stop thrusting. Needed to go over with her, needed that release to settle the raging anger that had been tormenting him the last few days. Sweat broke out all along his skin. His fingernails dug into the soft flesh of her ass and scraped along the cement wall of the building. He plunged into her again and again. Felt it coming, knew it was right there. Knew if he could just reach it—

Marley screamed, her cry echoed in his ears. Then her sex clenched down hard on his cock, dragging his orgasm straight out of his balls. He shoved in hard one more time and groaned as it ricocheted through him, blinding him with the intensity, until all that was left was darkness.

The sound of her heavy breaths slowly cleared in his ears. Against his skull, he felt her fingers softly drifting through his hair. Blinking, he tried to drag air into his tight lungs, then realized his head was resting on her shoulder and that somehow her feet were on the ground and one of her arms was wrapped around his back, holding him up against her.

A gust of cool air swept across the damp skin of his nape, sending a shiver down his spine, making him realize something else. They were outside in the cold. His gaze skipped past the soft skin of her throat to the remnants of snow littering the ground from last week's storm, then to the cement wall of one of the golf course's outbuildings where he held her pressed against the cold stone.

A dark feeling gathered in the pit of his stomach. A bitter reminder from the ghost of his father, telling him he was a disappointment, that eventually he let everyone down, that he'd never amount to anything more than his white trash mother. Closing his eyes, he tried to push the voice away, already hating himself enough, hating that he'd lost control, hating most of all that he'd done it with Marley. The only person who'd ever truly supported him.

He pushed away from her, pulled her skirt down, then cringed when he saw the seam was ripped along the side near the hem.

He tucked himself back into his pants and fixed his shirt. Against the wall, Marley shifted her weight. "Jake."

He held up a hand so she couldn't touch him. Wasn't sure he could handle that right now. Not after what he'd just done. "Go back to the party."

He took a step away, but she grasped his arm, stopping him from leaving. "That's it? You're just walking away?"

He looked up at a dark branch over his head. No, that wasn't it for him. It was never going to be it for him. But it had to be for her. All he was doing was making her miserable, and it had to end.

"I-I shouldn't have come to the party."

"Yes, you should have. I want you here, in case you can't tell. And you can't leave yet. You still haven't told me what you wanted to talk about."

His gaze slid to hers. And he saw then what he'd missed moments before. She wasn't upset. She wasn't even angry anymore. The emotions swirling in her eyes were warm and sweet and encapsulating. They were also everything he'd ever wanted and more.

She loved him.

His chest grew so warm, he thought it might explode. And every muscle in his body urged him to reach for her, to draw her close. Then he noticed her wild hair and swollen lips. And as his gaze drifted to her torn dress, he realized it didn't matter.

He drew back when all he really wanted to do was grab her and hold on. "This thing between us isn't healthy. You know that."

"I'm fine, Jake." Her hand dropped from his arm, but she stepped close, panic now filling her soft blue eyes. "I'm not hurt. I'm not even mad. I enjoyed that. God, I enjoyed it." She moved another step closer, reaching out for him. "There's something I need to tell you too. Something I was too afraid to say before." She swallowed hard and pressed a hand against her belly. "Oh God, I can't believe I'm going to say this, but I—"

"I need to go."

He stepped back quickly. Couldn't let her say the words. Knew he'd lose it if she did. All his life he'd tried not to be like his old man, but he'd just proved he was a carbon copy of the fucker. Cold. Selfish. Unable to love. Because if he really loved her like he'd thought he might, he never would have done this to her.

"You were right to resign," he said in a gruff voice. "Right to walk away. I-I'll have someone box up your things from the office and send them over."

Her hand dropped to her side, and her features darkened as he turned. "Don't do this," she whispered.

He didn't want to. God, he didn't want to. But he had to. Before it was too late. "It's past time one of us did."

Marley flipped off her flat-screen TV and tossed the remote on the coffee table, unable to stomach one more movie or TV show about happy people.

Two days had passed since the party, and she still felt as awful as she had the moment Jake had walked away from her down that cold, dark path. She hadn't tried to call him, knew there was just no point in trying anymore. A heavy emptiness pressed against her chest, making it hard to draw enough air to fill her lungs. Sitting back against the couch, she crossed her hands over her belly and stared up at the ceiling, refusing to cry, refusing to get mad again, refusing to do anything but just *be*.

A knock sounded at her front door, dragging her out of her self-inflicted melancholy, and she glanced out the wide windows of her living room toward her father's Mercedes parked in her drive.

Her eyes slid closed. Just what she needed. She'd been avoiding her father and Gray and everyone since the party, but she knew she couldn't go on doing it much longer.

Forcing herself to get up, she crossed to the front door and opened it. A gust of cool air whooshed into her entryway as she looked up. "Hi, Daddy."

Her father's disapproving gaze rushed over her and then returned to her eyes. "Pumpkin, you're still in your pajamas. It's three in the afternoon."

Marley glanced down at the flannel red-checked pajama bottoms and white T-shirt she was wearing, then stepped back and let him in. "I wasn't planning on going anywhere. Or having visitors."

He tugged his coat and scarf off and tossed them on the bench in her entry. "Amelia and I missed you at breakfast this morning."

She took a calming breath and moved past him into her living room, where she sat on her couch again and tucked one bare foot under her, pulled a throw pillow across her lap. He kept inviting her over for meals so she could get to know Amelia better, and she kept refusing. She liked the girl, she just didn't want to like her too much, especially if Amelia was sleeping with her father. Plus, going out to the farm meant she was bound to run into Gray, and she just couldn't stomach that yet.

She didn't know what she was going to tell him. She'd pretended to be feeling sick when she'd returned to the clubhouse after her scene with Jake, but she knew Gray had noticed her ripped skirt and wild hair. He hadn't argued when she'd said she was going home alone, but she knew he was anxious to talk to her. His repeated voicemails and texts were proof of that.

Her father dropped onto the couch next to her and exhaled a

long breath as he rested his hand on his denim-clad thigh. "I'm worried about you, pumpkin. Depression isn't attractive on you."

She frowned at him. "I'm not depressed."

"You're something." He fingered the edge of her white sleeve. "Have you talked to Gray today?"

Her stomach rolled all over again. "No."

"He came up to the house looking for you. I think he's worried."

He should be worried. That little announcement at the party had thrown her completely off-kilter.

Her father sighed and focused on the fire flickering in the hearth. "Relationships are hard. Your mother and I . . ." A faraway look filled his eyes. "We were like water and oil. Circling around each other. Clashing and then darting away. And when you added the hint of a flame . . . Well, let's just say we were more than explosive. We consumed everything in our path."

Marley watched her father's weathered face, surprised by his words. He never talked about her mother. When she'd been a kid and had asked about her mom, he'd always changed the subject. She'd only been two when her mother had left. Not even old enough to remember her. Most of what she knew about Faith Addison she'd learned from her brother Ronan.

"We burned hot for a while, then chilled. But it was like that with us. Passion and anger. Fire and ice." He turned to look at her. "It wasn't healthy, Marley. It wasn't any way to live."

Marley's stomach tightened, and, instinctively, she knew he was describing her and Jake. She shouldn't be surprised because she'd always known Jake was just like her father, but she was. One, because she hadn't thought her father had noticed what was going on between her and Jake, and two, because she'd never considered herself to be anything like her mother, who'd given up on life.

"A relationship like that," her father said, looking down at his hands, "it's either the best thing for two people or the very worst. If it doesn't lift you up and make you strive to be a better person, then it drags you down until there's nothing left. That's what happened to your mother. Our fire burned through her until it changed her from the woman I fell in love with to someone I didn't even know. And it threatened to do the same to me."

Marley's gaze slid to the fire, and as she watched the flames flicker over the logs, she saw herself in her father's story. She saw Jake. And she saw what they were doing to each other. Not making each other happy like two people should, but tormenting one another.

"Hot's fun and exciting in the short term, pumpkin, but it doesn't last. Marriage . . ." He shook his head and stared at the fire. "Marriage takes commitment. It takes two people who are compatible. Who bring out the best in each other. Who trust one another. At the end of the day, you don't want to be traveling that road with someone who will cut and run when times get rough—and trust me, they will get rough. You want to be on that path with someone you can depend on above all else."

He turned to look at her, and she saw truth in his blue eyes. A truth she didn't want to hear but knew she needed to face. "I know at your age, when it feels like you have your whole life ahead of you, you think marriage is something that should come from the heart. But if that heart's making you miserable, maybe it's time to think about someone who can give you what you need and want long-term without the anguish."

She knew what he was doing. She wasn't naïve enough not to recognize that he was talking about Gray. But she couldn't argue with any of the things he'd said. Because he was right. Jake would make a horrible husband. Even if they could get past the fact he was afraid to admit his feelings for her, he'd be domineering and arrogant and he would irritate her to no end. And she'd do the same exact thing to him. They'd argue and fight when they weren't burning up with passion, and even though that passion would flare hotter than anything else she'd ever felt, it wouldn't be enough. Someday it would burn out. Just like her parents' love had turned to nothing but cold, barren cinders.

Her mind drifted to Gray, to the difference between the two men, and she frowned at her father. "Five years ago you didn't even like Gray."

"Five years ago I was jealous that a man I barely knew was stealing my only daughter. I didn't know how you really felt about him until we lost him on that op. If I'd known . . ." He shook his head. "Well, let's just say things would have been different. I'm trying to make up for that now."

Marley knew he was. Their relationship had taken a hit after Gray had come into her life, and in the five years since the man's disappearance, it had never truly recovered. She knew she was partly to blame for that. Running off to work at Aegis had been easier than dealing with her—and his—guilt. But she wanted to mend that rift now. Wanted to do something to make everything better for all of them.

Her father placed his hand on her knee and gently squeezed. "Come by the house. Have dinner with us tonight. Amelia's making a roast. She's a really good cook."

Marley sighed. "I'm not sure how I feel about Amelia yet. She could be my sister, you know."

He grinned a mischievous smile that crinkled the skin near his eyes but brightened his face and made him look ten years younger. "Love sees no age."

She rolled her eyes. "You just sat here and told me that love shouldn't be a major factor in marriage."

"I'm not marrying her. I'm just enjoying our time together."

Okay, ew. She held up a hand. "TMI, Dad. TMI."

He chuckled and pushed to his feet. "Just come over for dinner and give her a chance. She might surprise you."

Marley doubted it, but for him she was willing to try. She walked him to the door, lifted to her toes, and hugged him. "I'll think about it."

"Think about everything." He let go of her, reached for the door handle, then swiveled back. "Oh, there was one other thing I wanted to talk to you about."

"What?"

"You mentioned the other day that part of the reason you left Aegis was because you wanted to work in the field and that Ryder wouldn't let you."

"Yeah?"

"You know I've never been a fan of that kind of work for you myself, but if it's something you really want"—his eyes held hers—"then I want you to be happy."

Marley's brow wrinkled. "Are you saying—?"

"I'm not saying anything yet. But I am making you an offer. If you come back to Omega, you can work in the field. As much or as little as you want."

Marley's eyes widened, and a smile broke across her face.

"On one condition." He held up a hand. "You do it with a partner. Someone I trust. Someone I know will take care of you if things get rough. Call me old-fashioned, but I'm not about to unleash my only daughter alone in the field."

Gray. He was talking about Gray. He was giving her what she'd wanted for longer than she could remember, but she had to do it with Gray. Her smile turned into a scowl. "Are you trying to manipulate me?"

"Absolutely." He kissed her cheek, then opened the door and stepped out onto her porch. "Dinner's at seven. I'm expecting you there."

Marley watched him walk down her drive, slide his sunglasses on to cut the winter glare, then climb into his SUV and pull away.

Closing the door, she leaned back against the hard wood and stared up at the chandelier hanging in her entry.

Her father's marriage announcement echoed in her head.

She'd be lying to herself if she didn't admit she wanted to get married. She wanted a partner. She wanted a family and a career she enjoyed, and yes, she wanted love too. And she was so very tired of waiting for those things to happen.

It was time to face facts. Marriage would never be on the table with Jake. She'd seen his reaction to the topic the morning after their wild night in the jungle. And if she'd learned one hard lesson over the last few weeks, it was that love didn't do anything but make people nuts. Maybe her father was right. Maybe what she needed most wasn't the fiery passion she had with Jake. Maybe what she needed was someone who appreciated her, who respected her, who wanted to make her happy. Love didn't have to be something to fear. It could blossom and grow and change. And it could be stable. Something she needed more than anything else right now.

Her stomach rolled. Pushing away from the door, she walked back into her living room and stared at the cordless phone on the end table while nerves bounced around in her belly. Thoughts of Gray, of Jake, swirled in her mind. And a future she'd always been too scared to imagine rolled out before her like a long red carpet.

Do it. Like a bandage. Just rip it off.

Nerves vibrating, she crossed to the phone, picked it up and dialed. Gray answered on the second ring, excitement filling his voice. "Marlene?"

"I'm not agreeing to anything yet," she said quickly, "but I think maybe it's time I heard you out." She bit her lip. "How do you feel about dinner tonight?"

chapter 21

"What do you think about pink for the flowers?" Amelia pushed a magazine in front of Marley and pointed toward an arrangement on the page. "Everyone loves pink."

Reminding herself her father's assistant was just helping, not purposely trying to annoy her, Marley glanced at the photo, then looked quickly back to the report she'd been scanning. "Fine. Whatever you think is best."

Amelia straightened in front of Marley's new desk at Omega Intel, her auburn hair falling over her shoulder as she moved. "I get the feeling you don't like pink."

No, Marley didn't like pink at all, but she wasn't about to say so. Drawing in a calming breath, she looked up, even though all she wanted to do was go back to the reports detailing the latest ops Omega had run, refreshing her memory on what her father's company had been up to while she'd been at Aegis. "I'm fine with whatever you want to do. The less I have to think about the details, the better off I'll be."

Amelia frowned. "Most brides are excited about the details of their own wedding."

Marley's stomach flipped at just the word—*wedding*—and she quickly looked back down at her papers. "Well, I'm not your typical bride."

Yesterday she'd finally given in and agreed to marry Gray, and Amelia was already rushing forward with the wedding plans. Yes, Marley knew saying yes was sudden—only three days after her father had gone to her house to have that little chat—but she needed a brand-new start. Gray was crazy about her. He'd made that more than clear ever since he'd come home, and she knew he'd make a good husband. Plus, everyone was so excited—Gray, her father, Amelia—it had to be the right decision.

Thoughts of Jake flittered through her mind. Their days in the jungle together. The night they'd spent at his house. Then the moment he'd walked away from her on that path at the country club. Her heart pinched. Pinched and ached so bad it stole her breath. But the hard truth was that he didn't love her the way she needed. And the sooner she put the past behind her and looked toward the future, the better off she'd be.

She smiled up at Amelia when all she really wanted to do was scowl. "It's just nerves. Don't worry about me. With the new job and all, I think it's best if I let you handle the details. The thought of whipping a wedding together while going through all this"—she looked down at the stacks of papers around her—"has me seeing stars."

Amelia relaxed, lifted the magazine from Marley's desk, and pulled it against her chest. "I understand. Don't worry about the details. I'll handle them all. Everything's going to be perfect. You'll see."

She left the room, and alone, Marley braced her elbows on the desk and dropped her head into her hands.

Two weeks from now she'd be married. Was she jumping the gun? Probably. But Gray had been so adamant they do it quickly, she'd let him talk her into it. Plus, part of her was afraid if she didn't do it fast, she'd chicken out. She kept telling herself the sooner she got through the ceremony, the sooner she could get on with her life. But the lifeline she kept holding on to was the fact that once she was married, she could work in the field, which was something she'd wanted longer than she could remember.

A knock sounded at her office door, followed by a familiar female voice. "Hey," Olivia said. "Everything okay?"

Dropping her hands, Marley looked toward Olivia, standing in the doorway, a worried expression on her face. Marley's stomach tightened. She could hide her anxiety from Amelia, but Olivia was another story.

"Hey," Marley said, working for calm when she felt anything but. "Yeah. Everything's fine."

Olivia stepped into the room, wearing slim black slacks and a red fitted top, and eyed her suspiciously. "I heard the news. Congratulations?"

Just the way she said the last word made Marley's heart speed up and thoughts of Jake ping around in her head again.

This isn't about Jake, dammit. It's about you. Stop thinking about Jake.

She forced a smile she didn't feel. "Thanks. It's very exciting."

Olivia's expression softened, telling Marley the woman saw right through her lie. "Are you sure about this? I mean, you and Jake—"

Oh no. Marley pushed out of her seat. She couldn't let Olivia go there. She and Jake were done. She'd put that behind her and only wanted to focus on what came next. "Yes, I'm sure. Gray and I are a good match. It makes sense."

"To whom? Him or you?"

"To everyone." Marley forced herself not to get worked up because she knew her friend was just concerned, but she didn't need to justify this to anyone but herself, and she'd already done that. "Look, Liv. I understand what you're trying to say, but I've thought this through from every angle. And I'm making the right decision for me. That's all you really need to know."

"Okay. If you're sure this is what you want."

"I am."

Olivia stared at her a long moment, then finally nodded. "In that case, someone needs to tell Amelia that pink is your least favorite color." She winked. "You can thank me later."

Olivia moved for the door, and Marley closed it after her so no one else could bother her. Leaning her head back against the hard wood, she stared up at the ceiling and blew out a long breath. Olivia's question swirled in her head.

Was this what she wanted? She wanted to be settled. Wanted a husband and a family. Wanted more out of life than just being someone's assistant. And she wanted to matter. With Gray, at Omega, she could have all of those things. And she'd have someone who respected and doted on her. Someone who could make her happy. Did it matter that she didn't love him?

Yes! her heart screamed. But her head ignored it. Because she was done listening to her heart. All her heart had done was make her miserable. Her father was right. It was time to be sensible. And the most sensible thing for her to do was marry Gray.

She pushed away from the door, returned to her desk, and went back to her reports. And told herself, for the hundredth time, that she was doing the right thing.

"Thanks for coming in on a Saturday." Jake pushed back from the conference table and reached across to shake Allison Witlock's hand. "I'll be in touch."

The late twenty-something slim brunette shook his hand, then grasped her bag from the floor and slipped the strap over her shoulder. "When will you be making a decision?"

A flutter moved through Jake's gut, one he couldn't stop anytime he thought of filling the vacant position at Aegis. It had been two weeks. Marley wasn't coming back. And after today . . .

That flutter moved to full-on nausea, and the moment he'd heard the news about Marley and McKnight whipped through his brain, dragging the air from his lungs all over again.

Miller had stopped by his house, four days after Mason's party. It wasn't like Jake to stay home, but he hadn't felt like going to work. Hadn't felt like doing anything but drinking. He'd pretended to be sick, but Landon—who'd been through a serious depression himself once before—had taken one look at him and known the truth. He'd tossed Jake into a cold shower, made him some food to sober him up, then dropped the bombshell Jake had never expected.

Clearing his throat, Jake tried not to think too much about Marley's—his stomach revolted again—wedding. But just the word . . .

How the hell could she marry the guy? She didn't love McKnight. She'd told Jake as much. She loved *him*, dammit.

And you pushed her away. Why wouldn't she marry McKnight? She loved him once. And he's made it more than clear he wants to spend the rest of his life making her happy. All you've done is mess with her heart and confuse the hell out of her.

Realizing his thoughts were drifting and that Allison Witlock was watching him with a perplexed expression, Jake forced a pathetic smile and refocused on their conversation. "Within the next two weeks if all goes well. I have several other candidates I'm interviewing."

"Of course." Ms. Witlock stepped toward the door. Her hair was pinned up in a stylish do, she was confident and assertive, and dressed sharply in navy slacks, a white shirt, and a crisp linen blazer, she was professional and courteous. And her résumé was stellar with experience at several defense firms and personal ties to the Middle

East and Europe that would benefit Aegis immensely. But something about her felt off. Something he couldn't quite put his finger on.

She turned when she reached the door. "I look forward to hearing from you soon."

As soon as she was gone, Jake dropped into a chair at the table, rested his elbows on his knees, and leaned forward. The ache he'd been living with the last two weeks spread outward from the center of his chest, making it hard to breathe.

Marley was going to marry the fucker. And there wasn't a damn thing he could do to stop it because it wasn't his place. He couldn't even warn her off because sometime over the last few days he'd realized she was right in that he was looking for a reason to condemn McKnight. He hadn't been able to find any link between McKnight and his Tahoe explosion, and there wasn't a shred of evidence that said McKnight's story about Colombia wasn't anything but true.

Which meant Jake was the asshole here, not McKnight. For accusing an innocent man. For hating the guy simply because he cared about Marley. For almost ruining her life when she had a chance to be happy.

He had to get out of his head. Had to stop thinking about her. He'd done the right thing by letting her go. What she did now was her choice.

Shoving down the emotions, he reached for the file in front of him, pushed to his feet, and headed for the door. Humming carried across the room as he drew closer to Marley's old office, and a flicker of hope whisked through him at the thought she was there. But when he rounded the corner and peeked past the doorjamb, the woman behind Marley's desk wasn't the one he'd hoped to see.

Eve glanced up. "Hey. I didn't know anyone was here."

Jake stopped at the doorway, couldn't seem to make himself step into Marley's old office, and eyed Eve, dressed in a slim-fitting red dress with a heart-shaped neckline and tiny cap sleeves. "Doing interviews."

"Oh. Find someone yet?"

Jake glanced down at the most recent candidate file in his hand and frowned. "No."

Eve tipped her head. "What was wrong with this one? Too tall?"

He didn't even care that she was being a smartass. Man, he was pathetic. "Just didn't click." He nodded her way before she could jump to conclusions about what that meant. "What are you doing here?"

Eve closed the desk drawer and held up the object in her hand. "Forgot my cell charger. Archer's waiting in the car." Her gaze swept over his slacks and the dress shirt rolled up to his forearms, and one of her slim brows lowered. "Please tell me you're not wearing that to the wedding. I'm pretty sure that's the outfit you wore yesterday. And is that ketchup on your sleeve?"

It was the outfit he'd worn yesterday. And yeah, that was ketchup from a burger he'd tried to eat but just couldn't stomach. On top of that, his clothes were wrinkled and dirty thanks to the fact he'd slept in his office last night, but he didn't want to tell her that. Nor did he want to tell her he couldn't quite bring himself to spend too much time at home lately because every time he was there he remembered Marley and the amazing night she'd stayed with him.

That ache spread outward from his chest again thanks to that word—*wedding*—and he turned away and moved for his office. "I'm not going."

He dropped the folder on his desk, moved around the piece of furniture, and slumped into his chair, wishing for alcohol, wishing for Xanax, wishing for anything that would make this damn day go faster so it could be over already.

Eve—never one for obvious cues—stopped in the doorway to his office, perched her hands on her hips, and glared at him. "Go after her."

Hedley had said that to him, and look how well that had turned out. Scowling, Jake moved Allison's folder to the stack of candidates he'd already interviewed and ruled out for whatever reason—some were too old, some were too young, one had a purple streak in her hair Jake just wouldn't be able to stare at all day, and another was a Florida State graduate. He couldn't hire someone from Florida State. He'd gone to Notre Dame, for God's sake. "Stay out of it, Wolfe."

"If you let her go, you're going to regret it forever. I know from experience."

The last of Jake's patience slipped away, and he looked up. "I mean it, Eve. This isn't you and Archer. It isn't even close. So save your advice for someone who needs it."

Eve crossed her arms over her chest and tipped her head. "With that sunny disposition, I can see why she decided to marry the other guy." She dropped her arms and turned for the door. "Since you're not bothering to go, I'll be sure to drink all your alcohol. Have fun sulking."

Lips pressed together, Jake picked up the binder clip on his desk and chucked it toward the door she'd just exited. It clattered against the doorjamb with a clack and bounced back.

"You missed," she called from the hall.

A muscle in Jake's jaw ticked, and he dropped his forehead into his hands again. He wasn't mad at her, dammit. He was mad at himself. Mad at the situation. Mad at—

The cell on his desk buzzed before he could put a lid on his temper, and he picked it up without looking at the number and then barked out, "What?"

"Ryder," a voice yelled across a crackling line. "It's Bentley."

Pierce. In South America. His focus zoned in on the call. "I can barely hear you."

"Chopper's about to lift off," Pierce yelled. "But I wanted to get you the info as soon as I could. That fourth guy? Sanders? He's alive. I found him in a Bolivian clink. He was working with McKnight."

Bolivia was a good fifteen hundred miles from Colombia. Not a quick jaunt. "We already know that," Jake said. "They were both employed by Omega. What the hell is he doing in Bolivia?"

"No. You don't understand. They were both working for the cartel," Pierce yelled over the whup whup whup of the chopper blades. "They double-crossed Omega. The cartel agreed to pay them five million dollars if they blew the hit on Jose Moreno. But McKnight got greedy. Instead of just killing Jones and Reynolds and splitting the money with Sanders, he turned on Sanders too."

Holy shit. Jake's adrenaline shot up, and he pushed to his feet.

"Sanders took a bullet to the abdomen," Pierce went on. "And McKnight left him for dead. The cartel, however, decided McKnight was too expensive, and instead of paying him off, they took him hostage. That buddy I've got doing merc work in Colombia? The one who tipped me off about Sanders? He says the word inside Colombia is that the cartel planned to ransom McKnight back to Omega at some point, but a shift in power after Moreno's death three weeks later resulted in McKnight being moved around and lost in the system. Not hard to do down here."

No, Jake knew it wasn't. "What happened to Sanders? How did he get out of Colombia? And how did you get this info from him?"

"Some local villagers found him in the jungle, took him in, and tended his wounds. Turns out he might just be a bigger shit than McKnight, though. He bolted, afraid Omega was going to find out what they did. Ran wild through South America for a while. Right now he's in prison in Bolivia for rape and attempted murder. I got him to talk by telling him about McKnight getting cozy with Mason Addison and the crew at Omega."

Which had to piss the guy off because he was rotting in a South American prison and McKnight was free.

A buzzing sounded in Jake's ears. He'd known McKnight was hiding something. Known and hadn't pushed for more. And he'd given up trying to make Marley listen.

Marley . . .

Jake scrambled for his keys from the top drawer of his desk. "Get your ass back here, Bentley."

"Already on it," Pierce said. "South America is not my favorite place. What are you going to do?"

Jake tucked the phone between his shoulder and ear, pulled the gun from the holster at his hip, and checked the magazine. "Stop a fucking wedding."

He clicked End and quickly dialed Miller's number as he headed for the stairs. The line immediately went to voicemail. Jogging down the steps, he tugged the phone away from his ear, then tried Stone and Hedley, but the calls all went to voicemail as well.

"Fucking idiots." They'd turned their damn cell phones off for the wedding. He quickly dialed Eve. Her line rang through, but eventually went to message, which meant she had hers on and was just ignoring him. "Goddammit." He left her a message, then as a last-ditch effort, he tried Marley.

He didn't want to drag her into this, but he didn't have any other choice. Pressing the phone to his ear, he listed to her familiar voice on the message as he stepped out of the building and hustled for his rig.

As soon as the beep sounded, he said, "Marley, it's Jake. I just got some information about McKnight." He tugged the car door open and slid behind the wheel. "Don't marry him until I talk to you. In fact, don't even go near him. Please. Just give me a chance to explain. I'm on my way."

He clicked End, hoped to hell she listened, then peeled out of the parking lot.

"Okay," Olivia Miller said at Marley's back in an excited voice as she brushed the curls she'd just put in Marley's hair aside. "Prepare yourselves, ladies. This is going to knock your socks off."

The zipper slid up Marley's spine. Olivia clasped the hook at the top, fanned Marley's curls out over her shoulders, then moved aside and grinned. "You're all set."

Stomach swirling, Marley stepped out from behind the screen in the upstairs guest suite of her father's main house where she and the other women were getting ready and glanced at Amelia, dressed in a slim black cocktail dress across the room. "Well?"

"Oh wow." A warm smile spread across Amelia's youthful face. "Oh, Marley." Tears filled her light-brown eyes. Tears that hit Marley as completely bizarre since she'd only just gotten to know the woman who was now dating—correction: sleeping with—her father. "It's absolutely beautiful."

"Isn't it?" Olivia moved next to Marley and fixed the train. "It's perfect for her. I'm so glad we were able to get a Lexi Lacroix gown on such short notice. I mean, it's off the rack, but you'd never know by looking at her in it. It fits as if it were made for her."

Nerves bouncing around inside her belly like Mexican jumping beans, Marley pressed the palm of her hand over the crisscrossed organza layers of fabric covering her stomach and the tight bodice of the strapless dress and stepped toward the full-length mirror set up in the corner of the room. As soon as she saw her reflection, her feet drew to a stop, and a gasp rushed from her mouth.

The mermaid gown was everything she never would have picked for herself. Her shoulders were bare, the heart-shaped bodice plunged between her breasts to showcase an ample amount of cleavage, and the tight sheath bodice followed every curve until it stopped just above her knee and then fanned out in waves of more organza that dropped to her feet and spilled out behind her like someone with a can of whip cream had gone crazy. And though it was beautiful, though it was elegant and flattering and made her look amazing in all the right ways—in ways she wouldn't have expected—panic pushed at her chest as she stared at her reflection. Panic and an overwhelming heat that prickled her skin and stole her breath.

Oh holy God in heaven. This was real. She was getting—she swallowed hard—*married*. And she was doing it with the wrong man.

The door to the suite pushed open, startling her. Her gaze shot to the door in the mirror, and Eve, in a blur of red, moving into the room.

"Holy mother of God," Eve muttered, her eyes growing wide as she stared at Marley. "Um. Wow."

"Isn't it?" Olivia exclaimed, stepping beside her sister and grinning. "We are definitely getting you a Lexi Lacroix dress for your wedding."

Eve's face went ashen. "Slow down, twisted sister. Let's not jump the gun here. I might have said yes to Archer, but that doesn't mean we're actually going through with it."

Olivia rolled her eyes and crossed her arms over her chest, pulling on the deep-blue satin of her dress. "Sometimes I don't know what Zane sees in you."

"I never know what Archer sees in me," Eve mumbled, her face still as pale as ever as she stared at Marley.

Marley's gaze slid back to her reflection, and the sea of white in front of her only pushed that panic higher. Until it was all Marley could feel, until her heart was thumping so hard against her ribs, she was sure it might explode right out of her chest.

"Ladies . . ." Darkness pressed in at the edge of her vision, and she gripped the edge of the mirror to hold herself steady. She was going to lose it. And she didn't want to lose it in front of them. "I need a minute alone. Please."

Amelia rushed over and reached for Marley's free hand. "Are you okay?"

Marley nodded, swallowed hard. Tried to sound normal when she said, "Yes," but knew her voice was an octave higher than normal and that they all had to know she was freaking the hell out.

Amelia looked toward Eve and Olivia. Marley couldn't see the silent exchange, but she didn't care. Right now she just needed a moment to think. To breathe. To calm herself down.

Eventually—after what felt like a year—Amelia squeezed Marley's hand. "Okay, we'll be right outside. Call us when you're ready."

The women filed out and closed the door. Marley looked back at her reflection and then sank to the floor.

Oh shit. Her eyes drifted closed. Oh, holy shit. What was she doing? She was getting married on the rebound, which was nothing but a monumental mistake. She couldn't marry Gray. She wasn't in love with him. Not even the tiniest bit. She'd let her father and Gray talk her into this insanity because she saw it as her way to work in the field. But marrying Gray wasn't the answer. It wasn't fair to Gray, and it sure as heck wasn't fair to her. Just the fact she was flipping out told her loud and clear that she was making the wrong choice.

Her eyes slid open, and she stared at herself in a heap in front of the mirror. She had to tell him. She had to call this craziness off right this very second. She didn't care what her father said, she only cared what she felt and knew to be true. And inside she knew this was wrong.

Stumbling to her feet, she grasped the waves of organza on the floor and lifted so she didn't trip and fall flat on her ass, then crossed the room and grappled for her cell in her pocket. A voicemail from Jake flashed across her screen, but she didn't have time for him. This wasn't about him, dammit. This was about her. About not falling into old patterns with her father, about standing up for herself, about fixing the gigantic mess she'd made all on her own.

She hit Dial and held the phone to her ear. As soon as Gray answered, she said, "It's me. I need to talk to you."

"Right now?"

He sounded irritated, but Marley didn't care. "Yes, now."

"Marlene, it's bad luck for the groom to see the bride before the wedding."

"I know. It's important though." She glanced out the window toward the trees beyond the edge of the yard. The ceremony was set to take place in front of the giant fireplace in the enormous living room downstairs. If she took the back stairs and snuck out the kitchen door, no one would see her. "Meet me by the footbridge that runs over the creek in five minutes."

"I don't think—"

"Please, Gray. Just do it."

She pulled the phone away from her ear and clicked End. Then drew in a breath for courage and bolted for the door.

Jake threw his SUV into park in the middle of the circular drive, jumped out, and sprinted toward the main house. A valet dressed in a black suit hollered, "Hey! You can't leave that here!"

Cars lined both sides of the paved, tree-lined drive, and patches of snow littered the ground. Thanks to the number of guests already inside for the wedding, cars were backed up at least a quarter mile down the road. Tossing his keys at the valet, Jake yelled, "Then move it."

He pushed one side of the wide double doors open and stepped into the entry, his chest rising and falling with his rapid breaths. Voices and laugher and music echoed from somewhere deeper in the house. A few people mingled in the outer rooms, drinking and chatting, but he didn't see McKnight anywhere. He was just about to head toward the music when Ronan Hamilton strode through the foyer, decked out in gray slacks and a white dress shirt, holding a beer bottle in his hand, looking completely uncomfortable in his surroundings.

He stopped, eyed Jake from head to foot, and muttered, "You look like shit, Ryder. I'm guessing things didn't work out so well for you after we parted ways in Puerto Asis."

"Where's McKnight?"

"How the hell would I know? I didn't like the dude before, I'm sure as hell not hanging around with him now. Why?"

The phone in Jake's pocket buzzed. Anxious it might be Marley, he jerked it out and held it to his ear. "Marley?"

"No, sorry," a male voice said. "This is James Douglas with the investigator's office. Sorry to bother you on a Saturday, Mr. Ryder. I tried to call your office, but no one's answering. I have some information about your Tahoe."

The bomb. Shit. "I don't have ti—"

"We've had ATF consulting on this with us, and thanks to their help we were able to trace the lot number for the caps on the bomb back to the manufacturer, then the distributor, and finally to the store where they were sold. It's a place in Louisville, purchased about a week and a half ago. Unfortunately, the caps were purchased with cash, but we do have security footage of the buyer. I just texted a video clip to you. We'd like you to take a look and see if the man in the footage is familiar at all."

Jake needed to get to McKnight, but something in his gut said not to blow this off. "Okay, hold on while I look."

He tugged the phone away from his ear, paged through his texts until he found the video, and hit Play. The camera was perched on a wall near the front door of the store, pointed toward the cash register. A man walked up and set items on the counter, but Jake couldn't see his face. He was big though, blond hair, dressed in jeans, boots, and a heavy jacket. Jake squinted to see better. The clerk rang up the purchase, the man paid with cash, then the man reached for the bag and turned toward the camera.

Everything inside Jake went cold, and he hit Pause.

It was McKnight. The son of a bitch had set that bomb. Had tried to kill him. Probably because he'd sensed what was going on between him and Marley. And that meant his reasons for marrying her weren't what she or anyone else thought.

"Something tells me that is not good," Hamilton muttered at Jake's side.

A new sense of urgency rushed through Jake. He clicked back to the call. "It's Grayson McKnight. He's at Mason Addison's farm outside Lexington." He rattled off the address. "Get a team out here now."

"We're on it. Mr. Ryder, don't—"

Jake didn't listen to the rest. He shoved the phone back in his pocket and turned to Hamilton. "Where is she?"

"Marley? Upstairs, I think. Ryder, what the hell's going on?"

Jake bolted for the stairs, took them three at a time, paused and looked around, then started opening doors. There was no sign of Marley. Fear shot through his chest. The last door at the end of the hall opened to a bedroom. Eve and Olivia both stopped packing up makeup and hair instruments and looked over.

"Well, wonder of wonders," Eve said in a surprised voice. "Look who decided to show."

"Where's Marley? I need to talk to her."

Olivia set down the brush in her hand and stepped toward him. "What's going on? What's happened?"

At his back, Jake sensed Hamilton move up behind him. "McKnight's not who she thinks he is. I just heard from the investigators. He set the bomb in my Tahoe."

"Are you sure?" Eve asked.

"They have video footage of the purchase. It's him."

"Shit," Eve breathed.

"He also double-crossed Omega," Jake added. "That op five years ago went to hell because of him. He was working with the cartel."

"She freaked out," Olivia said quickly. "I think she was having second thoughts."

Eve grabbed her phone from the counter beside her. "She went to talk to McKnight. I didn't try to stop her. I didn't think anything of it. I didn't . . . Shit."

No, not just shit. Holy motherfucking shit.

"Where?" Jake demanded.

Eve shook her head, then talked rapidly into her phone. "Zane? No, we've got a problem. Gather the guys."

"Outside," Olivia said to Jake. "She went somewhere outside. I don't know where though."

Dusk was transitioning to dark. Jake's adrenaline shot up. They only had a few minutes before it would be pitch-black outside and he'd never find her. Jake twisted for the door.

Hamilton's eyes hardened to cool blue stones. "I'm going with you."

Jake pushed past Marley's brother. "Just don't get in my way."

chapter 22

Hand gripping the train of her dress so it wouldn't get dirty, Marley paced the length of the small bridge and shivered in the cold. The creek rippled beneath the wood slats below her heels, and darkness slid over the copse of trees surrounding the bridge. A twig cracked off to her right, and she turned to look, anxious to talk to Gray, then exhaled a long breath when she realized it was just a bird moving in the branches.

She shivered, rubbed her free hand over the opposite bare arm, and wished she'd thought far enough ahead to grab a coat. Wished she'd thought through agreeing to marry the man so she wouldn't be out here in the first place. She paced back in the other direction. Knew he was going to be pissed when she called things off, but hoped—no, prayed—he'd see it for what it was—the best decision in the long run for both of them.

She caught sight of him approaching from the direction of the house, wearing a dark suit. Her feet slowed their frantic pacing. She swallowed hard and waited while he crossed the bridge.

"Wow," he said, his gaze sliding over her dress. "You look beautiful."

She steeled her nerves. She wasn't there for compliments. She wasn't there for anything but to call an end to this madness before she made things worse.

"Gray, I can't marry you."

His shoulders tensed. "I know you're nervous but—"

"No, it's not nerves," she said quickly. "It's not. It's . . ." Shit. She needed to tell him the truth. It wasn't fair to go on pretending anymore. And after everything he'd been through, he deserved the truth, if nothing else. "I was crazy about you once. But I always knew something wasn't right between us. I don't even know how to describe it now. It was just a feeling. Something that told me our relationship wasn't built on anything solid. Maybe it was my father's interference, or maybe it was just the fact I was too young. I don't know. I just knew before you even left that we were never going to work in the long run."

"I'm different now. I told you that. I'm—"

"I know. And maybe if I'd met the man you are now back then, maybe things would be different. But the truth is, Gray, I'm not the same girl I was five years ago, either. I don't want the same things I wanted then. And marrying you now just because I'm trying to make my father happy or because I feel guilty about what happened to you isn't the answer."

His jaw ticked beneath his freshly shaved skin, and his features hardened. "Is this about Ryder?"

"No," she breathed. "This isn't about Jake. This is about a split-second decision I made that was the wrong one. Admit it, Gray, you know I'm right. You haven't even once said you love me."

"You know how I feel about you."

"If you can't say it, then it means it's not important enough to matter."

And didn't she know that all too well with Jake?

Pushing that thought aside, she took a step toward him, desperate to make him understand, and reached for his hand. "I care about you. I do. And I want you to be happy. But I'm not in love with you anymore. And marrying you . . ." She shook her head. "It's not right. You deserve a woman who loves you with all her heart."

His eyes narrowed and held on hers. "You're right. I do." His hand twisted around, capturing her by the wrist. He pressed his fingers against her skin until pain shot up her arm. "But first I deserve retribution."

Her mouth fell open. She tried to pry her wrist free of his vise-like grip. "Gray, I—"

He jerked her hard against him. She stumbled, let go of the train of her dress, and fell into his rock-hard chest. "And you're gonna get it for me."

He dragged her across the bridge, into the trees, and up the hill. Her heels sank into the soft ground as she tried to catch up, her dress dragging along the dirt and patches of snow, hindering her movement. Rage twisted his features. A rage she hadn't expected or anticipated. "Gray, what the hell are you doing? Let go. You're hurting me."

"Don't worry, Freckles," he sneered. "This won't take long. It does throw a wrench in my plans to take your fucking money, but the end result will still be the same. And plan A was always my first choice anyway. If your friend Ryder hadn't showed up in Colombia with you, your father would already be suffering like he deserves."

He stopped on the side of the barn up the hill, swung her around so her back was to his front, slapped his hand over her mouth, and jerked her head back against his shoulder. In her ear, he hissed, "Don't make a sound or I'll snap your fucking neck."

He pulled his cell phone from his pocket and dialed. Seconds later, in a calm voice, he said, "Mason? Yeah, it's Gray. We've got a slight problem. Marlene's got cold feet. I'm trying to talk some sense into her, but she's making crazy threats about bolting. Yeah," he said after several seconds. "I know exactly how she can be."

Marley tried to pry his hands away from her mouth and screamed, but the sound came out muffled and he only pressed his hand harder against her face, cutting off her oxygen.

"Would you?" Gray went on. "That would be great. I'm sure all she needs is a little reassurance from her father. We're in the barn. Okay, I'll keep her here until you arrive."

He clicked End on the phone, then released his hold. Marley stumbled forward, the heel of her dress catching in the long train. Fabric tore. She fell against the building and turned back.

His eyes were hard, menacing pools of simmering charcoal. His features twisted until she almost didn't recognize him. In a moment of clarity she realized this was not the same man she'd rescued in the jungle. This was one who wanted her dead.

"You're going to wish you hadn't done that," he growled.

Fear rushed down her spine. Fear and a burst of adrenaline that told her to *run*.

She pushed her legs forward and darted to the right. He stepped in her path, grabbed her by the shoulders, and hurled her back into the side of the barn. "Where do you think you're going?"

She bounced off the side of the barn. Pain ricocheted up her side. She pushed herself upright. Before she could find her footing in the mud around the barn, he grabbed her by the arm and dragged her into the building through a side door.

"We're not done, Freckles." He pushed her hard, hurling her against a tractor in the middle of the building. A burn sliced across her arm. Her cheek and shoulder hit the machinery, and then she tumbled to the ground. "Oh, we're not close to being done. Before this night is over, your father's going to wish he'd never met me."

- - - - - - - - - - - - - - - - -

Gun drawn, Jake rushed outside and stopped in the middle of the sloping lawn, scanning the yard and the trees beyond. Dusk was turning to dark quicker than he'd anticipated. A gray haze seemed to settle over everything. He looked through the trees into the darkness beyond, searching for Marley. She had to be out here. She had to be. She—

"Look." Hamilton tapped his arm and pointed past the trees to the hillside rising beyond. "There."

Jake's gaze swung that direction, and he squinted as he watched a shadowy figure appear from beyond the trees and disappear into the old barn three hundred yards away.

"That look like Mason to you?" Hamilton asked.

"Yeah." Apprehension slid down Jake's spine. "And there's no reason for him to be heading to the barn when he's supposed to be hosting a wedding."

"My thoughts exactly," Hamilton answered.

They jogged through the trees, across the creek, and up the hill toward the barn. As they drew close, Jake slowed his steps and checked the ground so he didn't step on anything that snapped, then held a finger over his lips.

Hamilton nodded, gripped his Sig in both hands, and tipped his head toward the front of the barn. They both moved toward the closed main doors carefully, then pressed their backs against the wood and listened.

"Calm down," Mason said in a panicked voice. "Just tell me what you want. Son, there's no reason for this."

"Don't come any closer," McKnight growled. Marley yelped, and Jake's adrenaline shot sky-high because he couldn't see what was going on. "You did this. You took everything from me that mattered. You left me there to rot."

"I made a mistake," Mason said frantically. "I made a mistake that's haunted me ever since. But this isn't the answer."

"You don't have a fucking clue about the answer," McKnight yelled. "Because of you I lost my money. I lost my dignity. I lost five years in a Colombian shithole filled with rats and filth you can't even imagine up here in your cushy mansion."

"I know," Mason said quickly. "I know, and I want to make it all up to you. Put the gun down and let Marley go. We'll figure it all out. We'll make it right."

Jake's pulse roared, and fear shot through every inch of his body. He glanced at Hamilton, pointed toward the front doors, then tipped his head to the side of the building. Hamilton nodded in silent agreement, slid his weapon into the back waistband of his slacks, and stood upright.

"No," McKnight said in a dead voice. "The only thing that's going to make it right is for you to suffer the way I did. For you to lose everything you care about. That's what she's for."

Jake's heart rate spiked. He sprinted around the back of the building and prayed Hamilton could distract them long enough for him to get in position.

He found a back door, quietly pulled it open, and slinked inside. Darkness made it hard to see, but he picked his way around farm equipment and focused on the light coming from the main room. Voices echoed. He slipped out of the back room and stepped behind a towering column of hay bales. Through the crack he could see McKnight, holding Marley in front of him as a shield, a gun pointed right at her head. Past them, her father stood with his hands at his sides, his face frantic, while Hamilton held his hands up in a nonconfrontational way and reasoned with McKnight to let her go.

"No one wins here if you shoot her, McKnight," Hamilton said. "But if you let her go, you can walk away from this. No harm, no foul."

"Fuck you," McKnight growled, his voice higher, the menace in his words even stronger. He pulled Marley back a step with him. "If you're here it means someone else knows."

"No one knows," Hamilton said quickly. "I came looking for Mason, wondering what the delay was on the ceremony. No one else knows. No one has to know. Let her go and you can walk out of here a free man. But if you don't listen to me, I guarantee this isn't going to end well."

"You can have anything you want," Mason added. "Money, transportation. You name it, it's yours. Just don't hurt her."

Hamilton was a good negotiator. Jake had to hand it to the man. He was keeping McKnight distracted.

Focusing on the gun in McKnight's hand, Jake thought through options. The gun was angled in front of his body, pointed down at Marley's head. Jake could shoot the fucker in the back of the head, but if McKnight's trigger finger pushed down in reflex, Marley would be dead before McKnight even hit the ground. That meant he needed to distract the man long enough for her to get away.

He slid his Glock into the waistband at his back, crept out from behind the hay bales, and inched forward. Hamilton was still pleading with McKnight to let her go. This close, Jake could see and hear Marley struggling against McKnight's hold. Stepping up behind McKnight, Jake said, "Hey."

His voice caught McKnight off guard. McKnight swiveled his head to look behind him. The momentum pulled his gun hand up and away from Marley's head, just enough so it wasn't pointed right at her skull, but it was still too close.

Jake closed his hand around McKnight's wrist, jerked the gun farther away from Marley, and yelled, "Run!"

She shoved her elbow back into McKnight's ribs. He grunted, doubled forward, but grabbed on to Marley's hair. She shrieked, reached up to try to pry his hand loose. Jake twisted McKnight's gun arm behind his back, forcing his momentum around. The movement gave Marley the chance she needed, and she tore free of his grip and then stumbled forward. Hamilton caught her and pushed her toward her father. Voices echoed in the barn. Jake tried to wrestle McKnight to the ground, but a left hook slammed into his jaw, then McKnight roared and shoved him back into the stack of hay bales.

Jake didn't let go of McKnight's arm or the gun in his hand. They both went over. Hamilton shouted. Marley screamed. Footsteps echoed close as Jake and McKnight rolled across the dusty floor of the barn and wrestled for control of the gun. From the corner of his eye, Jake saw Hamilton's gun pointed right at him and McKnight, but he knew Hamilton couldn't get off a shot. McKnight was weaving all around, grappling like a street fighter. Jake's fingers wrapped around McKnight's on the handle of the gun. He struggled to twist the weapon away. McKnight shoved him over and slammed him into a tractor tire. Pain raced up Jake's spine. The gun caught between their hands went off. The gunshot rang out through the barn. Followed by a second.

Jake wasn't sure who'd been hit, but there was blood. Everywhere there was blood. He yanked his arm back. McKnight let go of the weapon, slumped against the barn floor. Pushing himself up and back, Jake scrambled to his butt, the gun in one hand, the other pressing against his chest, his arm, his stomach, searching for a wound, looking for the source of all that blood.

"Jake!" Marley rushed to his side. She dropped to her knees. Her hands gripped his shoulders. Her eyes were wide ovals in her face as her gaze raced over his bloody shirt. "Are you hit? Oh God. Where?" She pushed her hands against his chest, his belly, his arms. "Where is it?"

"It's not me." He let go of the gun and gripped her hands when he realized she was doing the same thing he'd just done. "Marley, it's not me."

She froze. At her back, Hamilton stood over McKnight's lifeless body and muttered, "Fucking bastard. I told you it wasn't going to end well."

Her father moved up, saw McKnight, and stilled. "Dammit."

Marley's eyes slid closed. A plethora of emotions rushed over her bruised and dirt-streaked face. Then her shoulders slumped and she fell back on her heels.

Jake scrambled forward, caught her in his arms, and pulled her close. Her hands gripped his biceps as if he were her last lifeline. Her shoulders shook against him and her face pressed against his throat.

"I've got you," he whispered, pulling her closer, needing her heat and warmth to shove aside all the fear and anxiety still vibrating inside him. "I've got you."

She held on for only a moment, not nearly long enough to satisfy him, then sniffled and pushed out of his arms. "I'm fine. I'm okay, Jake. You don't have to . . ."

Her gaze drifted up. She spotted her brother, then quickly pushed to her feet. "Ronan."

"You're good, Marley." Hamilton hugged her tight. "It's over."

They embraced for several seconds, and then she moved for her father.

Mason's arms closed around his daughter. Against her, he whispered, "I'm sorry, pumpkin. I was wrong about him. So, so wrong. I thought I was helping. I thought he could make you happy. Forgive me. I'm so sorry."

Voices echoed from the front of the barn. Jake didn't have to look to know that his team was finally there—Eve, Zane, Landon, Mick, and Raleigh. Because he was too focused on Marley being consoled by her father.

Too focused on the fact he should be the one holding her close.

"The cut's not deep," the EMT said as he placed butterfly bandages across the wound on Marley's upper arm. "You're not going to need stitches. Shouldn't even scar."

"Thanks." Seated on the back of the open ambulance, her feet hanging down to dangle in the shredded train of her dress, Marley pulled the blanket back up over her shoulder and shivered in the cool night air. "That's one positive in all this, I guess."

The EMT, a young kid who looked to be no more than twenty-two, flicked a grin her way and grabbed a couple bandages and gauze pads. "I'm gonna check on the other guy. Be right back."

He headed into the main house where Jake was still talking to the police. Picturing Jake covered in all that blood sent fear coursing through Marley's body all over again. She drew a deep breath to beat it back, then glanced over her father's front drive and the emergency vehicles dotting the turnaround.

Most of the wedding guests had left, and the majority of the ones who remained were either family, her father's Omega employees, or the crew from Aegis, helping the police put the puzzle pieces of Gray's plan back together. People like Ronan and Jake and her dad, who were used to this kind of chaos. People who dealt with the fallout of an op gone right—or wrong—fairly regularly. People like her.

A sinking emptiness filled her belly. No, not people like her. This time it was very different. Not just because she'd been so involved, but because Jake had tried to warn her about Gray numerous times and she'd ignored him. She'd been so upset over what was happening between her and Jake personally that she hadn't wanted to listen to reason when it came to Gray and what he was after. Hadn't wanted to see. And then she'd gone and agreed to marry the guy just to prove that she could. That didn't make her a great operative. It didn't even make her a good one. It made her stubborn and bullheaded, and in the field, that kind of behavior wouldn't just get her killed, it could get someone else killed too. Someone she cared about.

Olivia wandered her way wearing a long, black wool coat and carrying a steaming mug in her hand. She stopped near Marley and handed her the mug. "Tea. Thought you could use it."

"Thanks." Marley lifted the mug to her lips and took a tentative sip, hoping the liquid would sweep away the heartache and stupidity she felt, knowing it never could.

"Are you okay?" Olivia asked. "They're not taking you to the hospital, are they?"

Marley shook her head and swallowed around the growing lump in her throat. "No. I'm fine. Just needed a few bandages, that's all."

Relief swept over Olivia's face. "That's good. I was so worried. Everyone was. I still can't believe that Gray . . ."

Yeah, neither could Marley. She took another large sip as Olivia fumbled for the right words. The level of rage inside Gray hadn't just shocked her, it had horrified her, and even now when she thought of it, a shudder ran down her spine.

Olivia's gaze dropped to Marley's muddy, ripped, and bloody dress, and she sighed. "It's really too bad about the dress, though. I mean, a Lexi Lacroix gown. It's like a piece of art. You may as well have torched a Monet."

For some insane reason, in the middle of this entire nightmare, that comment hit Marley as hilarious. She chuckled. Snorted. Lifted the back of her hand to her mouth to keep from exploding in laugher, then giggled until tears streamed down her face and the sound turned to uncontrolled hysteria.

"I guess it was a little funny," Olivia said, "but geez, don't choke. I'm no comedian here, and I'm rusty on my Heimlich."

Marley swiped the tears from her face, swallowed several times so she didn't do just that, and tried to settle her emotions. But she couldn't. Because suddenly it was as if all the stress and fear and misery were suddenly coming out as crazy laughter. And her body just couldn't stop. "My boss kills my fiancé in my father's barn minutes before my wedding, and the only thing you're worried about is a stupid dress."

Olivia shot her a look, clearly not seeing the humor in the situation. "First of all, it's not just a stupid dress. It's a Lexi Lacroix gown, so get it straight. And secondly, as awful as all of that was, the dead fiancé isn't the guy you're in love with, now is he? And he sure as hell isn't the one you should have been marrying. No, the one you *should* be marrying is right in that house. And he was frantic to get to you, even before he knew you were with McKnight. I've never seen Jake so scared or desperate when he charged into that room looking for you."

Marley's laughter died, and the humor quickly fled. She swallowed hard, glanced toward the double front doors of her father's house, and watched as Jake stepped onto the porch with an officer. His once white shirt was covered in blood. Straws of hay were still stuck in his hair, and his black slacks looked gray from the dust in that barn. A small bandage covered a gash on his right cheek, and even though she knew he was safe and that it wasn't him who'd been hurt, her heart squeezed just as tight as it had when that gun had gone off.

"Frantic and love are not the same thing," she said softly.

"No, but frantic *in* love is definitely an affliction stubborn alpha males tend to experience," Olivia tossed back, "especially when the person they love is in danger."

Marley drew in a deep breath as Jake shook the officer's hand, knowing Olivia was referring to her own struggles with Landon and everything they'd gone through to be together. But Jake wasn't Landon Miller. "I don't think he knows what to do with love, Olivia. To him it's all business."

"He's scared, Marley. Just be patient with him. He'll come around."

Marley wasn't so sure. She couldn't go back to just being friends or colleagues or whatever they'd been to each other before. And as much as she loved the man, she couldn't settle for anything less than everything. Not anymore.

Jake moved up next to Olivia, slid his hands into the pockets of his ruined slacks, and nodded toward Marley's arm. "How's the cut?"

"Fine," Marley answered. "No stitches."

"That's good."

"Yeah." Marley lifted the tea to her lips.

Olivia exhaled a long breath. "I'm gonna go find Landon. Marley, I'll call you tomorrow."

"Okay. Thanks for everything, Liv."

Jake turned and watched her go. "I didn't mean to run her off."

"It's fine." God, now that everything was done and finished, this just felt sad. "How's your cheek?"

He brushed his fingers over the bandage. "Fine." Then dragged his thumb down the left side of his jaw. "It's this I'm more worried about."

His jaw was a little swollen, but he'd been punched in the face before, so she figured he'd be okay. "It doesn't look too bad."

He sat next to her on the end of the ambulance and braced his hands on the edge of the vehicle. After several quiet seconds, he said, "I'm sorry about what happened to McKnight. I didn't mean to kill him."

She tugged the blanket up higher with one hand, hoping to ease the chill growing inside her. "It's okay, Jake."

"No, it's not. When I got the call from Bentley and discovered he'd killed those Omega operatives in Colombia, I knew I couldn't prove it. I knew we couldn't arrest him. I just knew I had to get him away from you. I didn't come here to kill him, Marley. I came to tell him to get the hell out of your life. I thought if he knew I was onto him, he'd just leave."

Her heart sank even lower. He'd told her in the jungle that killing someone stayed with a person, and even though Gray had turned out to be one of the bad guys, she knew this one was going to stay with Jake. Because it was connected to her.

"But you never got the chance because I messed up his plans by turning him down." She stared into her mug. "He snapped, Jake. I saw it when I was standing on the bridge with him. It was like a light just went on, coloring everything red around him. You were right. I should have listened to you. I shouldn't have been so stubborn."

"And I shouldn't have been such an ass about it. I'm sorry about that."

They sat in silence for several seconds, neither seeming to know what to say to the other. Finally, Jake said, "You know, the night of your dad's party, when I showed up? I went to tell you something." He bit his lip, then said, "I went to tell you that I need you."

She turned to look at him, afraid she'd heard him wrong.

"I was miserable without you, then," he said softly, his eyes as tender as she'd ever seen them, "and I'm miserable without you now. We both know what's happening between us is more than just friend-ship. It's bigger. And even if you don't come back to Aegis, I want a chance to see where it goes. I want you back. I miss you, Marley."

They were the words she'd wanted him to say for way too long. But her heart didn't skip like she expected because he wasn't saying the one thing she needed to hear most.

Carefully, she set the mug on the floor of the ambulance, then pushed the blanket off her shoulders and stood. Her muscles were tight, her legs sore, and she knew when she took this mess of a dress off she'd have bruises everywhere, but right now, the physical pain in her body didn't even compare to the emotional pain ripping through her heart.

"You're saying all the right things, and there was a time when that would have been enough, but things are different now. The night of my father's party changed things for me. It changed everything.

You changed it. Because you made me realize that what I want, you just can't give me."

"Marley." He stood, regret rippling over his face. Regret that tugged on her emotions and made her want to throw herself into his arms, but she held back. "I know what you're talking about, but if you just give me some time to—"

"Time for what?" Sadness filled her heart. Not because she was mad or upset or disappointed, but because she wanted him to be happy. Wanted to be the one to make him happy. And she never would be. "To realize how you feel about me? It's been three and a half years, Jake. If you don't know yet, you're never going to know. But I'm okay with that. I really am."

She stepped close, laid a hand over his warm, solid chest, lifted to her toes, and kissed his cheek. Before he could touch her or react, she lowered to her heels and stepped back. "Thank you for saving my life tonight. I may act tough on the outside, but every girl wants a knight in shining armor now and then. Tonight you were mine. I'll never forget that."

She turned and headed for her car, parked at the end of the circular drive, needing to get away from him, from her father, from everyone, and just *be* for a while. Behind her, he didn't call her name, didn't try to stop her, and she forced herself not to look back.

Inside, though, she knew she was always going to remember this moment. And the way it felt to walk away from the love of her life.

chapter 23

"Sounds good. Call me if you have any problems." Jake hung the phone up on his desk and flipped the folder in front of him closed. Raleigh Stone was heading to Honolulu to run a security test on a client's new property in the islands. For a fleeting moment, Jake had considered taking the assignment himself and getting away from everyone and everything, then changed his mind.

He had too many responsibilities, too many people depending on him. And with his new assistant so green on the job—she'd only been working for him for three damn days—he didn't feel comfortable leaving the office just yet. Not when she could fuck everything up and make matters worse for him.

Almost as if she'd heard his thoughts, Allison Witlock wandered into his office, wearing crisp black slacks, a white blouse, and a slim jacket, her hair twisted into some kind of knot, and small silver balls twinkling at her ears. She set a stack of neatly organized papers in front of him. "These are the day's reports on each of the operatives stationed in the field. I've created preliminary overviews on the two potential clients you have scheduled next week, and I organized the State Department's contract on Richard Burton, which you mentioned you were considering bidding on. Oh, and don't forget you have a meeting with the contractor at two p.m. to discuss the remodel."

Jake glanced at his watch, then up at her in utter disbelief. It was nine freakin' a.m. on a Wednesday and she'd done more in one hour than he did all day. Who was this chick? Wonder Woman?

"I'm heading to the break room to get some coffee," she said. "Can I get you any?"

And she was getting him coffee. Jake's irritation with the wonder assistant ticked up. No, he didn't want any coffee. If he wanted coffee, he could get it himself. He wasn't an invalid, for crying out loud.

"No, thanks." He clenched his jaw so he didn't say something he'd regret, then waved his hand so she'd just leave. "That's all for now, Marley."

"Allison."

His irritation got the best of him, and he dropped his hand. "What?"

"My name is Allison, not Marley." She turned for the door. "Buzz me if you need anything. I'm going back to reorganizing the personnel files. I can't believe where some of those records were filed."

She disappeared into the hall, and as Jake watched her go, all he could think about was the fact she was right. She wasn't Marley. She was never going to *be* Marley. She was efficient and logical and professional and she didn't challenge him with cute blue eyes or call him out when he was being a jerk. And even though she was everything he'd ever wished for in an assistant, all he wanted to do was scream at her to stop being so precise.

He let go of the papers, sat back, and rubbed his fingers over his eyes. He had to stop comparing her to Marley. Had to stop thinking about what he'd lost. It was for the best anyway, right? If Marley had wanted him, she would have given him a chance.

He slumped back in his chair, swiveled to the side, and kicked his legs up onto his desk, trying to make himself relax, trying to think about something other than her. But he couldn't stop his mind from wandering, and his memories kept skipping over that night in the jungle. When the fire had been roaring in the middle of the camp and he'd watched Marley dance and laugh and smile his way as if she were dancing just for him. As if they were the only two people in the world. As if he was all that mattered to her.

She'd been so beautiful that night. Beautiful and alive in a way he'd never seen her before. And she'd been happy. So happy when she'd dragged him in, when she'd kissed him, when she'd stopped worrying about everything else and let herself go.

He'd been happy, too. Happier than he could ever remember being. Yeah, they'd both been a little high, but that jungle juice hadn't done anything but lower his inhibitions. It hadn't changed what he felt. That night he hadn't been worrying about the future, hadn't been worrying about the past, hadn't been focused on anything but her. And for a moment, for one precious night, everything had been perfect.

His gaze dropped to his dress shoes on the surface of his desk, then his socks where his slacks had ridden up, and finally the bulge beneath the houndstooth pattern. Leaning forward, he pushed his sock down and stared at the braided leather band around his ankle.

His throat grew thick, his palms damp. Emotions raced through his chest. So many he couldn't name them all. But the strongest, the one he knew had been there for a long time but which he'd been too afraid to face, was love.

He already did love her. He loved her smile and her laugh, loved the way she put him in his place and never backed down from a fight. Loved that she organized things in bizarre ways and challenged him even when she knew he wasn't going to give in. He even loved that she was stubborn and bullheaded because it made her passionate. But most of all, he loved the way she cared about him—loved the way she cared *for* him—because no one else really ever had.

He wasn't his father. Not yet, anyway. But if he sat back and let her go without telling her how he really felt, he would be.

Hand shaking, he dropped his feet to the floor and reached for his phone. His fingers hovered over the keypad as indecision warred inside him. If he called her, she'd just let it go to voicemail. He had to do this right. Had to prove to her that this time things were different.

He dialed her father's cell, but Mason didn't answer. Biting his lip, he thought through who at Omega might be willing to help, then remembered Olivia.

He found her number in his phone and hit Dial. Olivia answered on the third ring. "Hey, Jake. I was just about to head into a training class. What's up?"

"Hey." *Play it cool.* "Is Marley at the office? I'm trying to find her. My new assistant has a question about . . . stuff." *Stuff? Shit.* That was so *not* playing it cool.

"I'm sorry. She's not here. She decided not to work for her father."

"She *what*?" Panic pulsed in Jake's chest. "Who is she working for?" He hoped like hell she hadn't already packed up and moved to DC. There were a number of firms there he knew would jump at the chance to hire her. And thanks to the fact it had taken him so freakin' long to figure out that he was already crazy in love with her, he knew if she'd already taken one, getting her back was going to be nearly impossible.

"I don't know. I don't think anyone yet. I'm pretty sure she's taking some time to herself."

Jake released a breath. Okay, time to herself could work. "Thanks. I'll try her at home."

"She's not at home. She's in Carmel. At your house."

"I have a house in Carmel?"

Olivia laughed. "Yes, you do. A pretty nice one, too. It's one of the properties you told Marley to list."

"What's she doing there?"

"Finalizing details with the realtor, I think. I'm not a hundred percent sure. I think it was also a good excuse to get away."

Carmel. She was in Carmel. At *his* house. She hadn't let go of him, not completely, not yet. Not if she was working on something that wouldn't benefit her in the least, but him. He still had time to make her believe he loved her.

Plans, details, a future—all of it swirled in his mind, lifting him out of his chair with hope. "Do me a favor, Olivia?"

"Sure. Anything."

"Don't tell her we had this conversation."

"Okay. Why not?"

"Because I want to surprise her."

"Well," she said with a smile in her voice. "It's about damn time."

It was way past time. He tugged the phone from his ear, then drew in a deep breath. And prayed he could get to Marley before she made up her mind for good.

- - - - - - - - - - - - - - - - -

Marley closed the front door of the beach house and dropped her purse on a chair in the entryway. She's spent three hours wandering the shops on Ocean Avenue in downtown Carmel, hoping a little shopping therapy would bolster her mood, but it hadn't. Blowing out a long breath, she kicked off her flip-flops and carried her shopping bag down the hall toward the massive kitchen at the back of the house.

It really was an awesome house, and part of her wanted to kick Jake for even considering selling it. He hadn't even seen the place, but she knew if he did, he'd fall in love with it as much as she had. It was all natural wood and glass and granite and stone, situated on a rocky cliff that overlooked the Pacific. A wide deck ran across the back of the house, and steps led down to the beach. And the view out across the water . . . her pulse slowed just thinking about seeing it again. It calmed her when nothing else these last few days had done anything to make her relax.

She stepped out of the hall and into the combo great room and kitchen with its wall of windows that faced the ocean, then stilled. A man stood on the porch past the windows, hands on the railing, looking out at the view. A man dressed in faded blue jeans, a loose light-blue T-shirt, and—yes, even—blue flip-flops. A man who *never* wore flip-flops.

Almost as if he'd sensed her, Jake turned and looked at her through the glass. And Marley's pulse shot straight up into the triple digits.

He crossed the deck, pulled the sliding glass door open, and stepped into the house. "Hey. This place is pretty amazing. Why didn't you tell me it was like this?"

Hey? *Hey?* That's what he had to say to her? She'd come here to get away from him, not to have him track her down like he'd done in Colombia. This was supposed to be the one place he never wanted to visit.

She set her shopping bag on the kitchen counter and told herself not to let her emotions get the best of her. Those emotions were the reason she was in this mess in the first place. He was obviously here for something that had to do with Aegis, so this time she'd listen, stay calm, and not get worked up.

"What are you doing here, Jake?"

"I was planning to ask you the same question."

Crap. It was his house. She'd forgotten that for a moment.

"The realtor needed me to sign some papers." She pulled the milk she'd bought out of the bag and turned to place it in the refrigerator. "I didn't want to bother you with it."

"You don't work for Aegis anymore, though. Your signature won't be valid."

Dammit. He was right. Her excuse didn't hold an ounce of water. "I didn't think of that." She closed the fridge and turned to face him, reminding herself to stay calm. "Is that why you came all the way to Carmel? To tell me that?"

"No." He moved up to the other side of the counter and eyed her over the sleek black granite surface. "I came to tell you that I love you."

For a moment, the words hung in the air, and she wasn't sure she'd heard them right. But she was listening this time, not with her heart, but with her head. And sure enough, the words were definitely there.

"I know you love me," she said quietly.

"You do?" His brow lifted in complete surprise.

"I've known for a long time."

"Why didn't you say anything?"

She reached into the bag and pulled out the eggs and cheese, surprised that she wasn't falling apart. "Because it wouldn't have made a difference."

She opened the fridge again and slid the eggs and cheese inside, then closed the heavy wood door that matched the rest of the cabinets in the kitchen and jerked back. Jake was standing right beside her.

"It does matter. It's the only thing that matters, and I should have realized that sooner but I'm—"

"Really fucked up?"

318

The words were out before she realized they'd escaped, and she pursed her lips as she stared up at him and berated herself for reacting with her heart instead of her head.

One corner of his lips curled. "Yeah. That. I am. As you well know." His smile faded. "But I need you to know why."

Dammit, she didn't want to hear this. It wasn't going to matter anyway. She turned back for her groceries. "Jake—"

"Eight years ago, when I was in the navy, there was this woman. She was an officer with the CIA, focused on uncovering the whereabouts of high-ranking al-Qaeda officials. She worked with our SEAL team on several occasions, providing intel on ops and terrorist locations. We hit it off. It wasn't anything serious, I mean, she was stationed in Kabul and I was all over the damn world, but there was something there. Whenever she was back in the States and I happened to be on leave, we'd hook up. But Gabby was . . ."

He glanced around the kitchen as if looking for the right words, and Marley's stomach tightened as she watched, unsure if she wanted to know more, curious at the same time about a woman who'd clearly meant more to him than any other he'd dated in all the time she'd known him.

"Independent," he finally said. "She didn't need a guy in her life, and she didn't have room for one to mess up her career. And though we had this thing, she was stubborn when it came to what she decided."

Like me, Marley realized, suddenly seeing a parallel between her and this mystery woman who'd obviously messed him up.

He rubbed a hand over his brow, and the guilt she saw in his face, it softened her. Way more than she ever would have expected. "What happened?"

"My team was in Northern Africa. Just hanging around the base, waiting for orders. She uncovered intel that the number-three ranking al-Qaeda leader was supposed to be in the Yemen area. She told me about it in confidence, said someone from her office needed to travel there to meet with a contact to confirm, but she was nervous about the meeting. Yemen wasn't all that far from our base. I wanted to see her, and I talked her into making the trip herself. Our team was the closest one to the area; we would have been called to take the hit. I knew if she was the one to make contact, I'd get to see her. I knew she was hesitant about it, but it was just a contact. It wasn't the cell itself. She finally agreed."

Marley's stomach sank. She knew instinctively that something bad had happened.

"It was an ambush," he said quietly. "She and two others from her team were killed. The cell knew the CIA was onto them."

Her heart hurt for him. Because he'd taken a chance on caring for someone after all the neglect and abandonment he'd lived through as a kid, and in the end, it had ended tragically.

"I'm sorry, Jake. That's awful. But it was an accident. You didn't know. It wasn't your fault."

"It was though. If it weren't for me—"

"If it weren't for you, someone else from the CIA would have died. They were going to that meeting regardless of what you said or did. You can't blame yourself for something someone else—a terrorist of all people—does."

"Yeah, but *she* would have been alive. That's the difference."

Marley looked down at her bare feet against the hardwood floor as understanding dawned. No wonder he'd freaked when she'd run off to Colombia. No wonder he'd tracked her down and stayed by her side the entire way. And no wonder he felt so bad about what had happened with Gray and the fact he'd given up trying to warn her.

"Marley." He stepped toward her. "I've overreacted. I haven't trusted you. I haven't tried to see your point of view because I've been too afraid of what will happen if I opened myself up. But I don't want to do that anymore. I love you. I love the way you make me feel when we're together. I even love it when you're arguing with me because it means you care."

Marley's heart squeezed tight, and all those emotions she'd tried not to think with came raging back. She pressed both hands over her face as she struggled to sift through them, and remembered what her father had said.

Yes, she believed Jake loved her. Yes, she believed everything he was saying, but at the end of the day, they were just too volatile to make this work. Their relationship was too much like her parents'. And she didn't want to ruin him the way her mother had ruined her father. Didn't want to ruin herself, either.

She dropped her hands and looked at him. Really looked at him. At the scratch his cheek from that fight with Gray, at the heartache and hope reflected in his dark eyes. And she knew in her heart that she was always going to love him, but that it wasn't enough.

"I love you too, Jake." He took a step toward her, but she held up a hand to keep him back, needing to get the words out before his touch distracted her. "But you were right the night of that party. We're explosive together. It's not healthy. If we let this go on, we'll just make each other completely miserable. I don't want that for you."

"Marley—"

"No." She stepped back, out of his reach, fighting back the rush of emotions begging her to give in. Knew she needed to leave fast before that happened. "You're too much like my father and I'm too much like my mother for this to ever work. And that ended so badly, my father's still reeling from it thirty years later. I won't do that to you. I can't."

She moved around the opposite side of the counter so he couldn't touch her and swallowed hard. "Stay here, enjoy the house." She glanced over her shoulder toward the gorgeous view. "Do yourself a favor and don't sell it. You need this kind of peace and quiet."

"No," he said softly, "I need you."

Marley stared at him, wanting nothing more than to give him that and so much more, but her brain took over, pushing her feet out of the living room and down the hall toward the door.

Hands shaking, she pressed her fingers against the wall in the entry and slipped on her flip-flops. She was just about to reach for the front door when she spotted a contract on the entry table with her name typed across the top.

She stared at it. Picked it up. Read the front page, then read it a second time. Heat rushed to her cheeks. Heat and disbelief and bone-jarring shock.

She rushed back into the great room and lifted the contract in her hand. "What the hell is this?"

Jake turned from the fridge where he was putting away the rest of her groceries and folded the paper shopping bag, not showing any kind of surprise that she was back. "The proof you need."

Her heart raced beneath her ribs. She looked down at the contract in her hand. "You're giving me half of Aegis. Just giving it to me for no reason?"

"Not for no reason." He moved around the counter to stand in front of her. "It's partly because of you that it's grown into what it has. The guys are all loyal to you, not me. They only put up with me because I sign their paychecks."

Her hands grew sweaty. "But this is your business. This is what you love."

"No, Marley. *You're* what I love. Aegis doesn't mean anything to me unless you're part of it. And before you go jumping to conclusions, it's not because I need you in the office. I don't. I want you to be as involved in whatever part of Aegis you want. And if that means working in the field, then I'm okay with that, so long as you let me tag along."

He smiled, a warm loving smile, but she was still too shocked to process. "I-I don't even know if I want to work in the field anymore."

"You don't?"

"No, I mean, yes. I mean . . ." She threw her hands up. "I don't know anymore. I obviously have trouble listening to directions."

That sexy little smirk made her heart beat even faster. "That's true, you do. We can work on that. And I can work on not taking unnecessary risks. I have to do better with that. I have something important to live for now."

She stared down at the papers in her hands. Swallowed hard. He was giving her half of Aegis. He really *really* loved her. More than her father had ever loved her mother. Mason Addison *never* would have done something like this for his wife. For all his talk about how bad he felt regarding their failed relationship, he'd never sacrificed anything for her. And never, not in a million years, would he have ever sacrificed his precious company for her.

"I . . ." Her legs grew weak. He stomach swirled. She backed up until her butt hit the sofa behind her. "I-I didn't expect this."

"I did." He moved closer, until the heat of his body swirled around her and made her lightheaded. "And I knew you'd be stubborn about it. I wanted you to be. Because I needed to prove that I love you. And that I'm not going anywhere. I can't. You own half my damn company."

Unable to find words, she watched as he tugged something slim from his pocket and held it up. "You took this off," he said softly. "You weren't supposed to do that, you know."

Her gaze dropped to the leather band in his hand, then shot to his face. His smiling, warm, gorgeous face. And she watched as he stepped back and pulled up his pant leg so she could see the leather band around his ankle.

Oh . . . "You put it back on?"

"I never took mine off." He dropped to one knee and carefully tied the band around her ankle. Her skin tingled wherever he touched, and heat gathered in her belly. A heat only he could create. "I think you're stuck with me, Addison. I mean, I know you tried to marry someone else, but I'm pretty sure it'd be damn near impossible to find that village again and get this thing annulled." He looked up at her, and his voice turned so sweet and dreamy her heart felt like it was about to lurch out of her chest. "I know I don't want to."

Love and a future she'd been too afraid to hope for reflected in his eyes, and all the reasons she thought she'd needed to hold back from him drifted away.

"That was completely unfair," she whispered, blinking through the tears.

"No, this is unfair." He pushed to his feet and pulled a ring from his pocket. A ring with a large blue stone. The same color as his shirt. "Call me old-fashioned, but as much as I love the Amazon wedding bands, they're just not very visible. And I want everyone to know you belong with me."

Her eyes widened. "Is that a sapphire?"

"No. A very rare diamond. You said you liked the color blue."

She had. During that op in DC he'd changed without telling her. He'd been listening. She blinked back tears. "Oh my God."

He chuckled, took the papers from her hands and dropped them on the couch behind her, then he slid the ring on her finger. "Wilson did not give me a deal on this, just so you know. Wouldn't even take back that sapphire I bought for you, so you'll get that when we get home. I didn't bring it with me."

Her gaze darted from the ring to his face. "You bought me a sapphire? When?"

"That night, in DC. I wanted to give it to you when I got back, but, well, I was afraid you might read too much into it."

She couldn't stop the laugh that slipped from her lips as she looked down at the ring through watery vision. "As opposed to now."

"This time I want you to read into it." Closing his arms around her, he drew her into the warmth and safety of his embrace. "I know we're going to fight. I'll make you so crazy sometimes you'll want to rip your hair out. And I fully expect you to put me in my place when I get out of line. But I also know I wouldn't want it any other way. And I know I am never going to stop loving you. No matter what happens in our lives or where we go or how nuts our kids make us, this right here is the only thing that matters. Because you are everything to me."

Kids. He'd just said kids. Ankle bracelets, rings, and kids. Tears blurred her vision as she pressed her face against his throat.

"All I want," he whispered, "the only thing I need, is to make you as happy as you were that night in the jungle when you danced around the fire for me. If it takes my whole life, that's exactly what I plan to do."

"Jake." She sniffled, pressing her hands against his solid chest. "I was higher than a kite that night. Are you sure that's the measure you want to go by?"

"Absolutely." He drew back and gazed down at her. "Because that's the night I fell crazy in love with you, wife."

Wife. He'd called her that in the hut. The morning after their wild night. And just like it had then, her heart warmed and skipped, spreading heat throughout her entire body. Only this time, she knew that heat was love.

She lifted to her toes and kissed him with everything she had in her. And as his arms tightened around her and his body came to life against her own, she knew everything—finally—was different.

"Oh." He drew back a breath. "One more thing. We're not selling this house."

She wrapped her arms around his neck and rolled her eyes. "Geez, already back to being bossy. I should have expected it. Fine. If you really want the house, I guess I could force myself to vacation here now and then. I'll call the realtor in the morning. *After*, that is, you spend the next few hours proving just how sublimely happy you can make me."

He grinned and lowered his lips to hers, then kissed her until she was breathless. "That I can do, wife. That I can most definitely do."

about the author

Photo © 2010 Curtis Almquist

Before topping multiple bestseller lists—including those of the *New York Times*, *USA Today*, and the *Wall Street Journal*—Elisabeth Naughton taught middle school science. A voracious reader, she soon discovered she had a knack for creating stories with a chemistry of their own. The spark turned into a flame, and Naughton now writes full-time. Besides topping bestseller lists, her books have been nominated for some of the industry's most prestigious awards, such as the RITA® and Golden Heart Awards from Romance Writers of America, the Australian Romance Reader Awards, and the Golden Leaf Award. When not dreaming up new stories, Naughton can be found spending time with her husband and three children in their western Oregon home.